Small Things

Out of the Box, Book 14

Robert J. Crane

Small Things
Out of the Box #14
Robert J. Crane
Copyright © 2017 Ostiagard Press
All Rights Reserved.

1st Edition

1.

"Any last words?" Greg Vansen asked, wagging his finger at Percy Sledger. Sledger stood at the edge of a precipice that overlooked the Columbia River and Interstate 85 several hundred feet below. Greg figured that in daytime it was probably a stunning natural overlook, for those who were interested in such things.

For his purposes, though, Greg saw only its utility as a perfect place to corner the running man in front of him.

A light breeze rustled the trees around them in the cool, Oregon night. Rain was in the air, but Greg hoped he would be on his way home before it started coming down. May rains in Oregon were not typically very warm affairs, and while Greg did have a poncho secreted away on him, he had no interest in deploying it and working around the rifle clutched in his arms. He had it pointed carefully at Percy Sledger's heart, and Sledger had his hands raised high, his thinness making him look like a particularly wretched scarecrow.

Greg had looked him over carefully; unless Sledger was hiding a secret like Greg's—which Greg felt calmly assured that he wasn't—the man had no weapons on him, and was thus no threat at all. He was just a man standing cliffside, his mop of brown hair drenched with sweat from his run, a look of fear twisting his long, skinny face as he pondered the drop ahead or the bullet that had his name on it as surely as if it had been carved into the lead.

"Please ..." Sledger said.

Greg sighed. "Disappointing. I tracked you from Georgia to Oregon and the best you can muster is 'Please.' How trite. These are your last words, you could at least try to make them mean something. You will die, there is no escape, no point in pleading." Greg felt a cool blossom of anger in his breast, wishing Sledger would just get on with saying something that had some meaning. The ones who begged only annoyed him, refusing to accept their fate. "I suppose next you'll mutter some irrelevancy about how you don't deserve this."

"I—I don't—" Sledger started.

Greg made a show of checking his watch without moving the muzzle off his target. "I don't care whether you deserve it or not. I get paid either way." His timing was precise as ever; he had gauged down to the minute without even checking his watch. Still, it was nice to have it in case he needed a more definite measure, perhaps down to the seconds.

Sledger stared at him, gape-mouthed, eyes twitching back and forth as he apparently tried to come up with something to say in response to that. Greg cut his juddering thoughts short. "Since you have nothing coherent or interesting to say, let's be on with the business at hand. It would be in my best interest if you jumped, landing on the Interstate below and ending your life and my problems all at once. If however, you wish to inflict further discomfort upon me ..." Greg adjusted the gun slightly in his hands for dramatic effect, keeping it trained on his target. "Well, there is a distinct possibility that the fall will cause enough damage to your corpse that the coroner may not notice the bullet hole."

"I don't want to die," Percy Sledger said, his shaking hands still aloft.

"I don't particularly care what you want," Greg said. Sledger was actually shorter than Greg, which was no mean feat. "It's not as though you've respected my schedule these last few days."

Sledger made a face at that, all bawled up as though he might cry. Greg felt a prick of annoyance. He was tempted to make a show of checking his watch again while evincing his distaste. Hopefully Sledger would see the futility of his delaying actions soon and jump, putting an end to this annoying endeavor once and for all.

"Well?" Greg tapped his finger along the side of the rifle. "We don't have all night. Make a decision."

"I don't—"

"Reason should compel you to recognize the inevitability of your death," Greg said, impatience bleeding through. "I've pursued you to the edge of a cliff. Two options remain—I shoot you or you jump. Both end in a fall and your death. Choose which you prefer. I will give you to the count of five. One."

"You can't—"

"Two."

"Aughhhhh!" Percy Sledger let out a primal scream, but his feet stayed anchored at the edge of the cliff, unmoving. It was a sad display of misdirected rage, and Greg would have rolled his eyes at the sheer silliness of it were he not otherwise engaged.

"Three."

"Please ... I'll give you whatever you want," Sledger said. "I'll give you everything I have. Just—don't—"

"Four."

Sledger wobbled on his legs, looking suddenly downcast. "Oh, God."

"Fiv—"

Before Greg finished the word, Percy Sledger looked up at him, eyes seemingly wider than his thin body, and took a step back. He started to slide, foot catching on the face of the cliff.

Greg took a step forward, rushing the edge of the cliff as Sledger slid down the edge a foot, bending his legs in the process. The second before he vanished over the edge completely, Sledger shoved off against the vertical surface of the cliff with extreme force, doing a backwards swan dive out of sight.

Greg stopped at the cliff's edge with precision, using his metahuman strength to halt him just before he slid off the overlook. Sledger was airborne below, but he was not angled to land on Interstate 84, as Greg had hoped. No, his last minute maneuver had been calculated, a shove-off to try and give him enough distance to land beyond the interstate, to come splashing down in the Columbia River beyond.

"Damn," Greg said mildly and then drew up his rifle. He acquired his target in a quarter of a second and fired three shots in rapid succession. The muzzle flash lit up the night, the gunshots cracking over the Columbia River Gorge.

The shadow of Percy Sledger bucked in midair, twisting, and Greg knew at least one of his shots had hit true. Probably more than one; Greg was very efficient with a variety of weapons. As an assassin, it paid to be good at your trade.

And few, if any, were better than Greg Vansen.

Percy Sledger landed in the waters of the Columbia River, a splash about twenty feet off shore swallowing him whole. Greg did the mental calculus—Sledger's speed, angle of impact, force of the water—it only took a few seconds, and he was mathematically certain that Percy Sledger was, in fact, dead.

"Good," Greg allowed himself, watching the water for signs of a disturbance. Something about the fall bothered him, but the math was certain. No human could have survived that, the probabilities, especially given Sledger's angle of entry, prohibited it.

This matter was settled.

"But it shouldn't have been necessary," Greg muttered to himself as he secured the rifle, putting it away carefully. How had Sledger been sure-footed enough to—

"It doesn't matter," Greg said, shaking his head. The math was certain, so he was certain. The clouds above were hiding the moon. They suggested that the rain was indeed coming.

Patience was a game of picking one's battles, and Greg had no interest in wasting any more time now that Percy Sledger was out of the picture. And so he scuffed his feet along the forest floor, making his preparations. He could be home in just a few short hours. Greg Vansen was done wasting his time.

4

2.

Augustus

"Wait for me," Reed Treston said, voice crackling into the earpiece I had couched in my right ear. "I'm en route."

I was standing on an overlook in Steelwood Springs, Colorado, heart of the mountains, a town of ten thousand nestled in a valley surrounded by peaks, trying to decide whether to take the boss at his word. He probably was on his way, but that could mean he'd be an hour—or five minutes. A wise man might ask for clarification. A smaller man might meekly accept his fate, waiting for help and the cavalry and the forces of truth and justice to arrive before charging blindly into battle.

But was I a smaller man? Ohhhh hell no.

"They're coming up the road," I said, just riding right past his previous statement like I hadn't heard it. "They've got five cars of local cops on their tail." There was so much red and blue flashing beneath me that you could have mistaken it for a K-Mart back in the day. Blue light specials, yeah. I don't know what a red flashing light would have meant, other than the cops, though. Maybe a nuclear meltdown? So it was like a K-Mart blue light special crossed with a nuclear plant going boom.

Yeah.

What I'm trying to say is that there were a lot of cops, and they were chasing up a mountain road after a new-model Chevy Acadia with two guys hanging out the window and

5

firing energy shots at the cops in pursuit. I couldn't tell whether the blasts were coming out of the eyes or the hands or what, because it was dark and they were down the mountain from me, threading their way up the switchbacks trying to escape the Steelwood Springs valley, but they were definitely throwing some metahuman hurt at the pursuing cops, who were wisely keeping their distance.

They were doing their job.

And I was about to do mine.

"Do not engage," Reed said. "I'm coming to you."

"And by the time you get here, they could be up the pass and gone," I said. I needed to lay a little groundwork to justify what I was about to do. This wasn't government service or anything, but Reed was still my boss.

And he thought of everyone on his team as kids he was in charge of, so …

It was time to show him differently.

"Augustus—" he started to say, but I thumbed my earpiece, rocking it back and forth in my ear canal, messing with the slight vacuum it created in there.

"I can't hear you," I said, moving it back and forth. "Reed, are you there?"

"Augustus, don't—"

"I'll catch you when you get here, Reed!" I said, and then pushed the button to turn off the earpiece. Once it was off, I said, "Alone at last," and stared down the mountain at the approaching car.

This was going to be over long before Reed got here.

The getaway car was rolling closer to its inevitable intersection with the rock beneath my outcropping. It was a straight shot for me down the mountain, a ninety-degree cliff face that dropped down into oblivion.

I stepped off.

Rock reached out and caught me lightly, touching my wingtip shoes as it surged out from the cliff face, riding me slowly down like a living elevator of stone. It rippled its way down the vertical face of the cliff, an escalator that made way for me. I hunched over, leaning forward in my guided descent.

It was a real shame no one could see me right now, because I was pretty sure I looked *cool*.

I raced toward my rendezvous with the getaway car, still snaking its way up the S-curved road, energy blasts hurtling out the side windows at the cops behind it. The police were receding in the distance, the criminals slowly getting away from them.

My little segment of rock intersected with the getaway car's hood, two tons of stone T-boning its way through a Chevy's engine block and holding its ground. My new, expanded powers allowed me to treat earthy elements like rock and stone as though I had telekinesis. I could hold rock in a wall shape, and I did, causing that Chevy to rip damned near in half.

The Chevy's hood crumpled like cellophane wrap, and the windshield shattered, sending glass flying at me. Using my power over sand, I guided it gently around. Not that it would hurt me much, but the last thing I needed was one of those little pebbles getting caught in my eye and blinding me.

About a half second behind the glass came two of the criminals who'd prompted this manhunt. I couldn't see them very well because the car headlights—the only source of light up on this winding road—had shattered when I'd sheared them off in the collision. Still, I watched two astonished, fearful faces go flying by, arms pinwheeling, screams echoing in the night.

This, kids, is why you should always wear your seatbelt.

They both made a soft landing on rock as I caught them, gently as I could given what I was working with. I molded the rock around their arms, their heads, their faces, giving them room enough to breathe and little else. I locked them into squatting positions, like large gargoyles in the middle of the road, and then swept away the excess stone I'd used to pin their smashed car right to the cliff face just as the first cop car was pulling up.

I held my hands up and waved. "Hey, yo."

The first cop came popping out with his gun drawn, but had the decency not to point it at me. "You get 'em?" he called to me. I could see his face in the streaky blue and red light his car was casting over the accident scene, and I recognized him as Officer Duc. I'd met him earlier in the day, when we'd confabbed with the Steelwood Springs PD before this all unfolded.

"I got 'em," I said even as a whirling wind rolled over me, making me blink away. The sound of feet landing lightly behind me was like an alarm over the roaring police sirens as the cops started to swarm into the scene.

"You didn't wait," Reed said accusingly as he stepped out of his landing. Dude could walk out of the sky now like he was stepping off a city bus. He was looking a little petulant, too, like he might be about to give me a hard time about my failure to comply with his orders.

"I must have lost signal in these mountains," I said with a shrug.

He extended a hand, and a tiny wind sucked my earpiece right into his grasping fingers. He gave it a cursory look then tossed it back. I caught it. "You turned it off," he said.

"Hey, man, they were driving up a mountain road at night," I said. "I had this."

Reed gave the shattered car a wary once-over. "Looks that way." His voice was laden with doubt, like I hadn't just handled it.

"You don't have to worry about us, you know?" I tried to give him some confidence via our shared look, but he'd been pretty enigmatic lately. Leadership had changed Reed. Or maybe it was his time in the clouds that had done it. "You put together a great team. You just need to trust us, you know? Let us do our thing."

He looked at me with smoky, inscrutable eyes, then looked past me, his face alight with red and blue. "Tell you what: why don't you go do your 'thing' with the press, who are crawling their way up the mountain right … over there." He pointed down the mountain, at an onslaught of cars slowly working their way up the switchbacks toward us.

"You want me to … talk to them?" I asked, straightening my shirt. I was wearing a suit, because that was the dress code, but … suddenly I wondered if I was done up enough. I started to adjust my collar self-consciously.

Reed never let anyone else talk to the press. Not that they had shown up much at our scenes until recently, but it was starting to happen more frequently. "Sure," he said, though I was having a hard time telling whether he was being sarcastic or not. "Give it a shot."

"Thanks, man," I said, picking past him, waiting for him to say something, to call me back, tell me he was just kidding …

He didn't. So I headed toward the cop cars and beyond, where the police were already starting to set up a cordon, and a few people were already out of their cars gawking up the mountain, cameras in hand.

Hell yeah. It was time to make my big debut.

3.

Sienna

I was in the middle of doing a thousand rep set of curls with my three-hundred-pound dumbbells when Augustus came on the TV. I wanted to drop my weights and shout, "I know him!" because my human contact had been limited over the last couple months, but I was still self-aware enough to know that a person with six hundred pounds of weight in her hands shouldn't leap to her feet in a sixth-floor studio apartment.

Because I had dignity, dammit. And a very, very thin subfloor that I didn't want to break.

Instead I sat on the edge of my seat and kept curling my dumbbells furiously as I watched. "Dayum, boyee," I said softly as reporters thrust microphones in Augustus's face and asked him stupid questions like, "How do you feel right now?" and, "Was this level of violence really necessary?" Like there weren't still-living criminals in the wreckage behind him.

Clearly, the world was suffering from a deficit of Sienna if they considered that to be a level of violence that bordered on the unacceptable.

Every new age brings with it a softening of the people, Wolfe said with a trace of regret.

"It's called civilization, Wolfey. Most of us consider it a good thing."

Your fragility compared to the folk of my era is appalling, Bjorn opined.

10

"That's okay," I said, grunting as I curled again, "because your savagery is still pretty appalling to many of those living nowadays."

But not you, Eve Kappler said.

"Not entirely, no," I said. "But then, my savagery is appalling to a lot of people who live in the modern world."

Could you possibly stop exercising for one minute so I can pay attention to this? Gerry Harmon asked with vague disgust. *Not that I'm complaining that you've whipped yourself into shape, but it's really distracting to have all this grunting and straining going on while I'm trying to keep informed about the events of the day.*

"Why, thank you, Gerry," I said, not stopping. I wasn't Crossfit-crazy, but I'd definitely upped my game since I'd come to Portland to hunker down for the summer. I was still a shut-in for the most part, but I was filling my hours with fitness, with training—as much as my apartment floor could bear.

I should have rented an actual house. Stupid explosive Portland real estate market, blocking me from ground-floor opportunities at reasonable prices.

"You know, we're really just working hard to curb the instances of … uh, rising metahuman crime …" Augustus went on in the background.

Someone finally noticed the number of metas has gotten jacked up these last couple years, huh? Bastian asked.

"Scott knew," I said, pumping my iron. I couldn't stop. After this, it was going to be two thousand sit-ups while I watched the cooking channel. Which might end up costing me my gains when I made dinner. "That means the FBI knows. So it's out there."

"Trouble like this is on the rise," Augustus said. "We're just trying to do our part to make sure it's dealt with responsibly."

I could see Reed in the background, watching and listening. I'd caught him on a few shows lately, the face of this new agency, and while I loved my bro, it was nice to see Augustus putting his face forward.

You're actually sick of your brother's canned answers, aren't you? Harmon asked.

I stopped pumping iron for a sec. "Look, he's been on all

these shows, and I'm constantly watching—"

Just give me a straight up yes or no.

"Yes," I said, and resumed my curls. "Reed's a great conversationalist, but dealing with the press? It's not like conversation. More didacticism, and he repeats his talking points across every network until I'm ready to slap him in the back of the head just to see if he'll reboot."

Gavrikov chuckled. *But at least you see him. You know he is safe.*

"They're all safe, Aleksandr," I said. "Klementina's probably filming another season of Beyond Human or something. She'll pop up again soon."

I'm sure you're right.

In the meantime, Zack said, *do you think you'll ever take a break from this non-stop exercise? I mean, I'm not complaining, since I do get to see your new and improved ass in the mirror every morning, but—*

I paused. "New and improved ass, huh?" I strained my neck trying to look. I'd been working it too, all low weight (relative to my meta strength)/high rep stuff because ... well, it would have been a floor breaker to bring a set of weights into this apartment that would actually challenge me.

Your shoulders are pleasingly tighter as well, Eve said, a little too casually.

I ignored that, but flushed a little as I curled again. "No breaks, Zack. No stopping. I can't get slack again, and besides, imagine how being all thin and taut is going to improve my disguise when I go out in public." Plus I felt better. I was eating better (mostly). And I wasn't letting myself get down anymore about the pressure I was under. "Dr. Zollers says I need to take positive actions, steps forward toward my goals in order to keep my sanity, and that's what I'm going to do." My forearms and biceps strained. "I'm not letting doubt creep up on me again. I will be prepared for trouble, because trouble will inevitably—"

Come knocking at the door? Harmon asked.

"Yes," I said, only briefly taken aback at his helpfully finishing my sentence for me. "Trouble always comes knocking, eventually."

No, I mean you're going to need to answer the door now, because—

Knock knock! The sound was loud and urgent.

"Who's that?" I muttered.

Trouble, Harmon said. *You should open it and see.*

I gently set down one of my dumb bells and kept hold of the other one, readying it to use as a club if Harmon was underselling it. I creaked across the rickety old floor and unlocked the door, wondering if I was making a mistake by answering it.

I threw it open at top speed and immediately backed up because a painfully thin guy came staggering in, drenched with water and blood, coughing, and flopped down only a few feet inside. He was skinny to the point of bony, sodden, hair hanging in limp ringlets over a pale face that was covered in a couple days of scraggly beard growth. I couldn't recall ever seeing him before, but as he fell he grabbed my arm with meta strength and squeezed hard enough to get my attention. "Sienna ..." he wheezed, and then I saw that he'd been lung-shot, the wound already starting to heal over. "... you have to ... help me ..."

"Who the hell are you?" I asked without tempering my response. It wasn't every day that total strangers came looking for me at my safe house, soaked to the skin and nursing a sucking chest wound. I kicked the door closed because I didn't want to chance any of my hipster neighbors overhearing this. They probably thought I was weird enough (compared to them) without adding any fuel to that fire.

"It's me ..." he said, staring up at me, his eyes rolling back in his head, hand clutching at the leg of my yoga pants (yes, I was wearing them unironically, shut up). "It's ... me ..."

"You who?" I brandished the dumbell. "Explain or I'm gonna make that gunshot the least of your probl—"

"It's me, Sienna ..." he said, rasping, "... Guy Friday ..." And then his body relaxed, grip letting go of my pants leg as he passed out without another word.

Well, Harmon said with undisguised amusement, *you wanted to be ready for trouble ... here it is.*

"Son of a bitch," I said, "how do these assholes keep finding me?"

4.

Augustus

It's not easy to disengage from a whole raft of people that
are asking you questions, especially when you were raised by
a momma who smacked you in the back of the head every
time she felt like you weren't being polite. Ignoring people
isn't polite, but eventually I had to stop talking to the press
because Reed had made his way off camera and started to
signal to me that he needed my attention elsewhere, a stern
look on his face and the local police chief standing
impatiently next to him.

I made my way over to them, feeling of nervousness
rising in my stomach. "Did I do okay?" I asked as I
approached.

Reed stared at me blankly for a second. "I'm sure you did
fine. We need you to 'unlock' the bad guys, though."

"Oh. Right." I'd forgotten about that, and started toward
the place where I'd left those boys all gargoyled up in a stony
covering. The police chief trailed me, Reed a couple steps
behind him.

"Really impressive, this takedown," the chief said as we
made our way past the wreckage of the Chevy, smoke
wafting gently off its hood in the combined glare of fifty
headlights. The chief's name was Smithson, and he'd been
kinda standoffish when we'd first arrived to consult with
him. Seemed to be warming up now, though. "And no rock
left on the road for us to clean up, either, except for the stuff

14

still wrapped around those fellas."

"Let me take care of that, and you'll have nothing left to clean up," I said, making my way over to them. They were both shouting from inside their stone encasements, voices sounding scratchy from non-stop screaming to be let out. A few cops were admiring my handiwork and chuckling to themselves. I had left those criminals on all fours, and they looked a little like stone-carved dogs.

"Really impressive," the chief reiterated. From some people it might have sounded ironic, but the barely concealed awe in his voice made it obvious he was being genuine.

"This is what we do," Reed said.

"Pros from Dover," the chief said. "I get that."

"From Minneapolis, technically," Reed said, and nodded at me. "Go on."

"What? I'm from Atlanta." I pushed back a layer of the rock from the backs of the criminals, and waved a cop with a syringe in his hand forward to dose them with suppressant. He did his thing, and then I waited about sixty seconds, then broke apart the statuettes. "There you go, chief. Two meta criminals, declawed and ready for transport."

"Oh, hallelujah," one of the crooks said, gasping for breath like I'd suffocated him. He kissed the ground and started to get to his feet, but a couple of cops wrestled him back down and metacuffed him. He didn't seem fussed by all the extra weight and power muscling him down; he wore a slight smile as he seemed to savor the cool mountain air. "Another few minutes in that thing and I would have told you everything I'd ever done wrong just to get out."

"I can put you back in if you'd like," I said, drawing his wide, fearful eyes to me as the cops dragged him to his feet.

"Dude, I will tell you whatever you want to know," he said. "Just don't … put me back in there."

I shrugged, looking at the chief, who shrugged back. I could tell he was thinking the same thing—that it'd be a shame not to take advantage of this fine opportunity.

"What's your name?" I asked.

"Keith Davidson," the guy said. I looked to see if his

15

compatriot was going to try and get him to shut up, but that guy was quiet as a mouse, and the cops were already culling him from his friend, dragging him toward a cop car to have their own conversation with him. Reed followed slowly behind, providing a watchful eye.

"Where do you live, Keith?" I asked. He spat out an address, chattering almost pleadingly. "And when did you get your powers?"

"Last week," Keith said, suspended between two bulky officers.

I went through the timeline in my head. We'd just gotten called about these guys last week. "Did you even wait a day before you started doing these home invasions?"

He nodded eagerly, like a dog. "Well, we were high as hell for the first day, so ... yeah? We both got our powers at the same time, Jacob and I. And we decided, you know, because we were both between jobs—"

"Do you two live together?" I asked, drawing a pissed-off look from the chief. I'd cut off his confession, I realized, and there were three cops standing around with recorders going.

"Yep," Keith said. "We have for about three years now. We met after high school and y'know, got to be friends."

"Tell me about what you did after you found out you had powers," I said, and let him start rambling on in a full confession of his crimes while I did some thinking of my own. The chief was nodding, smile on his face, and the other cops were watching with plain satisfaction as well.

He said he'd gotten his powers last week, but looking at Keith Davidson, he had to be nearing thirty. The fact that he and his accomplice had been roommates was also suspicious. They both manifested powers the same day, were unrelated, and lived in the same house.

This situation was setting off all my alarm bells, because everything about it suggested that they were not natural-born metas.

It was a dirty little secret of our business that for a while now the number of metahumans had been increasing in an unnatural way. Metahuman powers were originally a genetic pass-down; if your parent was a meta, chances were you would be, too. Sienna had told me early on that only a small percentage of people were born with metahuman genes, and even at the height there had only been about six thousand on the entire earth. An attempted genocide had brought that number down to less than a thousand, most of whom had been concentrated in the United States.

But based on everything we were seeing lately … someone was making new metahumans in the US at a rapid pace. I wasn't a natural born meta. Neither was my brother, Jamal, or my girlfriend, Taneshia. My old boss had invented a serum that unlocked meta powers, and he'd tested it in my house's water, among other places, which had accounted for the sudden appearance of powers for the three of us, well past the age when a natural meta would have manifested their abilities.

Either Keith and his buddy had somehow encountered the same serum, or else they'd suddenly developed late-in-the-game powers simultaneously, without being related.

Yeah … that was pretty damned unlikely.

Keith was wrapping up his confession, and I waited for a pause in the conversation to ask my next question. "Do you have any new friends, Keith? Anyone you've met recently?"

"Ahh, there's a girl, Danica," he said, racking his brain. "I was kinda seeing her a little bit. Took her out last night."

"What's her last name?"

"Shore," he said. "Her roommate went out with Jacob, too."

"Anyone in the week before that?" I asked. "New friends? Met anyone? Had a … I dunno, a plumber … do any work at your house?"

"Yeah, our sink sprung a leak last week," he said, frowning. "How'd you know?"

"Just a guess," I said, suddenly feeling a whole lot of excited. Another wild coincidence? I doubted it. "You know what plumbing company they were from?"

"I dunno, our landlord called them," Keith said, shrugging as expansively as the metacuffs and the cops hanging on him would allow. "He was Arabian, maybe? Omar, I think? Last name was, uh … Sharif?"

17

"Oh, the guy who fixed your sink was Omar Sharif, huh?" I quipped. "Must have been a real step down for him, coming back from the dead to fix sinks in Steelwood Springs."

"I don't remember his name, man," Keith said. "Ask my landlord. The guy was quiet. Mumbled a lot. I didn't even know if he spoke English, cuz he just sort of nodded whenever I'd ask him something."

"If you think of anything else, have the cops here let me know," I said.

"Hah," Keith said, and now he was smiling. "I'll come tell you myself. I'm going to be out in like five minutes."

The chief rumbled with a big belly laugh. "How do you figure that? You just confessed to at least ten felonies, and we got it all on tape."

Keith grinned. "You didn't read me my rights."

Every cop around him exploded into laughter, including the chief, and, with a few guffaws, me.

Keith's grin faded. "What? You didn't read them to me! That means you can't use my confession."

"Check with your lawyer about that, see what he says," the chief said, laughter drifting off. "That's funny. Didn't read him his rights. Gentlemen ... do this man the courtesy of reading his Miranda rights to him, will you?"

"You have the right to remain silent," one of the cops started.

"You can't do that now!" Keith said, suddenly alarmed.

"Oh, yeah, he can," I said, and Keith's jaw dropped. "As a suggestion ... you really shouldn't take legal advice from TV shows and movies. Writers aren't lawyers."

"Awww, man," Keith said as they dragged him away toward a patrol car.

"What was that about?" Reed asked, sidling up to me.

"Dumb criminals, part eight hundred and seventy three," I said. "I got a lead on something."

Reed cocked an eyebrow. "Do tell."

"These boys manifested last week," I said. "After a plumber did some work on their sink."

"You're thinking it feels like how you—"

"Yep," I said. "And I'm also thinking … we might have our first actual lead on this case of the suddenly exploding meta criminal population. Keith here seems to remember a plumber named Omar, last name possibly Sharif—"

"His plumber was a dead Egyptian actor?"

"I dunno. I was going to check with the landlord, who supposedly called the plumber. Figured it might be worth a look."

Reed stayed quiet for a second, and I waited with bated breath. We had other cases pending. A whole bunch of them, in fact.

But this was big. Potentially huge. It was like an apple that had been dangling in front of our faces for months, maybe even years, and now was tantalizingly close enough to grab a bite of … if only Reed would let me.

"All right," he said, nodding once. "It's about time we got a break in this." He went quiet again for a second. "You want to look into it on your own?"

"You got better things to do?" I needled him lightly. He had a dozen requests for help from local and state police forces requesting help. Legitimate needs, actual requests backed by cash paid from those departments for aid in catching problem metas. These were the things that paid the bills, whereas what I wanted to look into …

Well, if I managed to somehow stop all these unnatural metas from appearing, it'd kinda put a kink in our business.

"I've got brushfires to put out," Reed said. "But you've got a line on the arsonist. So, yeah, I want you to look into it. And if you need help—"

"I'll call," I said.

"Good," Reed said with a curt nod. "Then if you'll excuse me … I think I have business tonight in Oklahoma City." He froze, thinking. "Or was it Yuma, Arizona? Hell," he said mildly and fumbled for his cell phone to call the office. "Hurry up on this, because we need you elsewhere."

"I'll get right to the bottom of it," I said, trying to hold in my jubilance at having a case of my very own, one that I'd unearthed myself. It was a little unseemly, glorying in the idea of getting to work alone for a change, to tackle something serious that fundamentally affected all our lives.

"Keep me in the loop," Reed said and stepped up onto the air, letting it carry him away as he held his phone up to his ear. He wafted straight up, a blast of air the only sign of his passage, and left me alone on the mountainside as he headed off to the next destination.

Hell yeah. Now it was time to do things my way.

5.

Sienna

I tossed a glass of cold water in Friday's face. "Wake up, jaghole."

He sputtered as he woke, icy water coursing down his face and dripping onto his torn, damp clothes. He looked like he'd gone for a moonlight swim somewhere before he'd shown up on my door, and as he shook his stubbly, bone-thin face in response to the water, he peeked up at me. "What the hell?" he asked pitifully. I recognized the voice, though it wasn't as deep as Friday sounded when he was bulked up.

"What are you doing here?" I asked. "How did you find me?"

He looked down at the light nets wrapped around his chest, securing him to the chair. "Did you … tie me up?"

"Yes," I said. "Breaking out of them would give me the half-second I'd need to vaporize you, so I'd learn to love the feeling of light webs if I were you."

He gawked, then composed himself, breaking into a leer. "Kinky."

"This is going to turn into Fifty Shades of Skull Trauma if you persist in being a dipshit," I said. "Now answer my questions or I will turn you over and feed you into my garbage disposal, because it looks like your pin head would fit perfectly down my drain, Beaker."

"I've got an assassin after me," Friday burbled, dropping

the stupid leer and adopting a deadly earnestness. I'd never seen him without his mask, but the lips looked about right, and so did the eyes, though they certainly evinced more fear now than I'd ever seen from him in the time we'd known each other. "He caught up with me tonight on a cliff over the Columbia River. I jumped and he shot me."

I took that in, glancing at the TV, which was still covering the events in Steelwood Springs, Colorado, though Augustus had vanished and now it was just a reporter talking with a bunch of police cars and a dark night for a background. "Why is an assassin after you?" I asked. I was marginally more interested in whatever Augustus had going on, but unfortunately, he wasn't here and Friday was. "And how did you find me?"

"I can't tell you how I found you," Friday said, straining lightly against the light nets.

"I don't like your attitude," I said, lighting up my finger with fire. "How long has it been since you've done the 'turn your head and cough' test? Because I'm worried you might have a hernia after that fall."

"No! Please, wait!" Friday said, and now that I could see him emote, I sort of realized why he wore the mask. He did not have a poker face. Nor a particularly pretty face, at all. But the mask was probably more for the first reason. "I—I can tell you, but only if you help me."

I laughed. "I can kill you, and then I don't have to help you."

"You can kill me, but then you'll never know how I found you," he said, sounding increasingly desperate. "Or if others are coming." He licked his lips. "Help me and I'll tell you."

"You're seriously negotiating with me right now?" I stretched my shoulders, which were still glistening with sweat from my exercise.

"Please," Friday said, and again he showed off his expressive range of emotion. The pleading, the worry, it was all written across his forehead, around his eyes. "I don't have anyone else to go to."

You should help him, Harmon piped up.

Yeah, Zack agreed.

I made a face at Friday, one that he probably thought he caused. *Are you out of your minds? This is Guy Friday we're talking about. We've stepped on more sympathetic dog turds than this guy.*

Yes, Gavrikov agreed, *but …*

But what? I prodded, keeping my thoughts from springing out as I favored Friday with a hard stare during this little dialogue. He looked back with rising alarm, as though he thought I was trying to make him spontaneously combust with my mind. Which I could have done, technically, I suppose.

You're bored, Wolfe said.

You have been training, waiting for a case to appear, Eve said. *Well, here one is.*

But this is Friday, people! I said. Friday! He once locked himself out of his own cellphone because he forgot that his password was 1234.

I don't see anyone else knocking down your door looking for help, Bjorn said.

Any old port in a storm, Bastian agreed.

But. It's. Friday! He's tried to kill me—

So did Scott, Zack said, *but you helped him.*

And didn't you nearly add Jamal Coleman to our ranks once upon a time? Eve asked. *Yet when he asked for help, you came running.*

"I feel like you're going to make my brain explode," Friday said nervously.

"You would need a brain first in order for that to happen," I snapped. Those guys were different. Scott was mind-controlled. And Jamal had a history of helping me. There was context. There is no such pleasant history between Friday and I.

You were colleagues once, Gavrikov said.

Isn't there a code that says you should help the people you work with? Wolfe asked.

Bullshit, Wolfe. *If you've ever helped a co-worker, I will commit an act of cannibalism.*

Wolfe worked for Omega, remember? There were many, many co-workers. Once I helped Bastet move a box. Wolfe smiled smugly in my head. *Now … about finding some tender meat as a reward—*

I ate Sovereign, I said, *so there. Promise fulfilled.*

Not fair. You spat him out. That doesn't count.

Sienna ... Zack said. *You've got nothing else going, and you live for this kind of thing. Give Friday a hand, and then he'll tell you how he found you. It's win/win.*

Helping Friday doesn't feel like winning to me. I frowned, causing Friday to subtly flinch away from me. *And what if he's setting an elaborate trap?*

Look at him, Harmon said. *You just know he isn't.*

Why don't you just tell me how he found me and spare me this Faustian bargain? I asked.

Because then you'd just kick him out and move to another safe house, committing us to months and possibly years more of boredom while you endlessly pump iron and watch TV. Please, Harmon said, *let's break the monotony.*

"I ..." I said, staring at Friday through narrowed eyes, "... I am considering your offer. The payment is that you'll tell me how you found me?"

Friday nodded. "I also have a few bucks—"

"I don't need your money, Friday," I said. He was dripping all over my floor, but this safe house was basically burned now that he'd found me here, so it didn't bother me as much as it might have otherwise that he was ruining things. I glanced back at the TV and my weights arrayed around the couch. Harmon was, as always, annoyingly on point: if I didn't help Friday, I'd be sitting around somewhere else, head down, working out endlessly while irritating myself and my souls with a constant IV of cable news broken by the occasional grocery trip and On Demand movie.

It was a formula for madness.

You said it, sister, Eve agreed.

"Fine, you have a deal," I said grudgingly and dissolved the net holding him to the chair with a wave of my hand.

"Whew," he said, rolling his shoulders around. "I was getting kinda worried there for a minute."

"You had good reason," I said. "Now ... tell me everything, Friday."

"My name's not Friday."

"I know that. I'm the one who first called you Friday,

remember?"

"Oh. Right. So, for a while I worked in this paramilitary outfit," Friday said. "We were totally awesome, like Spec Ops with superpowers. We were so badass, we were like kryptonite for every jerk dictator and terrorist on the planet." The chair creaked under Friday's skinny ass. "Anyway," he said, "one of the guys in my group was named Greg Vansen. He didn't recognize me, but ..." Friday's small frame seemed to somehow deflate further. "Greg was the guy who tried to kill me tonight."

"How did he not know ... oh." I stared at him, blinking in disbelief. "Did you wear your mask the whole time you were with them, too?"

"Yeah, always," Friday said. "It's my totally awesome thing. It adds mystique, makes me an enigma. Plus I have a fake name now. Percy Sledger."

"Percy ... Sledger?" I snorted. "You stole your name from the guy who originally sang 'When a Man Loves a Woman'?"

"He's Percy Sledge," Friday said with irritation. "I was Percy *Sledger*. And how do you know about Percy Sledge?"

"My mom was a big fan of oldies," I said. "So, I'm just going to call you Friday, because it's easier for me and Percy is a lie anyway. Why does this Greg Vansen guy want to kill you? I mean, as a former co-worker, I kindasorta wanted to kill you at various points, but does he have a specific grievance, like you always left the coffee pot empty? Or is it just sort of 'He knows you, therefore he wants to murder you'?"

"I don't know," Friday said. "We seemed to get along fine when we were working together. Like you and me, you know—"

I tried not to laugh. Not very hard, but I tried. "We did not 'get along,' Friday. Why is Greg Vansen trying to kill you?"

"I don't know, exactly," Friday said, and then he sat there, stiffly, not looking at me. "But I know this: Greg Vansen ... he's the best assassin there is. You never hear him coming, never see him coming—"

"What the hell does that even mean? Does he turn invisible?"

"As good as," Friday said. "He's like a magician. And he has an array of weapons at his disposal you wouldn't believe. Every gun imaginable—"

"Wait, wait," I said, holding up the hand to get him to stop again. "He uses guns? What kind of meta is he?"

"I don't know what his power was," Friday said, and he shuddered a little. "He was like magic, though. If he needed a rifle, suddenly he had a rifle in his hands. If he wanted to disappear, he was gone—poof! I saw him do things I've never seen any meta do before, and whenever you'd ask him how he did it, he just did this kind of smug smile and said, 'Preparation.'"

"What ... does that even mean?" I asked. "And why is this guy suddenly after you? You must have some idea."

Friday settled back in the chair, thinking hard. It looked painful, that concentration, like he was trying to get a thought out, or maybe like he was about to break a streak of constipation. "Well ... there was this one mission we went on that might have something to do with it ..."

6.

Friday

Torrijos International Airport, Panama
December 20, 1989

Sienna note: I'm pretty sure Friday made this shit up.

There was a band playing the most metal version of the
"Star-Spangled Banner" you've ever heard when we came
dropping out of the plane. It was like Metallica crossed with
Nirvana but dipped in a little AC/DC, like the hard
chocolate coating on a Nestlé Drumstick. It RAWKED!
Which was good, because we came parachuting into Panama
like the fallen angels of hell coming down on fluffy little
unsuspecting kittens! RAWR!!!!

Sienna note: Sigh.

Stop interrupting! It was the awesomest awesome ever,
falling out of the sky on wings of fiery hell angels spitting
metal tunes like—

You mean you were wearing parachutes?

You're such a buzzkill, girl.

"HELL YEAHHHHHHH!" I screamed as I parachuted
down, a full-sized Gatling gun in each hand, belts of ammo
rolled around my huge, oiled-up biceps. My veins throbbed
with   pure   power   as   the   metal   rocked   my   soul.
"YEAHHHHHHHH!" I lit up the anti-aircraft batteries
hanging out below, my Gatling guns screaming along with
the metal badassness playing around us. It was so diesel, you

27

could almost imagine bald eagles flying with us and ripping the shit out of the Panama soldiers running around screaming below.

"OH MY GOD," they screamed, "IT'S THE AMERICANS WITH THEIR HUGE MUSCLES AND HUGER PENISES!"

Oh, yeah? They said that?

Damned right they did.

Just like that?

Well, hell yeah. Exactly like that. Every word.

*In … English? *SMACK**

OW! What the hell was that for?

They speak Spanish in Panama, pendejo.

Hey, uh, well, uh, the Panama-ians—uhh, Panama-ans -

Panamanians.

Yeah, the Panama guys, they really said it, I'm telling you. One look at me—throbbing biceps, heaving chest, you know—you see these cobras coming, it's like Ah-nold and Stallone coming for you all at once, you know?

Sigh.

I ran my Gatling gun over their positions anyway, listening to the Panama-ia—uh, those Panama guys— screaming about, you know, our huge junk as they abandoned their posts and ran off into the night. I blew up their AA guns, running my line of tracer bullets over a fuel tanker sitting on the runway. It took a few Gatling rounds and BOOM! Like an explosion right out of a movie, man, it goes off like a little nuclear bomb in the night! KAPOW! It lit up the whole airport!

"Hell yeah!" I shouted into the night as I landed, sweeping off my parachute in one move, explosions going off all around me as I walked in slow motion away from the tanker blowing up on the tarmac behind me. My gats were rolling, tracers streaking toward these dug-in sandbag positions—

*I thought everyone abandoned their posts and ran off into the night? Because of your huge penises. *Snicker**

—and I was pounding them with heavy fire, both my gats roaring. Hot, blazing brass was tinkling around my feet as the ammo belts streamed off my heaving, muscled chest. But most of the bullets were hitting the sandbags and stopping. I strode toward that main position, trying to get up on them, but a guy popped up and took a shot at me before I could whip my gat around and take him out.

"Ow!" Sexy blood went rolling down my arm where the Panama-guy stung me with his pop gun. Felt like a bee stung me, but I knew it was nothing. "You will pay for giving me a flesh wound that will mar my sexiness when I lay siege to your bars later tonight and quench my deepest desires many times with your Panama women! And none of your wives will ever want you again, because they will never be satisfied with your inadequacy after tasting the awesomeness and hugeness of me! FREEDOM!"

... *Really?*

I'm just ignoring you now because you're totally breaking my flow.

I felt a couple more stings and roared in the night. "Just flesh wounds!" I screamed, blasting away again with the gats. I could hear Panama guys scream, too, probably thinking about how my guns would kill them and my other gun would leave their widows—

I will toss you out of this apartment via the window and you can give the pavement a more sincere kiss than any Panamanian woman— or any woman, period—ever gave you.

"Are you all right?" A shouted voice from overhead caused me to look up.

"I'm fine! I've got them on the run and fearing for the lusts of their women!" I shouted back.

Jon Wiegert came streaking overhead, bulletproof surfboard attached to his feet and two Uzis clutched in his hands. He flew over me and raked those Panama guys that were hosing me down, causing them to jerk like they'd been shocked with an electric cable.

"Those were my bad guys!" I screamed, raising my gats to the sky and letting them hammer out a rhythm to match that metal version of the "Star-Spangled Banner" playing around me. The screaming whine of the gat mirrored my own feelings; with the last of the Panama guys dead or running, that was the end of my non-Panama-lady fun for the night.

Sigh.

"What took you so long?" I turned and saw Greg Vansen standing on the tarmac behind me. He wasn't a really tall guy, but he was standing next to a Concorde … he just looked small, like maybe 5'4" at most. He had a look in his eyes of irritated disappointment, and I knew that he was no competition for me with the Panama ladies, and his jealousy was thick as his abnormally stocky torso. Seriously, he was shaped like a fire hydrant.

But he was standing on the bodies of like fifty Panama guys I hadn't even seen. It was so metal, like he was on a pile of bones. Except they still had skin on them. For now.

Jon flew back overhead and hovered, just standing on his surfboard, Uzis smoking in the night. "Whoa, Greg. Nice body count."

"Thanks," Greg said, his raspy, lizard-like drawl and totally expressionless face kinda creeping me out. I thought about spinning up the gats but he was on my side. "We should get out of here. Now. Before—"

Shots cracked off, and again someone got me in the arm. "Flesh wound!" I shouted as a little blood sprayed in the night like a money shot to my mask, making me look even tougher and more awesome—

Sigh.

—Ignoring you! I started to go for them, and I saw Jon do the same, using his surfboard as a shield for the bullets that were coming our way, but suddenly those guys were all like, "Whooooa!" And they all jerked like someone had stuck a Taser up their asses, and suddenly Greg was just standing there over their bodies, standing on one of their heads, out of freaking nowhere, man!

"Whoa, Greg! How did you do that?" Jon asked, completely taken aback by his sudden disappearance and reappearance.

Greg just ignored us, kneeling down to talk to one of the Panamia-uh—those guys. He grabbed the dude by the head and looked him in the eyes, totally pissed off. "I hate a coward," he said, really steaming. "Any last words?" The guy blathered something I didn't understand—

Clearly it wasn't about huge penises, then.

—and Greg just looked at him for a second, all pissed and stuff, and he just stood and the guy's head just ripped right off! I was like, WHOOOOOOA! And Jon was like, WHOOAAAA! And together we were like, "Whoa, Greg, that was totes awesome!" I said. "I mean, I'm strong, and can do that, of course, but you're a tiny little man with probably a very small penis, and you just tore that guy's head off! Awesome!"

Greg just gave me that lizard look and said, "On the plane," as he tossed that guy's head and kicked it like a soccer ball. It flew across the tarmac and into the night.

"Dude, that's a field goal for sure," Jon whispered as we trudged toward the Concorde. "Also, I swear this Concorde wasn't here when we flew in."

"Whatever, dude, Greg is a magician," I said, shrinking down my leet muscles a little bit so I could climb up into the plane. Greg was already up there, and in the cockpit as I slipped in. The passenger section was all nice and clean, and I threw down my gats—

"What the hell are you doing?" Greg screamed at me from the cockpit. He was there in a second, like he teleported and appeared, his face all burning and furious, twisted like he was gonna pop a vein.

"Yo, you need to calm down, check yourself before you wreck yourself," I said, and Jon snickered as he stowed his bulletproof surfboard.

"Get those smoking, burning Gatling guns off my carpet!" Greg shouted, and I looked down. My gats were kinda making a mess of his carpet. Also, the place kinda smelled like the inside of a dispensary.

He seemed like he was about ready to pop a blood vessel, so I said, "You need to take a chill pill, Greg."

Greg swooped down and grabbed my gats. They freaking disappeared right in his hand! He just stood there and shook in pure anger, while I looked to see if he'd stuck them up his sleeve like a magician or something. I mean, they weigh a few hundred pounds, and he'd just disappeared them like

Copperfield with the Statue of Liberty.

"Dude!" I said. "My guns!"

"Don't make a mess in my plane or your guns won't be the only thing to disappear," he said, grinding his teeth.

"Well, what else is there?" I asked. "You already took my guns. I mean, what else could disappear—" I gasped, and covered my crotch. "No! You wouldn't!"

He just narrowed his eyes at me. "Sit down and shut up." And he poofed back to the cockpit.

"Dude," Jon leaned over to me across the aisle between our seats. "Greg is crazy, man."

"I think he just threatened to disappear my penis!" I said. "Good thing it's so huge he could disappear it by half and it'd still be bigger than—"

Pavement. Kiss.

"What do you think that guy's power is?" Jon asked, stealing a look at Greg, who was now hunched over the controls in the cockpit. We were whispering really low, so Greg couldn't hear us.

"He like, disappears and reappears, he tears peoples' heads off with his bare hands … I don't know," I said. "But they're pretty metal. Like KISS opening for Rammstein with a whole orchestra of electric guitars." The plane started to move, jerking a little.

"Yeah, that's crazy," Jon said, leaning back in his seat as the Concorde jerked down the runway. It didn't even taxi first, just started right into takeoff. "I don't know, man. Good thing he's on our side."

"But what if he's really not, Jon?" I asked, stroking my chin like a super smart private detective guy. "What if one day he finally snaps because he's jealous of our junk? He might just come after us, ready to—"

7.

Sienna

"—kill us all," Friday said, actually stroking his chin like it made him look smarter. Honestly, a well-worn copy of Newton's *Principia*, a beret, and a degree from Cambridge tucked ostentatiously under his arm couldn't make him look smarter.

I was trying very hard during his entire story to contain the sort of eyerolls that would break every muscle in my skull, but now I released and it felt so, so good as I threw my head back for an epic one. "You did not say that at the time."

"I did!"

"And your theory for why? Because he's suffering from penis envy? Seriously?"

"It's as good an explanation as any." Friday looked a little crestfallen, and his hand fell away from his chin.

"Admit it," I said, "you have no idea why he wants to kill you."

"Maybe not," he conceded. "But it was probably something to do with that Panama mission. He only showed up at the end, after all, and he could, like, teleport, so maybe he could have crisscrossed the whole base in the time we were there, tracking down secret intelligence and executing other mission targets we didn't know about. There probably a hidden objective, like he had to secretly assassinate Manuel Noriega."

"Noriega went to jail after Panama," I said. "Hell, he's still in jail, but back home now, I think. He wasn't assassinated."

"Well, I don't know what Greg was doing, then." Friday shrugged. "Maybe Jon knows. It had to be something secret. Something cool. Something which threatens the lives of everyone who knew about it." He was talking in a low, serious voice, like he was narrating some sort of docudrama about his own life.

I scratched my hair, the sweat from my earlier exercise having dried on my scalp and left me with that kind of sticky, itchy sensation you get after a workout. "Huh. So you have no idea what this guy's powers are, you don't have a clue why he wants to kill you … Basically, you know nothing."

"But it's probably related to Panama," Friday said. "Or his jealousy over—"

"Panama, huh?" I leapt at the thin gruel with which I'd been presented just to avoid any further discussion of Friday's privates. He'd already proven himself about as reliable a narrator as a drunk surgeon with greased up hands about to perform micro brain surgery. Now, if the target of said brain surgery was Friday, he'd have a wide margin for error …

"Definitely," Friday said, and he suddenly got a little more earnest. "Please … will you help me?"

I wanted to eyeroll, but I couldn't. Friday had come across the country seeking me, a person he'd never gotten along with, and fear, genuine fear, was showing plainly on his face now. And based on everything he told me …

He had good reason to be afraid.

"Yes, I'll help you," I said. A chorus of voices exulted in my head.

Yay! A case! Harmon said with less sarcasm and more sincerity than I would have thought him capable of.

Time to put those tight shoulders to good use, Eve said.

"It's going to be great working together again," Friday said. "It's been a long time since I've had someone close to my level to partner up with. Tough to find good help, you know, compared to this." He flexed, ripping off his soaked, half-shredded shirt.

"Yeah, whatever," I said, partially ignoring him. "I will say, though … in spite of your disastrous storytelling—"

"My storytelling was awesome."

"Ignoring you because you're breaking my flow," I said. "In spite of that … I did get one thing out of it."

He cocked an eyebrow at me. "Oh yeah? What's that?"

"This Greg Vansen guy?" I shook my head, thinking about what Friday had said. A seeming ability to teleport? Enough strength to rip off heads? This guy was a top-of-the-power-scale meta. "He sounds like a real, implacable badass."

8.

Greg

"Would you like some more eggs, dear?" Greg Vansen asked, holding the ivory-colored porcelain dish out and letting the spoon hover, little bits of yolk clinging to its silvery surface.

"No, thank you." Morgan Vansen favored her husband with a smile, her youthful features aglow in the morning light. Sun streamed in through the windows of their breakfast nook, no clouds on the horizon. Greg could see the shingles of the house next door from here, but it was a good ways off. They lived in a pricey Chicago suburb, in an older home where there was actually still space between the houses, that rarest of luxuries in a metropolis as massive as this one.

Greg swung the egg dish back down to the immaculate white tablecloth. He always cooked breakfast when he got back from fulfilling a contract, up early the next morning with the rush of exuberance that accompanied a success. It might have taken longer than he'd intended, and not come off as cleanly as he might have hoped, but Percy Sledger was dead, and that was all that mattered. "Eddie," Greg asked as an afterthought, looking at his son, his only child, who sat to his right, "would you like some more eg—"

"I want to be a zookeeper when I grow up," Eddie declared. His voice was high, the pitch appropriate to a baying dog or an overexcited five-year-old, which Eddie was.

Morgan beamed at her son across the table. "What kind of animals do you most want to take care of, sweetie?" She asked in a sugary tone.

Greg shifted the eggs on his plate, trying to keep a mild twitch in his right eye at bay.

"I like the lions," Eddie said. "I want to get five lions as my pets when I grow up." He shifted his gaze to Greg, a kind of worshipfulness in his eyes. "Daddy, can we get lions?"

"I thought you said you wanted them when you were an adult?" Greg speared a small cluster of egg and placed it daintily in his mouth. Greg didn't particularly enjoy being pedantic, but it came naturally to him, with his focus on details.

"I want them now," Eddie moped, "but you said we can't have any pets."

"We can't have any pets," Greg spoke around the egg in his mouth.

"Why not?" Eddie asked.

"Because I said so," Greg said firmly, ignoring that sudden blush of heat in his cheeks. He didn't like to be questioned.

"But why not?" Eddie asked.

Now Greg's face felt like it was steaming. Getting asked the same question more than once was a particular peeve of his, sure to push his dial. "Because I said so, young man. Now finish your breakfast."

"But why n—"

"Eddie, you heard your father," Morgan said firmly. It was good that she did. Being asked the same question a third time would not have done anything good for Greg's patience.

Greg's cell phone trilled in the distance, and Morgan sat up straight. "Do you want me to get that?"

Greg hesitated, another forkful of eggs paused halfway to his mouth. "No. I'll get it." He set down his fork carefully, pushed back from the table, taking a look around the sunlit breakfast alcove, and paced toward the kitchen, light sparkling off the white granite counters.

"Why do you want lions for pets?" Morgan asked as Greg passed through the arch toward his office in the front of the house.

"Because they're so cool, Mom," Eddie replied.

Greg scooped up his phone from the charging station where he'd left it as he stepped into his beautifully appointed, oak-covered office. He stared at the number flashing on the screen for only a second before answering. It wasn't in the phone's memory, but he knew it nonetheless, as he knew every number that normally might have been stored in his contact list—if he didn't change phones frequently.

"Mr. McGarry," Greg said as he answered, keeping his reply pleasant and professional. Mark McGarry was his most regular employer, the one who'd hired him to kill Percy Sledger. "You received my confirmation?"

"That the contract was fulfilled?" McGarry's voice was rough, American accent shot through with a faint hint of something from Europe, though faded and only audible every few words. "Yes, I got the message. Unfortunately, I got another one shortly after from one of my sources ... Sledger's still breathing."

"That is physically impossible," Greg said, keeping his tone in realm of polite disbelief. "He fell into the Columbia Gorge. No human could have survived—"

"Sledger is a meta," McGarry said, causing Greg to freeze in place.

Greg's face burned, internal temperature rising fast. This was a humiliating miscalculation. He kept his voice low, but avoided any ice in his reply. "That would have been useful information to have before I undertook the contract."

"Yeah, well, you didn't need it, so I didn't tell you," McGarry said. "I assumed you'd be able to work your usual magic."

"Magic requires a certain element of preparation," Greg said. "Preparation requires knowledge of what you're facing. Had I been fully informed, I would have been able to calculate the probabilities of Mr. Sledger's escape differently." More accurately, he meant, but that was irrelevant at this point. Greg was steaming again, set to a simmer by Eddie's inane questions, and now brought to a boil by McGarry's failure to inform of him of vital information. To think, in addition to running him around for more than a week, Sledger had survived his impossible fall because he'd possessed powers, a durability that Greg hadn't known about.

Greg's cheeks burned, the hot embarrassment and sensation of being utterly fooled causing his fingers to tighten around the phone. This was deeply upsetting, being caught out unaware. It shouldn't have been like this. His stomach felt like it was in free fall, as though he'd made a complete idiot of himself, even though it wasn't his fault. "I'll leave immediately and try to reacquire the target—"

"I can help you with this," McGarry said. "He's in an apartment in Portland. I'll send you the address when we get off the phone. He's with someone else."

"Do you know who?" Greg asked. Better to be sure; metas tended to group together, after all. "I don't want to be caught unawares." Again, he did not say, from humiliation. This whole conversation was pure, fury-inducing embarrassment at having been so very, very wrong, and in front of a man who was his boss.

"No idea. A lover, perhaps."

"I'll take care of it," Greg said, already running through the list of things he needed to do to prepare. It was, fortunately, short, because he'd done most of it before retiring to bed last night.

"Both of them," McGarry said. "I don't want any witnesses."

"Are you paying me for the girlfriend?" Greg asked.

"Call her a bonus. To make amends for your screwup." And McGarry hung up without another word.

Greg hung up as well, face now aflame with anger, heart thudding in his chest. To make amends for *his* screwup? How about McGarry's failure to inform him that Sledger was a metahuman? That would have affected his preparations. If he'd known, he would have been more ready to execute—

Setting his phone back on the charging station, Greg drew a deep breath. None of this mattered for the moment.

There would be time for recrimination later. For now, Percy Sledger was still alive, and needed to die, desperately, so that Greg could save face and renew his professional reputation, for it had just taken a hit, and in front of Mr. McGarry, no less. He had never yet failed the man, and now, to deliver this stinging result, after a week of chasing Sledger around the country?

Greg grabbed the two cases he carried in his coat pockets, then took up his phone, putting it in his front pocket. He was already wearing a suit, fortunately, so he was most of the way ready to go.

He started toward the garage but stopped himself. He couldn't just leave without informing Morgan, after all. He altered his course, angling back down the hallway and through the kitchen where he found Eddie and Morgan still at the table, sunlight streaming in around them.

"… and then the lions will—" Eddie was saying as Greg entered the room. Morgan was watching, enthralled by their son's story, leaning on a hand.

"You can't have pet lions," Greg said sharply as he approached. Eddie turned to look back at him, peering between the slats of the back of the chair. "They're dangerous, and will eat you."

"But when I get older—" Eddie started.

"No," Greg said sharply. "Not now. Not when you get older. Never. Also, being a zookeeper is a ridiculous occupation. Do you want to be poor?"

"Greg …" Morgan said softly, with a hint of warning that he ignored.

Eddie stared at him through the chair back, wide-eyed, eyes glistening. "No," he said in a small voice.

"That's the smartest thing you've said all day," Greg said, making his way over to Morgan and kissing her brusquely on the cheek. "Work called. I have to go."

"All right," Morgan said quietly, disappointment evident.

"Eddie," Greg said, making his way over to his son and ruffling his hair with a stray hand. It was done out of affection, but Eddie did not look up at him and kept his head bowed. Eddie didn't say anything. He didn't need to, really;

he'd taking his chastening properly, Greg reflected as he headed for the door. It was good to get him accustomed to reality, to the way things were. He belonged in the real world, not in some imaginary zoo where he lived among a menagerie in some fantasy that would never be.

Greg heard the slow wail start as he walked out of the kitchen, the mewling sound of Eddie breaking down and Morgan rising to tend to him. That was her task, to pick him back up and gently instruct as to why he needed to learn these lessons now. Greg's was to do the hard work he'd chosen, to pay for this roof over their heads, the food in their bellies, and the stellar school district that Eddie would begin attending in the fall. That, and to occasionally bring Eddie back to reality at moments like this.

Morgan would pick up the pieces; she always did. And Eddie would be all the better for it. They all would, Greg thought as he entered his office, ignoring Morgan's hushed whispers of reassurance and the sound of gentle sobbing he left behind him in his wake.

9.

Augustus

Sunrise in Steelwood Springs found me knocking on the landlord's door at the apartment building where Tweedledee and Tweedledum had been living before I'd taken their car out on the slopes. I found myself appreciating the raw beauty of the Colorado morning. They didn't exactly have mountains in the part of Georgia where I'd grown up—unless you counted Stone Mountain, and no one really did.

"My name is Augustus Coleman," I said to the guy who opened the door at the building. "I'm here on behalf of the Steelwood Springs police."

The landlord was a stocky guy, wearing a stained white shirt and plaid pajama pants, gut overflowing the bounds a little. He had a mustache that looked like it was straining the bounds of his lip too, overgrown and brambly, but the growth had kinda turned in on itself rather than expanding outward, like he made sure and established clear boundaries with the thing. "Yes ...?" he asked with a little bit of an accent.

"Ah, what's your name, sir?" I asked.

"Yusuf," he said, looking at me with a little bit of a squint.

"Hello, Yusuf," I said. "Like I said, I'm with the police. We caught a couple of your tenants getting themselves into some trouble. I was wondering if I could take a look around their place?"

He squinted at me, impassively, then opened his door and opened up on me a little. "Was it those idiots Jacob and Keith? In 2A?" He waved me off. "No, never mind. I know it was those idiots."

"Good guess," I said.

"I will get the keys to their place," Yusuf said, dipping back inside for a second and emerging with an overstuffed key ring that looked like it might have a thousand keys on it. I glanced around; the apartment building had maybe eight units. He shut the door and led me toward the stairs. "I never liked those two. Always causing problems. Noise complaints. Breaking things."

"Yeah, they mentioned something about a broken sink," I said, fishing as we went up the staircase. It was an internal one with old brown carpeting, but the walls were freshly painted, a neutral beige. The place was old, but it was pretty well taken care of.

"I had to call a plumber for those morons last week," Yusuf said, throwing up his hands and causing the keys to jangle. "You know what they do? Try to put a pizza down the garbage disposal. Whole pizza, the idiots."

I frowned as we approached 2A. "What happened?" Because it felt like a pizza wouldn't be any match for a garbage disposal with a steel blade and all.

"Idiots not turn on water first," Yusuf said in disgust. "Motor burned out. Cost me five hundred dollars. Was fortunate that plumber give me discount."

That perked my ears up. "Did you know this plumber?"

"Referred to me by a mutual friend from the old country," Yusuf said, picking out the right key from his ring of hundreds on the first try.

"Where's the old country?" I asked.

Yusuf gave me a sidelong look, curiosity at my curiosity. "Turkey," he said flatly and then opened the door.

"Interesting," I said, doing my best to avoid any sandwich-related jokes. They would have been so easy to make, because I was in the mood for a club. Skipping breakfast does that to me.

I stepped into the apartment and was greeted with a

familiar, burnt aroma. "Damn," I said.

"Dammit," Yusuf said, recoiling from the scent. "This is no smoking apartment! Will cost a fortune to prepare for new tenants and get the smell out."

I passed by an ash tray filled to the brimming with old cigarettes and wondered how Yusuf could have missed the deep-seated aroma of cigarette smoke until now. I suspected it had seeped into the walls by this point. I noted the pipes on the table and had another suspicion confirmed. Naturally these boys weren't just sticking to tobacco. "Huh," I said, noting the bag of residual green they'd left on the table.

Yusuf made a sound deep in his throat, his fingers over his eyes. "You want to confiscate that?"

"That's not my jam," I said, making my way over to the sink. The apartment was a two bedroom, and the bedrooms were on the wall to the right past the living room area. To my left was the kitchenette, and I made a beeline for it, squatting down and opening the cabinets under the sink. I stuck my arm under my nose, burying my face in my sleeve to stave off the stink of smoke, cigarette and otherwise. It was pungent in there, and I was looking forward to getting out as soon as I could, because it was damned near making my eyes water.

"Dammit," Yusuf said mildly. "Do you think this will affect how soon I can put this place back on listings?"

"I have no idea," I said, looking past the garbage disposal that hung under the sink like a big, chunky black cylinder and felt for the water supply. I traced the pipes with my fingers until I came across something that felt like an offshoot of soft, plastic cabling. I grasped at it, giving it a squeeze. Yep, plastic, and roughly the strength of medical tubing. Following it back to its source, my fingers found a soft bulb that I pulled down under the disposal so I could look at it.

"What is this?" Yusuf said, coming up behind me.

"I'm thinking it's the reason you got a discount on your plumbing job," I said, staring at the clear plastic bulb. I tugged it down and found a mechanism at the bottom that looked like it functioned as a dripper to allow whatever had been in the bulb to seep its way into the water coming out of the sink at a slow rate. I unscrewed it at the source and was rewarded with a water drip. "Oops," I said, prompting Yusuf to get down on all fours to peer at what I was doing.

"Need to turn water off first," Yusuf said with worried urgency. "Otherwise you'll flood the apartment."

"Yeah, I got it." I cranked the little knob beneath the sink.

Without prompting, Yusuf stood up and turned the sink on. Water rushed out at first, then died precipitously. "Okay, you remove it now—but carefully." And he padded over to one of the drawers next to the old, yellow steel oven, throwing it open. "Ugh! Pizza in the drawer! Who does this?"

"These boys aren't exactly MENSA members," I said, unscrewing the device as a trickle of water bled out and into the bottom of the cabinet. If Scott had been here, it wouldn't even have been an issue, he'd have cleaned it up lickety-split. I lifted the bulb up and stared at it in the light streaming in through the small kitchen window.

It was a simple tube connected to a bulb that had been filled with liquid. I gave it a quick sniff, and it damned sure didn't smell like water. It had a chemical scent to it, and it wasn't the sort of smell you'd expect from a water softener or anything of that sort, either. "Yep," I said, "this is the thing." I took a snap with my phone and immediately texted it to J.J. and Reed.

"What is it?" Yusuf asked, alternating between staring at it and taking some worn yellowed towels and putting them under the sink to clean up the mess I'd made.

"I think this is how your boys developed super powers," I said, looking around for a plastic bag or something to put it in so it didn't drip everywhere. I finally settled on a cup from the cabinets, because there were no Ziploc bags or Tupperware to be found in the minimally furnished bachelor kitchen.

Yusuf just stared at me. "Super ... powers?"

"Yeah," I said, dangling the cup in front of him. "They developed metahuman abilities."

Yusuf looked at me inscrutably. "Hmph. They have been

mouthier these last few days. Filled with unearned confidence, I would say."

"Yeah, well, be glad you didn't tell them that," I said, "because they might not have appreciated the critique. Now … about this plumber … did you catch his name?"

"It's Omar," Yusuf said. "Omar Cardiff. You need his number?"

Hmm. Those boys didn't have his name as far off as I would have thought, though his last name made me kinda wonder what was going on there.

"Considering he did this?" I jangled the cup again. "Yeah. I need to talk with him. Preferably somewhere that doesn't have any other people around. Know any places like that?"

Yusuf shrugged. "I have property up the mountain a little ways. Currently for rent. I am using it for Airbnb right now. You could book it. Nearest neighbor is three miles away."

"Hmmm," I said. "And you can send Omar out there to meet me for a … 'plumbing job'?"

Yusuf gave me another noncommittal shrug. "I told him I would use him again after he gave me discount on sink." He frowned at the cup in my hand. "Now I find out he cost me tenants—bad tenants, but still tenants—and ruined my sink. Now I have to get another plumber out to fix this. Yes, I will gladly help you take him to jail so I can sue him without him running off. In jail, process server can find him, no problem."

"You got an interesting set of priorities there, Yusuf," I said, "but I appreciate the help." I looked at the little device in the coffee cup. "When can we get this thing rolling? Because I need to talk to Omar, like … now. Before he gets the idea to empower any other morons like he did these two."

10.

Sienna

"I'm looking for a Jon Wiegert," I said into the phone once my call was picked up on the other end. Friday was staring at me with his skinny face blank as ever, and a bare amount of sunlight streaming in through my thick curtains suggested to me that the sun was well up outside. I was feeling the fatigue from not sleeping, too, but what the hell were you supposed to do when an idiot collapses at your safe house door?

Certainly not take a nap on the couch with him in the place. I'd probably wake up to find it on fire or something.

"Y'all ain't got Google where you are?" Jamal Coleman shot back at me over a slightly buzzing connection. He sounded distinctly unimpressed. He was also keeping his voice down, which told me that one of his co-workers was probably in earshot.

"You are my Google, Jamal," I said. "Also, my sunshine."

He grunted. "Jon Wiegert is an extreme sports personality, okay? Famous. You didn't need me for this. Seriously, Google. It will save you and me time. Man's got a channel of his own with millions of followers."

I pulled the phone away from my ear and put him on speaker. "But if I didn't call you, how would I get my daily dose of human social contact?"

"Do … do I not count for that?" Friday asked, sounding genuinely perplexed.

"No," I said.

47

"Try getting out and talking to people," Jamal said. "Leave the house. Stop having Amazon ship everything to you, including your groceries."

"Should I take it as a weird sign that you've bothered to investigate how much e-commerce I'm participating in? Are you stalking me, Jamal?"

"No more than anyone else."

"Hey, while I've got you on the phone," I said. "Do you know who knocked on my door last night?" Friday pointed at himself. "Yes, I know that you know," I covered the microphone, "I'm asking him."

"Uhmmm," Jamal said, and I could tell he didn't really want to even bother to pretend to care. "The pizza delivery guy?"

"You're a terrible stalker," I said. "I haven't had pizza in weeks." Believe me, I felt it, too. Tight shoulders come at a price, and that price was cheese and doughy crust.

"You're not going to make me look this up, are you? For real?"

"Guy Friday," I said.

"I don't know who that is. Wait—is that the white ape in the gimp mask?"

"I'm not an ape," Friday said indignantly.

"More of a gorilla," I said. "Oh, here he is." Google results popped up for Jon Wiegert. "You weren't kidding, Jon boy is mildly famous."

"See how easy that was? Try before you dial next time. And why have you got a great white ape in your house?"

"Seriously, I am not even in the same species as those things," Friday said with rising irritation. "Not even the same—order, or whatever."

"Humans are part of order primates, so technically you're wrong," Jamal said helpfully. "Unless you're actually something else completely, like a mushroom."

"Can confirm," I said, and Friday looked wounded again. His reactions really did explain the mask. "So, here's something Google isn't answering—where can I find Jon Wiegert right now?"

Jamal took a deep, theatrical breath. "Hang on," he said,

like he was so put upon.

"You know, technically, you do work for me," I said. "You could act at least a little like you're eager to do the job at hand."

"Oh, I'm sorry," he said without an ounce of actual contrition. "I'm so excited to Google this for you—got him, by the way."

"You really are a magician," I said.

"Yeah, it's magical how I went to his website, clicked on the tab that says 'EVENTS,' and saw that he's in the High Sierras this morning so he can skydive into a snowboarding run. Amazing, in fact, like conjuring water out of air."

"Serious mojo," I said. "Speaking of which, I've got a new big bad that I'm dodging, and I need you to do a little digging for me."

Jamal groaned again. "Okay. Let's try this again from the top: have you attempted to Google yet?"

"Bleh. That would involve me having to type on this little bitty screen keyboard, and then I'd have to try and read through the results … I'd rather you just do it for me."

"You want me to pre-chew your food for you, too, baby bird?"

"No, I just want to know how Greg Vansen—V-A-N-S-E-N, a metahuman assassin by trade—manages to somehow appear and disappear at will. At least according to Friday."

"Maybe he's a teleporter," Jamal said indifferently.

"Maybe," I said. "It'd sure be nice to know for certain, though, wouldn't it? And I doubt that's Google-able. If Google-able is a word."

"If it's not now, I'm sure it will be soon," he said, and I heard him tapping away in the background. "You're gonna have to give me a while to try and find this Greg Vansen. Kind of a common name, I'll need to sift resul—hang on. What's this?"

"Wonderful news, I hope," I said, and Friday cocked his head at me like a curious dog. "Happy, happy, joyful news, the sort that involves gumdrops and peppermints and—"

"What? No, there's no gumdrops."

"But peppermints, right?" I asked.

"No, I'm looking for this Greg Vansen, and I managed to come up with an NSA map of active cell phones tagged to that name by sifted conversations, and—dammit, what the— Sienna, maybe this is a coincidence, but there's a Greg—no idea if he's a Vansen—whose cell phone is—shit, this sounds like a low-budget horror line, but—"

"Ohhh, man," I said, getting a sinking feeling.

"It's coming from inside your building."

"What does that even mean?" Friday asked, still unable to shake that stupid expression he seemed to constantly wear. Now I sorta missed the mask.

"It means—" I started to say, already in motion.

Greg Vansen appeared like magic, like he was throwing off his invisibility cloak. He was a short, stocky guy, about my height, and when he appeared, it would have been amazing enough if it had just been him.

It wasn't just him.

Because in his hands was an M2 Browning, a crew-served machine gun that the military usually either mounted on a tripod, or on the top of a Humvee. Somewhere that the impact of the massive .50 caliber bullets leaving its immense barrel could be absorbed easily, because those suckers, once they left the shell, were the length of one of my fingers from knuckle to tip. Probably the same diameter, too.

If you wanted to kill someone real fast, an M2 Browning was a damned good way to start.

"Any last words?" Vansen asked, as he brought up the Browning, aiming it at Friday …

… and me.

11.

Augustus

Birds were chirping, I thought I heard crickets making noise in the distance, the sun was shining down ...

And I was standing on the side of a damned mountain outside Steelwood Springs, in front of what Yusuf's Airbnb page had described as, "a rustic escape, situated in the foothills and with a commanding view of the Rocky Mountains."

Yeah, I had a "commanding view" of *a* mountain all right. It was up just a little ways from me, and I stared at it. It stared right back, covered in ice and snow from what I guessed was a recent snowfall, but not recent enough for there to be any on the ground down here.

Funny little side effect of the drug that President Harmon had hit me, Reed and Scott with—I could feel the rock in the peak now. It was a strange, almost vestigial awareness. I could go to sleep and not really notice it, but it was there, always, like an army waiting quietly for me to issue a command. Or maybe like an Amazon Alexa, just sitting there doing nothing until I asked it to do something.

I was still getting used to the new powers, honestly, embracing the scale of my abilities, but every once in a while, when faced with a massive lump of earth sitting in my view ... I did get this weird feeling like the earth was looking at me going, "Well? Whatchoo need? If you're going to do something, let's get on with this. I ain't got all age."

(Age, see, because earth doesn't move so easy or quick, get it? Get it? Aww, man, that joke kills with other earthmovers like me. All two of them that I know. Not even enough to put together a poker game.)

Yusuf's rustic escape had a front porch, and I was just sitting on it like an old hillbilly, rocking lightly in the chair provided, when I heard the sound of the van in the distance. Yusuf had called the plumber as promised, and I'd been waiting about two hours for him to show up. I craned my neck to look down the driveway as he rounded the thick copse of trees that sheltered the house from the road. Sure enough, my quarry had arrived.

I could see him through the windshield of the van as it rattled up the unpaved driveway, kicking up gravel and leaving a cloud of dust in its wake. I nodded in the general direction of the van, as I imagined one does when sitting out on a porch and rocking like you've got nothing else to do with your day.

The plumber brought the van to a stop, and I got a little better look at him as he paused to take a gander at a clipboard and make a couple notes. He had a bronze tone to his skin, jet black hair, and a beard that matched. Not a hint of grey anywhere. He took a minute to write something down, and then the squeak of the van door opening filled the calm Colorado day.

"Morning," he said to me as he got out, even though it was probably afternoon now. I'd been sitting out here for a while, so I didn't know. "Are you ... Augustus?" He tried my name experimentally, pronouncing it perfectly on the first time.

"That's me," I said with a nod.

"You're having problems with the sink, then?" He stretched as he got out. It was a little bit of a drive from Steelwood Springs to get here. Winding roads.

"Yeah." I stood up, and stepped down off the porch slowly. "Water flow issue."

"Let me get my tools," he said and circled around the back of the van. He wasn't doing anything dastardly yet, so that was a good sign. So far he just seemed like a genial plumber.

We'd see if that continued once he was back in sight and I confronted him. I had it in my mind that he was doing some contract work for someone, pushing out the occasional install for some interested party who wanted to … I don't know, stir things up. Omar here might be the key to discovering the truth behind this rising tide of metas, and I was determined to get that truth out of him.

I needed to make sure I didn't screw this up, because a whole lot was riding on it. Answers to questions we'd been asking for a good long while.

Omar rounded the van after slamming the back door, and now he had a big, grey steel toolbox in hand. He carried it lightly, well-practiced and with his head down, like he was lost in thought. He looked up when he saw me again, and smiled. "Yusuf said you are a short-term renter?"

"Yeah, Airbnb," I said. "Just here overnight."

"Bad luck to have the sink go wrong while you are here, then," Omar said, still smiling.

"Yusuf said you fixed his sink at another property last week," I said as Omar approached, gravel crunching under his feet from his even stride.

Omar just nodded, seemingly preoccupied, answering offhand. "Yes, an apartment."

"He was really pleased with what you did there," I said. "Of course, he might not have been quite as pleased if he'd known you were turning two of his tenants into supervillains."

I was expecting a subtle reaction from Omar. Something like him freezing in tracks, his eyes going wide, maybe a guilty look spreading across his face. I could even have believed him stopping, eyes going wide like pie pans, body all frozen in a rigor mortis at being caught.

Omar didn't do any of those things.

The only facial reaction was a subtle hardening of the lines. I didn't have time to work through it until later, but that wasn't a sign of guilt.

It was a hint that shit was about to go off the chain.

There was a rumble deep in the earth, and the ground

gave me a two-second warning that something was happening in the well behind me before the top exploded off the old thing and a stream of water powerful enough to dissolve a boulder came shooting at me with a velocity usually reserved for rockets trying to break out of the earth's atmosphere.

The water stream hit the ground where I was standing a second before as I leapt, a solid platform of gravel lifting me up twenty feet straight into the air like a makeshift elevator. Dirt and rock gave way for the water pressure, and Omar's stream carved into the ground some ten feet before it stopped, such was the power of his attack.

Holy crap.

That was not normal, not even for a Poseidon.

"Someone's been juicing!" I shouted down at Omar as he redirected another blast of water at me. It was surreal to see it pool and turn in the ten-foot-deep hole it had created when it struck the ground while trying to kill me. It writhed and moved like a living thing, like a snake composed of liquid as it coiled around to strike.

I yanked the earth from around the driveway and sealed the water in, pulling the gravel and letting it pile to slow the coming attack. I jerked my hand in Omar's direction at the same time, and he shouted in surprise as a landslide of pebbles beneath his feet stole his balance and left him right on his ass like someone had pulled a carpet from beneath his feet.

The stones covered him in seconds as the earth heaved beneath him. I was breaking up the dirt and rock, planning to swallow him whole and let him suffocate for a few minutes, blind and struggling so I didn't have to deal with his attacks up on the surface. That would give me time to wait him out, let the inability to breathe work him into unconsciousness. It wouldn't kill him, not based on the level of power he was displaying, even if I left him buried for half a year, but it'd damned sure take some of the aggression out of him.

Hopefully a lot of the aggression out of him.

I plugged that impending water spout of doom with more and more rock, burying it as I felt it pulsate in the earth, trying to loose itself on me. I also moved about thirty feet to my left, my cloud of gravel functioning as a hovering sleigh to carry me from immediate danger. I didn't want to go too far, because I needed to see to be able to stop him, after all.

Omar was struggling beneath the earth, and I got an abrupt warning that something was amiss. His water spout that I'd trapped had shifted directions, and worse, he was tapping the well again. I turned my head in time to see the water overflow the well's bounds, the aquifer deep beneath giving up its goods as a waterspout blew it out like Old Faithful going off in Yellowstone.

The water flowed from the top of the spout's arc, bending like it was magnetized and heading in a specific direction. "Awwwww, damn," I said to no one in particular as I watched it spear into the earth where I'd buried Omar, meeting up with the water I'd trapped earlier just below the surface.

This was going to be spectacular, I thought, and a second later, I was right.

Omar burst out of the earth in a cocoon of water, arms held out in the center of a pulsating membrane of H2O the size of the Unisphere at Flushing Meadows Park in New York City. I'd seen Scott pull a similar trick before, and there was only one way to match this maneuver.

"So that's how it is, huh?" I shouted, and summoned the forces of earth to my disposal.

It took me less than two seconds to build a hundred-foot earth golem out of rock and dirt. I buried myself in the head, leaving a little space so I could see out, since even with all this earth at my command, it wasn't like dirt had eyes. I could feel what it felt, brushing against people, against water, against elements I couldn't control, but it still left me blind if I stayed entirely in its embrace.

Omar apparently didn't feel the need to do one of those chats before the battle. I respected that, though the lack of smack talk left me feeling a little like I was dueling a deaf man or something. It was weird.

He came surging at me in his ball of water, a thousand spikes jutting out and attacking my golem, water ripping through as the two of us engaged in combat like the titans of old, sounds of our battle spilling over the trees and woods and echoing down the mountainside.

12.

Sienna

"Dude!" I said in my best impersonation of a West Coaster, maybe a California transplant to Portland. I wheeled on Friday, who was standing next to me, frozen in place, eyes wide and terrified at the specter of Greg Vansen magically appearing in front of us with the biggest damned machine gun that could be carried. "You got any last words?"

"Whut?" Friday said, blinking at me, dragged out of his fearful paralysis by my attempt at mocking conversation. My gambit worked; Greg Vansen hadn't let loose with the Ma Deuce machine gun yet, which was fortunate for at least two of us in the room. I was keeping a close eye on his finger out of the corner of my eye, ready to start rolling with a plan of my own the second I saw his grip tighten even a hair. "I—I can't think of anything—"

"I have a few words, then," I said, turning back to Vansen. Based on his lack of reaction, I didn't think he recognized me. If he did recognize me, he was really dumb for letting me distract him this way. If he'd known Sienna Nealon was in the room, he would have been better off shooting me the second he appeared. "What's your beef with this guy, anyway?"

"You'll have to speak up," Vansen said and inclined his head slightly so I could see—he had earplugs in. Smart move, because the Ma Deuce he was holding tended to produce the sort of noise that would make the apocalypse

57

sound like elevator music played on low.

"What's your problem with old Percy, here?" I shouted. "Did he sleep with your mother or something?"

"No," Vansen said curtly, "he did not. It's nothing personal. I don't even know him—"

"Yes, you do, Greg," Friday said with amazing self-pity. Seriously. I almost teared up for him.

Greg Vansen just froze, looking at Friday the way a kid with a magnifying glass might look at a struggling bug he just ripped the wing off of. "Excuse me?"

"We were on the team together, man!" Friday said, his face all bawled up like he was going to cry. "We served together. We bled together! Panama! Desert Storm! Revelen!"

Vansen's eyes narrowed in calculation. "Wait. Were you the idiot Hercules that always wore that mask?"

"You don't even remember me!" Friday shouted like a scorned teen whose parents had forgotten her sixteenth birthday. Take it with some grace, Molly Ringwald.

"Bruce?" Vansen asked. "Bruce Springersteen?"

I blinked at Friday. "Seriously? Did you make that one up, too? So you could sound like the Boss?"

"I was a fan of his!" Friday said. "He rawked!"

Greg looked at me with that same coldly scientific look, like he was diagnosing me as a disease he was about to wipe out. "Aren't you a little young to know Springsteen? What's your name, Bruce's girlfriend?"

"Oh, no, you did not just call me—" I sputtered. "We are not—I am not *with* him, okay? I have dignity. And standards. And a life, which is more than I can say for you in about two seconds, you gargantuan ass nugget—"

He pulled the trigger on Ma Deuce as I lit off a blast of Gavrikov and shot it out of my palm at him while lunging sideways at Friday. I hit the big man under the armpit and tackled him down toward my couch as the sound of the machine gun cranking fifty cal bullets into the exterior walls of my apartment began in earnest. It was like the voice of God shouting extreme amount of displeasure directly into your eardrums, and as I knocked over my couch and dragged

Friday behind it, I reflected that there really was no good place to hide in this entire apartment.

I pushed Friday's face into the faux wood floor and saw his mouth was open. He could have been bellowing at the top of his lungs and I wouldn't have heard it because the Ma Deuce was belting out a symphony from hell; it was like every church bell on the planet had been crammed into my skull and was going off continuously. Pieces of couch stuffing were raining around me like the first snowstorm of the season in Minnesota, and with only slightly more likelihood of death (because everyone forgets how to drive).

The compression waves from the machine gun were so powerful that I could feel my heart fluttering and my skull rattling like someone was actually tapping it with a hammer. It made me dizzy and sick all at once, but I couldn't just lie there until the couch disintegrated under the withering machine gun fire. I kicked the sofa in Greg Vansen's direction and scrambled on all fours toward the TV stand as it slid away, tossing a fire blast at it as it went. It lit off like a Viking funeral, the cheap stuffing going up in a blaze of glory. I'd never liked that couch anyway. It was lumpy.

Vansen disappeared for a second as the couch passed through where he'd been standing a second earlier, flames licking their way upward. He appeared again and the intense hammering of the machine gun fire continued once he did. It had stopped for a second, and he didn't look like he'd raised his legs, so whatever he'd done to dodge it hadn't resulted in him becoming invisible but still solid, and it hadn't required him to jump, which left me scratching my head because I couldn't remember any metas who could just turn insubstantial, like smoke, at least not without any outward signs.

He really was starting to look like magic.

I didn't have to ponder the problem any further, though, because he had plainly picked me out as the biggest danger to him and was stitching the fire from the Ma Deuce across the floor after me. For my part, I was lobbing flames at him, trying to throw off his aim enough to buy me a second to throw something bigger at him, like my TV and its stand. I was kinda regretting having gone for the seventy inch until now.

Flames were spreading up the wall from where I'd lit the couch on fire, and I just let them go for a few seconds more, burning their way into the drywall and wood. I had a plan for them, but it wasn't mature just yet, and it was going to require the distraction of a thrown TV, at least. I also had two barbells in relatively easy reach after that, and was already scheming how best to lodge those in his skull.

Fragments of my faux wood floor sprayed my legs as I reached the base of my TV stand and toppled it over. The TV caught two fifty cal bullets and sparked accordingly, pieces of glass and plastic peppering my abdomen and face. He damned near had me, so I shouted, "BJORN!" out loud.

Warmind! Bjorn yelled, and the machine gun fire was suddenly, almost magically, redirected upward, ripping apart my ceiling and showering me with bits and pieces of the warehouse-industrial ceiling that was probably a huge sell for the hipsters who usually rented these kind of studio apartments.

I kicked the TV right at Vansen and it soared like a soccer ball toward the goal that was his head. He was squinting hard, trying to get the Norseman's psychic attack out of his brain, and he got them open just in time to see the TV coming when it was inches away.

He disappeared but the TV actually struck him this time—or caught him for a second before he disappeared, at least, because it smacked into a physical obstacle at the position where he'd been and jerked around like it had encountered a wall, flipping and breaking in half as it hit the ground, shattered.

Vansen reappeared a second later, dazed and woozy, the Ma Deuce pointed at the floor. I took advantage of the opportunity to do two things before he recovered.

One, I hurled a ball of flame with dead-on accuracy at the blocky firing mechanism of the machine gun. It hit just above the ejection port, five thousand degrees of heat landing perfectly on the machinery that launched death in every direction it was pointed. The fireball seared through metal and diffused its heat into the gun, causing the barrel to glow like it was straight out of a blacksmith's forge and a few of the closest rounds to light off in random directions.

It also made Greg Vansen scream a little and drop the Ma Deuce, which was now slagged and inoperable, as he clutched his burnt left hand to his chest. As one does when one has been burned.

The second thing I did was yank all the fire that had been crawling its way up the walls, consuming the stuffing of my sofa and was now working on the wooden studs hidden in the wall, drawing it toward me in a wall of flame that converged on one central point that lay between me and its source.

That point of convergence? Why, it was Greg Vansen, that dick.

I covered him in flames and wrapped them tight around him like a cloak of fire. He screamed again, but this time he could just pull himself away from them. I expected him to go invisible again, maybe appear a few steps to the right, but he didn't. He just writhed in the depths of the fire for about a second, and then—

He shrugged off the inferno, and it just disappeared.

Poof. A wisp of smoke, and all my fire was just … gone.

I was left sitting there, on my haunches, Greg Vansen staring at me—half burned, furious, short as shit, brow tilted down like a hard triangle over his face, and a layer of black over him like he'd stuck his face in a coal bin.

"Huh," I said, and crafted a new plan right there.

I grabbed Friday and flew out the window, shattering the glass on my exit and hoping like hell this freaking magical, seemingly invincible assassin couldn't follow.

13.

Impossibly hard jets of water were carving their way through the rock I was using as my shield, the ones holding up my golem as I strode into battle against Omar the Poseidon. It knocked me back, threatening to send my giant rock construct onto his back where Omar could just rip me apart at will, but I leaned the golem over, balancing him forward, and thrust a rocky hand into the defensive bubble of water Omar had set up to shield himself.

That didn't go so well.

Gravel sprayed everywhere as he sliced pieces of golem and I pulled them back to me, trying to compact them into a new layer of armor to replace the ones he was peeling away.

I was really missing the battle banter right now. I could've use some witty repartee to lighten up the fact I was getting creamed by this dude and making no progress. I pulled my golem hand back and found it washed away and smooth, like it had gone through a rock polisher.

Omar stabbed out again, hitting me with an attack across the vulnerable midsection of my golem. He struck a joint where a couple rocks had been balancing together through force of my will holding them tight and hit them with a plane of water no thicker than a half inch, like a guillotine blade right through me.

If the laws of physics had been in effect, that might have mattered. But apparently he'd missed it earlier when I levitated on a sled of rock, because all he did was chop my golem in half without actually ripping any rock out of my control, and I just went with it, dividing the golem and attacking him with both parts, separating them to avoid getting shaved again by his flat torrent of water.

I thought about forming a cone to boost my voice and shout at him, hoping to start a little unfriendly back and forth, but I doubted he'd even hear me, surrounded as he was in his own personal aquarium. Man, Sienna taught me this game her way and I just can't shake the old lessons. How were you supposed to fight someone when you couldn't talk smack to them?

It was pretty crazy looking, what we were doing. I had a kind of heady moment as I sat there, encased in my rock golem's chest as I came at him again.

I was getting pretty tired of this back and forth, so I readied a big spear of stone behind me, preparing to deploy it on a new limb I was crafting, like a scorpion's tail. Then I decided to make another one because who wouldn't want a stone scorpion with two tails? In case the first one failed, you know.

It damned near killed me inside not to shout out something like, "Feel the sting, baby!" before I came at him, but it would be stupid to telegraph a move like that. So instead, I just hit him with everything I had, attacking from below, and the minute I could see he was distracted ...

I launched both of those powerful tails at him, determined to punch my way through his bubble and right into the bastard's heart, even if it killed him. Because this dude? He was not playing around, and if I kept stringing this out, I had a feeling sooner or later he was going to end me.

Omar wheeled in his bubble the minute my attacks struck. I blasted another shotgun peppering of gravel and rock at him from below as my golem's disembodied legs renewed their attack in tripod mode, but none of it deterred him from his total focus, which was on me and my scorpion tails of jagged stone.

The tails were lodged in the water, and I shoved at him, and he shoved them right back at me. It was like a tug of war, except, dammit, I should have been winning. The stone was cracking against the force of his water shield, which ...

Hell, it should have been impossible.

Omar came belting around with something that looked like a fist of water, and it smashed my first tail, the one stretching up over the left side of my golem, shattering it into the component rocks. "Shit!" I said, wearing out on this not talking. I shot at him with a dose of rock from below, and he stopped that, too. It was starting to look like a good, old-fashioned standoff when I heard the rumbling in the distance.

The sound didn't trigger at first; I was stuck in my golem, after all, working to block his access to the water supply at the source of the well. But as the rumbling got louder, I couldn't ignore it anymore, and I finally turned my head from the eternal struggle with Omar to look at whatever the hell was making noise like an epic rockslide.

It wasn't a rockslide.

It was a damned avalanche.

And it had come from the top of the peak.

All the ice.

All the snow that dotted the foothills and up the mountain.

All of it was rolling down toward me.

And eventually, after it wiped me out and carried Omar off to celebrate his victory ...

It'd take out the entire town of Steelwood Springs and everybody living in it.

14.

Sienna

I streaked through the air, heading south out of Portland, the sun high in the sky above me as I headed into a cloud bank with Guy Friday clutched in my arms, avoiding the touch of his skin as though it were poisonous and plague-ridden.

Also, I was still really, really pissed that Greg Vansen had thought I would ever, ever, *ever*—you get the point, I guess—date Guy Friday.

"Where are we going?" Friday asked plaintively as I caught Interstate 5 and bumped up to way beyond the speed of sound. He sounded a little frightened as he asked.

"We're going to find Jon Wiegert," I said. "Apparently he's in the High Sierras today, jumping out of a plane, so …"

"Ohh, so we're going to California," Friday shouted over the gusting wind that swirled around us. It's hard to overstate how much wind resistance there is when you're traveling at supersonic speeds. He'd already bulked up a little bit, presumably to better weather the wind effects. I had him firmly clutched around his still-damp sleeves. There was no skin to skin contact, so as far as I was concerned, we were all good.

"Probably more like Nevada-bound, but it's right on the border," I said, probably not as snippily as I should have considering Friday had just cost me my Portland safe house, my weights, and my TV. Also, some clothes, and— "Damn! I dropped my cell phone when Greg appeared out of nowhere."

"Do you need it?" Friday asked.

"Eventually, yes," I said. "But it's not that big of a problem." I had another safe house in an apartment complex outside Reno, so stopping off along the way didn't seem out of the question since we were heading that way. Lucky thing, me having a network of safe houses everywhere. "So ... you really have no idea how Greg Vansen just appeared inside my freaking safe house?"

"Nope," Friday said, like the matter was just settled. He was hanging in my arms like he was quite content to just let me do all the work, including all the thinking—because clearly, I was here to do the thinking for him.

In fairness, that was probably a good idea, since his type of thinking had given me a story about how random Panamanians were screaming about how huge his genitals were.

"He didn't seem to know who you were when he went to kill you," I said. "Are you sure this has anything at all to do with your time together on that death squad or whatever?"

Friday was quiet for a minute. "Well, I thought so, but ... I don't know. Maybe not?"

"He said it wasn't personal," I said. "I'm not necessarily for believing everything our super-deadly magical assassin says, but he genuinely didn't seem to know your face. That tends to make me think that maybe hunting down this Jon Wiegert guy is going to be a dead end."

"Well ... what should we do, then?" Friday asked.

I shrugged as much as I could without dropping him. For some strange reason, I was treating Friday a lot more delicately now that he'd brought me a case than I ever had before. "Still go talk to Jon, just to cover our bases, I guess."

Actually, once I thought about it ... it wasn't all that strange.

This is what you do, Harmon said.

Speaking of which, I said, firing up the old synapses and talking in my own head, *howzabout you put those super telepathy powers to work and tell me what was really going on in Greg Vansen's head when we were fighting just now? Why is he after Friday?*

Gerry Harmon gave me a sparkling, presidential smile of the sort a politician gives when he wants to be a hugely condescending dick. Or maybe it was just Harmon being Harmon. *That would take all the fun out of it for you, wouldn't it? You'll figure it out.*

"Asshole," I said, only half meaning it. He knew me.

"What did I do?" Friday asked, sounding a little hurt.

"Other than wrecked my cozy little life in Portland? Nothing," I said. I didn't put much oomph into it, though. Instead, I sped up, eager to find this Jon Wiegert in hopes that he might give me another thread to chase ... and that maybe I'd find another after that, and another, and another ...

... in fact, if it could go on forever? That wouldn't be so terrible.

"Oh, well, no big deal, then," Friday said. "Your place was a dump, anyway. All that fire and shooting probably raised the value."

On second thought, maybe a short, easily solved case wouldn't be so bad ...

15.

The whole damned mountain looked like it was coming down, or at least the frosty cone at the top of it was, heading right toward me at the behest of the Poseidon who was locked in my death grip, grinning at me from beneath the surface of his shield of water. A thought occurred to me pretty damned speedily—a Poseidon shouldn't have been able to affect ice, which meant—

"Damn," I whispered under my breath, shoving both golem hands against the water bubble and trying to get away from Omar before the coming avalanche slammed into me.

Omar had been juicing, all right. He hadn't just used the serum that gave entry-level superpowers. He'd taken the one that President Harmon had given me too, leveling his powers up to epic-water-god level.

And then, apparently, he'd also taken the upgrade that allowed him to use powers that were similar in nature. Ergo, while Scott Byerly could stare at a cup of ice all damned day and couldn't make it do anything until it melted, Omar here was bringing down an entire mountain of the stuff with the apparent intent to bury me like an Everest expedition.

"Oh, shittttttt!" I shouted out the rocky, tunnel-like cone that was my only viewport to the world from inside my golem. This catastrophe was at least partially my fault; I might not have brought the ice and snow down, but I was the only superpowered person between it and the city with a chance of stopping it.

I reared back with a rock hand and slapped against the side of the water bubble hard as Omar was already pulling back. The effect was immediate; he shot forward like I'd spiked his little watery volleyball and headed for the trees lining the driveway. Apparently he was already trying to use this opportunity to get away, and I just gave him a little push. I couldn't have known that, though, because I couldn't see his face through the layers of water between us.

Before he'd even fully disappeared into the trees, I was already turning back to deal with the oncoming crisis. The avalanche was rumbling hard, a cloud billowing up and above the fatal slide of ice and snow, following it down the mountain like a storm warning.

I reached out into the rock in the distance and started to fracture the earth where I could feel the rumbling slide of cold sluicing its way down the mountain. I thought about those metal panels cops raised when they wanted to seal off a street—square pieces of metal that you just lifted up a couple feet and boom—car couldn't pass.

An avalanche wasn't a car, but it operated on a similar principle, didn't it? Momentum and matter, running away down a hill. It wasn't as solid as a car body, but that worked to my advantage, too, if I could slow the bulk of the mass. Strip away most of the mass and it'd just be a little trickle coming down the hill.

Ripping up the rock plates facing in the opposite direction seemed the natural choice, so I started doing it. I jetted into the air on my rock avatar like it was launched with a rocket. Levitating solid rock used to take a lot out of me. Now, while not optimal for traveling long distances, it was fairly easy to maintain for a couple miles, at least.

I got a bird's eye view of the avalanche, and it sent chills through me. It was a big mess, sliding on down that mountain, and I was already wondering if my idea was even going to slow it. It had runaway train speed going for it, too, but I was working at setting up my system of rock brakes, slightly ahead of where the avalanche was coming. It looked like a river of white, roiling currents in it seething with pure, furious power as it took on the appearance of a storm surging down the hill.

"Okay, here we go," I said, two hundred feet above the cascading white. My brakes were ready, and the avalanche was only a hundred feet from them. Fifty. Then ten …

I lifted the segments of rock, pulling them up at a forty-five degree angle in lines across the path of the avalanche's advance. The brakes were ten, fifteen feet high and stretched a mile across the slope. There were twenty of them, and it looked like a vent had opened in the ground, gills for some massive, earthen creature that was hiding beneath.

The avalanche hit like a hurricane running up against concrete jetties I'd seen on TV during storm season, and boom! White snow launched into the air when it clashed with my brake, rolling over the first brake, then the second, then the third …

I could feel the front lines of my brake system start to fracture. "Uh oh." I'd never tried anything like this before, and the idea that it could fail hadn't really occurred to me.

It was failing, though, and right before my eyes. The first line broke cleanly off, sheared by the force of the downhill slide of the avalanche. When it let loose, the mile-long line of rock shattered and was carried downhill, slamming into the second brake and catching on it immediately, creating a kind of ramp for the avalanche to launch off of.

It looked like a waterfall had been set up on the hill, a spray of white cascading over it at a near-horizontal angle because of the slope. If it lasted, it might have been considered one of the wonders of the world. It was, after all, a mile-wide cascade of snow, rock, trees and ice down a hill. A few pines went floating down below me, buffeted by the currents.

"This is crazy," I muttered, wondering if maybe I was the one who was crazy. Maybe I would have been better off building one giant brake—like a Great-Wall-of-China-type thing, buttressed by all the rock I could summon. But then, if that had busted, there would have been no chance to do what I was doing now, which was …

… Well, which was trying to adapt to my failure by

doubling down. Yeehaw.

The avalanche had slowed now that it had reached the tenth or so brake I'd created in the line. I ripped up five more down the line, and was activating a couple up the slope a bit, trying to slow the advance before it reached the waterfall the breaking of my first line had caused.

I felt like I was directing a symphony in chaos, watching snow and debris roiling below. Another tree trunk disappeared—just completely disappeared, full grown pine—into the snow like it was sucked into an undertow.

Yeah. This was crazy. And I was crazy to try and stop it. It was like a man trying to hold back a hurricane.

But I wasn't facing nature here, not really.

I was facing a madman meta trying to save his own ass and unleashing hell on an unsuspecting Rocky Mountain town in the process.

But if Reed Treston could stop a damned tornado ... well, I wasn't one to be outdone.

"Ahhhhhhhhhhhhhhhh!" I shouted, ripping deeper into the earth, channeling the rock beneath me in ways I'd never tried before. The thing I'd done with the well gave me inspiration, and I shuffled rock to create pits a hundred feet deep beneath me, a couple dozen feet wide, just to slow things down a little.

This avalanche was an elephant, stampeding its way down the mountain, destroying everything in its path. With every tree it uprooted, with every piece of rock it tore from my breaks, it added to the inevitable mass that allowed it to increase speed down the hill toward town. This elephant didn't mean to stop, either, and it wouldn't until I took care of it.

An old joke popped to mind: How do you eat an elephant?

One bite at a time.

I opened more of those pits, crunching together rock, siphoning it, moving it down the slope and adding it to my brakes. This was like deadlifting a ton, moving this much earth. I'd never done it before, and it taxed me in ways I couldn't recall being taxed. My brain was already stuttering from the exertion of the fight against Omar, but this—

This was vital. I had to do this.

Below me, the roaring snow was running downhill like rapids on a wild river. But it was swirling and eddying more now, caught up having to fill those sudden pits I'd created. The brakes were starting to have some effect, too; the avalanche had blown through the first round of them I'd pulled up, but it was slowing now. I could see the top of the fifth and sixth lines, poking their heads up out of the snow. Trees stuck out like snowy toothpicks.

My brow was covered in sweat, and I cast off the last of my golem, joining the rocks to the last barricade. The snow was oozing downhill now. It just needed one last thing to arrest its momentum. I raised the other brakes, just a little higher, my hands shaking as I mimed the motion I wanted the earth to make. I normally didn't even have to do that anymore, but I was so worn out I felt the need to, just to make sure it got done.

My hands were shaking as the front wave of the avalanche slid up against that last barricade, the Great Wall of Augustus. I lowered myself, the spitting cold of the cloud that the avalanche had let off chilling my skin like an icy shower. I set down on the top of my wall and felt some strength return to me, now that I was back in touch with the earth. I wanted to kick off my dress shoes and let my feet go against the rock, so I did. I shredded my socks off with pebbles, and it felt good, like a massage as I stood there, commanding the avalanche to stop.

And it did.

"Damned right," I said, as the wall beneath me groaned under the weight of tons of ice and tree and snow and rock. I was gradually reasserting my control over the latter, adding to my makeshift dam that was holding back the tide of hell that Omar had brought down.

Omar. I looked back, trying to see if he was lurking out there, maybe trying to sneak up on me.

There was no sign of bubble man, no hint of him beneath the untouched pines that covered the slope beneath me. Way, way down there, I could see the house where we'd begun our little clash. His van was still in the driveway, and off—way in the distance—I could see trees moving like something was passing between them roughly enough to disturb them.

Omar. Still in his bubble. Heading west, out of the valley, and at speed I'd never be able to match.

"Damn," I said, sagging against the rock wall beneath me. It felt good to be against the earth again, and I lay there, contemplating my next move, and didn't even realize when I fell asleep there in the sun.

16.

Greg

Greg's skin burned, and not just from the flames that had scorched him. It was strange that his circulatory system was still able to funnel blood to his capillaries, to let him feel like he was blushing in humiliation even though it was probably just his metahuman healing working to repair the burn damage that had been inflicted on him before he'd remembered how to put out a flame.

This whole scenario had been a cascading series of mistakes. Embarrassing ones, again. That he had burns seemed appropriate, since the burn of shame was perhaps the most acute and long lasting of the injuries he'd just acquired.

He steadied himself, head back against the soft cloth seat. He had time, and reliving his stupidity might just be the best cure for preventing it in the future.

1. How had he not known that Percy Sledger was, in fact, that idiot Bruce Springersteen? Because Mark McGarry hadn't told him, of course. Was it intentional? Probably not; Greg's past association with Springersteen, or Sledger, or whatever he was calling himself now, was irrelevant. He would have taken McGarry's contract to kill Sledger even knowing full well who he was.

2. What were the odds that after failing to report that Sledger was, in fact, a metahuman, McGarry would fail to tell him that the accomplice that Sledger had sought shelter with

was, in fact, Sienna Nealon? And how had Sledger found her where every major law enforcement agency in the country had failed? Had he been in constant contact with her since her flight from the law? These were questions that he had no answers for, and it drove him slightly mad. Greg did not care for the unknown or the uncertain.

3. Nealon certainly seemed to be helping Sledger now. She'd cost Greg his M2 Browning, which was one of his favorite tools. Not that it was irreplaceable, but it was another annoyance heaped on those already caused by Percy Sledger. He'd already cost Greg time with the chase, and now the contract—which paid a flat rate—was rapidly working its way from a profitable short-term contract with minimal risk into a longer-term amorphous quagmire with a risk quotient that would have sent any reasonable actuary fleeing in fear.

4. Normally he didn't even ask this question, but since this case had caused him so much trouble, it was practically begged—why the hell did McGarry want Springersteen dead? He was an idiot, true, and Greg had known that when they'd worked together. An annoyance? Even more true. But worthy of spending the money and time of a high-dollar professional assassin to kill? Debatable. No, there was probably something more going on here, something Greg would likely never have access to, in terms of a motive. Normally, he was fine with these unknowables; he made it a practice not to examine the reasons for the contracts he took, because it was better not to open that door. But now that it was open …

No. All of this was irrelevant. Greg still had a job to do, though it was getting to be a more troublesome one with every encounter. The last two attempts had ended in failure, so perhaps now it was time to do something even bolder, more destructive. Unfortunately, McGarry had now tacked Nealon on to the pile of trouble that Greg had to deal with per the contract, and without any additional fee.

But … he'd done that as an almost casual aside, when he hadn't known who it was. The contract itself was typically Greg's guide—the words, not some offhand instruction given after a series of failures.

Killing Nealon wasn't worth the trouble. Sledger was the contract. It wouldn't bother him to kill Nealon if it were easy, but it wasn't a coincidence that a great many people who had thought that killing Sienna Nealon would be easy were now dead.

Perhaps, though, he could make one final attempt at her. If he failed, then he'd at least make sure he killed Sledger, and grandly, to be sure it was done. After that, he would disappear from the scene, making sure she couldn't find him—which would be easy, of course—and leave her to her mourning, or whatever she might feel over the death of Sledger. Based on his own feelings, Greg expected it would be a sort of casual indifference to knowing the idiot was dead. *Oh, what a shame,* and move on with life, as one would do when hearing that an old co-worker had fallen down an elevator shaft.

Of course, the manner of Percy Sledger's death was destined to be rather more dramatic. Now it was just a matter of following his clue to them ...

Greg lifted the phone he'd picked up in the ruins of the Portland apartment. It had, fortunately, still been unlocked when he'd picked it up, the owner clearly not setting the screen to go off in what he would have considered an intelligent time frame.

As a result, now Greg had in his hand a very large clue as to the next stop on his quarry's itinerary. It would be a pleasant enough reunion, he supposed, to see Jon Wiegert again ...

17.

It was, surprisingly, not too difficult to find Jon Wiegert's plane over the Sierra Nevada mountains. It was flying a little lower than a commercial airliner, and of course looked different, as planes designed for skydives tended to. It didn't have one of those cool back ramps, instead opting for a rear door that wasn't open yet as we approached, which, I hoped, meant that Wiegert hadn't ejected himself out of the plane to perform his dope-ass, insane stunt yet.

When we were about two hundred yards behind the plane, being buffeting by its wash, Friday started scrambling around in my grip, fishing in his pants for something. I was prepared to close my eyes in case things went lewd, but he lifted his gimp-like mask out of his pocket a moment later and started to put it on.

"Do not put on that ridiculous mask," I snapped. I probably could have been a little nicer about it, but frankly, seeing his stupid expressions had given me insight into his personality that I'd never possessed when I'd worked with him. Also, the prospect of hanging around with a dude wearing his mask seemed more likely than anything to draw the sort of attention that runaway fugitive Sienna Nealon did not need at present.

"Do I tell you not to put on your ridiculous face?" Friday shot back, not even slowing in his quest to put the damned thing on.

"Lose the mask or lose your head," I said succinctly.

That stopped him for a second as he pondered my threat. "Literally?" he shouted over the rotor wash.

"Very literally," I said. "That propeller up there will literally be the last thing you see, the last thing that ever happens to you. And possibly the worst," I added as I increased speed, bringing us forward and up, as though positioning to drop him into the left wing prop.

He chewed that one over for a second. I could practically hear the thought bouncing around in an elaborate Rube Goldberg machine in his head while he contemplated my threat. "Worse than the time I accidentally got my pubes caught in the bowling ball return and it waxed me?"

I almost stopped dead in flight. I only caught my sudden decrease in momentum when I felt the wind resistance slacken obviously and the plane started to pull away. "... I ... do I even want to know how *that* happened?"

"It was an honest mistake."

"..." Because what the hell do you say to that?

"Also, it kinda bruised my junk. Maybe gave me an impromptu circumcision, but fortunately it grew b—"

"Okay, stop," I said, trying to keep from vomiting on the top of his head. But not trying very hard, because honestly, he had earned it. "Yes, me dropping you in a propeller would be worse than everything, ever ... except for that, I guess."

"I *need* to put my mask on." Now he was dangerously close to whining.

"Why?" I asked.

"Because Jon's not going to recognize me otherwise!"

He had a point there, based on Greg Vansen's reaction to him. Still, that prompted a question: "Why the hell do you wear that mask all the time?"

"Oh, who cares?" he asked, shoving his face into it and mumbling something I couldn't hear over the muffling effect of the leather and the roar of the plane's props. "There. That's better," he said once he got the mouth hole properly aligned. "Hey, the door is open!"

And sure enough, the door on the side of the silvery plane's body was, indeed, open, and a guy was standing there, a surfboard-like apparatus strapped to his feet. He was standing there, ready to jump, a GoPro camera strapped to the top of his helmet, and talking to someone behind him in the cabin of the plane. I couldn't see them, but I assumed it was a camera crew, catching his EXTREME AWESOMENESS (I imagined lots of exclamation points to indicate the EXTREME-ness of this feat) from both sides of the jump. Hell, there was probably a ground crew watching from below, too.

I lit my hair on fire, because I didn't want the new, raven shade to be caught on film. If there was a ground crew filming, I'd probably already blown that, but whatever. I'd been too busy contemplating how an idiot got his genitals caught in a bowling ball return to consider the importance of preserving my flimsy disguise.

Jon came jumping out of the plane a second later, and he wasn't flying, at least not obviously. He had a parachute on his back which he'd clearly planned to use in order to hide the aid his powers were giving him to pull off these stunts, but he didn't deploy that immediately either, instead launching into a downward spin, which was kind of mesmerizing since his snowboard was painted in seriously psychedelic colors, complete with prismatic coating that caught the reflection of the sun.

I bet it looked great from above, which was probably why they'd done it, but I didn't have a ton of time to pick a less auspicious moment to approach Jon. For all I knew, it could take hours for him to get down on the ground and away from any entourage he might have, in order for us to undertake a calm, reasoned discussion about why Greg Vansen was currently trying to kill the idiot clutched in my arms. By then, for all I knew, Friday might be dead. Which would be a shame for several reasons, the leading one being that I'd have to go back into hiding, or possibly avenge him. Neither of those options were very appealing, especially when considering that avenging a moron like him would probably extend beyond simply tracking down assassins and expand into a broader quest that involved the destruction of an unsuspecting bowling alley's ball return.

How the hell did he …? Never mind.

"Hi, Jon!" Friday screamed as I maneuvered in closer to Wiegert, who was doing some pretty wicked tricks now, inverting himself and pointing the snowboard down as he broke his spin to look at us. The way he arrested his corkscrew momentum was a dead giveaway to me that Jon Wiegert could fly like I could, but maybe on camera it could be explained away. I didn't really care.

"What the—Bruce? Is that you?" Jon asked, his expression only partially readable beneath a thick set of safety goggles and partially obscured by a helmet and breathing mask. I hadn't even noticed the air being thinner up here, but it was.

"It's me!" Friday shouted. I still didn't know what to think of his penchant for picking singer names as his nom de plumes, but I suspected if I went much deeper down this rabbit hole with him, it wouldn't have been a stretch to find out that he'd once called himself Brit Spears. You know, because it sounds vaguely dangerous, even absent the association with a person who once attacked a paparazzi's car with an umbrella, something that was now totally on my bucket list.

"What are you doing here, man?" Jon shouted over the rush of air. All I could see was his eyes blinking furiously, probably trying to figure out why his most annoying co-worker ever had suddenly appeared in the middle of his skydive freefall, carried by America's Most Wanted, a woman with her hair presently *en fuego* like I was a politician's pants.

That's hateful rhetoric, Harmon opined, *unfairly maligning a particularly vulnerable segment of the population.*

Oh, shut up. You know you're a silken-tongued liar and a sack of shit like the rest of your kind.

"Greg Vansen is trying to kill me!" Friday shouted over the roar of air blasting past us in our fall. I would have suggested we stop, maybe have our chat right there, but it seemed rude to either make Jon blatantly display his powers or else seize him by the parachute and force him to make conversation with us.

"What?" Jon ripped at his mask and popped it off, and

his confusion was obvious once I could see his expression. "Why?"

"We thought you might know," I said, figuring the sooner I inserted myself into the conversation, the less awkward it would be when I tried to box Friday out of it so we could, you know, direct it like reasonable adults.

"You think I might know why Greg Vansen is trying to kill *you*?" Jon just sounded flummoxed at that.

"Yeah!" Friday said, defying my mental wish that he would go silent. "I think it has something to do with Panama!"

"Like what?" Jon asked, as perplexed as a man could be while strapped to a snowboard and dropping toward the earth at almost two hundred miles an hour while being quizzed about random events in his past.

"Friday—err, Bruce," I said, "was hoping you might remember something about Panama that … uh … explained why Greg might want to kill him." When I said it out loud, I realized how enormously flimsy that chain of reason sounded, and it kind of made me want to plummet to the earth so I could find a hole and hide in it. Or maybe just reverse course and zoom off at supersonic speed, dropping Friday and all his troubles somewhere in the middle of the Pacific, where they could trouble me no more.

Either/or.

"Dude, I don't have a clue why Greg would want to kill you," Jon said, shrugging his shoulders as expansively as his flight suit and safety gear would allow. "I didn't even know he did kill people anymore. I haven't seen him since … I don't know, Afghanistan, probably."

"Good times," Friday said reflexively.

"Yeah, no, not really," Jon said. "Look, whatever you guys got going on—"

I had a suspicion about what Jon was going to say, but I didn't get a chance to hear it, because a missile exploded about ten feet below me, and I didn't recognize the whine of the AMRAAM until it was already detonating. Pieces of shrapnel and the blast of the explosion concussed me, but fortunately I was insulated from it somewhat by the body I was holding in my arms.

Friday, however, was not so lucky.

Friday jerked as pieces of shrapnel from the missile peppered him, causing him to spasm in my arms. A piece of the missile caught me in the right hand and ripped off my pinky and ring fingers, and another hit me mid-forearm in the left, causing my nerves on that side to go dead, everything below the elbow going suddenly numb.

I gasped in pain, and instantly lost my grip. "Wolfe!" I screamed, but it was too late.

Friday's limp body fell out of my grasp, entering a slow spin toward the earth as I stared at him, my hands utterly useless, the Sierra Nevada mountains racing up to meet us.

18.

Greg

"The right tool for the job," Greg said. He liked to elucidate his thoughts out loud; it made it easier to solidify his thinking when he did.

In this case, the right tool for the job was an F-35B Lightning II, a military aircraft with short takeoff and vertical landing capability. Greg steadied the plane as he brought it in close. He'd already loosed one AIM-120 AMRAAM missile and watched it detonate just beneath Bruce Springersteen, but that was not nearly good enough.

He had to confirm this kill, lest the slippery Hercules somehow survive.

Guiding the plane close, he thumbed the weapons display to the machine gun mounted in a pod beneath his wing, and pointed it toward the rapidly falling figure of Springersteen.

No, this time … he wouldn't get away.

19.

Sienna

"Sonofabitch!" I screamed as Friday tumbled out of my grasp. I tracked around as I spun and fell, finally catching the source of my current troubles: an F-35B that was closing and switching to vertical flight mode, coming to a hover as it pointed toward Friday. I could see the engine in the rear of the aircraft rotating down like a spray nozzle, redirecting the thrust it had been using to fly at supersonic speeds so that it could hold position and rake the hell out of me and Friday.

And in the cockpit, hard-eyed and staring at me from beneath a pilot helmet that couldn't hide his identity, was Greg Vansen, that little bastard.

"Get Friday!" I shouted at Jon Wiegert, my hands yet to heal. I'd done the whole air-to-air combat against fighter jets thing before, and one thing I knew was that my ability to dogfight was a lot better than theirs.

Or so I thought, until Vansen unleashed the 25 mm cannon under his wing at me as I streaked across the distance between us.

"Yikes! Eep! Shit!" I shouted in the thin mountain air as I dodged the blazing yellow tracer rounds streaking through the sky at me. Last time I'd fought drones, not planes, and when planes had shot at me, they'd had the good sense to keep their damned distance. That had spared me from being shot at by this volume of fire, which was not that dissimilar from what Greg had unleashed on me in my apartment just a few hours earlier.

A round skipped off my shoulder and threw me into a spin as I closed the last hundred yards to Greg's F-35B. I'd planned to smash into him dead on, but instead I skimmed off the cockpits, bashing into the glass and injuring myself in the process as I bounced off and did an ass-over-teakettle roll, feeling the serious pull of the intake for the vertical flight mode as I over flew the back of the plane. It tugged at my shirt, and might have sucked me in, if not for the momentum I had going when I flipped over it.

I righted myself about a hundred feet past the F35, which was damned good timing since Vansen was already spinning the aircraft around to deal with me. He had the cannon going again, hanging off the wing on a mounted, detachable pod. That was annoying, so I shot a compacted light web at it as the barrel came around. It wedged solidly in there and the damned thing blew up as he fired, making a hell of a noise and leaving a bigass, black, smoking pockmark where before it had been hanging from the wing on a strut. It also made a few little holes in the body of the aircraft, one of which started to smoke.

"Take that, jagoff!" I shouted, wondering if Vansen could hear me through the cockpit. Hoping that he could, I added, "That's for calling me Friday's girlfriend!"

Vansen smacked the shattered cockpit out of the way as he started to bring the F-35 around again. "I've shot at you twice today and *that's* what you're upset about?"

"How about I kick your ass and make you his girlfriend, then we'll see how you like it?" I shouted, tossing a ball of flame at the right-side air intake. It shot in and flamed out the rear, hard, turning Vansen's supersonic jet aircraft into a glorified helicopter in one shot. And not a very good one, either, since it relied heavily on the rear engine for thrust.

The F-35 bucked hard as the engine flamed out, the rear sinking as the thrust nozzles designed to help keep it steady when aloft in vertical flight mode became the only thing holding it up. Vansen's eyes got wide as he feverishly worked the control panels, but he wasn't a stupid guy. He got, pretty quickly, that his aircraft was doomed, and within a couple seconds I watched him hit the eject. He was catapulted out of the plane and then disappeared about a hundred feet up, almost like he'd just vanished out of existence with his ejection seat.

"Huh," I said, wondering if he was going to reappear. I glanced back at Friday and Jon, figuring that Wiegert would have taken care of the problem of his old buddy falling out of the sky and heading toward death on the mountains below.

Nope.

Friday was still plummeting, and Wiegert was nowhere to be seen. I shot after Friday (instinctively, I swear), scanning for Wiegert, wondering if maybe Vansen had somehow teleported over to him and killed him.

I found him hot dogging his way down, doing extreme tricks with his snowboard and trying—and I do mean trying, since I knew the bastard could fly as fast as I could—to look like he was making an attempt to save Friday. He was a few hundred yards back by now, though, Friday having somehow outpaced him in the fall, which presumably Jon was going to use as an excuse to justify not helping. He deployed his parachute while I watched, the sudden arresting of his downward momentum yanking him so hard that his snowboard jerked before it disappeared beneath the rainbow parachute. "How could I possibly have caught him? He was so far ahead," I imagined him telling anyone who dared question his version of events. And there'd be at least two cameras with a record to back him up.

Zooming down in a dive, I realized Friday was about five hundred yards from hitting the upper slopes of a snowy mountain. When he did hit, I imagined his insensate body was pretty well going to disintegrate on impact, because … well, that's what bodies tended to do when they hit hard surfaces at terminal velocity.

It was going to be a near thing, and I needed to be careful, because if I caught Friday at full speed, it would technically be worse than him hitting the slope below. Terminal velocity was about 200 miles per hour when traveling down with your arms all tucked in, after all, and I was traveling much, much faster than that in my attempt to save his big, dumb ass.

I got close and matched velocity as best I could, with only a couple hundred yards to go, then grabbed Friday under the arms, snaking mine beneath his in an attempt to end this as gently as possible. I applied my version of the brakes, then shot hard down the slope of the mountain, intending to ride it down as much as I could before I brought Friday to a complete stop.

It didn't take as long as I thought it would have.

"Gyahhhhh!" Friday woke up like he was coming out of a nightmare, waving his arms so hard he broke my grip, escaping me like an angry bull. He dropped twenty feet to the earth and landed squarely on his ass, producing an "OOOOF!" and the sound of a tailbone cracking as he struck the snow-dusted slope. He was already bleeding down the front of his chest and out of his gut, so I circled lower and figured I'd take a peek at the damage. Friday hit a tree in a way that would have played well in an old episode of *The Three Stooges*, stopping when he grabbed the thin trunk to arrest his further downhill momentum.

"Are you—" I started to ask as I came in for a hover close to him.

Friday vaulted to his feet like a drunk, staggering a few steps while dusting off the small amounts of snow he'd gathered to himself in the landing. "I'm okay! I'm okay, everyone! Nothing to worry about here." And then he promptly fell over and damned near went tumbling down the slope.

"Wow, you guys, that was crazy!" Jon shouted as he came in for his own landing. He unslung the snowboard neatly from his feet, and I figured he must have missed his preferred landing zone and decided to feign helpfulness, because there definitely wasn't enough snow on the ground here for him to do his boarding. Tracts of exposed earth lay between tiny little patches of melting snow that was barely an inch thick. I looked up the mountain and could see long, perfect stretches of white, the sort of zones he was probably looking to hit before his jump went all to hell. "You all right?"

"I'm good," Friday said, staying firmly anchored on his ass instead of trying to stand once more. I didn't really know where a Hercules lay on the power scale; I only knew that the higher up one was, the faster the metahuman healing tended to work. Friday brushed at his chest, and a piece of glittering metal caught the sun as he flicked it out of one of his wounds, a three-inch gash between his ribs.

Since Friday didn't appear ready to call his buddy out on what just happened, I figured I would. "What the hell was that, Jon-boy?"

Jon shed his helmet and a wave of golden hair came flowing out, matted a little by sweat. He used the flourish of his move to delay his answer, and when he finally did, he gave me a kind of California pretty-boy smile. "What was what?"

"I asked you to save him," I said, jerking a thumb at Friday, "and you totally bailed on him. I get that he's an idiot—"

"Hey," Friday said, sounding a little wounded.

"—but you were going to let him die to avoid exposing yourself as a meta. Or maybe because you have your own axe to grind, I dunno—"

"Hey, shhhh," Jon said, looking around furtively and then zipping closer to us in a very short, one inch off the ground example of his flight power. "No one can know about that, okay? I'm in competitions sometimes, you know? Pretty sure the rules forbid metahumans in the—"

"Oh, I see," I said without bothering to disguise my disgust. "If someone has to die so you can continue to cheat in your little games—"

"It's not cheating!" Jon said, but he was looking a little guilty. "There are others who do it, too. It's, uh … you know, kind of an … un-talked about, kinda common practice …"

"Shut your mouth, Lance Armstrong," I said, shaking my head. Something was buzzing faintly in the distance, over the steady breeze running over the mountains around us. "I just have one question, and you will answer it."

Jon swallowed heavily. "Or … you'll kill me?"

"No," I snapped, "I'll tell everyone you're a cheating meta asshole chickenshit who's been gaming the system."

Jon pursed his lips tightly. "Ouch. Some real talk there. Harsh."

"Gentler than death, though," I said. "Now steady yourself, surfer-boy, because here comes the $64,000 question: Do you have any idea why Greg Vansen is trying to kill Friday—Bruce—whatever his name is?" I pointed at him, just so I could make sure Jon was clear on who I was talking about.

Jon shrugged widely. "I have no idea, dudes."

That buzzing sound was getting louder now, and I was having a hard time deciding where the hell it was coming from. It sounded like it was behind me, but the slope down was thick with trees—another argument for why Jon would have been an idiot to snowboard here. Though I suppose with meta reflexes and the ability to fly, he was unlikely to end up kissing a trunk and dying spectacularly.

"Hey, do you guys hear something?" Jon asked, looking into the sky like a dragon was going to come down on us all at any time. I could only hope it would eat him first, because he was annoying me.

"Yeah, what is th—" Friday didn't even get out the full sentence before something roared down the slope, a black, shadowy shape appearing as if out of nowhere.

It was an RAH-66 Comanche helicopter, an unapproved American design that incorporated stealth technology into an attack helo. Designed to exterminate the hell out of ground-based targets, it was a project that had never been brought into production because it was just too damned expensive for a redundant function. There were, after all, lots of ways for the military to kill the shit out of people on the ground without sending a hovering helicopter to hang out just overhead.

Unfortunately for us, the Comanche being weak as shit was not one of the reasons the project got cancelled. In fact, from what I remembered, it was a pretty damned efficient killing machine.

And it was pointed right at us.

20.

Augustus

The slope above the cabin was a disaster-area-level mess, and I was in no position to do any kind of clean up, even after I awoke to the sound of the Great Wall of Augustus groaning in strain under my back.

So I did what I always did.

I called the cops.

"Hmmm," Chief Smithson said, standing with me and about fifty other cops about a hundred yards below the wall, listening to the creaking and cracking of the rocky bulwark as it resisted the weight of snow and tree and other debris. (I'd replaced the other rock that had broken loose back into the earth. It helped.) "Is that thing going to come busting down?"

"Nah, it's under control," I said, stretching. My back should have been knotted after sleeping on a rock for hours, but I was feeling surprisingly good. Rested, even. "It'll hold it all back until the snow melts and probably even after it evaporates. I might need to drain a little here and there, though." As the idea occurred to me, I immediately popped open a few more pits in the earth behind it. Smaller ones, this time, to drain off some of the fluid that was accumulating at the bottom of the snow pack.

The wall creaked its reply to the sudden relief of stress, and the cops all took a step back, led by the chief. "Well, all right, then," he said, sounding pretty skeptical about the whole thing.

"Did you catch any sign of Omar the Bubble Man?" I asked.

Smithson didn't bother to tear his eyes away to answer me. "Someone reported seeing something like that on the west highway out of town. Smashed two cars as he crossed the pass. Be pretty difficult to track him now that he's out."

I hid my disappointment well. "It's better you didn't get a chance to cross paths with him," I said. They were in no way ready for what Omar brought to the table. He would have left a bunch of crushed-up, soaked-out police cruisers in his wake.

A roaring sound above made me look up, and then the clouds parted and the late afternoon sun shone through for just a second as a figure descended from the heavens. One of the cops shouted something about the second coming, and I almost snorted, because I knew it wasn't that.

"What happened?" Reed asked as he set down, pants legs flaring as his vortex cut out. The effect would have been a lot cooler if he'd been wearing parachute pants, but given the dark look on his face, I doubted he was in the mood to hear that suggestion.

"I'm gonna suggest that you wouldn't be here if you didn't already know," I said, trying to keep some of the snide out of my tone.

"You could have called," he said, way more gently than I was expecting. "You could have asked—"

"Mother, may I?" I shot at him as Chief Smithson sauntered off, a little too casually.

"—for help," Reed said. I doubted that was what he was originally going to say.

"Help and permission are starting to feel real close to the same," I said, and I might have let a touch of resentment drip out.

I watched him take a couple extra breaths, composing himself and his reply. "What's that supposed to mean?"

"It means you got an iron-fist thing going, Reed." He cocked his head in confusion, so I went on. "You're a good boss, Boss, but you're kind of a micromanager. Get fixated on the small details of ops that you're not even running. Like this."

When he answered, his voice was so full of irony it could have been his sister talking. "Nearly getting a town destroyed by an enemy meta's avalanche is not a small thing, Augustus."

"Yeah, well, I wasn't expecting that," I said. "And I don't think you were expecting it either when you said I could pull on this thread. This guy I found, the one who helped make our troublemakers from last night? He was sipping his own cocktail, if you know what I mean. And not just the regular version, either."

Reed shook his head. "No, you're right. Pulling down the ice off a mountain? Your garden variety frost giant couldn't do that."

"He wasn't a Jotun," I said, and Reed frowned. "Or I should say … he wasn't just a Jotun."

Reed froze. "You're telling me—"

"I think he was using both the enhancement formulas we know about," I said. "The boost to grow his regular power, the one Harmon gave us … and the other one, the one Sienna discovered in that lab in Portland, the one that unlocks your secondary abilities. Whatever you want to call it. Because this dude? He attacked as a Poseidon at first."

"Holy hell," Reed whispered. "Then this is—"

"Yeah," I said. "It's not just some little rinky-dink conspiracy to swell the meta ranks in the US with Edward Cavanagh's serum." I took a deep breath. "They've got access to *everything*—absolutely everything that's been developed that we know about. And it looks like to me …" And I cast a glance over my shoulder, as though I could see, far off in the distance, Omar rolling over the hills as he made his escape, "… that they've got a hell of a lot of cards up their sleeve that they're not playing yet."

21.

Sienna

"Any last words?" Greg Vansen asked, voice amplified by some artificial means, like he had speakers mounted on the outside of the chopper.

"You know, I had the actual military hunting me last year and they didn't deploy half the cool toys that you have," I said to Vansen, staring up at him in his badass Comanche chopper. I admit, I was kinda jealous.

"Thank you," Vansen said with a sort of sincerity. "Now … any last words?" I counted at least a dozen missiles ready to light us up. Even I couldn't move fast enough to retrieve Friday and get the hell out of Dodge before they started landing on us. Not at this range.

"Why does he keep asking us that?" I wondered.

"It's his thing," Jon Wiegert said, and then waved at Vansen in the cockpit. "Uhh, Greg? Bruce here says you want to kill me, maybe?"

Greg peered down at him. "What? No." He sounded a little offended about it. "I have nothing against you, Jon. I only want to kill him." He looked a little pointedly at me. "Only him."

"Well, cool then," Jon said, very California dude and sounding pretty relieved. "Cuz, uh … I got a filming to finish and then, later, a calendar shoot, so …" He chucked a thumb over his shoulder. "I'll just go, if that's cool with you?"

"Yes," Greg said. "We're good."

"Awesome," Jon said, and then waved his hands at the two of us. "Good luck, guys." And then he flew off into the trees, backwards, snowboard under his arm.

"I should warn you, I have my finger on the firing mechanism," Greg said. "Any further attempts to distract or incapacitate me with the Warmind will result in immediate death. Any hint of your flames, and—well, I'll fire, obviously. I know your other tricks as well—light nets, flight. Even a hint of your Quetzlcoatl straining at the edges of your skin and I will saturate the area around you with so much destruction that even you won't survive, Ms. Nealon."

"You're talking an awful lot for a guy who's supposedly holding my life in the palm of his hand," I shouted up at him. "Why not just pull that trigger and be done already?"

"My employer did not contract me to kill you," Vansen said a little archly. "He specified some unnamed girlfriend—"

"You keep calling me that and I'm going to go to Quetzlcoatl form up your ass, Vansen."

"—not the most dangerous meta on the planet," Vansen said, ignoring my completely sincere threat. "I don't believe that my earlier failure to kill Bruce here compels me to do something for free that many of the best and worst in my profession have already failed to do for considerable recompense. Therefore ... you may go, provided you give me no more trouble in my endeavors. If you persist in this ... well, I think you know where we stand. I know you. I know what you have available to you. Now ... without further ado ... any last words?"

"Friday," I said, "tell the man your regrets." And then, in my own head, *Harmon ... I need to pull a hidden ace.*

Gerry Harmon sighed. *Fine. I'm not one of your servile souls, but...just this once. What did you have in mind?*

"Uhmm ..." Friday started, still lying flat from his fall and cringing, both from the pain and being put on the spot. "I feel really bad about that time I peed in the baptismal font. I didn't know what it was, and I couldn't find a bathroom ..."

Ignoring him as he started to ramble, I thought, *I have in mind that I need to know what Vansen has in mind—and if there are any paths out I can't see.*

There are always ways, Harmon said. *You want to know what it feels like to read a mind? Here, have at it—*

I suddenly felt like someone had inserted an umbrella in my ear and opened it, releasing a flock of wild monkeys high on amphetamines who promptly went tearing through my skull, smashing everything they could get their filthy ape hands on.

I clamped my jaw shut tight as the fleeting sensation of a screaming parade of lunatics running through my brain quieted after what felt like an eternity but was probably only a few seconds, ignoring the sudden, clammy feeling that was sending cold sweats down my scalp. I hadn't even realized that my hair had been doused and was back to tickling my shoulders and neck, but there it was, fire out, and I was left staring up at Greg Vansen, who was looking down at me from his helicopter perch of death.

And I could see myself through his eyes.

There was a board before him, at his fingertips. He knew how to pilot, and he'd done it so much it was instinctive, so thoroughly practiced that he didn't even have to give it much conscious thought anymore. Which freed him up to concentrate entirely on me, and, to a lesser degree, Friday, who was still lying in a heap with a lot of little superficial wounds spread over his upper body, going on about the time he got caught "accidentally" pulling his taffy in the girls' room at school, to Greg's rising disgust.

I sat there for less than a second, and it occurred to me that his brain was basically on autopilot when it came to the piloting, because his attention was almost entirely on me and the increasingly horrifying confession taking place in front of him.

Yes, Harmon said. *You see it.*

Well, yeah, I said. *He's watching us …*

And meanwhile, I was watching him from the inside. Which meant …

I could feel the collective, the stick that he used to pilot the Comanche. His grip on it was solid, if a little sweaty, as he started to run out of patience with Friday's recollection of horrors past. Time was slowed, thick as jelly, moving at a glacial pace. I snapped back to my own eyes for just a second, to check if what I remembered about the position of the helo was right ...

It was. His tail rotor was less than ten feet from a copse of pine trees, the ones he'd miraculously appeared through.

Zipping back into his head, I tested my control by yanking back on the collective with all his arm's strength and metahuman speed.

I could feel Vansen's alarm a quarter second after I did it, that sensation of pure freakout that comes when the solid ground beneath you—or in this case, the steady helicopter— suddenly drops. The Comanche bucked radically as the top rotor spun up, hard, the RPMs raging and causing it to show us its belly instead of the fierce, deadly nose.

Popping back into my own head, I raised a hand and blasted at him with a fireball to each of the wings as the helo started to fall backward, inverting. The tail rotor, that vital component to the operation of any helicopter, slammed into the trees behind him. The whine of engines straining against resistance was almost lost under the whooshing noise of the main rotor railing at full power. Then that, too, hit the trees and the sound of splitting metal got even louder.

The four helicopter blades suddenly blew off, explosive bolts launching them in all directions. The top canopy of the helicopter was buffeted by a small series of explosions, and then the entire cockpit launched off over the trees, successfully ejected as the Comanche spun in and exploded, its fuel tanks combusting as it crashed to the earth down the slope.

"Wow!" Friday shouted, pumping his fist. "That was awesome!" He looked straight at me. "We really kicked his ass."

"'We'?" I gave him some crazy eye.

"Yeah, I totally distracted him," Friday said, "you know with all that, uh ... blatantly made-up stuff that totally never happened to me."

"Whatever," I said, "I need to go confirm the kill."

"Oh, yeah." He popped up, fresh as a daisy and hulked

out, little shards of metal popping out of his wounds as his muscles swelled, the red, crisscrossing cuts healing right there before my eyes and leaving nothing but faint traces of crimson like tiny scars across his skin. "Let's do it!"

It didn't take us long to find the ejected cockpit, since it was caught in the top branches of a tree. I was surprised a tree would support it, since it looked to be at least a half ton of metal and equipment, but there it was, cradled in the boughs of a big pine, parachute only half deployed and the canopy still down. I dropped Friday in a nearby tree with an admonishment to, "Shut the hell up and stay here!" because I was kinda done with politeness, and then readied my approach.

I zoomed right up to it and lit up my hand, ready to saturate the entire area with fire the moment I opened the cockpit. Then I reached down and ripped it open, prepared to burn everything to ash.

Of course … there was no one in the cockpit.

"Dammit," I muttered, and then lit it on fire anyway, figuring better safe than sorry. I made my turnaround sweep and picked up Friday, who had been hanging off a branch like a gorilla. It was a good look for him. "Let's get out of here."

He jerked a little in my arms as his weight settled and he started to shrink back down to normal human size. "What happened?"

"He was already gone," I said, heading high into the sky in hopes of avoiding Greg appearing again with—hell, I don't know. An aircraft carrier, probably. Maybe a helicarrier.

"Wow. See, he really is a magician," Friday said with not even grudging admiration. It was obvious, blatant, bordering on lusty admiration for the guy trying to kill him.

"Yeah," I said, without nearly so much appreciation for the magic since I was the one tasked with defending Friday against it. "Any idea how he's doing it?"

"Nope," Friday said with a surprisingly happy demeanor—you know, for someone targeted for death by a magician who could seemingly appear at will with billion-dollar military killing machines. "He always used to pull these sorts of miracles when we were working together, too. Everyone thought it was *awesome*."

"If you keep calling everything 'awesome,' I'm going to reach into your brain and rip that word out, replacing it with, 'kittens.'"

"That would be totally *kittens*!" Friday said with immediate enthusiasm, his face all lit up like I'd just given him the bestest Christmas present ever. "I love it! I'm gonna start saying it all the time now."

I held in the agonized scream that threatened to burst out of me because, honestly, what was the point?

Look at all the fun you're having, Gerry Harmon said with rich amusement. *Isn't this so much better than lifting the same weight over and over again a million times a day?*

Yes, so much fun, I said. *Sedative-free limb amputation couldn't be any funner.*

Shame you didn't get to see how Greg Vansen was managing his little disappearing act while you were in his head, Harmon said, oh so smug. *If he still had a face, I would have reduced it to a fine jelly with a single punch right then.*

I don't suppose you'd be willing to—

Nope, Harmon said with a smile. *Figuring it out is the point of the case. Telling you would be taking out the mystery, and thus, the joy.*

Oh, I'm feeling the joy, I said. *Anyone else ever seen anything like this? Wolfe? You've seen everything. What am I dealing with?*

For the first time ever, Wolfe actually sounded uncomfortable. *You need to work this out for yourself, Sienna.*

Seriously, you guys? Zack? I searched for support.

No can do, he said. *I don't know what this guy is, but … if I did, I wouldn't tell you.* He smiled wanly. *You need this.*

I need Friday like I need a case of flaming hemorrhoids, you guys. Seriously. Help a sista out.

This is the work that fulfills you, Sienna, Gavrikov said with all the Russian solemnity he could muster. *For us to spoil the—*

The hunt, Wolfe said.

—It would be wrong, Gavrikov said. *It would cheapen this. You need the fulfillment, and a shortcut … it would not end this thing in a satisfying way.*

You're all conspiring against me, you bastards. I would have shaken my fist at them, but unfortunately, they were in my head. Also, shaking my fist would have meant dropping Friday, probably. So ... aces all the way around, then.

Work it out for yourself, Sienna, Harmon said, but with much less smugness this time. *Take the chance while it's here. You may not get another case anytime soon.*

Fine, I said with grudging acceptance. I took a long breath, and listened because over the whistling of the wind around us, I could hear another kind of whistling—it was Friday, singing ... "Hungry Like the Wolf"?

"What the hell? Friday," I said, and he stopped, blessedly. "Can you think of anyone else who might know why Greg would want to kill you?"

"Theo might." Friday's empty, expressive face seemed to sink into thought, his eyes staring off into the distance above as we passed into a cloud. Fortunately, I could still see him, and the slow nod as he started to speak again. "See, there was this one time ..."

22.

Friday

Baghdad, Iraq
February 20, 1991

*Sienna note: Do I even need to remind you that this is probably 100%
bullshit?*

It was hot and heavy, right at the tail end of
OPERATION: DESERT STORM, and we were flying the
flag of aweso—err, I mean—BADASS KITTENS! And
America! And doing badass stuff behind the lines! And—

Get to the point already, before I drop you.

Ooh, okay. We were crammed in the body of the
Concorde like sardines, Greg had blacked out all the
windows, and the pressure was so intense it was like—like
being in a popcan before it's ready to explode! The five of us
were huddled in together, not meeting each other's eyes. The
pressure was intense, like being at the bottom of the ocean
without a submarine to protect you from the ... uh, the
pressure. And the eels! And sharks! And uh ... anyway, it
was intense, like looking into the sun. But without the
blindness.

"Gonna be glad when this is over," Theo said. You could
always tell who Theo was because he was our black guy.

*I would facepalm right now if it didn't mean dropping you. Hell, I
might anyway.*

But—but he was really good at what he did! I'm not a

racist, I swear!

If the only characteristic you remember about him is that he was black, then yes, that literally does make you a racist. What did Theo do for the team?

I don't remember. Something. Anyway, Chase spoke next. She was our girl, our resident chick, and a badass. She was totally KITTENS and totally hot for me. We were boyfriend and girlfriend—

This poor girl, not even here to defend this casual defamation of her character.

—and had been HOT AND HEAVY IF YOU KNOW WHAT I MEAN *wink wink*—

Sienna note: He actually turned his head to look up at me and winked here.

—for six months, ever since she'd gotten on the squad. It had been all killing and sexytimes and more killing since we'd come to the desert, and it was all joy from my end.

But tonight ... tonight was the finale, and here we were, in a blacked-out plane, with Greg locked in the cockpit and the rest of us without a clue where we were going ... except to know that DANGER WAS AROUND EVERY CORNER!!!

... There are no corners when you're flying a plane high in the sky ...

Muh flow! Knock it off! Anyway, the Concorde shuddered as Greg steered her low. I had no idea what was going on in the cockpit, only that we were heading into the most dangerous danger we had ever faced! The most perilous peril—

I want to drain your brain of all adjectives.

What's an adjective? Never mind, no one cares. This would go a lot smoother if you would just stop talking.

I'll take, "Things Hookers Say to You for $1,000, Alex."

Not listening to you anymore. This is all super important. And awesome. I mean KITTENS.

Greg got on the overhead speakers. "In precisely five minutes, we'll deploy." Then he clicked it off.

"That guy is not one to mince a lot of words, is he?" Chase asked, looking nervously at the ceiling, as though she could see him instead of the speakers he'd just spoken through.

"It's okay, baby," I said, threading my arm around her. "I'll protect you."

"Oh, my big sexy sugarbear—"

vomit Oh, sorry, couldn't contain it in my mouth any longer. My bad.

Ignoring you, because you totally didn't really throw up, you just made the sound to distract me. Anyway, five minutes passed like an eternity. Jon laced up his sneakers and strapped on his board. I readied my fifty cals—wait, what was the thing Greg was carrying earlier?

A Browning M2 machine gun.

Yeah, I was totally carrying two of those, one cradled in each arm like kittens. I was swole, had been working out for months, and these GAINZZZZ made me look totally awesome.

"You look so sexy right now," Chase whispered. "I totally want to have your babies and stuff when we get back."

If you don't knock this shit off, I'm going to throw up on your head for real next time. Stick to the story. What happened next that is actually relevant to us finding out why Greg is trying to kill you? No more of this sexual fantasy bullshit you're concocting in your head.

Fine. Ruin everything.

Greg came on the speakers again, "We are on final approach. Prepare to deploy in sixty seconds." We waited in silence, the tension eating us alive like kittens eating mice. "Thirty seconds," Greg said coolly.

"Fifteen seconds," he said, and this time, I swear, he sounded a little tense. "I will open the boarding door in just a moment, and we'll deploy.

"Blindfolded."

"What?" I asked as the cockpit door opened and Greg came out, sauntering his short ass down the aisle like a stewardess, holding blindfolds instead of my in-flight peanuts. "What the shit?" I asked as he extended one to me.

"Put it on," he said, and when I didn't, he reached up and put it on me—

Wait. Friday, he's like my height, five foot four. How did he reach the top of your head to put it on if you were 'swole' enough to hold big guns like a Browning?

I don't know, he just did—

Did he jump?

No. He just reached up and blindfolded me while I whined—err, I mean … while I told him what I thought of that bullshit—

Yeah, I think you accidentally got it right the first time.

Anyway, he blindfolded Jon, Theo and Chase, and then shoved us down the aisle to the boarding door. I was like, wtf is this shit all about?! But I didn't say it, because I was blindfolded, obviously.

And that interferes with your mouth how? Hell, I wonder if a ball gag could shut you up at this point.

He opened the door and we waited, all stacked up. Chase was pressed against me, all frightened, and I—

Death.

Anyway, the wind was whipping through, and he pushed us out the door. Theo screamed like a girl. So did Jon. Chase held tight to me, and I to her. "If these are going to be our last moments," I said, "I think we should be together—one last time—in the air—while the world spins around us and the metal chorus plays." And the electric guitars started up right then, on cue, playing my favorite Metallica song, and we—

STICK TO THE STORY, FRIDAY.

Suddenly our feet hit solid ground, which was weird, because we weren't wearing parachutes. It happened fast, too, like we were only five feet off the ground when we jumped or something.

… So there really wasn't time for an amazing, mid-air lovemaking to a pulsating Metallica tune, was there?

What, no, there totally was!

Only you could pull that off on a five-foot jump, Friday.

Thank you!

… That really wasn't a compliment …

Sure it was.

… Endurance champ …

Whut? Never mind. Doesn't matter. We landed, and Greg disappeared the blindfolds from our eyes. And we were in a corridor, like he'd tossed us out of the plane and we'd teleported right into this dark, concrete block construction corridor, with electrical piping overhead and metal doors like you find on a ship.

"Where the hell are we?" Chase asked, looking around as she adjusted her camo tank top sexily.

Greg stood there behind us, and I looked back to see him fiddling in his coat pocket for a second before he replied. "We're in the bunker of Saddam Hussein."

"This is so kittens," I said, my two giant machine guns held in my arms. "Let's kill this mofo!"

"We need to—" Greg started to say, but then, without warning, fifteen bad guys poured around the corners on either side of us.

"NOOOOOOO!" Jon shouted as he was gunned down horribly in a blaze of bullets, blood squirting everywhere as he fell down. I grabbed him as he dropped. "Bruce ..." he whispered. "I'm so sad ... I'm not going home ... and I never got to tell you the thing I've wanted to tell you all this time ..."

"What is it, Jon?" I asked, holding him tight, trying to give him solace in his final moments.

"That you were always my hero ..." he choked out, and then went limp, dead in my arms, tongue hanging out of his mouth like a roadkill dog. Dead. Super dead. Dead dead dead. So sad.

What the ...? WE LITERALLY JUST SAW HIM ALIVE. He did not die in Desert Storm, you brain-damaged idiot!

Oh. Right. Well, I mean—Jon sprang back to life. "Flesh wound!" he shouted, pulling his Uzis and mowing down the enemy as they came down the corridor, full of confidence that they were soon to lose!

"Yeah!" I shouted, and "Enter Sandman" mixed with the "Star-Spangled Banner" was playing, and it was the most diesel awesome KITTENS song you've ever heard as I added to the chorus with my M2s lighting up the place. Muzzle flash was going like strobes and fifty cal cartridges were filling the ground at my feet. Iraqi soldiers were dying like crazy, heads exploding, chests exploding, legs, feet and arms exploding and flying off as I doused them with crazy amounts of bullets, the big belts of ammo rolling across me as the Browning sucked them up like Chase on—

STOP.

What? She liked cherry sodas. In a bottle. With a straw.

... Whew.

But seriously, we were killing them all. Hundreds of Iraqi soldiers died in that corridor, my machine guns going off like car alarms in a parking lot where a twelve-year-old mischief maker is going nuts with a baseball bat.

"We're winning the war right here!" Theo shouted, his own M249 Sawsall—

It's SAW. Squad Automatic Weapon.

—right, SAW, he was butchering with it.

"I have never seen this much sexy killing in my life!" Chase screamed, ripping her top off and letting those bad boys flop as she lit up her totally badass lightsaber power and jumped into the battle at the rear, her glowing green beam cutting into enemy soldiers and tearing them apart. She whirled and spun, and heads flew off, Iraqi soldiers clutched at their chests where she plunged her light blade in through their lungs and hearts. When they were all dead, it was a pile of bodies everywhere. We'd killed more Iraqis than the entire US Army and Marine Corps combined.

... I kinda doubt that.

And then we walked tall down the hallway and I kicked open the door, my machine guns smoking from all the shooting I'd just done. There were bullet holes in all the walls, and it smelled like sexy gunpowder everywhere, including my oiled-up, sweaty biceps.

There were a bunch of guys in the room just cowering in fear, and I was ready to squeeze the trigger on them when Greg pushed past me. "Stop," he said, "this isn't the mission."

"Whatever," I said, and lifted my gun. Saddam Hussein was right there, and I wasted him with a hundred rounds from the M2. He screamed, his little mustached lip quivering as he opened his mouth wide and trilled a note high enough to make me believe he had no nuts.

Then I shot his nuts off, blood spraying everywhere as his crotch exploded like a pastry cake I'd put my fist through. If he was screaming before, he was screaming louder now, and I turned his entire upper body into red Jello paste with the big .50, and finally turned loose on his head to make that stupid noise stop. Once he was dead, I said, "YEAHHHHHH!" and jumped over there and teabagged his corpse—

... Saddam Hussein was hanged to death in 2006. He did not die at your hands in 1991. Dipshit.

Well, that's how I remember it, but maybe I missed my shot. I dunno.

"That's not our mission," Greg said, brushing my M2 aside as I pulled the trigger and killed some random stupid dude in an Iraqi military uniform. His chest turned into shredded mozzarella and spaghetti sauce and he made wheezing noise as he died. The shooting sound made a ringing in my ears too, so I didn't hear what Greg said for a few seconds. When it faded, he said, "... and if you continue to press your luck, you and your sons will end up like your general over there. There is nowhere we can't get to you." And he made Saddam Hussein or maybe his secret imposter or something, anyway he made the guy nod, eyes wide and full of fear.

Also, pretty sure Saddam, fake or real, peed himself. Real profile in courage, that guy.

"I believe our mission here is complete," Greg said with irritating precision.

"Not mine," I said, and hosed down the room with ammo! People screamed, died, cried, begged for mercy. Chase shook her boobies with excitement, those puppies flopping wildly about as I wildly sprayed bullets everywhere.

Greg slapped my gun barrel down before I could have too much fun. "Not ... the ... mission. Come on," and he waved for us to leave the room, which we did, sealing the metal door behind us.

"That was amazing," Theo said. "Greg, you were amazing."

"Yeah, he was totally kittens," I said nonchalantly. "But you know who else was amazing?" I pointed with two thumbs at myself. "This guy."

Greg got right up in my face, and suddenly he was taller than me, and his face was huge, like the moon eclipsing the sun, and I was like, "Ohhhh, shit, I dun it now!"

"Do your job," Greg said, all up in my face. I felt like he spat all over me as he spoke, and then he kinda … went back to normal. But mad. And he tossed me a blindfold. "Put that back on. The rest of you, too."

"Say it, don't spray it," I said, and he gave me another look that I gave him right back. And then I put on my blindfold like he asked, because I'm a polite guy.

"I think we just won the war," Jon said as I stood in the darkness with the others, waiting for Greg to do … whatever the hell Greg was going to do. I could hear him moving around out there, and he touched me for a second on the arm as he went past.

"Because we are totally kittens!" I said, nodding my head. I knew we'd be back at base, soon, and I was looking forward to getting Chase alone so we could—

Okay, that's it, you're done, unless you have something germane to the story to tell me.

Oh! Right! So, I was just standing there, thinking about what I was going to do to her when we got back and I heard Greg snap at Theo. "What are you doing with your blindfold off?" He sounded super pissed.

"I didn't—I'm not—I mean, it slipped for a second, I don't know how it—

I heard a scuffling, and then Greg shoved me and the others, you could tell by the grunts, and I was climbing up a set of stairs and then the door shut, and he ripped my blindfold off along with everyone else.

Greg's face was purple with rage, and he was pointing a finger at Theo. "So help me … if you ever tell anyone what you just saw … no one will ever—EVER—see you again. Do you understand me?"

Theo looked like he'd swallowed a live kitten. "Yes," he said, and his voice cracked like he was going through puberty. Which he probably wasn't. I mean he was young, but not that young.

Greg just stared at him, all furious and stuff, and then stormed back into the cockpit and slammed the door, only opening it a crack so we couldn't see anything as he went in.

"What the hell did you see?" I asked after he was gone, whirling on Theo.

"I don't even want to know," Jon said, and he zipped to the back of the plane.

"I don't think I want to know, either," Chase said, and she spider-monkey climbed over the seats to head back to the middle of the plane with Jon.

"Baby, no!" I shouted after her, but I couldn't pull myself away. "Seriously, Theo ... tell me, brutha ... what did you see when you took the blindfold off?"

Theo just stood there, shaking, and then he looked right at me, fear filling his eyes like my own penis in my hand. Huge. Huge fear. "I didn't see anything, man. Nothing." And then he went forward, locking himself in the bathroom for the rest of the flight, as I sank into my seat and pondered the infinite mysteries of the universe that had just been opened to me, at the tip of my grasp—

Oh, shut up. So you really don't know anything else about what Greg can do?

No, but Theo does. Clearly.

Maybe. But I'm guessing you don't know where Theo is.

Come on. We can find him together. Like we did with Jon.

What? We didn't find Jon, Jamal did. And when we did find him, you were useless.

I distracted him!

Sigh. So now we have to find someone else, in the faintest hope that this Theo maybe—just maybe—has a clue about how this Greg works his mojo. Great.

He's a real killer, that Greg. You should have seen the shit he did later, when we were in Operation Enduring Freedom. It was off the chain.

I have a feeling I've seen something similar. Because I've dealt with this Greg all of twice ... and honestly? He's kind of impressing me with what he can do. Which ... for me ... is more than a little scary.

Well ... now I'm scared, too, Sienna. Hold me!

I will drop you right now, you giant dipshit.

23.

Greg

Greg didn't feel comfortable taking so much as a breath until he was safely back in his plane, headed east, vector locked toward Chicago. He stroked the plush leather seat that he'd had refurbished, replacing the straightforward military style plastic and vinyl bucket arrangement in this, his very own SR-71. "At least I still have you," he said to the empty cockpit.

It was hard to fathom exactly how much damage Sienna Nealon had done to his arsenal in just two encounters. A flawless Browning M2 that now needed replacement because she'd turned it to slag. An F-35B that he'd painstakingly stolen—those were still incredibly rare. Though not so rare as the Comanche, which was nearly irreplaceable, one of only two that had ever been built. He'd stolen it when it was still in the testing phase; now that it hadn't been adopted by the military, he was going to be hard pressed to find the only other model. He might have to step down to the AH-64 Apache if he wanted to fill that particular gap in his lineup.

Greg pressed his damp palm to his forehead, mopping the hair out of his eyes. The slight sweat he left behind caused his eyes to sting. "No one has ever humiliated me this badly," he said to the empty cockpit. And no one had.

Planning had always been his hallmark. Where others failed, he succeeded at tasks because of exceptional planning and preparation. Preparedness was the grease that made any mission go smoothly.

But Mark McGarry had failed to adequately prepare him for his mission. First in failing to inform him that Percy Sledger was actually a metahuman. One ounce of information could have insured that Greg killed him the very first time, never giving him a chance to slip the noose at the Columbia River Gorge. Greg could have switched weapons if he'd only known. He could have used something even more lethal. Perhaps a Mark19 grenade launcher. A round or two through Sledger's midsection and he'd have been Humpty Dumpty as he fell, splattered into so many pieces that even his metahuman healing couldn't have put him back together again.

But no, the information had been denied, and Greg hadn't been able to plan accordingly. If he had, Sledger would already be properly dead, because Greg would have been able to use the right tool for the job. Overkill was a messy business, a wasteful philosophy that Greg simply did not subscribe to.

If only he'd known Sledger was Springersteen ... if only he'd known what to use to insure the kill ...

Then he never would have had to run across Sienna Nealon. And he'd have his M2 Browning still in flawless condition, as well as his pristine F-35B and his RAH-66 Comanche in perfect working order.

Greg heaved a sigh. This was becoming a costly contract, and logic would seem to suggest cutting his losses before entangling himself further.

But pride wouldn't allow it. Greg held tightly to the center stick, his strength threatening to leave clamp marks where his fingers gripped the plastic and steel. He'd been humiliated here. The gauntlet had been thrown down, and Sienna Nealon had made no secret of her intention to defend Sledger.

If preparation was truly his calling card, then Greg's course was clear. Now that he knew what he was facing, in precise detail—a Hercules and an unleashed succubus with flame power, near-instantaneous healing, faerie light nets, Quetzlcoatl transformational abilities, an Odin's Warmind ...

And apparently, now, telepathy. That was an interesting twist.

"The right tool for the job," Greg said under his breath. How did one approach a foe as canny and destructive as that? A Hercules was an easy matter, and if it was just down to dealing with him, Greg might have gone with a sniper rifle again, at a distance, with an exploding shell.

But Sienna Nealon had declared her intent to insert herself in this private matter, this dance of death that Greg planned with Sledger, and that was not a wrinkle to be casually overlooked. No, intense preparation would need to be taken. Planning would have to be adjusted. Certain ... items would have to be used, ones that Greg had never intended to see use.

Then again, what was the point of having these weapons if not to eventually use them?

"Unfortunate," Greg said, though he lied, a little, to himself. It wasn't entirely unfortunate.

After all, what was the point of going to the trouble to steal a nuclear bomb if you never got a chance to use it?

24.

Augustus

"Staff meeting!" Reed shouted as we walked into the bullpen back at the agency office in Eden Prairie, Minnesota. We'd left a pretty damned glorious, warm spring afternoon outside when we came in, which was a shame because I was shivering after the long, plane-less flight from Colorado. Apparently, the cold of being in the upper atmosphere did not bother my co-flyer, because he was bopping along into the building like ice hadn't been building up in his undies.

Well, it had in mine, and I had to shake it loose in big chunks when we came down. Also, I had to take a big breath, because that air up there? Thin like Kat the week before filming a season of her TV show.

I passed my desk and touched the surface, leaving behind a little trail of moisture from what I was sure was ice buildup on my fingers. I would have happily thrown myself into my chair, but Reed had called the staff meeting, and I could already see everybody filing into the conference room at the far end of the bullpen, so I soldiered on, figuring I'd just sit once I got there.

"You all right?" Reed asked with a ready smile as I entered the room. Scott Byerly was standing next to him, and the two of them were like twin poles of good-looking, white-boy stereotypes—the blond, short-haired preppy Scott and the dark-haired, ponytailed, swarthy Reed in his ragged leather jacket.

"I know the cold don't bother you, Elsa, but my nuts are not winter-safe, okay?" I shook a leg as I passed the two of them, and watched Scott snicker as a few flakes of ice fell out of my pants. I bet he'd flown with Reed a time or two and knew what I was talking about.

"You get used to it," Reed said with a smirk.

Scott shook his head as if to say, "No way," but what he actually said was, "Unless you're a man of the wind, I doubt it."

"You guys just aren't tough enough, I guess," Reed said.

"This from a dude who looks like he's part of the cast of *Saved By the Bell: The Surly Post-Teen Years*," I shot back as I headed into the conference room. Scott let out a loud guffaw and I added, "You shouldn't laugh too hard, curly-haired Zack Morris." That didn't stop him, though; he had a good sense of humor and he kept laughing.

J.J. and his girlfriend, Abby, were already sitting at the conference table, Abby's wild-pink hair shading looking like she'd popped some bubblegum up there. J.J. was looking less plump lately, but he still wore those thick-framed glasses. "I never really noticed that before," J.J. said, peering at Scott and Reed, "they kind of do look like a couple of, uh—I don't know—"

"Like the cast of a CW drama," Abby said, not looking up from her phone.

"Does that make us part of it, too?" Jamal asked. My brother sat just down the table from them, tapping his finger against the conference table, suspiciously lacking a phone or any other sort of electronic device. I hadn't asked him about it, but it looked to me like he'd been trying to limit himself or something, put his nose in books and in the real world more often the last few months, keep his computer time to working hours only. It was pretty weird considering he'd been a full-on electronics geek for as long as I could remember, but we weren't the kind of close that made me feel comfortable asking him about the change. "Because I don't want to be the black dude that dies once the second one joins the cast."

"Shit, I think I'm the one that's going to die, then," I said, taking a seat next to him. We both exchanged a look. "It's always the one that's been there longer that gets the axe once the new hotness comes in, you know." I pretended to look at him. "Guess I'm safe, since you're older and also not hot."

"Oh, that is not true," Abby said, putting down her phone, in full motherly protective mode, even though she was probably younger than my brother. "Jamal is very cute. I like a guy in glasses." She smiled at him.

"Lucky for me," J.J. said, staring at his screen, apparently oblivious to his girl talking about another guy's attractiveness. He struck me as a kind of dense dude in a lot of ways. Abby could probably climb up on the table and cuckold ol' J.J. right there, and if he was staring at his computer, he might not notice.

"Is Angel coming?" Reed asked, looking out over the bullpen again. I sat up a little straighter in my seat. I had forgotten about Angel, which wasn't usually an easy thing to do.

"No idea," Scott said. "I think she's out for the day. Migraine or something."

"What about Veronika?" I asked. She was another one that made me uneasy. Girl had never yet met an innuendo she didn't want to tongue in front of everyone else. It made her an uncomfortable person to be around. "Or Colin?"

"Colin's home in Seattle," Reed said. "Same with Veronika, in San Fran. They're enjoying their paid vacation benefit."

"Lucky them," I said under my breath. I was wishing I was taking advantage of mine right about now, since I'd damned near helped destroy a town just this morning.

Scott worked his way around the table and sat down with a lot more grace than I had when I plopped into my chair. He made it look cool. "I trust this meeting has a purpose behind it?"

"Why?" I asked. "You got better things to do? Like get some Manny's take-out for lunch in your Ferrari?"

Scott shifted in his chair a little self-consciously. "Manny's isn't really a, uh ... take-out kind of place. And I don't drive a Ferrari."

A low chorus of snickers around the table was interrupted by a fierce buzz from my brother's cell phone. He scooped it up off the table nervously and spoke into the receiver. "I'm going to have to call you back."

"No, you don't," a hard female voice replied.

He looked around the table, and said plaintively, "I'm in a meeting."

"Get out of it." Everyone at the table was staring at him, wondering who the hell would be giving Jamal orders like that.

"It's my girlfriend," Jamal said, looking around self-consciously.

"Why does everyone want me to be their girlfriend today?" the woman asked. The voice sounded pretty damned put off, but it was faint enough I couldn't really recognize it and could only hear it by virtue of my turned-up meta hearing.

"'Scuse me," Jamal said, and practically ran for the door. "Just—hang on, will you? Damn. Patience, please."

"Somebody's whipped," Scott said, and made the whipping noise. "Ka chish!"

Abby just shook her head at him, sternly. "No. Just don't."

Scott looked fully crestfallen. "But—"

"No. Just no." She centered her gaze on him. "Because someday, probably not with the same girl, that will be you, harking the sound of *your* master's whip."

"Why did you even throw that in about the 'same girl' …?" Scott asked, now looking confused. "Isn't that just automatically implied?"

"Sure," Abby said, looking a little frozen.

"As much fun as it is to watch Jamal have to run from the room while a girl—" Reed started.

"Woman," J.J. said. Abby patted him on the hand.

"—*Woman*," Reed corrected, raising his eyebrows like he was pained having to say it, "we've got other fish to fry. Augustus ran across a meta in Colorado that had some … peculiar properties. Augustus, you want to share with the group?"

"Oh, is it story time?" I asked, then I launched into an explanation of what had happened. My brother came trudging back in around the time I had gotten to setting up my meeting with Omar, taking his seat while looking a little downtrodden himself, like that call hadn't gone super well. "... And then Mr. I-Thought-He-Was-Just-A-Badass-Poseidon brings down all the snow and ice off the peak in a runaway crazy avalanche that I had to stop through insane, and personally trying acts of heroism—"

"You can spare us the commentary," Reed said. "Point is, you ran across a meta that seems to have used that drug that Sienna discovered in Portland—the ... I don't even know what to call it—"

"Oh, we're going with Skill Tree Unlocker," J.J. said as Abby nodded along. "Not to be confused with the power-up potion Harmon gave you guys, which we have dubbed 'the Stat Boost.'"

Reed looked like he wanted to argue for about a second. "That's ... not bad."

"Who will save the world?" I asked rhetorically. "Geeks. It's geeks all the way down." I looked at Scott. "You can't control ice, right?"

Scott shook his head. "Not until it melts."

"This is why you're not invited to my parties," J.J. said. "If you could make ice, you'd be the biggest hit. Especially if you could shape it like a miniature Death Star—"

"But we bought those tumblers for that," Abby said.

"Yeah, but you have to admit, one of actual ice would be so much cooler—"

"Come on geeks, we gotta save the world here," I said, trying to bring them back on point. "I'd say this is confirmation that our perps, the ones that are spawning all these new metas—"

"Points for using the word 'spawn' in this context," Abby said.

"—have access to the full repertory of chemical enhancements that Edward Cavanagh was developing across *all* his enterprises." I looked around the table. "Anyone care to take a stab at how that's happening?"

"Well, President Harmon was trying to pull all that together, wasn't he?" Abby asked. "With Cassidy Ellis's help?"

"Yeah, but Sienna stopped him," Scott said uneasily.

"Are we sure about that?" Reed shifted at the table. "Do we have any confirmation other than behind-the-scenes rumors that Harmon is actually, genuinely out of the picture? Not that my sister has ever been reticent to kill people, but the President of the United States—"

"Yeah, he's dead," Scott said, then hesitated. "Ish."

"Oh, I bet there's a good story in that 'ish,'" I said.

"Yeah," Reed said, leaning forward, "and I kinda want to hear it."

Scott stiffened up, like he was becoming a wall before our eyes. "It's not really mine to tell."

"Come on, man," I said. "This is important. If Harmon somehow escaped his encounter with Sienna—"

"He didn't," Jamal said, causing everyone at the table to look at him in surprise. "She was carrying him off to deal with him, and he pawed at her. Like, a lot. And she fended him off, until she realized he wasn't trying to hurt her." My brother looked down at the table and gave it a couple taps. "He was trying to make contact with her skin so he could—"

"Holy shit," Reed said, leaning forward almost double. "You mean he's in—" He touched the side of his head.

"Another soul in the collection," Scott agreed. "A willing sacrifice this time, apparently."

"I don't know if I believe that," Reed said, like a wall had come down on his face, all serious suddenly.

"Believe it," Scott said. "When we were working that case together in Florida, Harmon talked to me in my head, from Sienna's. He did it to himself."

"Look, you may want to believe my sister is blameless in this—" Reed started.

"No, it's true," Jamal said. "He thought she was going to kill him, so he took the only way he saw out. They were antagonizing the hell out of each other when I worked with them, though."

I stared at Jamal. "You been working with Sienna?"

Reed sat back in his chair like he'd been punched. "Anyone else at this table been secretly working with my sister?"

"I wasn't doing it secretly," Scott said. "You knew about it."

"I worked with her before I came to work for you," Jamal said. "Didn't know I needed to mention prior hangouts with your family members."

"It would have been nice," Reed said, a little testily. "Just a little heads up, you know, something like, 'Hey, I saw your sister just before I started here. Worked a case with her. Probably killed five hundred people in the process, FYI. Let your lawyers know.'"

"Your lawyer already knows," Jamal said with an offhand shrug, "so I guess you're covered."

"You told Miranda?" That almost caused Reed's eyes to pop out of his head, but Jamal just shrugged again. Reed whirled on me. "Did you know about any of this?"

I shook my head. "No. I been Sienna-clean for months now."

"Me too," J.J. said. "Though you kinda say it like helping her is a bad thing. She did help capture that dangerous meta in Florida."

"And she kept all of your secrets, dirty and otherwise, from being exposed when the two of us teamed up to stop an uber-hacker down in the Virgin Islands," Jamal said.

"Wow," Abby said, "she's on the run and still heroing. That woman is a badass."

Reed stared at the surface of the conference table, shaking his head. "Unbelievable."

"I find it totally believable," I said, drawing an ireful look from Reed. "Come on, man. You know your sister. She was on the run from the law when that whole Harmon thing came to a head, too, and that didn't stop her from wading in and deposing the sitting president to the point where he felt the need to commit suicide via absorbing himself into her head in order to 'win' against her."

"Not sure how putting yourself in my sister's head is considered 'winning,'" Reed said.

"Better than dying, right?" I asked. Scott gave me a wary look. "Maybe I'm the only one thinking that. Anyway ..."

"Anyway," Reed agreed, dragging himself back up but looking a little wearier and more pained than the effervescence he'd started the meeting with. "So ... someone's out there with all the chemicals. Harmon's dead—or at least trapped in Sienna's head. If he could talk to you, Scott ... what are the odds he could still be pulling strings from in there?"

"No idea," Scott said. "You'd have to ask someone who knows telepathy from that side, like Zollers. I mean, we all know firsthand that when Harmon had a body, he could yank our puppet strings with all the ease of a kid playing with dolls. Now that he's disembodied—"

"Heh," Abby said, looking at Reed. "He's sis-embodied."

Reed swore under his breath in reply, and Scott went on, "—he is still powerful. He transferred all the memories Sienna stole from me back into my head. Whether that power extends to being able to run some kind of ... behind the scenes continuation of his earlier world domination scheme ..." Scott shrugged. "Hell if I know."

"You really think Sienna would fail to miss him actively scheming from inside her own head?" J.J. asked, all afrown.

Scott drew a deep breath and then held it. "Maybe. I don't know. They didn't have the best working relationship when I dealt with them, but that was a couple months ago."

"When did you work with her?" Reed asked Jamal.

"January," Jamal said.

"How did the two of them get along when you were playing detective together?" Reed asked.

"Not that well, I don't think," Jamal said. "He didn't talk to me like Scott, but I know she was arguing with the voices in her head back then, so ..." He shrugged.

"You're ignoring the big piece that's still on the board in favor of one that's on the sidelines," Abby said. "Cassidy Ellis is still out there somewhere, and if she was in charge of President Harmon's attempt to bring all this power together ...?"

"That's a damned good point," Reed said, pulling out his

ponytail and rubbing his hands through his hair self-consciously. "Cassidy is no gentle flower, I can tell you by experience."

"Because she blew up your car?" J.J. asked. "Oh! Is that why you're stroking your ponytail? Because it burned your hair off when that—"

Reed stopped playing with his hair. "Yes, probably. Thanks for pointing out that little psychological tic I hadn't even noticed." He left his hair flat, hanging over his shoulders. "So ... two leads, maybe. Cassidy Ellis and President Harmon. One's in the wind, the other is in my sister's head. How do we get after them?"

"I could, uh ... call your sister," Jamal said uncomfortably. "Errr ... call her back." He touched his phone.

Reed just stared at him, jaw slightly open. "That was ... that was her ...?"

"My subconscious totally nailed that 'master's whip' thing," Abby said to Scott, smiling with incredible self-satisfaction. "My 'with the same girl' comment is looking pretty prescient now, isn't it?"

Reed erupted from the table and a wind stirred the blinds, rattling them against the window to the bullpen. "Fuck's sake! You're still talking to her?"

"Hey, not all of us have an axe to grind with her," I said under my breath. Everyone heard it anyway.

He fixed me with an icy stare. "You don't know what I'm thinking, Augustus." He looked down the table at J.J. and Abby. "Find me Cassidy Ellis. If she's involved in this, I want to know." He snapped his attention to Scott. "Give Dr. Zollers a call, ask him about—about all of this, about Harmon. See what he thinks." He turned his gaze to Jamal. "And you ... go talk to my sister." He looked like he wanted to say something else, but he just gave up and left it at that, hair flowing over his shoulders as he walked out of the conference room, the wind stirring the blinds wildly in his wake, as though a tornado had passed with him.

25.

Sienna

"Where are we going again?" Friday asked as we shot over Bakersfield, California, at an altitude of 5,000 feet and over a thousand miles per hour.

"I told you," I said. "Los Angeles, to talk to your pal Theo about what he saw when he lost his blindfold."

"Oh," Friday said. He was sweating profusely and so was I; May was a warm time in California, even at this altitude. "Are you sure he's even there?"

"Jamal said so." I'd called Jamal again, of course, because this time Google had failed me. Honestly. I had actually tried this round, and it came up with like a million results that didn't seem all that related to Theo Moreau. I mean, was that even his full name? Or was he Theodore? Or something else, like Theophilus? Sounded like a job for Jamal to me, no matter how displeased he sounded when I dragged him out of that meeting.

Besides, he got me my answer in like two seconds and got back to listening to my brother bellow about whatever was on his mind with no one the wiser about it being me who called him.

Hahahahah, Harmon said in my head, but I ignored him, because I was pretty sure he wasn't going to answer me if I asked him why he was cackling like an old hen.

"What if Jamal is wrong?" Friday asked. He sounded pensive, and he looked … worried.

"Jamal's not usually wrong," I said. "He tends to be solidly on target for these things. And hey, maybe if we're lucky, this Theo might be able to point us in the direction of a motive for Greg wanting to kill you." But I wasn't holding my breath on that, because based on our experience with Jon, I had an inkling this could be another wild goose chase.

But at least it got me out of the house, which was pretty key since my Portland apartment was now a charred ruin. Whatever. That town was too ironic for even me.

"Maybe Greg just resents my good looks and sexiness, did you ever consider that for a motive?" Friday asked. Way, way too earnestly.

"Strangely, no." I kept the eyeroll to a swift 180 degrees and back. "Did you ever consider that maybe you just really, really pissed him off?"

"Impossible," Friday scoffed.

"Oh, trust me," I said a little warily but with surprising good cheer, "you pissing people off is more than possible."

"I think he just has the smell of a bigger, more dominant alpha dog in his nostrils and he can't get it out," Friday said.

"That would explain why he keeps coming after me. But why is he still trying to kill you?"

"Oh ha ha," Friday said. "Let's just put it out there … I have a nemesis."

I yawned theatrically, trying to express my eyeroll without eyerolling. "Yeah … that's why I just kill all my enemies. That way I'm not constantly dealing with these pain-in-the-ass revenge seekers."

Friday thought that over for a minute. "That really worked well for you in Eden Prairie last year."

Not gonna lie, my cheeks burned a little when he scored with that jab. "Touché. But it proves my point, no? If I'd put those bastards in the ground over the last few years instead of in the Cube, that little incident might not have happened." And by incident, I meant "that time I made a smoking ruin of my life." I didn't really believe what I was espousing, having more or less passed the indiscriminate killing phase of my career, but if he was going to snark at me—at *me*, of all people—I wasn't going to just lie there and take it.

"Maybe," Friday said. "Still, if Theo doesn't have the goods on what Greg is, or why he's trying to kill me ... what do we do then?"

"Well, then," I said snidely, "I'm sure you'll favor me with yet another fable from your tall tales that draw upon your adventures with the Inglorious Bat-turds."

He stared up at me blankly for a good ten seconds before he dissolved into laughter so fierce I was afraid I'd drop his ass five thousand feet into the chaparral below where I'd have to waste my valuable time and innocent eyes pulling a stray scrub brush out of his nether regions. "Hahahahahahahhahaha!" he said, doubling over, slapping his thigh and making it infinitely harder to hold him. "'Inglorious Bat Turds'! Like *Inglorious Basterds*, that movie, but with Bat Turds—"

"Yes, that's the joke," I said, wondering maybe if this Theo thing didn't pan out if perhaps my civic duty had kind of reached its apex and I could go ahead and call the whole case quits. "What's Theo's power, just out of curiosity?"

Friday got grim on me. "His power is incredible. Enemies quake at the sight of his coming, and even his friends shudder at the thought of him unleashing—"

I blew up. "If you don't know, stop trying to blow smoke up my ass, all right? For crying out loud."

Friday went quiet, taking his chastening with a bowed head. "Yeah. All right, you got me on that one. I don't know."

"Geez, just say it, next time, okay?" I shook my head. "I'm here helping you, all right? Just ... be honest with me. I don't have a high opinion of you, so it's not like you're impressing me when you lie. In fact, my opinion of you couldn't get much lower. You could literally tell me you've shit yourself in fear twelve times during the last day and I could not possibly think less of you. I'm still here, helping you, all right? But if you don't start being straight with me, Friday—so help me—I'm gone, and you can just die at the hands of Greg Vansen. Capische?"

"I ... yes, I understand," Friday said quietly, and settled with his head down so I couldn't see his face as we flew onward, toward the fading western sky, trying to get to Los Angeles and maybe—however unlikely—some answers.

26.

Greg

At work in his shop was a pleasant enough place for Greg to be. He didn't usually have any interruptions here; Eddie couldn't get in yet, and Morgan … well, she tended not to come and visit him here, especially since she didn't know he was back.

He looked out over the lines of all the machinery he'd collected over the years. There were racks of weapons, rows of tanks and bombers and planes that would have been perfectly in place in any military base the world over. He could see them from his place under the SR-71, where he tinkered with his tools, the smell of oil and aviation fuel a little too thick in the air. He'd have to take care of that shortly.

If any of his neighbors had known how close they stood to these awesome engines of destruction … but no, that was the secret, that they were here, in the outskirts of Chicago, unbeknownst to anyone but him and Morgan. And Greg suspected Morgan tried to forget what all his workshop contained. She wasn't a squeamish woman by nature, but …

Who really wanted to contemplate having such engines of destruction in their home?

Doing the mechanical maintenance on all these things, all his wonderful toys … it was practically a full time job, but Greg treated it as an aggressive hobby, demanding of his time. Sometimes he wished he could have a little more help on these things, but ... well, it was probably better that Morgan kept to the house now. This wasn't a fit place for nearly anyone, and certainly not someone tasked with the care of a child.

"I thought I heard you come back," Morgan said, appearing as suddenly as he might have if he'd wanted to. "You didn't call."

"I took the SR," he said, waving a tool at the black body of the plane. "Too high for cell phone coverage until I was on final approach, and by then ..." He waved the implement again, trusting she'd take his meaning, which was that he needed both hands to fly the plane to a safe landing.

"How much longer do you think she'll run?" Morgan brushed her dusky auburn hair back, then folded her arms. She looked like she was anticipating something.

"The program was canceled in '98. I was able to acquire a modest amount of replacement parts and supplies, but ... not too much longer, I expect." He dropped the tool, setting it down with a clank in the massive box and shutting the drawer. Trying to perform even ordinary maintenance while conversing with Morgan would probably result in negligence on his part. It wasn't as though he serviced this plane every day, and his hands weren't as practiced at it as perhaps they should have been.

"What will you do then?" Morgan asked.

Greg frowned. He wasn't quite sure where she was going with this. "I could switch to the Concorde full-time, I suppose. I managed to pilfer enough things to keep it running for another fifty years."

Morgan's eyes flashed, and she moved past him to stroke the forward landing gear on the Blackbird. "You think you'll still need to be flying all over the globe in fifty years?"

Greg felt his face twist, unasked, into a hard frown of concentration. "The money doesn't just keep flowing in if I'm not working, Morgan. As careful as I've been with our investments—"

"I thought they were performing well." Not accusation, but disappointment.

"They are performing modestly well," Greg said. "But

not well enough that I would feel confident stopping work."

"What about doing something else?" she asked, breaking contact with the forward landing gear. "Something safer? Something ... closer to home?"

Greg made a gesture at the Blackbird, and the Concorde parked down the row. "I have taken measures to make certain that I'm never more than a short commute from home, you know that."

"Not when you have to fly around the world."

"I seldom work outside the US," Greg said. "I'm home almost every night, and often for weeks at a time between contracts. I don't understand where this sudden querying comes from—"

"I'm worried about you," Morgan whispered, stepping up close to him. She didn't have to look up to look him in the eyes, and that did bother Greg from time to time. She actually looked down just a little bit, sometimes. "Did you know that Eddie cried for an hour after you left? After you blew up at him?"

Greg let out a sigh of annoyance. "He was prattling on about that stupid idea of keeping lions as pets. Someone needed to disabuse him of that foolish notion before—"

"He's five," Morgan said, finally breaking loose a little on him. His wife wasn't the most emotional woman, but she let a little out now. "Five, Greg. Not fifteen, not twenty-five. Five years old. And he wants a pet."

"Perhaps a pet rock might settle him some."

"He wants something furry because he thinks it will love him in a way his father doesn't," Morgan said, and though she spoke without accusation, Greg felt a certain prick as the blow landed home.

"I ..."

"I'm sorry," Morgan said. "I didn't mean to hit you with that. It's just ..."

"You're the one who picks him up," Greg said. "I can't help it if he's weak."

"He's a child," she said softly. "You could take it a little easier on him."

"This is just a difference in approaches. Morgan, we

chose these roles when we decided—when you wanted to have a family." She deflated a little at his mention of her being the driver of that decision.

"You miss the good old days before Eddie?" Morgan asked, and it was hard to tell whether she was nostalgic or hurting, perhaps, for seeing Eddie mentioned so casually, almost cruelly, as if he were an unwanted thing by Greg.

"You were a good partner to me when we worked together," he said, and Morgan casually brushed her hair back, stroking it self-consciously. "Working alone is … more solitary. Perhaps less enjoyable, though it still has its perks." The quiet was a benefit, he thought, away from the decibel level that Eddie brought to any room he entered. "We have different pressures upon us now. I wouldn't wish to be in charge of Eddie's day to day care and I doubt you'd want to take up the job again, working without me—"

"I wouldn't," she said, shaking her head. "I'd rather you not be doing it, either."

"It pays the bills," he said, understating it.

"It gets you out of the house, away from us, and gives you something to do," she said quietly.

"Not away from you," Greg said quickly.

"You always told me you wanted to be a father."

"I always did," Greg said.

"Until you had a child and realized it wasn't like in the movies? That it wasn't all love and sweetness and good parts? That it's exhaustion and cleaning up vomit in the middle of the night and—"

"And having to listen to inane talk of 'bottle flips' and Minecraft and heaven knows what else, yes," Greg said. "I found it easier to relate with Eddie when he was a baby, and his primary mode of communication was cooing and filling a diaper." He looked toward the exit door at the far end of his workshop. "I understood the basic needs—fill his belly, empty his diaper, put him down for a nap. Perhaps hold him for a while. I don't love that, but I understand it—" Greg's emotions burst out in a flare of anger. "But this—these things that he does now—the craven, desperate attention seeking—"

"He loves you, Greg," Morgan said. "He wants your approval. Your notice."

"Well, he's not going to get it like that," Greg said. "How can I approve of such stupid frivolity? Lion pets and other such idiocy? You know what he told me last week? That he wanted to be Iron Man when he grew up. As though that's a career choice you can educate yourself toward—"

"He's a child. Try to show some understanding."

"I *don't* understand, Morgan," Greg hissed. "He's gone beyond my understanding now. He makes no logical sense. When I was his age, I wanted to be an engineer, like my father—"

"Well, we can't tell him what you do," Morgan said.

"What *we* used to do *together*," Greg said.

Morgan sunk slightly. "I asked you to find another line of work when I left."

"Nothing pays like this," Greg said. "Nothing I can do. There is no other out for me. You want to live in this house? Send Eddie to these schools? Not accumulate enough debt to bury us over our heads? This is what needs to be done."

"You haven't even looked," Morgan said. "Maybe the government—"

"They pay peanuts, comparatively," Greg said.

"Compared to the field where you have to kill people," Morgan said. "Kill them. For money. Snuff out human lives in exchange for cash—"

"You weren't this sanctimonious when you were in the thick of it with me. And you know damned well we didn't kill any innocent people, Morgan."

"We killed them when they were doing innocent things, though," Morgan said. "Don't you remember that man in the park? Who had a brain aneurysm, unexplainable?"

Greg resisted the inclination to smile. "How could I forget? It was some of your finest work. He was a drug lord, if I recall. Looked like natural causes."

She stared at him like she was examining a bug. "You sound like Sam, so proud of doing it that way."

"You used to be proud of a job well done," he fired back. "Comparing me to Sam, though ... that's low."

SMALL THINGS

"It felt right," she said. "I've changed. And if you have, it's because you've gotten colder, darker. Like—"

"Don't compare me to Sam again," Greg said, raising his finger to point at her. "I'm not like him. Which is why I don't work with him anymore."

"None of this has turned out like I hoped it would," Morgan said quietly, look up, high above them, to the ceiling somewhere in the distance.

"Life never does," Greg said.

"Spare the philosophical bullshit," Morgan said. "I should have known it would go this way, as hard as I had to fight to get you onboard with even having Eddie—"

"I'm sorry I wasn't ready to give up the life I'd grown accustomed to," he said, temper rising.

"You were ready at the time," Morgan said. "But now that you know what you're in for, now that things have gotten tough, it's like you've withdrawn. We truly are on different roads now. And we're getting farther apart all the time, Greg."

Greg just stood there, strangely frozen. "What is that supposed to mean?"

She stared back, unmoving. "What you're doing … the way you're becoming? It's carrying you away from us."

"I'm home every—"

"Stop being so damned literal about everything!" she almost screamed at him. "I'm not talking about how much you're physically present. I'm talking about how much you're mentally present. About how you're not here—really here— for Eddie. About how little patience you have for him, because your patience is all spent in other activities, or maybe because you're simply not choosing to understand your own child the way you try to understand the people you hunt to their deaths."

"What do you want from me?" Greg shouted, all the frustration finally boiling over in one exquisite explosion of emotion. He preferred to keep these things contained under at least a veneer of control, but Morgan seemed to encourage this—this hemorrhage of emotion, as though emotional incontinence were something to be gloried in rather than abhorred.

"I want you to be a family man first and an assassin—not at all, probably. It's not good for you. You cheapen human life—"

"We used to—cheapen it together," he finished lamely. It sounded stupid even to his ears. "We used to be in this together, Morgan."

"I'm not with you on this anymore," she said. "What we did … Greg, it was … we took other people away from their families. With some distance … it gnaws at me. Every day. And I'm not saying we turn ourselves in or anything, but … I wish you would stop." She lowered her voice. "I don't ever want you to be like Sam. To enjoy it like Sam does. And because it seems as though it's an escape from your life and your problems here … it feels like you're starting to."

"Do you wish the money would stop coming in, too? Do you wish we would lose our house? That we would have to move to—to a shitty school district and—and—" he started to stutter, "—and live in a shack and—"

"Is that what a human life is worth to us?" she asked quietly. "It's okay for us to live in a lovely slice of the American dream—four bedrooms, two baths, manicured lawns—and all we have to do is commit a blood sacrifice for it every once in a while. Execute a few people a year, and it's all taken care of. They die so we can live in luxury. You like equations, Greg—how does that balance strike you? Is X worth Y? Their death worth our life of luxury?"

There was something in Greg's chest like a slow grinding of metal on metal. "I don't know how else to provide—"

"Then maybe this isn't worth being provided, if that is what you have to do to get it," Morgan said. "If you're going to pay to finance our lives with other peoples' blood … I don't think we should live like this. Not anymore. If that's the sacrifice in order to keep you from having to—to murder others—then let's just make the trade. Yes, we'll move to a smaller house. Yes, we'll probably be in a less impressive school district. Oh, no. Our little suburban dream won't be flawless—except it wasn't to begin with because we've been cheating, we've been building our perfect little lives on the wreckage of other peoples'. Greg, we can't—*I can't* live like this anymore."

"You need to stop this," Greg said, waving a finger at her. "This is—it's like a disease, this emotion you're grappling with. It will spread. You say, 'We can't do this anymore', today. But tomorrow, after I give up this—this work—it'll morph. 'We need to atone', you'll say, because these thoughts, unchecked, will metastasize. And soon, you'll be saying we need to confess. To go to jail for—"

"I'm not saying that—"

"Not yet—"

"I am not—don't you see what you're doing?" She sagged. "Don't you see the toll this is taking on us? You don't get lighter and happier as the years pile on, Greg. Eddie should be a bright spot in your life, but your soul—your mind—they're all tied up in dark business, and it's eating you alive. You can't kill people during the day and just—leave it out here at night to pick up tomorrow morning. You carry it with you, always. Everything except the guilt, apparently."

"I don't feel guilt because I choose not to feel guilt," Greg said, lowering his head to stare at the hard metal floor. It had a speckled sort of sheen. "Anything you feel is an emotional, chemical reaction to stimuli. This remorse, for instance. You could shut it right down if you wanted to badly enough. We used to talk about this all the time when we worked together—"

"And it was always your philosophy, not mine," she said. "But assuming it's true ... how do you explain the emotions you display when you blow up at Eddie? Shouldn't it be easy to account for nonsense from a child and just ... adjust your parameters for it?" She said every word with dripping sarcasm. "So it doesn't smash the emotions of your son?"

"It's better that he learns to live with disappointment now," Greg said after a few seconds. "To understand the importance and rigor of controlling himself. It's good ... training for life."

"Sadly ... I think you really believe that," Morgan said, and she folded her arms in front of her and backed away, leaving him to his maintenance and repair, alone as ever.

27.

Sienna

East Los Angeles was looking pretty dusty and worn as the sun was heading low ahead of us. The sunset caught on a glassy building in downtown LA and gave me a good reflected glare in the eyes for a few seconds until I altered my course to compensate for it.

Friday was still dangling limply from my grasp, trying desperately not to talk to me, like that was some kind of punishment for me.

I didn't want to drop him to check my GPS, so I slowed my pace, trying to work out where my destination was from the overhead map I'd studied briefly before setting out on this quest. I was usually pretty good with this sort of thing, spatial memory, but using a GPS was quicker. Still, for the occasions when my passenger was obnoxious but finally silent, and I didn't want to break the equilibrium, it seemed acceptable to try to go on memory for a bit before yielding to checking my phone.

Once I'd circled East LA a couple times, I was pretty sure I'd locked on to the general area of the gym that Jamal had flagged as Theo's current location. I couldn't check my phone to be sure Theo was still there, but that was okay, because I had his residence address too in case he wasn't at the gym. That would require a little more GPS work; residential neighborhoods were much less differentiated on overheads than strip malls and the like.

"Ah ha," I muttered as I caught sight of a long, L-shaped mall that looked a hell of a lot like the one I'd set as our destination. I steadied us as I flew in overhead, preparing the swift descent that was always required to keep my visibility to a minimum. Jetting toward the ground at a couple hundred miles an hour to come in for a landing behind a commercial building carried its own risks of sighting, but more acceptable ones than slowly drifting to the ground like a feather on a breeze or something.

Friday was still being quiet, and I took that as a personal challenge now that we were almost there. I set us up, prepared to drop into the weed-choked parking lot sandwiched between the mall and the high fence behind, only a few employee cars to mark its use. The front parking lot wasn't close to full either, but I didn't really care about that. The fewer people, the less likelihood there was of me getting spotted and phoned in to a police force that was probably nominally still looking for Sienna Nealon.

I turned headfirst and accelerated toward the ground, clutching Friday under the arms. My fingers and wrists were cramped from holding his ass up a lot of the day, and as we shot toward the earth, he went limp in my grip for a second. I heard a snort from him and realized ...

That son of a bitch had gone to sleep in my arms.

He woke with a jerk and became aware of our descent about a second later, letting out a long, loud, girlish scream that hit an upper register that would have sent a banshee running in the opposite direction. "Shut up, you idiot!" I shouted into his ears as we rocketed past the roof of the mall and I applied the brakes.

Friday started to writhe in panic as I slowed us from a couple hundred miles an hour to zero in the space of a couple seconds, and he escaped me about ten feet from the ground and headed straight down, fall uninterrupted.

He took the landing in a big old bellyflop, swelling as he struck the pavement. I actually felt bad for him as he smacked into the asphalt in a slap that was only just quieter than a gunshot. He bounced about a foot and came back down, neck snapping back from the impact. He crashed again and stayed down this time, splayed out on the dark pavement like a suicide jumper who'd taken a dive from the top of a skyscraper.

I hung there above him in silence for a minute, cringing at what I'd just seen. "Friday?" I finally asked. "Are you all right?"

He didn't answer at first. Of course he wasn't all right; he'd just plummeted to the pavement at high speed. I feather-glided down and crouched next to him, my worry escalating. "Friday?" I started to reach for him—

"That … was … *kittens*!" he said, bouncing up, cracking his neck, and swelling his chest and muscles as he sprung to his feet. There was a little trickle of blood running down his lip, and he touched it with his finger and then licked it, grossing me out.

"Stop saying that," I said reflexively.

"What? You didn't like awesome, so you said 'kittens.' Now I like kittens and you don't, so—I'm just thinking it's because you're a difficult person."

I stared at him, and strangely, my urge to kill was flat, even after that devastating personal assessment.

Probably because it was true, Harmon said.

"You're not wrong," I said and then waved him toward me as I headed around the corner of the mall. "Come on, let's just go talk to Theo."

"Okeydoke," Friday said, falling in behind me. We rounded the side of the mall quickly and then stepped onto the covered sidewalk out front. The place was clearly decaying, and in a decaying area. Weeds sprouted between the joints of the sidewalk, closed storefronts displayed prominent graffiti. Only three out of about twenty storefronts in the whole strip mall were even open—a lawyer's office, a place with the name written in Spanish that I couldn't decipher, and one that read, GYM in big letters on a sign that hung from the awning above us. It was the closest, fortunately, only about six doors down, and occupying what looked like a double storefront, as though they'd expanded when things around here had gone on the downturn.

We came to the gym doors and I opened them up, popping inside to find a lady with dark hair behind the front desk. She said something in Spanish, and it wasn't one of the five words I know: *Uno, dos, tres, gracias* and *margarita*, so I just nodded politely and said, "I'm here to see Theo."

She stared at me blankly for a second, and then nodded. "*Si.* Theo." And she pointed to her left.

"I'm here to get SWOLE!" Friday declared, and I turned back to see that he'd gone and inflated himself again, his body comically over-muscled to an extent that would have looked ridiculously out of place even in a Mr. Universe competition.

The lady receptionist took him in with wide eyes, and I shook my head as I headed in the direction she'd pointed. "Come on, Bane, let's just get this over with before someone calls the cops and reports you as a van committing a major parking violation."

"Whuuuuut?" Friday called after me as I headed round the bend into a free weight area. He trotted to keep up, having to dodge to keep from knocking over a bar that was already set up for someone to do some pretty heavy lifting.

"Eyes on the prize, stupid," I said, trying to get his pea brain focused on the task at hand. I noticed that this particular gym catered to a certain-ish ethnic make up, and spotting the black dude at the back of the gym working out with earphones in was kinda like playing a game of "Which one of these things is not like the other?"

"Is that Theo?" I asked as Friday stomped along behind me, like a Tyrannosaurus rex in desperate need of an extinction.

"How'd you know?" Friday chirped.

"From your description combined with a general application of common sense."

"Yo! Theo!" Friday waved at him from halfway across the room.

Theo perked up from where he'd been setting up the weights to do some serious curls. I mean, not as serious as my curls, but pretty good for most people. He wasn't trying to load the weights so as to not out himself as a meta, but he

135

was well within the realm of challenge for a normal human, a hundred or so on each dumbbell.

While I was admiring his weights, kinda wishing I was doing some lifting of my own, Theo took one look at Friday and turned to bolt. He was about halfway through the large free weight room, fifty feet or so from the rear door marked by a green, faintly glowing EXIT sign when he took off.

"You bastard," I said and reached down, scooping up a free weight from a nearby rack and spinning once to hurl it like a discus.

It shot across the room like a homing missile and caught Theo right in the back of the knee. It hit him just as he was about to take a step and it ripped his leg right out from beneath him. His body followed the sudden momentum and he got all tangled up and hit the ground, rolling into a rack of weights that rattled as they threatened to fall.

"Theo!" Friday said, and he turned to me with mouth-gaping astonishment. "What did you do that for?"

"Oh, shit!" I said. "I saw him bolt and I just forgot—shit. See, this is the problem with not being myself." I fluffed my jet-black hair, so very un-Sienna, by several shades. Also, my attire was urban hipster all the way, down to the plaid flannel shirt and old work boots. "I lose the intimidation factor that causes people to freeze in place in fear."

"I think he's intimidated now," Friday said as we picked our way between weight sets to Theo, who was rolling around, clutching his knee and moaning. Friday knelt down next to him. "Theo, it's me, Bruce. You okay, buddy?"

Theo had his eyes pinched tightly shut until Friday spoke, then he opened one a slit to look up. "Bruce? Bruce who?"

"Bruce Springersteen, man," Friday said, but that only prompted Theo to raise his eyebrow a little higher. "You know … from Desert Storm?"

"I was never in Desert Storm," Theo said, still grimacing in obvious pain. Then he stopped, his eyelids fluttered. "Oh. Shit. You mean—oh, you're that idiot from when I was with that sketchy, supposed spec ops group that took on any meta they could get their hooks into?"

I looked down at Friday. "This explains a lot about how

you got hired."

"What?" Friday almost bellowed. "We were totally elite."

"Elite nothing," Theo said, still holding his knee. "We were a bunch of posers except that one guy." He hissed through gritted teeth, stretching his leg. "What was his name? Gary?" He looked right at Friday. "You know, I didn't even recognize you without the mask. You just looked like another one of these jokers I owe money to, come to collect."

"Good news, we're not here about any money you're owed. Bad news ..." I eyed his leg, "... I might just have broken your leg anyway."

"Well, I think they're aiming to kill me at this point, so a leg's not so bad," Theo said, eyeing me warily. "So long as you stop there."

"Yeah, I'm done," I said. "Sorry. People run, I get this automatic instinct to stop them. It's reflexive, you know, like a dog chasing a moving car."

"Well, then that outfit that hired us back in the old days would just love to get their hands on you," he said, then paused. "Wait ... are you the girl that was working with us?" He looked me up and down. "No. You're too young. Too pretty, too."

"Sweet talker," I said. "I already told you I'm not going after that other leg, so you can lay off the flattery. Unless you want to keep going, because I'm not going to throw a weight to stop you." People never complimented me anymore.

You're incredibly vicious, Wolfe said.

I told you repeatedly that I like your newly toned shoulders, Eve said.

I admire your ability to destroy your relationships with the people you care about most, Harmon said. *There's no one else I've met who can truly salt the earth in a relationship as well as you.*

Thanks, dickweed, I said. *I'm working on that, you know.*

Yes, and you've made marvelous progress, Harmon said. *How long has it been since you talked to that brother of yours?*

"Soo ..." Friday said conversationally, "... how've you been? Other than the debt to mobsters problem, I mean."

Theo was almost done nursing his injury, and the gym

was kinda settling back to normal after the initial rush of people heading for the door to get the hell away from our little altercation. "All right, I guess," he said. He sucked air between his teeth painfully. "Can't complain. You know, other than that thing with the owing money."

"Got a job?" Friday asked.

"Bouncer at a club on weeknights," Theo said. "You?"

"I was working for the government for a while," Friday breezed, "but I kinda had a falling out with my boss's boss, so I told them to stick it and bailed on that shit. Crappy job anyway."

"Pay good?" Theo asked.

"Decent," Friday said. "Better than we got back in the old days."

"Yeah, nobody paid nothing back then," Theo said, "unless you were like—well, you know. He was raking it in, I bet."

"You talking about Greg?" I asked.

Theo looked at me like I'd sworn at him, except I doubted he would have been nearly so offended if I had. "Yeah, that was his name. I've been trying not to say it these last few years, guess I forgot it somewhere in there."

"What, is he like Voldemort?" I asked. "Is he going to appear if I say his name? Because that would actually explain him better than any other theory I have right now."

Theo looked around like he expected exactly that. "Man, I don't know. He could, though. That dude ..." He stopped scanning the room and looked around. "... That dude was crazy. The things he could pull off ... I ain't never seen nothing like that."

"About that," I said, getting to the point, "Friday—err, Bruce here ... says that back in the day, you took off your blindfold when you weren't supposed to. Saw something that Greg didn't want you to see."

Theo stiffened up and started looking around again, full blown paranoia setting in. "I don't know what you're talking about."

"How much would it cost for you to suddenly, unexpectedly, realize what I'm talking about and cough up the story I need?" I asked pleasantly.

Friday frowned, squinting at me. "Wait, are you offering to bribe him?"

"He's not a cop, Friday," I said, "so it's not a bribe. It's a cash payment in exchange for him telling us a story. I'm paying him to be a storyteller, like in the days of old when humans sat around fires and gave the guy with the good stories a piece of meat in exchange for keeping them distracted from the reality of their shitty lives and inevitable deaths in their twenties at the vicious jaws of nature."

"Ohh," Friday said, nodding. "That makes sense."

"How much you offering?" Theo asked. He wasn't cradling his leg anymore, and his attention was wholly on me.

"How much do you want?" One thing I knew about negotiation with small-timers who were desperate: they either never want as much as you would think they would, or they ask for the whole damned world and you can grind them down to a reasonable amount. Theo, tragically, struck me as small-timer all the way, a victim of circumstance and an intellect that was probably only marginally more impressive than Friday's. Like that was some kind of accomplishment.

"A thousand bucks," Theo said. "Cash. Right now."

"Five hundred," I countered. I had the thousand, having picked up a packet of cash at the safe house when I'd grabbed my new phone, but if I caved immediately, he'd think he'd been taken advantage of, get greedy, and immediately ask for more. Which would prompt me to threaten and possibly beat him for going back on our deal, doing no one any favors.

Theo's eyes darted as he considered my offer. "Eight hundred."

"Seven fifty," I said, "final offer. And maybe I'll pay for a meal at the Mexican restaurant around the corner." I'd seen it when I came in for a landing. It looked festive. And they probably had margaritas, my favorite Spanish word.

"Deal," Theo said, and offered me a hand. I yanked him to his feet quickly, before my powers had a chance to work on him, and he put a little weight on his leg, testing it. It didn't collapse. "Why are you guys coming around now, looking for info on Greg?"

"Because he's trying to k—" Friday started to say, and I smacked him in the kidney hard enough to make him shriek and bend backward, writhing through the pain on his tippytoes.

"Because I want to hire him," I lied, watching Theo for reaction. He hadn't been looking at Friday when I'd swatted the dumb bastard; the last thing we needed was a fearful Theo hearing the words, "Because Greg is trying to kill me!" and deciding to go back on our bargain. Theo stared, perplexed, at Friday's contortions. "He's passing a kidney stone right now," I said to explain it away.

Theo seemed to take that explanation in stride. "All right, let's go eat and have a talk." He didn't look super pleased about the deal, but then, he was caught between a rock and a hard place. He didn't really want to tell us what was going on with Greg, but clearly, being in the ranks of the economically disadvantaged had put a few screws to him as well. He motioned toward a back door to the gym, the one he'd been headed toward when I took his leg out from under him.

"After you," I said, and as soon as he turned his back, I grabbed Friday's ape-like head and pulled it close to me, as though whispering my dreams into a seashell before casting it into the ocean. "Say nothing." And I let him go, following after Theo in hopes to get some damned answers about this magician meta who'd been troubling me all day.

28.

Augustus

"Jamal?" Reed called across the bullpen. We'd all scattered after the meeting, heading back to our desks to tug our own individual threads. Reed's question was not a question; it was a request for an update, and we all knew it, our heads down as we pretended to work but listened in. Most of us were metas; it'd be hard not to listen in to a shouted conversation.

"She's not answering," my brother called back. Like he couldn't have just spoken at a normal volume and had everyone hear him anyway. We followed weird formalities.

"Let me know when you get her," Reed said, and turned his attention to J.J. and Abby, in their shared cubicle just across the way from mine. "J.J.?"

"Reed, don't bleed," he said, and I wondered why the hell he would say such a thing before remembering they had some kind of joke about name rhyming between them. "I got no twenty on Cassidy so far. She's a smart girl, y'know. Good at hiding her footprints. Might want to put Jamal on that and me on dialing Sienna, you know, smarter division of labor—"

"I've got a location on Ellis," Abby said, and you could have heard a pin drop.

"You … found the smartest woman in the world?" J.J. asked, and I wondered if he was going to insult his girlfriend and get himself kicked out of bed for a year by expressing skepticism. Fortunately, for him, he didn't: "This is why I love you!" he exclaimed with pure joy.

"Well, that and the thing with the—"

"No one else needs to hear about that," J.J. said quickly, saving us all from a potentially very disturbing detail of their love life.

"Cosplay and fantasy are very natural things," Abby said matter-of-factly, ending the stay of execution for those hoping to maintain the good-hearted fiction that those two never knocked boots. "Costumes—"

"Please stop," Jamal said.

"You need a girlfriend, Jamal," Abby said pityingly. "I know someone I could set you up with. If you're interested."

"You know what I'm interested in?" Reed asked, sounding like a boss from a fifties sitcom that had lost patience with the banter. "Cassidy Ellis's location and nothing else. Just the facts, none of your personal business."

"Reed's an old school stoic like that," J.J. said.

"Am I an old school stoic, too?" Scott asked. "Because I'm cool with not oversharing personal stuff."

"Yeah, that's what Veronika is for," I agreed.

"Cassidy. Ellis." Reed said again.

"You're not going to believe this," Abby said.

"I'm willing to believe anything if it keeps us on this conversation instead of the one that keeps rearing its ugly, cosplaying head," Jamal muttered so that only us metas could hear him.

"—but it looks like Cassidy is right here in the Minneapolis area," Abby said. "She's in Richfield. Twenty minutes away."

"I'm on this," I said, barging for the door.

"I'll go with you," Scott said, jumping to his feet.

"I'm the captain, I get to go on the damned away team—" Reed said.

"—I am not staying behind here," Jamal said, snatching his coat and barging for the exit.

"Oh, wow," J.J. said as we all fled for the exit, "who would have thought all it'd take to get a bunch of big, strong, badass meta policing dudes to flee was to just talk about naughty stuff?"

"I figured that one out a while ago," Abby said as the four of us turned the corner into the reception area. Still, I could faintly hear the squeak of one of their chairs, and the smack of someone's lips on a cheek as Abby sighed, "Alone at last."

"Who wants to drive?" Reed asked, stepping up his pace and throwing up the front door for us. The receptionist, a local girl named Casey, looked at us quizzically as we all practically threw ourselves out the front door like a bunch of clowns piling out of a little car.

"I got this," I said, motioning toward my black Mercedes E300, parked in the front row.

"And you gave me shit about a Ferrari," Scott said as we made our way to the car.

"I'm willing to declare a blanket forgiveness for all shit given provided we all never talk about the geek sex horror that we nearly witnessed back there," I said.

"Agreed," Scott said, entirely too quickly, as I stepped down into my driver's seat.

"Witnessed," Reed agreed.

"So sworn, or whatever," Jamal threw in.

Once we were all settled in, I let the uncomfortable silence hang for just a minute before popping it with a kinda obvious question. "None of us has the address, do we?"

"I'm not going back in there," Reed said from the passenger seat, "and I don't expect any of you to, either." He turned back to my brother. "Jamal ...?"

"Yeah, I got it," Jamal said. He pulled out his phone, giving it a quick tweak, little sparks of electricity flowing out of his finger almost unnoticeably. He sat like that for a second, then touched my car.

"Calculating route," my built-in GPS said as the screen mounted in the middle of my dashboard set up for a trip. "You will arrive at your destination at 5:59 PM."

"That's handy," Reed said. I put the car in gear and started to back out, using the park assist to keep from sideswiping the row of vehicles behind me as I damned near burned rubber to get the hell out of here, as though leaving the area could somehow cleanse the thought of nerdy sex from my mind.

"Most new cars have GPS now, don't they?" I asked absently as it put the car into drive and damned near smacked the curb as I gunned it, heading for the outlet to the road. The sun was low in the sky, orange tint cast over the buildings in the office park around us. This place wasn't that dissimilar from the office park Sienna had detonated a few months ago, but it had the virtue of being on the other side of town so we didn't have to listen to the noise of reconstruction going on around us.

"I was talking about Jamal's ability to keep us from having to send a man back in there," Reed said as I signaled my turn and pulled out into the thickening rush hour traffic toward Interstate 494.

"Yeah, that was a real traumatic-image-burned-into-your-mind-forever lifesaver," Scott agreed.

"Way to be a hero, Jamal," I threw back over the seat.

"I'll take my bow now," Jamal said. "Hopefully this is the only act of heroism any of us has to display today."

"Knowing Cassidy, and the trouble she's caused us up until now ..." Reed shook his head. "I kinda question that. But ... yeah, let's hope for the best."

29.

Greg

"Eddie," Greg said softly entering his son's room with quiet footfalls. Eddie was on the floor, playing with a Lego set. Greg's eyes flitted over the tiny creation, a little version of Avengers tower that he recognized from the most recent movie. He'd taken Eddie to see it, and basked in the two hours plus of awed silence from his son. Of course, he'd had to compel the silence by threat of leaving the movie if Eddie talked … but still. It was a companionable silence, one punctuated by the expression of pure zeal during battle scenes and laughs during the occasional gags.

"Daddy!" Eddie sprang up, his assembly forgotten along with whatever ill feelings he might have had when Greg had left this morning. He hit Greg at the midsection, a hug turning into a near tackle. Eddie was tall for his age and Greg was short, and painfully aware of it. He grimaced as his son impacted him harder than he would have liked, but his metahuman strength and sense of balance saved him from being rocked back off his heels.

"What are you up to?" Greg asked awkwardly, trying to jump start some sort of conversation about the Lego project. Legos, Greg could understand and respect. They reminded him of the Lincoln Logs and Erector sets he built with his own father before graduating to model kits of the planes of the time—the P-38 Lightning, the P-51 Mustang, the B-52 Stratofortress. He actually had one of each of them now, carefully, lovingly maintained in his workshop with the same care and attention to detail that he cultivated when he and his father built the models together.

"Avengers tower got destroyed in an attack by Ultron," Eddie said, dropping back to his knees on the beige carpet. He was wearing shorts, and fibers of the carpet had left little impression marks on his knees. "Now we have to rebuild before he attacks again."

Greg felt a slight chuckle trickle through him like sweet relief, a breezy balm after a hot day. Talking about *Avengers* movies was no imposition on Greg; he certainly enjoyed them enough to discuss them in detail. He had copies of every single *Avengers* comic book from the first to now, also secreted away in the office in his workshop. And he'd read every one of them.

"Did you know that in the comics," Greg said as Eddie snapped together the sundered pieces of the tower, "Ultron isn't created by Tony Stark at all?"

"Oh?" Eddie answered by rote, not really paying attention to Greg's words. These were rare, the moments when Eddie cared more about his own project than bubbling with conversation all over his father or mother.

"Yes," Greg said, taking slow, ambling walk to the front window, which looked out over their idyllic street. "He was actually created by another Avenger. Can you guess who?"

"Umm ... Scarlet Witch?" Eddie was focused entirely on his project.

"You're not thinking this through carefully," Greg said, clucking his tongue. "Scarlet Witch isn't a scientist."

"Umm ... Bruce Banner?"

"No," Greg said. He felt a tiny prickle of impatience. He'd told Eddie this before, hadn't he? When they'd had this same conversation after they walked out of the movie? But of course, Eddie was so intent on being a babbling brook of excitement, he probably hadn't paid attention to a word Greg had said.

Still ... at least he was closer with Bruce Banner. "Dr. Banner is a scientist," Greg agreed, feeling like perhaps this would sugarcoat his disappointment in the wrongness of the answer with a pat on the head, "but he didn't create Ultron in the comics, no."

"Mmm ..." Eddie was putting together an Iron Man suit, a little minifigure smaller than Greg's pinky finger. "... Thor?"

Greg made a grunting noise in the back of his throat. "No," he said, trying to keep his patience. Maybe he remembered that in the comics, Thor had a secret identity as Dr. Donald Blake. It still irritated him that this little detail hadn't been in any way faithfully conveyed in the movies, ending up as nothing more than a wink-and-nod joke. "Not Thor."

"Black Widow?"

"No," Greg said, huffing now. "Black Widow is not a scientist, she's a spy. An assassin. Honestly, I don't think you're even trying at this point, Eddie. We've had this conversation before." He knelt down and tapped Eddie on the forehead—gently—trying to prod him to pay attention. "Think. Who created Ultron in the comic books? This is important."

Eddie looked up at him with a mixture of fear and confusion, looking a little like he'd been attacked. He reached up to his hairline and touched the spot on his forehead where Greg had just vigorously tapped him. "I ... I don't know—"

"He was my favorite Avenger," Greg said, trying to prompt him, but the statement came out bubbling with anger. "We've talked about this. A million times. Haven't you been listening?"

"I—I don't—" Eddie was stuttering now, and collapsed back on his haunches, his knees once more showing the pressed-in shell-like pattern from the carpet fibers. He was blinking, lip quivering.

"This is truly pathetic," Greg said under his breath as he rose to his feet and looked down at Eddie. He seemed so small. And he was a quivering mess again—and all over a question that he should have known the answer to. It was so simple! "Why are you down there like a baby, whining—" Eddie was whimpering, too, a sound low in his throat. Greg put a hand over his eyes. This wasn't the way this was supposed to go. He'd come up here to offer an olive branch. He'd started a conversation on a mutually agreeable subject. And now Eddie was just sobbing, fearful, like—

Like any number of people Greg had looked down on, asking them if they had any last words. He hadn't asked that here, though, so what the hell was the problem with Eddie?

Maybe Greg was just tense, he decided. Failing to kill Percy Sledger ... it was not the sort of event that conspired to put him in a good mood. If he could just kill the stupid bastard, things would get better. Morgan was wrong— everything had been fine before this contract. Some contracts were just like that, though he'd never had one go quite this wrong before ...

That was down to Sienna Nealon, though. She was beyond problematic, she was a day-wrecking trauma of the first order. He'd sort her out, though, once he figured out where she was. The nuke was loaded and ready to go when he headed out next. Sledger would be out there, somewhere, the fool. Probably predictable, too, since he seemed to be bouncing around, running to people he'd had past associations with—

Theo.

The name bludgeoned Greg in the head like a skyscraper coming down on him. His eyes widened as the idea occurred to him. Yes, Theo. Theo could very well be the next stop on Sledger's agenda. It was logical, tracking him down. Jon had been first, after all, and surely not for no reason. Sledger was seeking out his old associates, which left Theo and Chase. Chase would be the last one Sledger would voluntarily look for if he had a brain in his head—which didn't rule out him looking for that brand of trouble—but Theo ...

What was Nealon seeking? Answers.

Who would have had the clearest insight into how Greg could do what he could do? Theo, in all probability, because the idiot had lifted his mask that time, and Greg had let him live afterward.

"I have to go," Greg said, giving Eddie, still whimpering on the floor, one glance. Part of him longed to stoop down, to gather Eddie up in his arms. But that was weakness talking, and there was a wall of pride built between them. Greg had made his position clear; he loathed weakness. Detested it. Somehow, it was even worse from his own blood. He needed to make Eddie strong, to not indulge the boy in this pitiful quivering. Picking him up would be to tacitly condone such behavior.

And he could no more do that than allow this contract to slip through his fingers.

Greg had almost made it to the door when an answer came, weakly, from behind him. "Hank Pym."

Greg turned. He almost thought he'd imagined hearing it. "What did you say?"

"H—Hank Pym is your favorite Avenger," Eddie warbled out, biting his lip. "I think."

Greg's skin felt suddenly cold, a sick sense of guilt rolling into his stomach, stealing the life and strength from his hands; if anything had been in his clutches right now, they would surely have fallen out. He clenched his fist tight in opposition to the feeling that was weakening him. "Very good," he said, once he had composed himself. "I guess you were listening," he offered as grudging praise. "And do you remember which Avenger Hank Pym was?"

Eddie was still on the floor, but he wouldn't look at Greg now, his face down, eyes rooted to the carpet. "I ... no."

Greg couldn't find it in himself to be angry at the failure. Not this time. "Keep thinking about it," he said, and walked out the door, not daring to look back, especially when the sobbing started ... again.

30.

Sienna

"Does this place have good margaritas?" I asked Theo as we studied the menu. Mariachi music was playing over the speakers in the background, and a pleasant hum of conversation filled the room, which was yellow-toned and bright, a few festive piñatas hanging from the high ceilings. It kinda screamed either "Mexico!" or "Kid's Birthday Party!" I was fine with either as long as there were margaritas.

"Had one of those days?" Theo asked, looking sidelong at Friday with a world of suggestion.

"Oh, yeah," I said. "You know what I mean." Theo nodded subtly.

"I don't know what you mean," Friday said. He'd reduced himself to a much more basic size than he'd been in the gym, fortunately, now merely the size of a dude who was headed to Muscle Beach or Gold's Gym rather than impossibly large. "What do you mean?"

A waiter passed by and I almost ripped his arm off trying to get him to stop. "Margarita, please. Large. Large as you can make."

He nodded, and once Theo had ordered a top-shelf shot of Patron—I guess since I was paying—and Friday had ordered a Diet Coke with a slice of lime, which he was very particular about, the waiter disappeared and we were left studying menus while I avoided the topic of conversation I most wanted to get to. I knew Theo would get around to it sooner or later, he was just working up the liquid courage to broach the fearful subject.

"How long have you been in LA?" I asked, figuring I'd give him some alternative conversational topics to play with while we waited for the booze to arrive.

"Ten years or so," Theo said as the waiter came back with his shot of Patron and Friday's Coke. He disappeared again after saying something like, "*Un momento, por favor,*" to me, but I just assumed that meant the bartender was working on my drink.

"Things changed much in that time?" I asked.

"Oh yeah," he nodded, eyeing the shot. "Do you mind if I ...?" He looked at the glass with significance.

"Go right ahead," I said. "For the pain, you know." He looked at me blankly. "Your knee?"

"Yeah. Exactly." Theo downed the shot in one and held it up as the waiter passed. Still no margarita. The waiter scooped up the shot glass as he went by, nodding at Theo as our dinner companion silently requested a reload. "The world's changed," Theo said, waxing philosophical as the alcohol started working its way into his veins. "Hell, metahumans were still a secret ten years ago, and now we're the talk of the town. Probably every town." He looked around nervously. "I still ain't saying nothing, though."

"Why not?" I asked. Friday made a slurping noise through his straw and rattled his glass, his Diet Coke at an end. By a razor-thin margin of self-control I kept myself from slapping it out of his hand or performing amateur dentistry on him with it.

Theo smiled thinly as the waiter stopped back with another shot. What the eff was taking him so long with my margarita? He vanished without a word, and Theo said, "You probably don't realize this, sitting at the top of the scale, but for those of us way down there at the bottom, having powers doesn't make you all that powerful. It makes you a target."

"What are you going to get?" Friday asked, shifting his yellowed menu as he looked at it, ignoring Theo and looking at me. "The chimichangas?"

"Do I look like Deadpool to you?" I asked, giving him

the evil eye for his rudeness. "I'm going to get a burrito." And then I was going to avoid eating the shell, because the calorie count on that thing had to be nuts beyond measure. "Assuming our waiter ever manages to get his thumb out and bring me my margarita. I'm starting to suspect sexism."

"I have that problem, too," Friday said. "Sexy-ism. People ignore me because I'm just too sexy. They can't handle it."

"I doubt that's why," I said, turning in my chair so that I could face Theo. "You mentioned that being low-level makes you a target. For who?"

The waiter stopped off and delivered another shot of tequila and no margarita, and I let out a growl so low that he stopped for a second when he was already about five steps from our table, looking around like he'd heard something but didn't know where it had come from. Then he shot off again, not a word about my beverage.

"Humans thinking they can be a badass if they take down a meta," Theo said. "Governments and other sketchy groups looking for superpowered firepower. All kinds of people, I'm guessing. I don't want to find out for sure, so I just stay quiet about what I can do."

"What can you do?" I asked.

Theo looked strangely at Friday. "You didn't tell her?"

Friday was drinking a fresh Diet Coke, one I hadn't even notice the waiter had refilled, rattling the cubes. "Huh? Oh, I don't know what you can do."

"I'm a low-level earth mover," Theo said when he looked back at me, and I suspected shotgunning that second round of tequila had helped him loosen his tongue enough to part with this info without asking for more money. Judgment was always the first thing to go. "But I can't move much. That's why when Bruce and I were with that outfit, they called me Sandstorm." He eyed his shot glass longingly and licked his lips. It disappeared as the waiter went by and scooped it up, catching Theo's nod as he went past but not stopping long enough to answer any other questions.

"Okay, I'm about to make a scene here if someone doesn't get me my damned margarita soon," I said. Turning my attention back to Theo, I said, "Before you drink me into the poorhouse, what did you see in Saddam's bunker?"

Theo looked at me blankly. "Whose bunker?"

I didn't even bother to look back at Friday with an accusing glare for lying to me. "Whoever's bunker it was the night you lifted the blindfold and saw ... whatever Greg didn't want you to see. Describe it for me."

"I didn't see much," Theo said, looking at the table. "What Greg didn't realize is ... I pulled that mask up for a second. That was all. He caught me right at it, and you better believe I dropped it back down right then."

"Why did you lift it?" I asked.

"Because a few seconds earlier we'd been standing in a corridor in a bunker," Theo said, slurring slightly now, "and there were little grains of sand all around me from where people had tracked it in out of the desert. See, I can feel the bigger stuff—mountains and whatnot—I just can't control them, lift them, whatever, the way that cat that hangs with Sienna Nealon can."

He was talking about Augustus. I almost snickered; Theo hadn't recognized me. Which was good, overall.

"But the minute Greg did his thang," Theo said, "there was suddenly no dirt anymore. Not in the air, not in the distance. Nothing I could control, just—big-ass pieces of rock everywhere." The waiter dropped another shot in front of him and he took it down immediately. "So I lifted my blindfold because we were in the desert—well, a desert bunker—one second, and the next, there's not a single grain of sand anywhere around. You explain to me how that happens?"

"Magic," Friday said with certitude.

"That's what I think, too," Theo said, waving the empty shot glass at Friday. "I think he can teleport from one place to another, like a storehouse or something, and then booyah! Teleport right back in the blink of an eye with, say, a Concorde or a machine gun or something."

"What did you see that night?" I asked, trying to doggedly get to the question rather than the theory.

"I saw ... rough ground," Theo said. "Like we were

153

standing on a cliff's edge. It was pretty dark, too, but there was light from somewhere above. Faint, though, like we were in a big warehouse or something and someone hadn't bothered to lay electrical in the corner we were in. I couldn't see the horizon; we might have been indoors. I didn't get a good look, because I was focused on the ground for most of the moment the blindfold was up." He finished with a shrug. "That's what I saw."

"Really interesting," Friday said. "Thanks, Theo, that helps a lot."

I started to give him the stink eye, because that didn't help at fricking all and made me at least $750 poorer, but right at that moment, the waiter appeared and set a margarita in front of me the size of a toilet bowl. "And for the lady ..." he said, and suddenly I felt a whole lot warmer in my heart for him.

"Maybe you guys should check with Chase," Theo said as his shot glass disappeared in the waiter's hand again. "She was always sneakier than I was, and for about a quarter second while I was trying to get a look through my blindfold, I saw her looking, too. Just a little peek of an eyeball from under her blindfold, you know? 'Cept she didn't get caught looking."

"I don't even know where to look for her," Friday said so quickly that I knew he was lying. I didn't care right then, though, because I had a margarita in my hand, and I started sipping. Part of me wanted to take it down like Theo with a shot, but based on the service in this place thus far, it would probably take me until my eightieth birthday to get another, so I sipped slowly. Mmmm. Good. Sour. Tangy. Salt on the rim, which I licked like a pervert.

Theo was too gone to notice. "Yeah, I don't blame you for not looking for her after what happened last time you two met."

"What happened last time you two met?" I asked.

"Tell you later," Friday said, a little too quickly.

Theo stared at us, his eyes glazed. "Why can't you tell her now?" Friday looked a little trapped, but then Theo's head lurched forward a little, and he shook his head. "Man, I'm tired. Hurry up with the story, will you?"

"Well … all right, I guess," Friday said, looking nervously at him. A couple seconds later, Theo closed his eyes, and Friday sat up a little straighter. By the time he'd fully launched into it, Theo was snoring gently, right there at the table.

31.

Friday

October 8, 2001
Kandahar, Afghanistan

Sienna note: Bullshit bullshit bullshit bullshit—
They called it Operation Enduring Freedom, and let me tell you something—it was only day one and I was already enduring my freedom like a stone pimp back at the base with Chase every chance we got, if you know what I mean. SCHAWING!
slurp of margarita
"I bring you civilization, heathen devils!" I shouted as I jumped out of the Blackhawk helicopter at five hundred feet. I had a guitar specially made into a super duper grenade launcher gun, and it was the baddest of baddassity, barrel on the neck of the instrument, which I played as I fell, firing wildly at the enemy technicals—that's their name for their little shitty trucks with machine guns mounted in the beds—
I know what a technical is, thanks.
One of them went up to the furious thrusting of my grenades. BOOM! BOOM! Another! BOOM! I was single-handedly destroying the Taliban of Kandahar province!
Chase shouted, "You are singlehandedly destroying the Taliban of Kandahar province! Now let's hurry and finish this vital mission so we can get back to base and you can take all my clothes off and—"

I am going to bury a fork in your eyeball if you don't keep this story on track and out of the gutter. A knife will follow, and I'll save the spoon, which is guaranteed to be the most painful thing I use on you, for last.

So, anyway, I was killing my way through line after line of Taliban! I landed and was ripping off heads as I played my guitar—rocking and hitting the chords as I grabbed a guy in a black robe and turban and yanked his head off. I punted it into the next province to warn them I was coming. Boom! Grenade to an old jeep! BOOM! Grenade right to a guy who was shaking in his pee-stained robes, wishing he could surrender! He blew to pieces, it was so cool.

A Humvee on a parachute dropped down next to me and I ripped the parachute off and shouted, "Come on, team! We're going to liberate this province from these evil shitstains!"

"Yeah!" Chase said, and she shook her—

brandishing fork Carefully consider your next words.

"We're with you!" Theo shouted, shaking his M-16 in the air.

"I will follow you everywhere, Friday!" Jon shouted, flying overhead on his surfboard and hosing down the enemy with his dual Uzis. He only killed, like, ten guys. I'd already killed three thousand between my grenades and ripping heads off. It's a satisfying feeling, watching the pieces come hanging out little tissue streamers of red and—

slurp Stop.

I jumped into the Humvee and Greg jumped in next to me. "You will lead us to victory on day one of this war!" he shouted.

"Damned right," I said, and started the ignition. "Chase—on the gun."

"Yes, my lusty love with an immense—" Chase said, and—uh, stop glaring at me—anyway, she manned the turret and ended up killing a hundred Taliban. Which is good, but obviously not as good as me.

I drove across the mountainous desert, kicking up a cloud of dust that could be seen from a mile away, like a warning: THE STORM IS COMING!!!!

(I am the storm.)

*Oh, for f- *rattle of ice, slurp of an empty margarita glass* That went fast.*

I headed for an enemy position ahead. You could see a battle line etched across the hill, machine guns everywhere, a bunch of guys in their black robes and stuff, and they started making ululating yells when we were five hundred yards away.

And they started shooting at two hundred.

"I'll save you all, team!" I said and inflated to huge proportions.

"I'll get out of the way so you can do your heroic best!" Greg shouted, and then he disappeared, leaving me more room to get SWOLE.

"My love, they are filling your sexy chest with bullet holes!" Chase cried from the back while lighting those bastards up with endless fire from her turret.

"But I will bleed sexy blood and destroy them and then drink to my own awesomeness!" I shouted, steering toward the trench line the Taliban had cut into the hill. They started to panic and scream like girls and threw away their guns at the fear of seeing my bare, huge-normous chest taking round after round and still I came forward, playing my guitar, firing grenades and overwhelming them with my tight death metal. You could almost see them thinking as they screamed and ran around in the trench, their eyes flitting in fear—"If that's the size of his chest, imagine how HUGE he is below the belt!"

I crashed my Humvee into the trench, into the densest concentration of Taliban, killing like fifty of them at once. The crunch of bone and blood was lost as I leapt into the air with my grenade launcher guitar and hung there for a minute, pounding them with explosion after explosion, and a guitar solo that went on for like, ten minutes! IT WAS TOTALLY KITTENS!

rattle of ice in empty margarita glass *This isn't fair. This isn't right.*

I landed back on the ground lifted the smashed Humvee with one hand while I continued my raging, badass guitar solo/killing stream with the other. I smashed like twenty guys with one swing of the Humvee, then killed fifty more with a well-placed grenade at the end of the trench.

"You are the badassest badass of all time!" Jon said.

"You are so extreme you make Arnold, Stallone, and Willis combined look like the sissiest sissies!" Theo said. "When we get back to the United States, I want to become your manservant and follow you around and say catchphrases for you like, 'He's on fire'! and 'DY-NO-MITE'!"

Jesus, Friday. He's sitting right there, and you're being really racist.

What's racist about saying DY-NO-MITE!? Anyway, up at the cave mouth ahead, I saw a massive figure come striding out. He looked like an Arab version of me, except for that big beard and the white turban. I would never wear a turban. There's no containing these devastatingly gorgeous locks.

"That's Osama Bin Laden!" Chase cried. "We have to do something!" She looked right at me, eyes full of sexy desire and hope. "Bruce! You can win this war right now!"

"I *will* win this war right now!" I shouted and jumped into the air. Osama threw up his hands and screamed girlishly as he saw me and my massive package descending upon him, ready to smite him like I'd done to his men, who were all dead, all of them, except for one guy who came out from behind a rock with his pants down, running around yelling for like toilet paper or something, I dunno. I would have felt bad about killing him, so I let him live. Because I'm merciful.

"Aieeeeeeeeeeeee!" Osama screamed, trying to hold up his hands to protect him from the vengeful god of bronzed muscles and sexy bullet wounds descending on him from the heavens. I like to think he got religion right there, and that he knew the Furious Crotch of God when he saw it coming—

head in hands, weeping gently for my wasted time and my blackened soul, listening to this shit Why is the service here so sexist and slow?

Wait, the story gets better.

"I beg you to spare my life!" Osama cried as I landed in

159

front of him. I was twice as tall as he was, and I lifted him up into the air.

"Any last words?" I shouted, and big tears streamed down his face.

"Please don't kill me!" He peed himself right there, again, then shit his robes, I think. I didn't want to check. "Have mercy, with your big American heart and bigger American penis!"

I stared at him coldly. "I don't have one of those … and it's not the penis!" I spun him around and kicked him in the ass while simultaneously firing a grenade up there and hitting the high notes of my guitar solo all at once. He exploded from within, I nailed the hardest hardcore chord ever played heard in the entire world, and his corpse went tumbling back into the cave.

head in hands *You did* not *kill Osama Bin Laden. That's not how—or when—he died!*

Oh, it is. You just bought into the government lies, man.

"Nicely done," Greg said, appearing at my side as my team wandered up now that all the badass, huge-chested hard work was down. "Tight metal, by the way." And he lifted his pinky and index finger as he made a drum set appear and we rocked on the pieces of Osama's dead corpse—

What the actual fu—

32.

Sienna

"—ck is wrong with you?" I asked, head buried in my hands, as it had been for most of the story. "That story had nothing to do with Chase, or Greg, really, or anything other than you making up more horseshit about how awesomely badass you supposedly are."

Friday stared at me inscrutably for a second. "Earlier, you called my story bullshit. Now, it's horseshit. So ... what's the difference?"

"One comes out of a bull, the other out of a horse," I deadpanned, "but they're both shit, the only difference is in the consistency—and your stories have no consistency, no connection to reality other than maybe in passing. The people in your stories don't die when you say they do, I question whether the locations even exist—"

"You don't think there's a Kandahar in Afghanistan?" Friday snickered.

"Oh, I know there's a Kandahar," I said, "I just question whether you've ever seen it, and especially whether you've seen it on the days you claim to."

"But you don't doubt I was there with my badass team," Friday said, puffing like a peacock.

I stared at him evenly. "If you were, I think you were the guy that you were supposedly letting escape mercifully because he'd been busy taking a dump while the battle was going on."

Friday's face fell. "Ouch. So much hate."

"That's truer than anything you've said so far." I tossed enough money on the table to cash us out. Theo was still snoring gently, his last shot of tequila just sitting undrunk in front of him. Not wanting to be undrunk myself, I snatched it and took it down quickly, slamming it down hard enough to wake him. "Closing time, Theo. You don't have to go home, but you're not getting any more loaded on my dime here."

"Oh, okay," Theo said, getting slowly to his feet. "Did I miss anything?"

"Just a crazy story that you probably could have poked enough holes in to render it less seaworthy than the Titanic," I said, steering him toward the exit. "Also, Friday here seemed to be under the impression that you wanted to be his butler and follow him around when he came back to the States."

Theo made a rumbling laugh. "Shit. Bruce here can't take care of himself, let alone anybody else. He needs Supernanny or something." He broke into laughter.

"You guys are really mean," Friday said as we passed the hostess station. I was tempted to complain about my shitty waiter and my pitiful lone margarita, but what was the point now?

I stepped out into the long shadows of the LA evening. Sundown was coming, but not just yet. There weren't many cars on the street, which was weird for LA at this time of day, and I started to question how much margarita I'd actually had when something long, ovoid and steel started to drift down in a slow arc from above. It was small, maybe the size of a baseball, but shaped like a miniature bucket and I turned back to say something to Theo—

But he was gone. I was left alone with Friday on the sidewalk just outside the Mexican restaurant, the streets around us as deserted as if the rapture had come to town and swept them all away. "I got a bad feeling about this—" I barely got out before that bucket-thing hit the ground—

There was a flash of blinding white, the kind you saw in—

Nuclear explosions—

And the wave of heat and flame swept over me a millisecond later, before I even had a chance to say another word, register another thought—

Or prepare any kind of defense.

33.

Augustus

"All right, here's how we do this," Reed said as we parked a couple houses down from the address that we had for Cassidy Ellis. It was a clean-cut street in the Minneapolis suburb of Richfield, which was sandwiched between the burgeoning suburban landscape of south Minneapolis and the commercial metropolis of Bloomington, which boasted the Mall of America and the airport, and a few other things that city-dwelling me yawned at. "Two of us crash in the front, two in the back."

"Did he make that sound kinky or is it just me?" Scott asked.

"Just you," Jamal said. "Get out of the gutter."

Richfield just looked to me like another boring, post-war tract of small houses, at least on this street. The type of places thrown up to house residents of an expanding city, with all the inconsistencies of an aging, first-ring suburb. One house would have immaculately kept yard, trimmed and perfect, flowers planted in the beds outside the window and blooming already. The next house would be gone to seed, weeds already springing up even though the ground had only thawed a month earlier.

The whole street was pretty green, with leaves out on every tree and the dull roar of one of the freeways—probably 494—rumbling in the distance. A car passed by as we crossed the lawns, striding with purpose to a little white-

164

painted house that looked somewhere between gone to hell (which was on the right of it) and lovingly maintained (which was to the left). It was a Goldilocks house, kind of a "just right" balance between someone who really showed pride of ownership and someone who'd let the bank take the place having not given a shit about it for the decade before.

"House is set up to not draw too much attention," Reed said, casing it as we approached in the shadow of a tall maple tree. "Compared to the neighbors, I mean."

The wind blew through, bringing the smell of pine mingled with a little exhaust. "No steel door at the front," I said. "And it's got a window. We could reach in and unlock it, or kick it down."

"Kick it down," Reed said.

"Gee, why not just have him make a golem and do it that way?" Jamal asked.

"Trying to keep this quiet, since technically this is breaking and entering," Reed said, his stride a little uneven as the question was asked.

"We could just, y'know … knock," Jamal said. "Two in the front, two in back, like you said. Watch to see if she goes out a window, but sort of do the polite-society thing first before we come crashing in like fools."

That caught Reed by surprise. "No," he said. I had to wonder how much his judgment was being influenced by the fact Cassidy had once detonated him and his car. The only thing that had saved him was Sienna sucking in all the heat from the explosion. The car, tragically, was a total loss. Damned shame, too, because it was a beautiful Dodge Challenger. "Give us a second to get in position and then we'll knock knock, okay?"

"Ok—" I barely got out before Reed sucked Jamal up in a vortex and the two of them flew over the house. It was surprisingly soundless considering that the wind force necessary to lift up two dudes of their size had to have been something more than a light breeze.

"I think he might be letting his feels get the best of him here," Scott said after Reed disappeared over the roof of the house. He led the way up to the door, up three small steps to a concrete porch with a ragged old screen door that wasn't completely closed.

I scoured the area around us for any sign of cameras and found none. That didn't necessarily mean anything; Cassidy was one of the smartest people on earth, if not the smartest in terms of sheer technical, theoretical brilliance. For all I knew, she'd engineered cameras the size of a safety pin and was watching my pretty face right now in glorious 1080p. But probably not, I reassured myself. She'd been a schemer, but turning herself to tech stuff? Hadn't happened yet. And fortunately, people were predictable in a lot of ways, what with them not liking to change their spots and all that.

"What do you think the go signal is?" I asked, and then the sound of a door being split off its hinges echoed over the house and down the street.

"Probably that," Scott said, rearing back and giving the front door a mighty kick.

"Yay for our first felony of the day," I said, following behind him as he cleared the door and entered a living room that looked like it hadn't seen any use at all. There was a layer of dust on a flatscreen TV on the far wall, and the couch didn't look like it had been sat on in years.

The carpet looked freshly cleaned, though, which was weird considering the state of everything else. I started to open my mouth to say something to Scott, but he was already charging through toward the kitchen, which I could see through an archway ahead.

Once I was sure the living room was clear, I followed Scott. "Hey, I does this carpet look funny to y—"

I didn't even get the words out before Scott disappeared in front of me, a hole opening up in the floor, perfectly concealed by the shag carpeting. He fell through the trapdoor pretty as you please, the segments snapping shut behind him and once again leaving no sign that it had just swallowed my partner whole.

Reed shouted, "Jamal!" A gust of wind blew through the house and then stilled itself as the clank of machinery or something falling clacked from that direction.

"Dammit," I said, looking around with unease,

wondering where from or even if the attack was coming. "We really should have knoc—"

Something grabbed me from behind, strong metal arms scooping me up and yanking me backward and down, into the darkness as a door in the wall closed behind me and I fell down, down into the unknown.

34.

Greg

There was something beautiful about watching a nuclear bomb go off, especially from a safe distance. The small-scale nuke had started out as a 500-ton device, which was enough to destroy a couple of city blocks. Greg had done his thing, though, worked his magic, and now the blast radius was roughly the size of the street.

And oh, how the street was looking, with a mushroom cloud rising above it, and a blast of flame and compression wave of force shattering the windows of the Mexican restaurant.

Sure, there'd be some property damage. Of course there would be. You couldn't set off a nuclear bomb, even one with a blast radius the size of a trailer, without seeing some structural devastation spread out from the point of impact.

But Greg was far enough above it now that he wouldn't have to worry about said devastation. He'd done his part, evacuating the street of people so quickly they hadn't even known what was happening, and leaving it clear so that when the moment came it was just Sienna and that idiot Sledger standing there, gawking as the bomb went off in front of them.

Greg didn't have any illusions about Nealon surviving. She could, probably, but that was more or less irrelevant. Maybe she'd heal from the burns, shrug off the effects of the radiation that was probably going to toxify that segment of road for years to come.

But Sledger did not possess her healing ability, and she hadn't had any time to shield him or otherwise jet him out of there before impact. Greg had seen to that.

So this, he reasonably assured himself, should be the end of the contract. Fulfilled, at last. The only wild card factor was Nealon. Would she take this defeat, the death of Sledger, humbly and accept it as a simple, ordinary loss in a world filled with them?

Mmmmm ... perhaps not. Which was unfortunate but characteristic of her, Greg reflected as he watched the mushroom cloud rise over east LA, already banking the SR-71 toward home and throttling up to full speed. That was all right, though. If she couldn't accept her loss, if she wanted to settle things, Greg would make the necessary preparations to be sure he was ready for her if she came.

When she came, he corrected, adjusting his course slightly north, toward Chicago. It really came down to if she could find him. But if she did ... he'd be ready for her. After all, he'd just defeated her once. He could do it again.

Even if it took another nuclear bomb—a bigger one, perhaps.

One she wouldn't be able to survive.

35.

Augustus

I was locked up pretty tight in a series of plastic and metal cords, one around my neck biting into my flesh with a blade-like feel. Neither of my hands were free, and the sense of compression I was experiencing at being completely swallowed in whatever entrapping contraption Cassidy had fashioned for me was outweighed by that sharp feeling against my neck telling me that if I moved, my head and my body were going to part ways, hard and fast.

Fortunately, Cassidy had seen fit to allow me and the others to observe the pickle we'd been put in. Scott was visible just ahead, in a cylinder buried up to his neck in some kind of dusty sand. More was trickling in above him, and an ominous vent above his head shimmered with a mirage-like vapor that suggested gas was flowing into the chamber with him.

Reed had suffered the same fate, except he was only up to mid-chest in the grey sand-like stuff. That same shimmer was visible above him, though.

Past him, I could see Jamal in a vat of water, shivering and up to his waist. It rolled down the sides of the plastic container, grounding him from shooting electricity anywhere meaningful.

"Do I even have to explain to you guys how screwed you are right now?" Cassidy's voice, electronically boosted through a speaker system, rattled through every one of the plastic bonds that wrapped my body. A strong chemical smell threatened to overwhelm me. After a pause, the ominous tone evaporated, and Cassidy said, with undisguised glee, "Okay, I'll explain it:

"Reed, Scott, you are both swimming in a highly combustible sand I made out of kerosene resin and wood shavings. Above you, a pilot light is waiting to be lit by even a single stirring of wind or a change in the water pressure of the pipes from outside. If it lights ... you're going to end up looking a lot worse than the last time I blew you up, pretty boy.

"Jamal ... I don't think I need to explain this to you, because you're generally brighter than the rest of them, but ... zap, splash, drown. You got that, right?

"And as for you, Augustus ... I laced the ground outside with seismic sensors. They go off, and the French Revolution comes to visit you. *Comprende?*"

"Yeah, I get it," I said, "but you could have at least sprung for a real guillotine."

"I knew you'd get that," Cassidy said, coming into view in front of me, her pale skin almost aglow in the basement's soft light.

"Because I'm such a worldly, educated dude?" I asked.

"Because you're taking Western Civ at the University of Minnesota right now," Cassidy said, peering at me curiously, like I was a science experiment she was about to jot some notes on. "Now, hold still." And she grabbed a little hanging remote with a big button—

And pressed it.

I waited a breath for my head to get cleaved off my shoulders, but it didn't happen. Instead, all those hard plastic arms retracted from around my body and I stumbled out, surprised that I was suddenly set free. Scott and Reed's tanks started draining of their combustible material, the gas valve losing its shimmering mirage as the gas cut off. A few seconds later, the grey sand was gone, and the tanks lifted off.

Jamal came staggering out at roughly the same time, looking only a little damp. The hum of an industrial dryer clicked off from where his trap had been sitting, and I wondered why she'd bothered to design that into the thing.

"Now then," Cassidy said, "have we established that you are all my bitches, and that you really shouldn't break into peoples' houses? Crime doesn't pay? Were you guys not paying any attention when Sienna tried and tried to hammer that lesson home to me and all the others in the prison?"

"What's to stop us from letting loose on you right now, Cassidy?" Reed asked, pride burning in him to the point where he looked like he was on the edge of losing all reason.

"Human decency," Cassidy said, unimpressed. "Aren't you the one who's always going on about how there's a different, a better way than what your sister does? Because greasing the basement floor with me, while soothing to your wounded pride after you stumbled ass-backwards into my obvious ambush, is considered murder. Or assault and battery, if you were to stop short of killing me, so ..." She smiled brightly, giving her skeletal face a sinister cast.

"Why did you go to the trouble of setting all that up?" Jamal asked, wringing a little drip of water out of one of his sleeves. Scott looked at him apologetically and sucked it all out with a gesture, the wetness disappearing into Byerly's fingertips.

"Oh, I did this months ago," Cassidy said, dismissing the traps with a wave of her hand. "I would have done it anywhere, but since I set up here in Minneapolis, the likelihood of one or more of you discovering my location and eventually paying me a visit were extremely high, so it made sense to be prepared in case you came knocking. Or not knocking, in this case."

"You know why we're here?" I asked.

"I caught the basics from the lovebirds, after you left," Cassidy said.

"Wait, you're listening in on us?" Scott asked.

"Most of the time, no," Cassidy said, taking a hell of a chance in my opinion by turning her back on us as she started walking to a computer station in the corner. "But I've got this program running—kind of odious, I know, blah—that records conversation held in the vicinity of it and analyzes for certain words—'Cassidy' being one of them. When it hears it, it flags it for me and I listen in on what follows."

"That's illegal," Reed seethed.

"Nope," Cassidy said, shaking her head. "I'm not going to tell you who, but one of your staff? They downloaded the program from the app store, and when they clicked on the terms and conditions—"

"They consented to you monitoring their conversations," Jamal said, putting his head in a hand. "Evil. That's ... really evil. And kind of genius."

"Well, yeah," Cassidy said, "lawyers came up with the boilerplate, but you get the idea. Net effect—I get to listen to you anytime I want, but guys, really—I've got better things to do, so I only do it when—"

"We whisper the devil's name?" I asked.

"And now you hear the flap of my digital wings," Cassidy said. "Anyway, like I said, I got the coverage of your dilemma. Been working on it since I intercepted the convo." She slid into her chair, apparently assured none of us were going to commit bodily harm to her, because she turned her back without looking once over her shoulder. "I didn't have anything to do with this Colorado business, and I have no hand in what's going on with this rich blossoming of metahumankind. It actually works against my interest, albeit negligibly, to have more metas out there. I prefer a small marketplace where my skills are in demand because I'm the only one who can provide them, and someone passing around a serum that makes more of us while also selectively applying the ones that broaden their power set and strengthen their primary to godlike proportions does me absolutely no good."

"Your denials sound strangely like lies to me," Reed said coldly.

"Listen harder," Cassidy said, tapping away at the keyboard. "I have no reason to lie to you. I could have killed you just now. I could also have not bothered to explain truthfully how I knew you were coming for me; I could have just said I set those traps out and waited the last six months for you all to stumble into them. You wouldn't have known any different."

"So why are you telling us the truth now?" I asked, drawing a heated glare from Reed. He really was out of control of himself, at least in relation to Cassidy. "Uh, if you are, I mean. Because there could be a wilder explanation you're not telling us, you know."

"Because in spite of whatever you think, after my last conversation with Sienna—which was after the fall of President Harmon, just so we're clear," she grinned wickedly at Reed, apparently rubbing it in, "she got me thinking about something." Cassidy stopped tapping at the keyboard for a second and spun around to face us. "It was a real eye opener, coming from her, because really, I've never thought of her as—obviously not as an intellectual giant, but barely an intellectual dwarf. Anyway, she said something interesting, and I'm paraphrasing here to hit an old saying … 'If you're so smart, why aren't you rich?'

"And I realized … this dimwit was right," Cassidy said, sounding vaguely enthused. "The world, to me, has long been this series of interlocking pieces that I saw every edge and seam of. I knew how it worked—little fuzzy on the people part of it, but the gist, the systems—I got those. But I'm committing these stupid felonies to get money? Why? Because my boyfriend wanted me to? Bleh." She stuck out her tongue like a teenager. "I could do better. It wasn't like there wasn't opportunity out there. So …" She spun back around and started typing again.

"So you decided to make a fortune …?" Jamal asked, looking around the dingy, poorly-lit basement. Other than the traps and the computer, there really wasn't much of anything down here except bare, concrete block walls. "To prove you were smart?"

"Yep," Cassidy said, "and all on this side of the law, too."

"How are you doing it?" Scott asked, sounding like he was genuinely interested.

"Selling digital data in the third world to the highest bidder," Cassidy said without missing a keystroke. "See, in places like Venezuela, the government wants to control everybody and everything, and since they write the laws, they pretty much can. So if you can monitor the emails and calls and digital footprint of their declared enemies of the state, they tend to want to buy that stuff at a high price."

"That's … even more evil that authoring an app and EULA'ing it so you can eavesdrop on us," Jamal said.

"And illegal," Reed said.

"No, again," Cassidy said. "You're zero for two, legal eagle, you should probably consult a lawyer before you go for strike three. I'm fully compliant with the laws of the countries I'm operating in, and also paying my taxes like a good US citizen on my overseas contracting. I'm not operating in any jurisdiction forbidden by US law or treaty, and I'm not spying on anyone on US soil without—y'know, the kind of tools that require the consent of the person who downloads one of my spying apps. So-o-o … I'm in complete compliance with US law and the law of every country that the US has an extradition treaty with." She tapped the keyboard a couple more times as if punctuating her point, and said, "There."

"There … what?" Scott asked. The four of us were still just standing there, like we were afraid another bunch of doors were going to open up beneath us and whisk us off to the next round of traps.

"Been doing some digging on Augustus's case for the last half hour," Cassidy said. "I've emailed it all to each of you." She looked at Jamal apologetically. "Sorry about your phone, but you didn't really want to carry it anyway, did you? Trying to break the habit and all that?"

Jamal stared at her. "Yeah."

"I commend you for it," Cassidy said airily. "Anyway, you're going to find that the Omar that Augustus clashed with in Colorado is connected to a US branch of a foreign entity. I couldn't find a clear motive for them juicing people into metahuman status, but based on the skim of their communications, they're getting paid for it and taking their job very seriously. Head of US operations is a guy named Mark McGarry, based out of Raleigh, North Carolina, but it looks like he's on the road right now—reason and destination unclear." She spat all that out from memory, without turning back to check her computer once. "He doesn't seem to be directly involved in actually setting up the plumbing machinery that's producing the metas. He's a very high-level guy, but he's really just the mouthpiece for the big bosses overseas."

Reed looked like he was ready to either grind his teeth or give Cassidy a big kiss. "Overseas where?"

"Headquarters looks like it's in Bredoccia, Revelen," Cassidy said. "Lot of hubbub going on over there right now, but I'm not sure why they're making metas like crazy in the US, because although it's giving you guys a lot of work, running around to catch the nuisance ones, it's not really had any kind of deleterious effect on society as whole so far, at least not at the level they're running things."

"Is it the government of Revelen that's sponsoring this?" Jamal asked quietly.

"Not sure," Cassidy said. "It's kind of a failed state post Iron Curtain, so there's not a published hierarchy of government since the last big changeover about five years ago. Drawing any conclusions from the mess of muddled info that's made it out of their borders these last few years would take a lot more time and attention than I'm willing to give it, especially since I've got my own stuff cooking, and y'know, it's your job and I've already done enough of it for you."

"Answer me this, though," Reed said, still a step from grinding his teeth, "how did this McGarry and his crew get their hands on these chemical enhancements for meta powers?" Reed asked, looking to us for answers.

"Don't know, exactly," Cassidy answered before any of us could say anything. "But their supply is being made right here in the US of A, so ..." She shrugged. "I emailed you the facilities they're using, the names and addresses of the plumbers distributing it, everything I found in my cursory search." She yawned. "Which is probably better than your deep search, but, you know ... whatever. Happy to do the neighborly thing and help, at least this once."

I stared at her. "This once?"

"Yeah, just this once," Cassidy said, looking right at me. "Because this time, it gave me a chance to explain myself, acquaint you with what I've got going on here. You've had a chance to look around, I told you what I'm up to, and I gave you a little freebie to make the medicine slide down smoother."

"What ... medicine?" Scott asked, looking around as though the walls were going to come closing in.

"I *could* help you in the future," Cassidy said, twirling in her chair. "This is kind of a sample. Audition, if you will. But it's not going to be free next time. It's going to cost you. A lot. A prohibitive lot, which is why generally only governments that have control of entire economies can afford to hire me. So you're probably not going to want to do that unless you're truly desperate, because this ..." She waved a hand in front of her pasty, skinny self, "... this don't come cheap. Also—"

She stopped as a klaxon wailed through the room, and spun back around to the computer, tapping at the keys.

"Also, what?" Reed asked, eyeing the flashing lights in the corner, but apparently not deterred enough by them to get off his point.

"Blah blah blah," Cassidy said, half-distracted as she focused her attention on the enormous computer monitor, "I was just going to idly threaten you by reminding you of what happened this time in case you got the bright idea to try and force my compliance in the future. This is stage one," she waved a hand in the direction of the traps. "The gentlest stage. Subsequent stages feature confinements that very definitely skirt the edges of Minnesota and federal law on harming trespassers, so ... let's not ever explore those options, okay? Wait—what the *hell*?"

"What the hell what?" I slid up next to her, looking at her monitor, which was a blur of computer code.

Jamal squeezed up on the other side and started to put his hand up to the computer, but Cassidy slapped it away like a mom trying to keep a kid from snatching up an unasked-for sweet. "Read, don't touch," she said and focused back in on the screen as nonsensical strings blazed down way faster than I could make sense of them.

Jamal did just that, ignoring the slapped hand, and craned his neck down, eyeballs looking like they were going to shoot right out of his head. "Is this legit?"

"I think so ..." Cassidy said, still typing feverishly. "Trying to get confirmation through local sources, you know, stuff that's not blindingly illegal to hack and—oof. Yeah. Someone's got a camera phone with my app installed on the 50th floor of the US Bank building." She did a few keystrokes, and the screen fuzzed, the little wheel spinning as it tried to load something.

"What the hell is going on?" Reed asked, coming up behind Cassidy and standing over her shoulder, staring at the loading screen.

"There's a report of a radiological event in East Los Angeles," Jamal said as the video started, blurry at first, but resolving into a cityscape. I recognized LA after a couple seconds while the picture got clearer, and sure enough—

"That's a mushroom cloud," Scott said, easing up next to me and pointing a thick finger at the screen.

"Yes, that's what a radiological event is," Cassidy said with obvious impatience, still typing. "Trying to get something closer ..." She threw the live feed into the corner of the wide monitor as the mushroom cloud continued to rise over the city of Los Angeles, a fearful sight in the midst of the second largest metropolis in the United States.

"Ooh, got one a block away," Cassidy said, and another loading video screen popped up live, coming up more quickly this time. It went through the blurry stage quickly, showing us a street view of a city street, smoke wafting up and pieces of paper and debris floating down in the dust.

Up the street, closer to the cloud, I could see the bright yellow of a Mexican restaurant with all its windows blown out. A couple figures were visible in the haze, staggering, one thin and one large, making their way out of the cloud, the grey haze growing clearer with every step.

The big one emerged first, coughing, shaking, his chest swollen to comically large proportions. There was something about his gait, the way he moved, that seemed really familiar—

"That's a Hercules," Reed said, staring at the screen. He jolted upright. "Do you think that's—"

He didn't even get a chance to get it out before the second figure, female, smaller, came staggering out of the cloud of dust and fallout. It should have been obvious when he saw the glow, but now it was blindingly so—

The woman who emerged from the mushroom cloud was on fire, chest and legs covered, her hair aflame, but none of it appearing to consume her one bit. Instead it was like a bodysuit, protecting her from the dust and the elements.

She shoved the big Hercules clear and then stumbled herself, probably suffering from radiation sickness that even she hadn't been able shake off just yet.

"Sienna," Reed said, closing his eyes, his chin almost touching his chest, as the holder of the cameraphone shouted the same conclusion he'd come to.

"That's Sienna Nealon!" the voice came, excited and fearful all at once. "And she just blew up East LA!"

36.

Sienna

My first thought, when the heat kind of cleared out a little bit, absorbed without any thought into my hands, chest, feet and face was, "Holy shit, I just blew up East LA."

Then I remembered that I hadn't done it, Greg Vansen probably had, and also, that I probably should thank the person in my head who'd just saved my life. *Thanks Gavrikov. Reflexes of lightning, there.*

Faster than, actually, Gavrikov said. *A nuclear bomb goes off in—*

"Should probably save the technical precision for someone who would appreciate it," I said, then tried to hold my breath. I'd absorbed the heat from the blast, but not the force, which explained why I was planted against something kind of squishy, which was in turn up against the smashed-up facade of the Mexican restaurant. Which I felt by reaching back past the immediate object behind me and running a hand over the cracked stucco.

"Whuuuuu …?" The object beneath me let out a low, pained groan, and I realized that Friday had broken my horizontal fall with his immense hugeness. When the nuclear shockwave had kicked me back, he'd been standing right behind me. Apparently I hadn't even noticed smashing into him and then into the wall, probably because I was too focused on the waves of radioactive heat and flame rushing into my body while I screamed mutely and inhaled it.

"Friday?" I called back, pushing off of him. I was pretty close to nude at this point because absorbing the blast had burned through my clothing, so I did my thang and lit up my skin in order to give myself a little modesty coverage, and Friday's eyes flicked open, and he looked me over.

"Your tits are on fire," he said, and closed his eyes again.

"That's intentional," I said, keeping from slapping him. I doused my hands, just in case my restraint failed. I also killed the flame down both arms from wrist to shoulder, making my little flame outfit into a unitard tank top. Might as well show off these shoulders since I was bound to get some press attention within minutes anyway. I grabbed Friday and hauled him to his feet.

He grimaced at me, holding himself at an odd angle. "What just happened?"

"Greg Vansen just upped the ante in our little war," I said, grabbing Friday by his shirt, which was burnt and partially ripped. I shoved him forward, trying to suss out which direction was the shortest route to the end of this dust-filled mushroom cloud. "How much radiation do you suppose we just absorbed?"

"Whut? Are we radioactive right now?" Friday threw his hand up to his head self-consciously. "Nooo! I don't want to lose my hair! It's too pretty to die."

"Just be glad it's not you dying, stupid," I said, shoving him forward again through the impossibly thick haze as I sought the way out. I could almost see light in the distance, but it was tough to tell. The cloud was dense, closing in on all sides like a heavy fog. I might have been tempted to just wait for rescue if not for, y'know, the radiation danger and the fact that if the cops showed up they'd try to arrest me. "How big a blast do you think that was?"

"Nuclear bombs aren't small," Friday said, like he was suddenly an expert filled with completely useless, vague advice.

"This one was," I said, coughing. How bad would this stuff hurt my lungs? *Wolfe*— I said.

You should hurry out of the cloud. I'm working as hard as I can but you're absorbing a lot of rads, and it took me enormous exposure

181

over several years to build up immunity to them. You don't want to go through that, trust me.

"But nukes are big," Friday said, as I talked to Wolfe in my head. "I mean, they destroy cities."

"Not all of them," I said. "In the fifties, America built ones that were meant to be deployed in artillery strikes in case the Soviet Union came roaring through the Fulda Gap in Germany. They were supposed to be used to irradiate the area, make it impassable to stymie a Russian invasion because the Red Army was way, way bigger than what we had to defend with. They called it the Davy Crockett system, and the projectiles were—I dunno, I guess it's been a while since I read about it, but I wanna say a little bigger than a backpack."

"Well, how big was this thing?" Friday asked.

I tried to think back as I shoved him again through the haze of smoke and dust that completely clouded what had been a clear sky when we'd stepped out of the Mexican restaurant. I was feeling a little woozy, and I doubt it was because of that one margarita and the Patron chaser. "Really small. Maybe a little bigger than a baseball. And I don't think it made much of a bang, comparatively speaking."

"Maybe it was just a regular bomb, then," Friday said as we stumbled clear of the cloud at last, coughing and half-blind. My eyes were burning, and I heard somebody say the same thing I'd thought when I first came back to my senses in the cloud:

"... she just blew up East LA!"

The words broke through the desire to cough, the urge to just lie down for a while and let Wolfe work his detoxifying magic until I felt better, but instead I turned around to look at the mess we'd left behind.

A very clear mushroom cloud rose up several stories into the air, the size of a skyscraper plopped right here in the middle of the street, and crowned with a mighty bloom that was already extending out for miles in every direction.

"Nope," I said, feeling my heart sink. "That was not a conventional bomb. Come on." I snatched up Friday's arm and took care to place his tattered shirt between my fingers and his skin.

He didn't struggle. "Wait—we have to leave now?"

I bit my lip as we rose into the air. "Yep. A nuke going off in a major metropolitan area is the sort of thing that tends to draw attention, see. And I don't want to be around for the fallout—literal or metaphorical."

Friday went kind of quiet for a minute. "What do you mean?"

I took a minute to answer, and when I did, it was very curt, because I was trying—really hard—not to choke up. "They're going to blame me for this."

37.

Augustus

"Sienna ..." Reed said quietly as we watched her fly off into the sky on the feed from that pedestrian's phone camera, "... what have you done?"

"This is like Eden Prairie all over again," Scott whispered, "but so much worse." The mushroom cloud was billowing out from ground zero, spreading radiation all over East LA.

"She didn't do this," Cassidy said, shaking her head and tapping the screen.

"There's a massive nuclear explosion and Sienna just flew off from the middle of it," Reed said, hand over his mouth as he spoke, as though he could mask his emotions. He sounded drained. "How is this not her?"

"You said it yourself," Cassidy said, then waited, as though we lackwits would just get it.

Then I got it. "Wait, this was a *nuclear* explosion—"

Jamal went next. "Sienna can't go nuclear—" He pivoted on Cassidy. "You're sure this was a radiological event?" She nodded, but if she was pleased we'd all caught up to her line of reasoning, she didn't show it. "So if she didn't ... what happened here?"

"Someone she pissed off, clearly," Scott said, prompting all of us to look at him. He flushed, his ruddy complexion going dark red. "What? If someone launches a nuke at you, there's gotta be a reason for it, and let's just state a fact we all know—she's really good at bringing out the ragemonster in people."

"You just think this is part of the mess she's in with Friday?" Jamal asked.

"Look at the size of this mushroom cloud," Cassidy said, already back to look at the first feed, the one from US Bank Tower in downtown LA. The cameraman was moving around a little, and she hissed in impatience until it steadied, then froze the frame before it moved again. "The detonation? It was small. Like, really small. Smaller than anything in the US strategic arsenal. This is small even for a tactical nuke."

"That cloud is like fifty stories high ..." Reed said.

"Yes, the cloud is," Cassidy said, "but the actual damage you can see is incredibly tiny. I mean, if you look here," and she pulled up the footage from the other pedestrian, the one that had caught Sienna coming out of the cloud, "you can see the Mexican restaurant in the distance is still standing. Nuke goes off next to a building, it tends to lose structural integrity, you know what I mean?"

"Sure, like in Hiroshima and Nagasaki, where it flattened shit all around," Jamal said, leaning in.

"But here," Cassidy said, pointing the screen, "I mean—I doubt this restaurant was much to look at to begin with, but now—the exterior facade's a mess, the windows are busted, but architecturally ... it doesn't have a list, the roof doesn't seem to have blown off ... this bomb was small. Tiny." She leaned back in her chair, which threatened to swallow her minuscule frame, and she chewed her lip as she processed her way through what she saw on the screen. "Smaller than this country has ever made."

"So ... is there a country that has made bombs this small?" I asked.

She looked up at me and blinked a couple times. "I don't know. I mean, I guess I could spend a few minutes reading and finding out, but ..." She shrugged.

"But what?" Reed asked, looking like he was barely keeping himself from losing control right here.

"But it's the sort of thing I'd need to get paid for," Cassidy said. "I mean, I could get to doctorate level mastery of nuclear physics in an hour or so, but … my time's valuable, and this isn't really your case, is it?" She looked at Reed knowingly.

His jaw went so tight an ant couldn't have crawled through the gaps in his teeth, and I could tell he was working hard not to threaten her. "My sister just damned near got nuked by someone."

"Probably this Greg Vansen she's been after all day," Cassidy said matter-of-factly.

"Do you know anything about him?" I asked.

"Nope." Disinterest flooded out of her. "And I won't learn or search for free, either. Business is business, boys, and business—is booming." She favored us with a disingenuous smile. "I've given you about two million bucks' worth of my time for free already, for … old times' sake," she gave Reed an almost apologetic look. "Past history and amends and all that. But … I'm all about the future now, so … unless you guys want to hire me, you need to head out." She glanced back at the screen. "As interesting as this is, I'm about to have to shut it off and get back to the sort of work that clients pay me for."

"I know someone who might be able to get us some answers," Jamal said, like he was laboring to tear us away from Cassidy before something went really wrong here. I got the feeling he was reading Reed pretty accurately on that.

"Good luck finding her," Cassidy said with a smug smirk that reminded me she was one of Sienna's biggest pain-in-the-ass villains not so very long ago.

Jamal froze, but the rest of us turned to stare at him. "Who's she talking about?" I asked.

"No one." The answer came way, way too quickly to be convincing. Also, he had, "LIAR," written all over his face.

"ArcheGrey1819," Cassidy said.

"The cyber terrorist?" Scott asked, looking from Jamal to Cassidy in open-mouthed disbelief. "Are you serious? You want us to work with a criminal?"

"Says the guy who just finished running a manhunt with my sister," Reed said.

"That was different," Scott snapped, "Sienna is

innocent."

"As much fun as it is to watch you boys argue," Cassidy said, "I've got work to do. If you decide to come back with a big wallet, please call ahead or at least ring the bell next time." She made a little wave with her fingers, one at a time. "Stairs are in the corner. I'll close the trapdoors so you don't accidentally go for a repeat of your earlier drop." Then she made a shooing sign, and with Reed as our guide, clearly boiling over with a desire to reply to Scott's comment, we walked up the stairs in a silent line and out the front door.

Just as we came out, a window and door repair company van was pulling up to the curb to park. Reed took one look at it and seethed audibly. "She saw us coming a mile away."

"That's what happens you've got someone able to tap your communications," Jamal said, thankfully diverting the conversation into this new direction instead of back to Sienna, which sounded like it was poised to be a contentious topic for at least some of us.

"Yo," I said, sidling up to Jamal as we crossed the lawn and the repair guy sauntered past us on his way up to the front door, "you really trying to date a terrorist?"

"I'm not trying to—" Jamal got the same look he used to wear when Mama would humiliate him by calling out something obvious he was hiding, like the time that he broke my Stretch Armstrong and wouldn't cop to it. "I don't even really know her, okay? I was just putting her out there as someone who's better than me and cheaper than Cassidy."

"Uh huh." I didn't want to call him on it right then, because that was more a job for our mother. I was quite content to take the long way around, because Jamal clearly had some feelings going on there, a little story in the background that had me wondering.

"Don't act like you know what I'm thinking," Jamal said, looking at me hard as I came around to the driver's side and got in.

"Man, I didn't even know the last time you had a girlfriend until after she'd been dead for years," I said, slamming the door behind me a little harder than I meant to. "You're right; I don't know what you're thinking. Like, a lot of the time, and not just when you're programming or doing computer wizardry."

"This is touching," Reed said, "but why don't you drive now and have a deep, personal family conversation later?" He'd gotten in the back with Scott. The two of them had been bickering about something between themselves until Reed had leaned up and said that.

"Why don't you," I said, turning around and letting him have a piece of the irritation that had been building up in me since I'd gotten dragged into a dank, concrete basement and wrapped up in inescapable plastic bonds with the threat of beheading due to his "leadership," "get a double deluxe bottle of SuperEnema and use it to cleanse yourself of whatever bullshit you've got up your ass with regards to your sister."

That quieted the car down real fast.

I watched Reed in the rearview, and it only took me a second to realize I'd probably stepped real, real far out of line in my anger. "Reed, I'm so—"

"Just drive," he said, and settled back in his seat. After a moment of silence I pushed the button to start the car, and drove off.

We made it the whole way back to the agency in pained silence.

38.

Greg

The phone rang when Greg was over Chicago, close enough to the ground that he felt comfortable taking the call without worrying that it was too high in the air to go unnoticed by anyone monitoring calls above 10,000 feet. He started to answer it without thinking, assuming it must be Morgan or else McGarry, but when he looked down, he saw that it said something quite different.

Sam Bennett.

Greg shifted at the controls of the SR-71. It felt like he'd been flying most of the day, which was, perhaps, not much of an exaggeration given that he'd crisscrossed the country several times in the last twenty four hours. He hesitated. What could Sam want? They hadn't spoken in years, not since they'd dissolved their partnership.

Well, there was only one way to find out.

"Hello, Sam," Greg said, clipped, but trying to put his best professional spin on it.

"Gregggggg," Sam let his name drag in an enthusiastic, faux-friendly sort of way. Sam had a natural drawl that he seemed to turn up in moments when he was trying to be charming. It would have been a more appropriate greeting for two old acquaintances at a bar than for a phone call between two former work colleagues where a modicum of professionalism might be expected. "What did you do, little buddy?"

189

"I don't know what you mean," Greg sniffed. How much ruder could he get, launching into his accusation that way?

"You just nuked East LA," Sam said, laughing all the while. "I mean, I'm assuming that was you given that the explosion was so small. Could have been a mouse with a grudge, I guess. Anyone else would have let a nuke go off full force, but … they're saying someone evacuated people—physically dragged them away from the scene, as if by magic." He laughed again. "I gotta say, I wouldn't have bothered with that, either. I would have dropped that nuke full force and let it take care of my Sienna Nealon problem."

"I don't have a Sienna Nealon problem," Greg said. "I never had a contract on her."

"Oh, so it was for the big guy that was with her?"

Greg froze. How did he know that? "Yes," he said slowly …

"Yeah, they both walked out of that fallout cloud, Greg," Sam said, still laughing uncontrollably, but apparently in control of himself enough to squeeze the words out without much difficulty. "I'm afraid your little gambit failed to pay off, amigo. The only thing you killed today was that Mexican restaurant's margarita sales. I'll give you some credit there, though, little buddy—no one else I know would have bothered to steal a nuke, weaken it down, and then throw it at the world's most dangerous meta—well, second most dangerous, next to me, you know. No offense."

Greg answered out of habitual politeness. "None taken."

"I couldn't believe it was you, though," Sam said. "I mean, I knew you had one of those old nukes lying around in your collection, but … man! Never figured you'd use that sucker. Kudos."

"I wasn't trying to impress you by using it," Greg snapped. Was it possible for the man to even talk without being condescending?

"Yeah, you were looking to kill your target, but you whiffed wide on that one, pal, because they are still sucking air. Hey, who gave you that contract? Was it your man McGarry? Because if he saw that and is okay with the collateral damage—I mean, damn, he needs to talk to me and

I definitely need to talk to him because we can come to a working agreement. I could get behind some mass destruction, if you know what I mean. I've been doing this all wrong if that sort of shit is okay!"

Greg ground his teeth. Sam was always like this, no restraint, no preparation, no professionalism. "Sometimes things go wrong. This was obviously one of those cases."

"Hey, I thought preparation was the key to keeping things neat." Now Sam was needling him with his own words and ethos. "I'm just joshing you, little buddy. I would have thought that thing would have killed anybody but a cockroach meta. Still ... ballsy move. Nicely played. It's just your bad luck it didn't work out." He chuckled again. "But I got to tell you, man ... the things we can do ... and you play it the way you do. All reserved, taking forever. I really didn't think a nuke would fit into your stodgy old pattern there, Greg. You might just be heading for a working renaissance there, good buddy. Dropping a nuke in LA. I am so proud of you right now, you have no idea—"

A beep cut him off, and Greg looked at the number for the incoming call that had interrupted Sam. "I have to let you go." He glanced up; he was still six minutes or so from final approach. "I have to take another call."

"Catch you later, big shooter." Sam laughed as Greg hit the button to flip to the other call.

"Mr. McGarry," Greg began.

"Was that you?" McGarry did not sound like his usual self, sedate, controlled, only occasionally forceful. His voice was high. "In LA, was that you?"

There was a pause, a brief quiet, and Greg assessed the situation; McGarry did not seem pleased. Still, it did not occur to Greg to lie in this instance. "Yes sir, that was me, if you're talking about the ... event."

"Are you kidding me?" McGarry's voice went higher and tighter, and a strange noise like straining plastic made Greg wondering if he was gripping the phone tightly. "You dropped an atomic bomb in Los Angeles? To kill your target?"

"A very small one, but yes," Greg said. "I have, uh, heard

reports that the target survived—"

"Let me confirm it for you—yes, Percy Sledger is still alive." McGarry voice was clipped; he was clearly restraining himself by only a razor-thin margin. "Some dumbass posted a video to YouTube of Sledger stumbling out of the cloud with Sienna Nealon. What the hell is he doing with Nealon? You didn't tell me that the two of them were working together."

"I was trying to handle it internally," Greg said. This was just professionalism, not running to your employer whenever a contract went slightly wrong. He didn't bother to mention that McGarry had withheld a crucial fact of his own, because it wouldn't have improved the tone of the conversation. "You gave me an explicit order to kill Sledger's girlfriend—"

"Sienna Nealon is not Sledger's damned girlfriend!"

Greg blinked. "Yes, she's made that completely clear."

McGarry seethed in silence for a moment and Greg let him gather his thoughts. When he spoke again, it was no more collected. "Have you been operating under the assumption I wanted her dead all day?"

"Yes sir."

"Well, I don't," McGarry said, and that raised Greg's eyebrows. "I want the exact opposite, in fact, so let me say this explicitly—I do not want Sienna Nealon dead. If I'd known it was her, I would have told you to hit Sledger from a mile away, where she didn't have a hope of seeing you or a prayer of stopping you."

"She's doggedly defending Sledger," Greg said. "None of my distance measures would have effectively worked if you were looking to minimize damage to nearby targets."

"Clearly not," McGarry said in a dry fury. "This is the second time I've had to call you in a day to deal with a screwup. Greg, until now you've been our best but I'm beginning to think you might have met your match."

"I'm not outmatched yet," Greg said stiffly. "I just need to—"

"If you had to deploy a nuclear weapon to get the damned job of killing one Hercules done, I think you're out of your league," McGarry said. Now he was calm, lethally so.

"Consider the contract canceled. I'm handing it off to someone else, and I'm going to be re-evaluating your future work with our firm very carefully. I'm not so sure our relationship should continue based on the exceptionally bad judgment you've exhibited today. We wanted things done quietly. You've done the opposite."

"I've tried to simply do the job assigned—"

"Goodbye, Greg," McGarry said, and he hung up.

"That prig," Greg said, once he was sure the connection was dead. His hands were clenched again on the stick, his breath coming in furious starts, as though he were developing asthma on the spot. To lose this contract ...

McGarry had been a steady employer, keeping him busy for the last couple of years. He'd come to rely on that regular infusion of cash. It was the bedrock of his life at this point ...

He was still three minutes from his landing, and the only consolation, he supposed, was that he at least had the luxury of hiding out in the shop until he'd managed to find a way to put a positive spin on this devastating loss to Morgan.

39.

Sienna

I sat on the couch in my safe house—an actual house, this time—up on the hill in Juneau, Alaska, and pumped my iron furiously as I watched the cable news cover the incident in East LA ad infinitum.

Sienna … Harmon said as I completed my two thousandth lift. The dumbbells were about as good as I could have asked for. Clearly my minions who were responsible for setting up these safe houses were following specifications, which was good, because I needed failure in that regard right now like I needed another kick in the teeth.

"I don't want to talk about it," I said, continuing to pound out my reps. There was no point in discussion, after all. East Los Angeles had just taken a nuke in the middle of a public street because of me. There wasn't much to say after that.

Sienna … Gavrikov said.

"You're the last person who should be saying anything to me right now," I threw back at Gavrikov pointedly. "Remember a town called Glencoe, Minnesota? That used to exist before you decided to annihilate it into oblivion to prove a point to me and Old Man Winter about how badass you are?"

Then I am the perfect person to carry this message, Gavrikov said, apparently finding his courage. *You cannot control the acts of every madman to walk the earth.*

Also, Zack said cautiously, apparently more worried about pissing me off than Gavrikov was, *this assassin of yours went to some pretty serious lengths to try and minimize civilian casualties. No one died, so …*

Why are you acting like the entire city went up? Eve threw in helpfully. There was a pause as my souls gave her baleful glances. *What? We were all thinking it.*

I pumped my iron in the silence, driven by the anger that was rolling its way through my veins. "Because dammit, Phillips had stopped the shit. Or at least the shit had stopped. No one was chasing me anymore. I was sitting in my safe houses and I was feeling—safe." My arms collapsed, maxed out from however many thousand reps of five hundred pounds, and I barely got them to the ground before my shoulders started quivering. I'd been treating this like a cardio workout, and I'd found my upper limit of endurance.

The US Government doesn't just forget about its fugitives, Harmon said.

"Yeah, but the heat had died down," I said, sinking back into the overstuffed couch, which was layered in a corduroy upholstery. The safe house was bare bones, not a single piece of décor on the walls, which was how I liked them. "There were websites out there where they were calling me a folk hero, uploading footage of me trying to save lives. I had my lawyers on appeals to clear my name."

I closed my eyes. "Now a nuclear bomb goes off in East LA, and everyone's blaming me for it—wrongly, I might add, but what the hell else is new? I'm back to square one. I'm the evil monster that you painted me to be, Harmon, and the damned chess board I've been playing trying to reverse that damage just got turned over on me. Now I have to pick up the pieces again, and I just—I don't—" I made a growling sound of frustration in the back of my throat. "The lawyers I hired through my bankers in Liechtenstein told me this could take years, trying to fight these warrants and charges. But I don't want to live like this for years." I put fingers in my hair and tugged at it, gently enough that no strands came out. "I've been on the run for six months and I'm so over this already. I just want my life back." That last bit came out as a whine, pathetic even to my ears. "I just want my life back," I pleaded again.

Be strong, Harmon said.

"I'm trying," I said, the weariness now settling in. Friday was sleeping in one of the bedrooms behind me, probably trying to detox the radiation out of his system by meta healing. "But I have to ask … why the hell am I doing this?"

It's your job, Zack said.

"Nice," I said. "Toss my own words back in my face like a grenade with the pin pulled."

You're working to beat the bad guys, Roberto Bastian said. *That's a noble effort.*

To protect the people, Gavrikov said.

"Someone dropped a nuke while trying to kill me," I said. "While trying to kill Friday. And if he hadn't cleared the area himself, there would have been mass casualties. I ask again, beyond the easy answers, guys—what am I doing? Is Friday really worth this much trouble?"

If you don't do this for the least liked among you, Bjorn said, stirring after watching all this argument unfold, *then … why bother for the greatest among you? Such inconsistency … it is a violation of principle, is it not?*

"Sonofa," I muttered. "Did I just get lectured on my principles by Bjorn?" No one answered. Maybe they were as stunned as I was. "I mean, really, guys … you have to admit, coming on this mission may have been my worst idea ever, and that's saying something, because it means it'd rate above walking into a bank in Florida without checking my corners, above trusting Old Man Winter, and above that time I pulled Clyde Clary's finger when he asked me to." I reached up and ran fingers across my sticky, sweaty forehead like a gentle caress. It was the closest I'd gotten to anyone touching me in a positive way in a long time. "Yeah, my principles … defending people, protecting the world … but at a time like this, I have to ask … what am I doing this for?"

Because you owe a debt, Wolfe said. *254 lives. And it can never be repaid.*

My scalp tingled at his words. "This is all your fault," I said. "Because, yeah … it always comes back to that."

Yes.

"And it always will, won't it?"

Yes, Wolfe said. *Now ... as Zollers would say ... get off your ass.*

I stood up. "You're not the boss of me. I'm taking positive action because sitting on this couch isn't going to get me closer to any of my goals, and it's not a positive coping strategy. Though the near infinite reps do help a little. Burn off some frustration and whatnot."

So ... Zack said, *what are you going to do?*

"I still have to figure out why Greg wants to kill Friday," I said, "and I need to figure out what his powers are, which will hopefully tell me how to stop him. If Friday has either answer, he's not telling me, which means I need to talk to someone who would know."

You're going to talk to his old girlfriend? Zack asked. *Chase?*

"Let's not do her the insult of calling her that without checking with her first," I said. "I mean, honestly, I could totally see Friday saying that about poor, unfortunate, innocent women that he has no relationship with at all, like some stranger off the street he thought was pretty. 'Oh, she's my girlfriend, and we totally banged or whatever like a million times.' Because that's just kind of who he is." I paused. "Wait, why am I trying to save his life again?"

Principle, Bjorn said quietly.

"Dammit." I hung my head, the weariness of not sleeping in well over a day catching up to me. "That was a nice speech, Bjorn. Where'd you pick that one up?"

The Norseman took a minute to answer. *It was something my father used to tell me when he was ... displeased with what he considered my moral failings. "Principle is our anchor in times of storm," he used to say. I ... rarely listened.*

"Not a dumb guy, that Odin," I said. "All right. I'm back in the game. We need to find Chase and talk to her." I felt an overpowering desire to sit down again on the couch, and I did. Action could wait until tomorrow; it was nearing midnight here in Juneau, after all, which meant the rest of the US, including wherever Chase presumably was, would be sleeping right now. "Tomorrow. First thing tomorrow."

Yes, Harmon said, it can wait a day. *You won't do anyone any favors rushing into this half asleep. You'll need your wits about you if you're going to understand your way through this.*

"Or you could just tell me," I said, "given that the stakes are super high now. People are throwing around nukes. It's never been more serious."

You need this, Harmon said. *You need to see your way through this.*

"You're just lucky no one died," I said. "How did you not see him coming?" I leaned back on the couch, laying my head against the armrest and kicking off my tennis shoes, putting my feet up on the other end.

I wasn't paying attention, Harmon said tightly. *Trust me … it won't happen again.*

"I hope it doesn't," I said, my eyes closing involuntarily. Holy hell, I was tired. Maybe just a quick nap …

I passed out on the couch without enough energy left to hold a single thought in my mind, drifting off into a weary, fitful sleep filled with nightmares of what could have been; of fire and thunder, the sounds of my failure.

Of a city dissolving under the endless force of a bomb.

40.

"So we charter planes again now, huh?" I asked as the Gulfstream rolled to the end of the runway at Eden Prairie airport and left the ground with a last, gentle shudder, the wing dipping slightly from the crosswind as we said goodbye to the earth and hurtled into the sky at over four hundred miles per hour.

"I could fly you all on the winds, if you'd like," Reed said, staring at a tablet with the data Cassidy had given us dumped on it. He looked like he was reading intently and didn't bother looking up at my question. "But there's a low-pressure system over the Dakotas that brought a ton of cold air with it, and I figured considering how much you whined last time you came down covered in frost, you might appreciate some insulation."

Nevada was the destination; it hadn't taken more than a few minutes debate to hammer out the plan, because just outside Vegas was where the factory producing the serums seemed to be located, at least based on what Cassidy had told us.

"It doesn't bother anyone else we're hinging our next move on something told to us by a woman who just bound and gagged me like something out of *Fifty Shades*?" I asked.

"She covered us in combustible sand and threatened to light us on fire," Scott said, motioning to Reed. "Your charming bindings retracted when asked; I still smell like whatever that crap was she nearly drowned me in." As if to illustrate his point, he gave his suit's lapel a sniff and made a face. "Trust me, this whole thing is bothering me."

"I'm just gonna say it, since I know we've all thought it at one time or another," Jamal said. "All this increased business flooding our agency coffers and making Ms. Estevez smile as she counts the dollars rolling in? It's all because these people from Revelen are making more metas and meta-criminals for us to deal with. I know it's the right thing to do, but ... are we cutting up our credit cards here?"

"I hadn't thought of that," Scott said dryly. "Probably because I've been too busy chasing after dangerous metas to think much at all."

"Even if we clean up the supply side of the meta production," Reed said, finally looking up from his tablet, "you have to believe we're going to spend some time rolling up the ones that are already out there. No, I'm not worried about business dying if we clean this mess up. Also," he said, turning his attention back to the screen, and becoming a bit arch, "it's the right thing to do."

"Shouldn't that have been your first answer?" I asked.

"It came last because it's most important," Reed said.

"What about Sienna's LA misadventure?" I asked. "What are we going to do about that?"

Reed's mouth formed a tight line, parting only when he spoke. "Nothing. We need to focus on our mission. We're not a support agency to Sienna, and we just got handed a big target. We go after them. Now. Besides, the FBI is not likely to listen to us if we stick our noses into that LA business."

"Yeah, we're more likely to get punched in said nose," Scott said. "Director Phillips is not a huge fan of ... uh ... any of us, so far as I know. Unless he's secretly a Jamal groupie."

"I have no groupies," Jamal said. "Mine is a sad, groupie-free life."

"Mama follows you on Twitter," I said. "She's kinda like a groupie for you."

"What? Mama doesn't have a Twitter account."

"Yes, she does," I said. "Started one two months ago."

Jamal's eyes got big, and he gulped silently. "Ohhhh … oh, shit."

"She's not going to like that kind of language," I said.

"Why do you think I just said it now?" Jamal asked. "She's probably built a list of every time I've sworn on Twitter, waiting to smack me upside the head with it when I get home next." He drew a deep breath. "Well, I guess I'm just going to have to miss Thanksgiving and Christmas for … uh … the next couple decades."

"Back to the topic," Reed said with thinly masked irritation, "Sienna's not our problem. Hopefully when or if the FBI dumps her phone logs, once they track things back to her, Jamal's calls and voicemails won't implicate us in any of this. As far as I'm concerned, beyond that … we have our own work to do. There's nothing we can do to help Sienna now, and … let's face it." He looked at each of us in turn, stone-faced to the point of causing me to worry, "She doesn't want our help anyway."

"She asks me for help all the time," Jamal said.

Reed's right eye fluttered slightly. "I meant in the fight. She regards you as support, and yeah, she'd ask you or J.J. for help all day when it comes to information. But when it comes to active danger …" He shook his head. "She'd go it alone all the way into death and ten miles beyond. Mark my words—when it comes to whatever she does next, Sienna's not going to be asking us for help, and on a legal basis, we shouldn't go out of our way to give it."

His bit said, Reed turned his attention back to his screen and used his fingers to scroll.

"Wow," I said quietly.

Reed looked up. "Do I even want to know what the 'wow' is for?"

"Was just thinking we've gone full circle," I said, "back to when I first met Sienna, and you two were so on the outs you'd barely speak to her."

His face went grey to match his stony facade. "You don't know what you're talking about this time, Augustus."

"All I know is what I see," I said.

"Like I said …" Reed stared me down, and I finally

looked away because I didn't want to have a staring contest with my boss right now, "… you don't know what you're talking about this time. You don't know how I feel, and I'm not sharing, so butt out and let's focus on doing our jobs."

Once he'd spoken, Reed looked back to the tablet again, but this time, as I watched, his eyes didn't seem to be skimming the page, reading. Instead they stared at a fixed spot in place, just past the tablet, and didn't really move for a while as he got lost in thought, and none of the rest of us dared interrupt him.

41.

Greg

There weren't really any good ways to spin this, Greg decided as he sat in the shop, trying to come up with a way to explain that his number-one source of income over the last several years had come to a very abrupt stop. It wasn't even easy for him to explain to himself, but it was a fact that could not be ignored.

It was a mark of the moment that in spite of what he'd done, he wasn't thinking about how he'd dropped the bomb in LA—no one had died, after all, and the property loss was trifling, comparatively.

No, Greg's mind was on the impending loss to him. Even he could recognize, albeit dimly, that his fears were perhaps overblown. Yet his lifestyle changing, evaporating— perhaps he would have to turn to thieving in a very real way instead of simply stealing from the military as support for what he deemed his "legitimate" profession—caused his stomach to sink, even as he was aware that his fears were small in scale indeed compared to the more "real" concerns of others the world over.

Thinking about things in that way, though, did not seem to help.

It was quite dark when he entered the house, leaving behind his workshop. He did so as quietly as he could, though he could hear the TV playing in the living room, where Morgan was surely watching some overly dramatic program. He still wasn't entirely decided on what to tell her or how, which was a strange position for a man who prided himself on preparation.

"Hello," he said as he passed under the hallway arch into the living room. It was furnished tastefully, white cloth couch and loveseat with a glass-top rectangular coffee table in the middle. The table's wooden legs were an exquisite maple, the sort of thing he'd been able to easily afford before, without consideration.

Now, though, who knew? Maybe his next furniture would be made out of presswood. Ugh. And they'd live in a trailer in a school district without a Chinese language immersion program ...

Greg shuddered involuntarily and looked at Morgan. Her face was ashen, a whiter shade of pale than he remembered seeing her since she'd been in labor and had begun to bleed more than she was supposed to. "What?" he asked.

She blinked as though coming out of a trance, and her head jerked slightly as she turned to look at him. "You ... you did this, didn't you?"

"Did wh ...?" He didn't even get it out before he turned to look at the TV. It wasn't a dramatic scripted show at all.

She was watching the news.

Live from LA.

"I ... no one was hurt," Greg said.

"You dropped a nuclear bomb on East LA, Greg," Morgan said, narrowing her eyes at him as a look of horror unfurled on her pale face.

"A very, very small one," he said. "I estimate the yield at no more than—"

"What were you trying to do?" she asked, voice a hoarse whisper.

"My job," he said. "I was simply trying to fulfill my current contract—"

"Your current contract is insane," Morgan said, "if it requires you to drop a nuclear bomb on a US city!"

"It was so small it might as well have been conventional," Greg snapped. "It didn't knock down a single building or kill a single person. You're buying into this idiotic hype—"

"They're saying the area will be radioactive for—"

"I very much doubt that's accurate, but if true, that's the first time their so-called science reporters will have been right in quite some time. And in any case," Greg said, taking a deep breath, "we have a bigger problem."

Morgan's frown relaxed instantly. Now her brow went in the opposite direction, rising toward her hairline. "A bigger problem than that you just nuked a city?"

"It was not—" Greg almost exploded but caught himself just a step short. He seethed quietly for a moment, and Morgan, wisely, let him. "I was trying to use the heat energy from the fission reaction to kill my target. I didn't particularly need the nuclear component and certainly not the radiation. Perhaps I would have been better served using a napalm compound precisely targeted, but that's neither here nor there." Morgan was watching him like he was an invasive species that had wandered into the living room. "Mr. McGarry is indicating that he perhaps wishes to cancel our business arrangement—"

"So you used a nuke in LA and you lost your contract for it," Morgan said quietly. "Wow."

Greg stood in the archway, trying to decide what the look on Morgan's face meant. "I don't think you fully appreciate—"

"You're in no position to lecture me about what I appreciate," Morgan said coldly. "Not after what you did tonight."

Greg's face tightened. "I did my job—"

"Your job is murderous and evil—"

"You used to be good at it yourself—"

"—and even your murderous and evil employer thought what you did tonight was too much—"

"No, he was only upset that I could have killed Sienna Nealon. He didn't seem particularly worried over the fate of East Los Angeles."

"I don't even know you anymore," Morgan whispered. "When we worked together, you would never have considered doing this. You had that—that thing—"

"It was a bomb, Morgan. A fission explosive."

"You told me you'd taken it as a tribute to your father," Morgan said, rising off the couch. "You told me you took it from the government because he'd had a hand in creating it. It was supposed to be your touchstone to him—not some weapon you deployed when you got sick of trying to generate a body count in a conventional way—"

"You seem to think I've lost control. I haven't—"

"Then you are even more gone than I thought you were, if you think this—this metahuman leap beyond the pale—"

"I'm doing what I have to do!" Greg said and lashed out at the archway. His fist clipped the plaster and sent a shower of white chips flying back into the hallway. "Why can't you see that? I'm sorry I'm not gentle enough to take up the nurturing role with Eddie and his fragile little ego and insecurities the way you have!" He was shouting at the top of his voice now. "I am the man! I am charged with providing for this family, and I have one path with which to do that—"

"You are so full of it." Morgan's eyebrows were arched downward, eyes themselves dark like stormy skies. "You do it this way because you like the work. You've always liked the work. You loved it when we worked together. You even liked working with Sam, though God knows why. You only dropped him when it became obvious that he couldn't control himself, that he liked the killing part too much. Well, I think you might have gone his way, Greg—"

"Don't say that."

"—and I'm amazed I've never seen it before," Morgan said. "How could I not have? I've been thinking we were just growing apart, that I was going in a different moral direction, that you were staying the same. But you're not. You're getting worse. Wilder, somehow—"

"This is one isolated instance, in which I am up against the most powerful metahuman in the world—"

"—and less judicious. You're not preparing, you're flying off the handle. Using a nuke? Doesn't reflect on properly preparing for the threat, Greg. It's a reflection of a mind so desperate to win that you would throw your father's only legacy away in order to—"

"Only legacy? I have more of them," Greg said.

That stopped Morgan in her tracks. She paused, standing there, swaying behind the coffee table like a tree in the wind. "When did you take them?"

"I don't know. A year ago. Maybe three," Greg said, placing his hand on the shattered archway, feeling the cracks in the plaster where he'd lashed out and broke through it. It felt a little like rocks that had been busted open. "They were being decommissioned. It seemed a waste—"

"You didn't even tell me." Cold accusation.

"You didn't like the one," Greg said, "I can imagine how you would have felt about thirty."

"Because normal people don't store nuclear weapons anywhere near their children!" Morgan said, voice starting low but rising in intensity.

"Please," Greg said, "you know as well as I do that they're absolutely no threat to Eddie or yourself, even assuming they all went off, which is improbable to the tune of several decimal places. You're more likely to get killed by North Koreans bombing Chicago than by my little stockpile."

"What are you becoming?" Morgan asked.

"I am what I have always been," Greg said. "What you used to be."

"Then I never saw you clearly before," Morgan said. "Maybe you're right. Maybe we were once both like this. I don't think so, but … maybe. The difference is, I don't want to be like you. Not anymore, not ever. But you … you don't want to change, either. Not when you—when you do things like *this*," she had so much anger in her voice, "not when you crush Eddie the way you have been …"

"I'm not cr …" Greg didn't bother to finish the sentence. On a level of intellectual honesty …

… He found he couldn't.

"Even you know it's true," Morgan said, but there was no satisfaction of rightness in the way she said it. "You can't bring yourself to argue."

"I have room to improve—" Greg said lamely.

"You're destroying this family," Morgan said quietly, her voice gaining strength. "You're destroying us. I don't even know you anymore." Her eyes met his, and there was a hostility there that he'd never seen from her before, at least not pointed at him. "Get out."

Her last words were low and angry coming from deep within. He stared at her, and a million responses flashed across his mind.

You're wrong.

You used to be like me.

I'm not as bad as you say I am.

Things aren't as bad as you're letting on.

You've been watching too much news.

You're poisoned against me.

Eddie is fine.

… You've become a monster.

The last one stuck on his lips, hollow in his ears, a small voice within speaking to him like a stone wedged in the valve of his heart. It hurt in a way Greg could scarcely recall feeling, and it paired well with the pit in his stomach.

"I never meant to hurt you," he said, and looked toward the stairs. Somehow he knew—

Eddie was standing there, tears glinting on his face in the darkness. His shoulders were hunched back, fearful, as though he were waiting for Greg to strike at him.

But Greg had never hit him. Not once. The way he'd struck at the boy was deeper, somehow, less obvious. Maybe more painful; it was hard to say.

He looked back to Morgan and saw that same muted, horrified look. He felt … small. In a way that, ironically, he had never felt before. He wished he was smaller still, small enough to escape their notice, and the desire to retreat, to run away from this, his greatest failure, won out—

And Greg turned and left, halting steps carrying him back toward his workshop with uncertainty, wondering if he would ever feel welcome—or as if he even belonged—in his own home again.

42.

Sienna

I woke up on the couch to the sound of the TV playing at probably level one of fifty, so muted that only a meta could have heard what was being said on it. As I slipped into a dim consciousness, I became aware that the sun was up outside, shining faintly through the thick, yellowed window shades like light through construction paper. My mouth was dry and cottony, like I was working my way through a hangover even though I hadn't had a drop to drink last night. My shoulders were killing me, which was a thing that should not have happened with Wolfe on the job—

Sorry, Wolfe said. *Working on it.*

My shoulders unkinked, the healing power running through me and restoring vitality to my weary limbs. I felt a little of that morning weakness in my hands, though it faded quickly. Even weakened, my hands were probably still strong enough to break a few boulders. I clenched a fist with my right hand, then the left, and wondered what that crunching noise was, because it sounded like somebody else actually was breaking boulders—

I sat up to find Friday sitting at the table in the corner of the room, munching a bowl of cereal. He ate quite daintily, like he was trying to show off his table manners. Under other circumstances, it would have seemed odd, but given I was a fugitive on the run while trying to save him from a relentless assassin, Friday's delicate mouthfuls of cereal took a distant

209

backseat to nearly getting nuked last night. Strange days.

"Hey," he said, barely turning his head to acknowledge my wakeup. "I saved you some Basic 4."

"Thanks," I said, massaging my neck, not because it hurt, but because my fingers kneading the muscle felt soooo good. When no one can touch you without losing their soul, sometimes it's easy to forget how nice human touch feels. "You know, for saving me my own cereal." I yawned and sat up, glancing at the TV.

Predictably, it was all still coverage of my night in LA, a very serious news reporter standing in front of the scene with a yellow radiation suit covering most of his body and a slightly nervous look on his face. "—still have no idea of the whereabouts of Sienna Nealon, though the FBI is said to be more aggressively stepping up their hunt for her."

"Oh, that's good," I said, stifling another yawn, "because I'd hate to think they were just sitting around being lazy asses given everything they've done to me up to this point. Hunting me with drones and satellites and F-22s and metahuman tactical teams from Eastern Europe and whatnot."

That was me, Harmon said. *Without me, they probably won't use the military against you. Probably.*

"It doesn't really matter," I said, "since my current opponent has attacked me with a Comanche helicopter, an F-35B, an M2 machine gun, and a nuclear bomb so far. It's like getting hunted by the military, but without any rules of engagement."

"The good news is," Friday said, "there's only one other RAH-66 Comanche in existence, so if you can wipe that out, you won't have to worry about those anymore." He said that shit with a straight face, munching on his cereal.

"Yes," I said, trying to contain my sarcasm and oh, so failing, "but then he can just switch down to—what's the next step down in assault helicopters? The AH-64 Apache? And there are probably thousands of those?"

How do you know these military vehicle designations? Harmon asked. *I never paid attention to that and I was the Commander-in-Chief.*

"My mother made me study every major weapons system and all the firearms employed by every military around the world," I said. "It was part of my social studies and self-defense curriculum."

"Neat-o," Friday said, pausing with the spoon almost at his lips, milk dripping down into the bowl. "I bet that beat the hell out of my boring-ass World Studies course. And gym class."

"Maybe," I conceded, looking back to the TV. The chyron at the bottom was predictable, too: SIENNA NEALON TOPS FBI MOST WANTED LIST AFTER NUCLEAR INCIDENT IN LOS ANGELES. Big letters. Small minds. "Do you think they've noticed that I don't have the ability to irradiate an area?" I snorted mirthlessly, because inside I felt like I was dying. "Not that anyone cares at this point."

"Are you feeling sorry for yourself?" Friday was crunching cereal as he spoke, so I got a great view of him annihilating the multi-grain flakes and raisins as he chewed with his mouth open. "Because, if you ask me—"

"I didn't ask you," I said. "Because I was sure your opinion would be stupid."

Properly chastened, he shut his mouth and chewed. "Okay," he said, shrugged off my shot like it was nothing, and went back to watching the TV as the nervous anchor continued his report from the sight of his impending, lethal cancer—or at least that's how he made it sound. So brave, two hundred yards from ground zero on a nuke that didn't even bring down the building ten yards from where it went off. He probably wouldn't even see a dip in his fertility from this, though heaven knew the gene pool would have been better off if he had. Hell, he'd take more radiation from a dental X-ray.

"Regardless of the outcome," Mr. Serious TV reporter was saying, white with fear but talking in his I'M A SERIOUS PERSON TELLING YOU SOMETHING SUPER SERIOUS voice, "it's become very obvious that Sienna Nealon is a threat which simply can't be contained."

"Well, no shit," I said. "What was your first clue? That

the FBI has been hunting me for six months and come up with dick to show for it?"

"They're going to kill you," Friday said.

"They're going to try," I said tightly. Of course he was right, which was annoying. With Scott in charge of the investigation, and after my coercive truce with Phillips, things had reached a nice little detente. I wasn't going to go rubbing the government's nose in the fact that they weren't very good at tracking me or fighting me, and they weren't going to expend their limited resources in this ridiculous manhunt anymore. Or so it seemed.

And then along came this bullshit.

"I think the gloves are really coming off this time," Friday said. "Remember, I was on the team when Harmon ordered you killed. And don't get me wrong, we came after you hard. But coming after you that way and having you come back at us—it was kinda like a street fight. Short, brutal, over faster than you might think if you're up against Sienna Nealon."

"Thanks, I think?"

"But the way they're going to do this ... it'll be a steady series of fights like that," Friday said, crunching. "Over and over. Wearying. They'll just keep after you, no breaks, really, until they grind you down." He took a sloppy spoonful and it ran dribbling down his chin, which was covered in thin whiskers. "And then, sooner or later ... one of those first shots they take, the ones that come without warning ... it's gonna hit you. Maybe in the brain, make it over quick. Maybe in the spine, hobble you. Death by a thousand papercuts. But they'll get you. They'll make it as quick as they can. Merciful, almost, because they won't want to chance you healing. But that's how it's going to go."

I just sat there, realizing Friday had laid out a pretty reasonable scenario for the death of Sienna Nealon. It should have sent a little cold chill down my spine, but ... I'd recently looked death pretty hard in the face, and he was right about the weariness. Even after counseling with Zollers for the last couple months, and trying to take positive action to turn my life around ...

... There was only so much you could do as a wanted fugitive who was always on the run. My body was in shape, my mind was sharp, but ...

The US Government was going to hunt me and hunt me and hunt me now. Hunt me until I had nothing left or catch me unawares and splatter my brains in a wider dispersal than June Randall had done in that bank in Florida, really decorate a wall somewhere with them. And that'd be that. Maybe they'd hang a plaque to commemorate the spot where it happened.

"Shit," I said under my breath. These were grim thoughts, even for me, but I could almost feel the noose tightening around my neck. I looked back at the TV, where they'd switched to a panel discussion of how awful I was.

"—is just emblematic of how impotent our government's response is, in so many ways, to a critical threat to our security." This was coming from a congresswoman from New Jersey. "Seeing the FBI's hamfisted, Keystone Cops response to her is—well, it's very disheartening."

"I find myself agreeing with the congresswoman," a grinning pundit from DC said, dressed in a dapper suit with a purple pocket square jutting out of his left breast, all jaunty and flared. "If the FBI can't handle this very basic function, maybe we need to look at a new agency to handle this threat. Something more specialized, a sort of ATF for metahumans."

"You had one of those," I muttered under my breath. "And you decided to roll it into the FBI."

I decided that, actually, Harmon said. *Because the person who was running it was the very definition of a loose cannon.*

"Phillips was a loose cannon?" I cracked. I knew he meant me, though technically he was wrong.

"—but either way," the pundit was saying, "the response is, to use the congresswoman's phrase, impotent. It really is. Pathetic. The Gondry Administration may have inherited Harmon's weakness in this regard, but he could choose to right the ship here."

"Do you think," the anchor butted in, wearing what I assumed to be his version of a pensive look (but which I took as seriously constipated), "that perhaps President Gondry fears Sienna Nealon's response? Based on what is alleged to have happened to his predecessor?"

"You mean the rumors that Sienna Nealon killed President Harmon?" The pundit was still grinning while casually mentioning a presidential assassination, and I couldn't tell whether it was because he was enjoying the thought or because he was having fun tossing that out there.

The congresswoman looked like she'd caught some of the anchor's constipation. "We need to be a little careful about throwing that accusation around. 'Alleged' is the right word—"

"Oh, come on, Jane," the pundit said, still grinning, "why are we tiptoeing around this? Everyone knows that Sienna Nealon had some kind of hand in President Harmon's disappearance. She is an active threat to the safety of this country, our people and our very democracy." I almost had to admire the casual way he pronounced me a dire threat to every damned thing while still smiling.

"He seems pleased with himself," Friday said.

"Yeah, almost like he's not actually worried about me swooping down and Harmon-ing him," I said. I looked at the name at the bottom of the screen: Russ Bilson.

That guy, Harmon said. *Ugh.*

Ugh? I asked. *Why, ugh?*

He's a party functionary, Harmon said. *I inherited him from my predecessor. He gladhanded donors during the campaign, and got hired to do some policy work in the background of the administration. I showed him the door when I took over and started setting up my own team.*

So you know this douche? I asked.

Never met him, Harmon sniffed. *Too low on the ladder. Not worth my time.*

"—but what the Congresswoman is not saying," Russ Bilson, still grinning, said, "is that while they can't build the case, every major government agency knows that Nealon did it. Building a case against a meta who can fly and crash through walls and kill with a touch is a lot harder than busting some punk with a gun who held up a liquor store. So they may not be prepared to call it, because the evidence is lacking, but I'm telling you—serious people in the government know she murdered President Harmon. It happened. We may never know exactly how it happened, but my sources assure me it did. No doubt in their minds."

"That's stunning, if true," the anchor said, still serious and needing to poop. "What do you suppose the motive—I mean, what do your sources say the motive was for this action?"

"It seems pretty obvious to anyone with a brain," Russ Bilson said, so smug I wanted to slap all the teeth out of him. "Harmon was spearheading a manhunt for Nealon. She reacted as we've seen her react on any number of occasions—or overreact—and she went after what she perceived to be the source of her problems. And, honestly, she might have been very savvy in doing so, because since President Gondry took the oath, I think we can all agree that the effort to hunt her down has been halfhearted at best. Certainly not the response we'd expect for a multiple murderer and suspected presidential assassin who has just now gone and perpetrated a nuclear attack on one of our foremost cities—"

"Oh, you can stick your crooked, speculative head right up your ass," I said, snatching up the remote and clicking the power button so hard the plastic cracked a little. I did that sometimes—or worse—when things got heated on TV shows where I was the subject.

Friday had stopped crunching his cereal. He picked up the box and poured himself another, doused it with milk in the silence, then stuck his spoon in like he was about to dig a grave or something, leaving it sticking up slightly until it started to sag down. "This stuff really gets to you, doesn't it? People talking crap about you on TV and the internet?"

"Congratulations on having eyes," I said, fuming.

"Okay," he said. "You know you didn't nuke LA. You know you didn't murder Harmon in cold blood."

"Yeah. And?"

"So …" He picked up the spoon, but cradled it in his hand, not bringing it closer to his mouth, like it was in a

215

holding pattern. I could almost sense the flakes turning soggy. "Why does it bother you so much?"

"Because now everyone thinks I did," I said. Duh. Obvious. He didn't seem to get it, so I added, "Because perception is reality."

He shoved a spoonful in his mouth and then talked around it again. Gross. "No it isn't. Reality is reality. Just because I perceive pi is 8.9 instead of 3.14 blah blah blah, it doesn't make it so."

I looked at Friday, thinking … he seemed slightly smarter right now than he usually did. He was also deflated, no hint of the usual bulk, and I wondered, not for the first time, if his brainpower suffered when he used his powers. It would make a lot of sense, actually.

I could have pointed out to him that after his last couple of farfetched stories, he was the last person who should be lecturing me on reality, but …

Damn. He was right. Sort of.

He was also back to casually eating his cereal, as though he'd forgotten we were talking. "It's because I feel like … the world is against me, I guess." He looked up, stopping his eating again, so I took it as a sign to go on. "It's not easy to live knowing everyone hates you."

"Not everyone," he said.

"No, not absolutely everyone," I said. "But things like this don't help. I mean, I'm getting the blame for this thing, and that can't make people feel warmer and fuzzier toward me. It's a lie, but it fits their perception of the truth, so … boom. Some people—maybe a lot of them, maybe most, I don't know—believe it. And they hate me more." I half laughed. "And … in my head, I guess I shouldn't care, because you're right—the people who know me presumably know I don't have radioactive powers and that I wouldn't nuke LA, but … I don't get to see those people much anymore. My life's in ashes—err, ruins." Ashes felt too soon, given what had just happened yesterday.

"Yeah, your life is pretty corked," he said matter-of-factly. He seemed to realize that this wasn't a statement to make me feel better, so he added, "Sorry."

I sat back down on the couch and stared at my tennis shoes, which I hadn't removed before I had fallen asleep last night. They were new, of course, because I'd burned off the boots I was wearing in LA. "The funny thing is ... I've had lawyers working on getting me out from under those false accusations from Eden Prairie, but ... when a potential jury pool sees something like this? It doesn't help my case. When they hear I might have assassinated the president, it drives another wedge between me and the humans who are going to decide my fate. I don't really know where I could ever go in the world to get a fair trial, because I'm pretty sure most of the country believes what they hear about me, even though it's mostly bullshit. But ... being a public enemy means that ... well, you know, that a lot of the public is my enemy. Which makes me kinda sad, because I've done my best to save lives. Including theirs."

With that little depression grenade thrown out, we both settled into silence for a little bit. "That's a pretty bad deal," Friday seemed to agree between slurps of cereal. "Sorry," he said again.

"It wasn't your fault," I said. I left off the part about his damned case not helping, because it wasn't like he had any control over Greg the magical assassin coming to kill him. Which reminded me ... "So, I think I know what we need to do next."

"Oh yeah? What's that?"

"Chase."

Friday frowned, milk dribbling down his chin again. "Okay. Who do we chase?"

"No, we need to talk to Chase," I said. He stared at me blankly. "Chase." Still nothing. "Your girlfriend?"

That got him. "Ohhhh, Chase. Yeah. Okay. No." He shook his head. "We can't do that."

"What? Why not?"

"Because it's not a great idea."

I just stared at him. "She's the last member of your team. We still have no idea why Greg is coming to kill you, and we have even less of an idea about his powers, except that he can kindasorta teleport around, and draw objects from the air by magic. If you don't have the answers, and Jon and Theo don't ... I'm sorry, but she's the last one left before we start talking to random strangers. Which, right now, probably not the greatest idea for me."

"We can call your friends again," Friday said.

"Uh, no," I said. "We need to keep them completely away from me now." There was no way I was going to bring any more linkage between myself and them for the FBI to question. Jamal was savvy enough to cover his tracks thus far, I thought, but I suspected all my old friends would be under total surveillance now, if the FBI had any brains among them (and they did, in spite of Phillips being a serious downward drag on them in that regard). They'd be all over my friends' lines of communication by now, and the quickest way to lead them right back to me would be to call Jamal or any other employee of the agency.

After all, when they were escalating to the point where they were probably just going to shoot me the next time they got a chance, what the hell was listening in on my friends' conversations compared to that?

"I don't want to talk to Chase," Friday whined.

"Why not?" I bet this would be good.

"Because, uh ... we had a bad breakup." He nodded, as though reassuring himself. "Yeah. Really bad. Epic. Makes Los Angeles last night look like a peaceful night in the Pacific Northwest." He made a face like he'd tasted something bad. "But not like my last night in the woods in the Pacific Northwest, what with the getting shot by Greg and all."

"We have to go see her," I said.

Friday looked tinged with panic. "There has to be another way."

"There's not." Now I was going to dig in because I really, really wanted to meet Chase and hear how badly Friday had lied about her. I'd already estimated that no part of what he'd told me in those stories was true, but whatever she was going to say was bound to be entertaining, even if she didn't have a key to open up this case.

"Shit," Friday said. "What about—"

"No."

"You didn't even listen to me!"

"… Okay. Go on."

His eyes flitted around uncertainly. "What if we … uh … how about we … uhm …" His shoulders finally sagged in defeat. "Shit, I say again."

"Yeah," I said, "finish your breakfast and I'm going to start looking for Chase on the internet—"

"She's in Billings, Montana," Friday said, slumping down in his chair, his thin shoulders looking particularly pitiable given his posture. "Working in a lumberyard." When I stared at him, he shrugged. "What? I cyberstalk her every now and again. I like to know how she's doing."

"All right," I said, trying to steel myself. We were going to have to fly to Montana, crossing Canadian airspace and a little of the US, too, though fortunately not much. Now was the time when we were going to find out how serious the US Government was about hunting my ass down. "Let's do this thing."

"Can I finish my cereal first?" Friday asked, slurping another spoonful down.

I just stared at him for a minute. "Well, yeah," I said, "and you better have saved some for me. That Basic 4 is good stuff."

"I know, right?" Friday said. "It's a real winner, and especially good considering that they changed the formula on Frosted Flakes so they taste like ass compared to when I was a kid eating them."

"Yeah, what did they do there?" I asked. "It kinda feels like they did something to the flake, and also maybe decided that much sugar wasn't good for you."

"I think they actively started using ass as an ingredient," Friday said. "Like ground-up squirrel ass or something. Maybe possum. I dunno."

"Well, let's eat some cereal and then go talk to your ex," I said, watching him squirm slightly as I tossed out that statement while giving him the benefit of the doubt. I could tell by the way he held himself he was going to make a correction pretty quick.

"Maybe don't mention that around her," Friday said. "It

ended so badly, you know ... just seeing me is going to be hard enough on her. Better not to open up old wounds."

"Uh huh," I said.

"She took the breakup really tough," Friday said. "Probably sat around eating some of those new formula Frosted Flakes, just to punish herself, you know. Once you've had the best, everything else tastes like broken glass, probably." He took a bite and chewed self-consciously, mouth closed for once.

"Friday," I said as I poured my own bowl.

"Yeah?" He shifted in his seat.

"You're full of shit."

His thin shoulders sagged again. "Yeah."

We settled into another long silence as we ate, me in hopes of what we'd learn from Chase, and him, presumably, in dread of seeing her again. I'd hung out with him for all of two days and he'd found all manner of ways to annoy the hell out of me. I couldn't imagine what he'd done to a woman who'd worked with him for a decade.

But I was willing to bet her reaction was going to be priceless.

43.

Augustus

The production facility outside Vegas looked like a cross between a warehouse and a factory, the sort of thing you might drive by in any number of small towns in America, or maybe an industrial district in a city. It didn't have belching smokestacks, just a couple pipes on the roof that let out a small cloud of steam into an unseasonably chilly Vegas day. I would have guessed it was twenty degrees above freezing, at least, but it still felt weird to have flown into Vegas and have this greet me instead of burning heat.

"It's the lack of humidity that makes it so bad," Scott muttered, rubbing his fingers together as we pulled into the parking lot. The place was pretty full, but most of the cars were old and crappy beyond belief. I saw two bumpers being held on by duct tape, and a truck that was two tone because the bed that had been grafted onto the rear of the frame looked like it had come from a completely different model, and was navy where the cab was white. Both were dinged up like they'd been in a rollover crash, though.

"Damned sure ain't the heat," Jamal said, stepping out, "because that's gone missing like Augustus's ability to speak after that time he 'accidentally' walked in on Taneshia in the bathroom."

"We were twelve and it really was an accident," I said, shaking my head at him. "Now I walk in on her all the time. With permission."

"Head in the game, guys," Reed said as we threaded our way through the parking lot toward an industrial garage door about thirty feet wide and equally as tall. "Also … geez, guy. I make Isabella keep the door closed. There are few things that kill the romance faster than an open door to the bathroom."

"You guys aren't quite as bad at oversharing as Abby and J.J., but you're getting there fast," Scott said.

"How do you want to do this?" I asked. "Calm and quiet, or Miley Cyrus style?"

"Miley Cyrus—what?" Scott asked.

"Wrecking Ball," Reed said with a quick flash of a grin.

"Ah," Scott said as we reached the big garage door. It was partially open, probably about four feet off the ground, the corrugated steel looking like a symmetrical set of waves rolling down the door to the bottom. He ducked under it, taking a peek while the rest of us made a slower approach. When he didn't get his head knocked off, I followed a moment later.

The hum of industrial machinery reminded me of my last job, working on the factory floor at Cavanagh Technologies. I could see people walking around in plastic chem gear, masks on. "Looks they're taking some serious precautions here," I said.

"Probably don't want to accidentally create any superheroes that would lead directly back to them here," Jamal said.

No one was looking at us, and there wasn't a security guard posted at the door. I knew why they'd left it open just after stepping inside, though; the heat that Vegas was lacking right now? It was made up for and more by the warmth in this place. I was sweating in seconds.

"Still not sure about this," I said, though it was obviously too late to just turn back now. "Maybe we should have rolled up the distribution network first." I'd voiced this thought before and Reed had blown me off.

Now he smiled, but kept his eyes front, looking for any of these chem geared figures to come at us. "I've got Kat, Veronika, Colin and Angel on it." He looked right at me.

"Taneshia, too, if she's available. Ms. Estevez is coordinating with them."

"Sending in the B team," Scott said.

"Yo," I said, "don't call my girlfriend a B-teamer where she can hear you, all right? Friendly advice." He nodded in receipt of the information. I think he got it; I wouldn't have wanted to piss off his ex either. I turned my attention to Reed. "So you're doing this all at once?"

"Best we can," Reed said.

"Whose authority are we here under?" Jamal asked. "Not our own, I hope."

"I talked to Nevada about it," Reed said. "Offered to do this pro bono and they accepted. Probably still a little sensitive after those metas tore up the Strip a few months back. They'll be sending in their state police, but the perimeter is going up a ways back. I told them what happened with Augustus when he tangled these folks in Colorado."

"When did you get a chance to do all this?" I asked.

"When you weren't looking," he said, and stepped over to a steel staircase leading up to a catwalk above. "Let's see what we're dealing with here."

We all ascended, not bothering to walk softly because it was so loud that our footsteps couldn't be heard anyway. Once we were on the catwalk, the production facility looked much more impressive—chemical vats that had looked like simple cylinders from the ground were laid out throughout the place, hundreds of gallons of chemicals brewing before our eyes, valves spraying and adding liquid to them. Giant booms whirred overhead, stirring the vats like a giant witch's cauldron.

"There is not even one of these vats where the chemical composition is close enough to water to enable me to control it," Scott said, waving a hand experimentally around the cavernous room. "This is some seriously altered stuff."

"So … what now?" I asked.

"Any of you guys ever seen *The Untouchables*?" Reed asked, looking out over the place with a smile on his face.

"No," Scott said.

"Yeah, with DeNiro as Capone and Costner as Elliott Ness," Jamal said. "Why?"

"Because this … kinda feels like one of those old bootlegger raids for some reason," Reed said, still smiling. "And it makes me want to shout—*This is a raid! Nobody move!*"

His voice boomed out over the sound of the machinery and the chemicals percolating. Twenty guys in chem suits looked up to see who was shouting, and most of them froze right where they were, not a word said.

"Man, I hope we're in the right place," Jamal said, "because otherwise, it's going to be so embarrassing to explain why we're busting up a Clorox factory."

"Nobody's moving," I said. "I think they got the message."

"Well, that was eas—" Scott started to say … but he didn't get a chance to finish.

A blast of blue plasma shot within inches of Reed's face, and our fearless leader ducked back to avoid losing his face to it. A second later, a disc of red energy sailed through the catwalk in front of us, searing through the metal effortlessly and causing the whole thing to shudder, rattling as it started to twist under our weight, unmoored now that the energy burst had sliced through it.

It held steady for a second, and then we all pitched forward as the catwalk collapsed, throwing us all forward— and headlong into a vat of dark, bubbling green chemicals.

44.

Sienna

Billings, Montana, was looking surprisingly green considering how far north it was. When we'd flown through Canada, traveling at supersonic speed, there had been snow on the ground until well south of Calgary, where it had started to fade. I knew there were places elsewhere in the US where it was still on the ground, and was eminently surprised when Billings turned out to be green as a spring field instead of buried in ice and cold.

It was still chilly though as Friday and I ducked out of the woods across the street from Burnham and Scannell Lumber Co., a rural lumberyard that was surrounded by its own product, waiting to be harvested. I watched a truck laden with tree trunks rumble in through the gate while I cast furtive looks at the tall trees that cloaked the lumberyard from a view of town. Seemed kinda silly to truck in trees when there were an awful lot waiting to be harvested right outside the chain link fence, but whatever. There's probably a reason I don't run a lumberyard. Other than all those pending felony charges, I mean.

No one stopped us at the gate, probably because the lumber they had was pretty much all bound in huge pallets so that someone couldn't just walk off with one. I mean, I probably could have, because I'm super strong and my shoulders are diesel as hell—

Toot your own horn, why don't you? Eve asked.

—but most people weren't jacked enough to just carry off a pallet of lumber. Friday and I just sort of wandered in, feet crunching in the packed gravel as I scanned the workers milling around here and there, looking for a woman.

It didn't take too long. Most of the workers were dudes, which was obvious by their builds, their jeans, their shoulders, their hair—I mean, I probably grossly generalized, but when my eyes fell on a short, small-framed figure working in the corner next to a buzzing saw that was bigger than my chest, running the conveyor that ran the logs through, I kinda figured, 'That's probably Chase.' When I nodded to Friday, then at her, he nodded back, with enough reticence I knew he probably wasn't leading me astray.

I made my way over, Friday trailing farther and farther behind me as we went. The air was heavy with the smell of pine, sun catching little motes of wood dust that floated around us. When I was almost to her, Chase seemed to detect my presence in spite of her heavy ear protection and thick plastic goggles. She stiffened and turned to look at me.

She stared at me for a second, and I stared back at her. She looked serious as hell, scowl deep, her hair tucked back under a hard hat. But she also looked really familiar. "Oh. Hey," I said, "I know you—"

She spun all the way around, adopting a fighting stance, and stuck her right arm out. A long, red blade of energy like a freaking lightsaber popped out as though she had bound the handle to her wrist. She stood there, energy blade humming like an amped-up fluorescent light, and said, "Yeah, I know you, too, Sienna Nealon. The whole damned country is looking for you after last night."

"I didn't do what they said I did," I said.

"Wait, you two know each other?" Friday asked, catching up at last.

Chase squinted at him. "Bruce? Is that you?"

"Hi, Chase," Friday said, sinking back, one leg set like he was going to run if she said a cross word at him. He looked at me. "How do you two know each other?"

I looked back at Chase, who was still giving me the death eye. "We, uh, had an encounter in the US Virgin Islands a few months ago."

"She kicked my team's ass, my ass, and killed my principal," Chase said, glaring at me.

"Principal?" Friday asked. "That's so kittens, I didn't know you were a schoolteacher!"

"I was bodyguarding," Chase said acidly, "and she killed the body I was supposed to be guarding. It's why I'm working here now; tough to get work as a bodyguard when your last job ended in your boss getting killed."

"I totally did not kill him," I said. It was true.

"This is so cool," Friday said, gushing over the saws ripping like a kid, "my two favorite ladies know each other already! Small world, right?"

"So Disney would have you believe," Chase snarked.

I was stuck on something else. "I'm ... one of your favorite ladies?" I wasn't quite sure how to take that.

Chase favored us both with a look so sour it would have puckered a stoic's lips. "If your standards have fallen to the level where you could consider that a compliment, there's something seriously wrong with you."

"Hey," I said, violating a cardinal rule of not being stupid by forgetting that anything Friday told me was probably bullshit, "you're the one who dated him."

If I'd thought Chase's eyes were furious when she'd seen me coming, that was nothing compared to how flamingly pissed off she got now. "Is that what he told you?" Her growl was harsher than the saw shredding its way through solid wood.

"I—no," Friday said, already shaking his head madly. "No, I never said that."

"You liar," Chase said, and she started to make a threatening move on Guy Friday, like she was going to decapitate him with that energy blade.

I interposed myself between them, holding up a hand to stop her. "Wait, wait. We're not here to fight. In fact, we're really just looking to get a question answered and we'll leave."

She narrowed her eyes at me. "A question? Really? And then you'll get out of my hair?"

"Like we were fleeing from a Medusa," I said. "Promise." I could tell she was feeling skeptical, so I just launched right into it. "See, the thing is—uh, Bruce here is being hunted by one of your old teammates—"

Chase stared at him, hard. "Is it Greg?"

Friday still wasn't daring to look at her in favor of his shoelaces. I guess he was capable of embarrassment after all, something I wouldn't have guessed. "Yeah."

Chase softened just a touch, losing that jagged edge of anger, her body language suggesting that she might not rush him at any second. "What'd you do?"

"Nothing that I know of," Friday said, shrugging expansively. "I haven't seen the guy since Afghanistan."

Chase rolled her eyes. "We never went to Afghanistan. They said they were thinking about deploying us there, but we only ever ended up on that weird training op in the Arizona desert."

"Whatever, you know what I mean, clearly," Friday said, now refusing to look at me.

Chase just stared at him. "I can't think of anything you did there that would have pissed him off bad enough to kill you over a decade later."

"He said it wasn't personal." I stepped in. "Like he's a hired assassin or something."

She seemed to think things over. "Wait. Was he involved in that thing in LA?"

"He *was* that thing in LA," I said with feeling. "I don't know what you've heard, but I don't have the power to irradiate squat. Blow up, yes. Add radiation? Not so much."

She chewed her lip, and then the lightsaber blade retracted to half its size. Her body language continued to loosen up, her eyes still moving around behind those plastic safety glasses while she thought. "Deploying a nuke sounds extreme, even for Greg."

"We'd been clashing with him all day," I said, "while we were trying to figure out what the hell was behind this and ... you know, how Greg does what he does."

She stiffened right up, and looked straight at Friday. "Wait ... you never figured it out?"

Friday caught the attention of both of us and withered under it. "I ... no. And neither did Jon or Theo."

"You guys," Chase said, shaking her head with amusement. She looked at me and said, way more sympathetically than anything she'd said so far, "That team we were part of ... not exactly the best and the brightest."

"I kinda got that," I said.

"Ouch," Friday muttered. "This is totally not kittens."

"Except for Greg," Chase said. "He was good. Really good. I guess you saw that, though. How he could disappear and reappear, show up in places unexpectedly? Make something appear out of nothing, like—"

"Magic," I said. "Yeah. In addition to somehow keeping a miniature nuke up his sleeve ... he tried to hit us with an army arsenal that would have defeated most of the countries in the world."

"He likes flash, he likes tech, and he likes being ready for anything," Chase said. "And he could do it, because of what he is." She chewed her lip again. "Look ... it's not magic."

"I gathered as much."

"Whut?" Friday looked at both of us in turn. "It is too, magic. You can't explain it any other way."

"It's simpler than you think," Chase said, looking at him pityingly. "Like, if you throw something at him—"

"It doesn't pass through him if he disappears," I said, following along.

"Right." She arched her eyebrows, smiling, enjoying probably the most power over a conversation she'd had in months. "Because he doesn't go invisible, he doesn't turn to smoke or anything of the sort—"

"You know, a magician gets real upset when someone spills his secrets." Chase and I both turned; I expected to see Greg standing there, but the voice was more pronounced, had a drawl, and lacked the precision I'd heard in our assassin's tone even when he was furious.

There was a man standing there in a black suit with one of those bolo ties, a string around his collar with a metal circular thingie in the middle to keep the ends together. He had brown hair carefully combed over and slicked, and was

ROBERT J. CRANE

pretty handsome overall, looked like he might be in his late thirties.

"Who the hell are you?" I asked, since neither Chase nor Friday beat me to the punch. The fact that she didn't say anything to him clued me in that he wasn't the boss here, and probably didn't belong here at all.

"I ... am Sam," Mr. Bolo said with a wide grin. If he'd been wearing a hat, I get the feeling he might have tipped it.

"That's my second favorite book," Friday said.

"I saw that movie," I said, ignoring Friday's commentary. "Sean Penn didn't dress anything like you. And he sounded smarter."

"We were like brothers once, Greg and I," Sam said, ignoring my wisecrack. "Now ... I've been hired to bat cleanup where he failed. That feels ..." He drifted into thought. "Hmm ... what would you call it?"

"Stupid?" I offered.

"Poetic," Friday said.

Sam looked at each of us in turn. I wanted to preemptively punch him, but I was well past the point of doing that to people without feeling like I was getting overly violent. "I was going to say ironic."

"Should have gone with stupid," I said, shaking my head.

"I don't feel stupid," Sam said, still smiling.

"It's an annoying tic, stupid people never realize how much they're inflicting themselves on the rest of us," I shot back.

Sam just shook his head, and then—

He disappeared.

"Shit," I said.

"Whoa!" Friday said. "Another one! They really are like brothers!"

"Watch out!" Chase shouted, spinning toward me. "He's—"

Whatever she was going to say was lost on me as she started to distort. Her face receded in the distance, like I was getting yanked away from the lumberyard at Mach 1, except I didn't feel like I was moving. Something was definitely happening, though, something weird, because I could see the ground surging up at me, the grains of dirt hidden between the gravel rocks looking like pebbles as I rushed toward them.

I found myself staring at the world from a very, very different point of view. I could see Chase and Friday, standing like mountains over me, and miles and miles away. Suddenly, the thing that Theo had said about standing on a rocky cliff made total sense.

The floor in the bunker would have been pebbled and cracked, filled with sand that had been tracked in out of the desert. And because of that, it would have looked like a rocky landscape ...

If you were a millimeter tall.

"Welcome to my world," Sam said, and I turned to find him standing there, almost double my height now. "Well, mine and Greg's." His smile widened in triumph as he stared at me for only another moment, delivering his taunt, already growing again, returning to normal human size but offering a parting shot as he went, leaving me trapped like this, smaller than an insect. "I hope you enjoy it here ... because you're gonna spend the rest of your life this small."

45.

Augustus

The catwalk collapsed beneath us, pitching me headfirst toward the damned boiling, dark green liquid in the cauldron below. "Ohhhh, craaaaaap!" I shouted as I slid, trying like hell to find some sort of earth element to hold on to me. There was concrete beneath my feet, way, way down at the floor, the component pieces manipulable by my powers, but I'd have to break up the slab first, and that would take time …

Outside, in the desert, there was soil and dirt and rock to work with … but if I went for it with all my strength and concentration—an iffy proposition while I was falling into a toxic vat of chemicals—it wouldn't get here before I went splash. And turned into something horrible, like Jack Nicholson's version of the Joker, but, y'know, black. And young. And much sexier.

The wind flared beneath my feet, taking me off course and away from the edge of the chemical vat. It swept me to the side and gently lowered me to the floor below.

Just in time for some dude in a chem mask to blast at me with another of those blue plasma bursts like Veronika used.

I screeched, I'm not ashamed to say, and bolted my ass and the rest of me, meta speed as I sprinted from the site of impact. The plasma hit the side of the vat with a sizzle, burning through and filling the air with an awful smell of melting metal, a chemical aroma that might have threatened to make me sick if I wasn't so damned busy running for my life.

"Damn!" Someone shouted above me. It sounded like Scott. A geyser of chemicals went spraying out behind me, catching on fire as it sluiced out. It didn't blow up, fortunately, because that would have hurt, but it lit up as it came out, going like a napalm sprayer in 'Nam, a solid jet of flame that made me duck, warming my ass as I circled around another vat for cover.

"This shit's about to go off!" I muttered as someone came around the corner and screamed at me through their chem mask, waving their hands in surrender. They didn't wait for me to say anything, they just turned tail and ran, but at human speed. I came around the edge of the vat to see 'em joining with another group of similarly attired workers, all of them beating feet toward one those glowing EXIT signs they post so you can see where to run if the lights go out. They took that shit seriously, too, and when they hit that door, they didn't even look back.

In my mind, I'd already mentally divided the workers from management, figuring maybe those guys that just ran off didn't know what was going on here. Whoever was firing that plasma, though, they knew what they were doing. They had to be involved, running security for this place with meta powers.

Someone moved ahead and I turned in time to see a blast of blue come blazing at me. I ducked and it tore past, ripping into the corrugated metal past me and letting in some of that Vegas sunshine as it shredded a six foot hole in the wall.

That could have been me. Nice.

I dodged around the vat I'd been circling as another blast, red this time, and originating from energy dude's eyes came ripping after me. Liquid sprayed behind me as I sprinted like a track star away from the source of the crazy lasers and all else. A blast of bright green that looked like it was almost neon and shaped like a full-bodied version of a sound wave, complete with oscillation, came shooting around the curve of the vat after me. It made a humming noise as it ripped through the mighty steel of the vat like a scissor through paper.

"Sheeeeeeeeuuuuuuuuuuuuut!" I am not ashamed to say I was screaming really loud and high as I came around and damned near ran into Reed. There was a steady spray behind me, the vat opening up along the line where energy man had torn it nearly in half.

Reed looked at me in surprise as I ran toward him. "What?"

"There's a dude behind me that's shooting energy out of every damned orifice!" I shouted, stopping for a second to report. "Well, maybe not every one. I guess he hasn't taken his pants off yet."

"If you see him do that, I'd keep running," Reed said dryly. He stepped up next to me like we were about to present a united front on this fight. The chemical spraying out of the vat in front of us was causing a flood of reddish liquid across the concrete floor, like a bloody tide, and it made me wonder what the hell this one was.

"Something's coming," I said, my ears perking up. Something was indeed circling around the vat; I could hear it moving toward us.

A man emerged from the chemical spray like a monster from a horror movie. He wasn't a small little dude, either, he was big; swollen at the arms and chest, thighs the size of whole hog carcasses. He thumped when he walked, several hundred pounds of weight dropped down on his two feet. "That's a Hercules," Reed said.

"It's more than that." I looked the guy up and down; the proportion was all, all wrong. He was at least ten feet tall, and while our old pal Friday had been a Hercules and done the "hulking up" thing enough times I was familiar with it, he never really grew taller. "This guy's got a height thing going on."

Reed nodded once, understanding. "Atlas."

"What's an Atlas?" I asked.

"They can grow," Reed said. "Get tall. Probably a related power, next to the Hercules one, so it got unlocked by the Skill Tree Unlocker."

"Oh, well." I looked at Mr. Atlas Hercules, which

sounded like a great name for an eighties action hero. He had muscles piled on muscles, and had grown his proportions to the point where I felt like I was standing in front of the Incredible Hulk, just waiting to get pulped. "How are we going to fight this thing?"

"*We* aren't," Reed said, stepping forward and stopping just short of the line of spray bursting out of the vat. He motioned me back. "I got this."

I took a step back on command because it made good sense, but once I realized I'd done it, the other part of what he said clicked through for me. "You're gonna fight that thing?"

"Don't worry," Reed said, turning to look straight at Mr. Atlas Hercules, who was just standing there, looking intimidating, and staring down at Reed, who looked like he might be about a foot tall compared to the big guy. "I won't fight fair."

"Yeah, I don't think he will either, Reed," I said, but Atlas Hercules roared like an animal and came at Reed, so I didn't get a chance to hear a reply.

The beast took a quick step forward and swung at Reed, who looked for a second like he might just stand there and take it. Chemicals spraying all around him, orange light shading the scene, it really did look like it was ripped out of the frame of a horror film, and Reed had the monster coming right at him with a punch that would've leveled New York City.

I was expecting Reed to break into a dozen pieces when the punch landed, because he looked he was just going to take it with his feet planted like an oak, but at the last second Reed started to twist. He stepped sideways, turning his body and dodging, whipping out and slapping Atlas Hercules's hand like he was giving the big bastard some additional momentum. A puff of superfast air shot right into Atlas Hercules's hand, and the big man kept going like Thor's hammer and held on, his hand yanking him along to the side and off balance.

Atlas Hercules didn't just stagger; he was full-on ripped off his feet and did a face plant on the concrete floor, getting a snoot full of chemicals as he landed in a heap, tangled up in his own feet after Reed's jiu jitsu maneuver. His landing made a sound like a building falling down. I was all set to start applauding like Citizen Kane in that meme when Atlas Hercules made a "Mmmmmm arrggghhhhhhh!" noise, like he couldn't even speak anymore on account of being a brainless monster.

"Hey, Reed, you best get out of there before he gets m—"

Atlas Hercules launched off the ground, onto his knees and then back on his feet, swinging around for the fences— or more accurately, Reed's chest.

Reed didn't wait this time, he started moving right away. He fell back in a roll as Atlas Hercules came forward with his swiping rage punch, and Reed actually caught it between his hands, slapping them together on the monster's wrist like he was killing flies or clapping. He anchored his grip and dropped back gently, rolling as he landed, kicking up with his feet and planting both in the big man's chest.

A WHOOSH! of air caught Atlas Hercules on the roll as Reed pulled him forward and off balance again. Reed's back met the concrete, and he arched into a ball so that he distributed the force of landing in a roll from the small of his back up to his shoulders, and when he reached the shoulders, he arched and stuck his feet up; Atlas Hercules was trapped, about to pancake down on him, but that rush of hard air hit the big bastard in the stomach—

Atlas Hercules went airborne, forward momentum combined with Reed's sudden blast of air to flip him ass over teakettle (stole that from Sienna) through empty air and into the side of another chemical vat. He crunched, metal clanged, and he collapsed to the ground, landing on his neck at an ugly angle. Where he'd struck the vat there was a two foot indentation in the solid, foot-thick steel.

"Yikes," I said as Atlas Hercules slumped, legs still sticking up in the air. He gradually fell over, his body starting to shrink as he wilted like a flower, gravity taking hold and pulling him back to earth. "Damn, boy," I said to Reed, "that was really somethi—"

I was interrupted by another blast, this one a fresh, bright blue like Veronika's plasma again, except it was about five feet wide, the scariest, hottest kamehameha I'd seen this side of *Street Fighter*. It blazed past, so hot I felt like it burned my cheek even though it cleared me by three or four feet, tearing through another round of catwalks and ripping a massive hole in the ceiling. More Vegas sunlight streamed in from above, bright blue sky looking down on us.

"Reed, we need to—" I didn't have time to finish, didn't have time to think, because Mr. Energy followed up his plasma burst with a searing blast of red out of his eyes, and I was dodging back as it split Reed and me apart, dividing us up before I could get to him.

As I leapt back to avoid the red blast from my foe's eyes, another blast—the neon green wave from his hand—came streaking at me from the other direction, a pincer-like move that was going to split the difference—and split me—right through the middle.

46.

Sienna

The incredible shrinking Sienna was not pleased. I was a millimeter tall, standing in a land of giants, a tiny figure in a massive lumberyard I could no longer even see the ends of clearly. The world beyond was a blur, a miasma of colors, the clarity stripped away by the massive scale. Yes, there were trees in the distance, but they were not at all clear to me, just a blur of forest green.

What was clear to me were three things: Guy Friday, whose black, dirty, disgusting boots were only a mile or two behind me; Chase, who stood like a pillar slightly to my right, her lightsaber glaring down at me like a red sun; and finally ...

Sam, that bastard, who was a thousand feet or so away. Or at least the leading edge of his toe was. The rest of him stretched way, way up there, and when he spoke, it was like the heavens opened up and Alanis Morissette started speaking. I couldn't cover my ears fast enough.

"Now I've gone ahead and dealt with Sienna, dear," Sam said, his charm and drawl all blurred out by the fact it sounded like a banshee screaming, but deeper, his size amplifying his voice so that it was like a bass speaker behind my ear. "Young lady," I thought he was looking at Chase here, but from way down on the ground I was ill placed to see where his eyes were directed. Hell, he could have been talking to Friday. "I got no gripe with you. If you want to walk away right now, I'm content to let you go on. My contract is with your acquaintance Percy Sledger, and I see no reason to drag you into this."

"Shit, he's gonna kill Friday and I'm smaller than a fricking ant," I said, my voice sounding completely normal— which meant it probably didn't project to the titans above me.

I did not see this coming, Zack said, sounding a little disturbed. *Who knew there was really an Ant-Man meta?*

I did, Wolfe said, but he sounded surly about it.

You could have said something, Eve said.

I convinced him not to, Harmon said quickly.

"What the hell, Harmon?" I asked, taking flight. I wondered how long it'd take me to get to Sam's face and give it a good punch, even at supersonic speed. It was possible, given my size, I'd blast right through him and he'd maybe feel a tiny sting. Shit. "You trying to actively sabotage me now?"

I'm trying to get you off the bench and living your life, Harmon said. *At least, as best you can. You know, like that overly sensitive therapist of yours is always suggesting.*

"I don't think Dr. Zollers intended for you to use that as an excuse to hide materially important information from me in the middle of a case!" I shouted. No one except me and the souls heard it.

"Dammit all to hell," Chase said, her voice rumbling like thunder off the mountains. Except there wasn't a mountain, just her. But she was like a mountain to me. "I can't just let you murder him."

Sam seemed to take that in stride. "Suit yourself. But this here is a man who was deeply involved in the bombing of East Los Angeles last night. Whoever was to come after him … I feel like it ought to be personal. Come from a place of pain. Someone so angry, they're going to beat him right to death, but not quickly. They'll want to have a little fun with it first." God, he sounded like he was going to enjoy himself as he spelled out how Friday was going to die.

Chase set her feet in a defensive stance, lightsaber at the ready. She had to know she didn't stand a chance, knowing what he was and what he could do, but here she was, throwing down with this asshole Sam anyway, on behalf of Friday, of all people.

What a hero.

"Need some speed," I said, and jetted up. I was aiming for Friday's ear, and it took me a few seconds to get there. "Hey! Friday!"

Friday whipped around, looking for the source of the invisible voice he was probably hearing. "Whuuuuut?"

"It's me, you idiot! He shrank me to molecule size!" I shouted directly into his ear, which was not easy because he was moving his head around looking for me like I was hiding behind him if he just turned around a little farther.

Friday paused, looking dumbstruck. "Really?"

"Yes, really!"

Sam was staring at Friday quizzically, then he closed his eyes and threw his head back. "I forgot she can fly. Damn. Rookie mistake. Most people I do that to get stuck on the ground, see. Which leaves them pretty helpless."

"He shrinks people?" Friday asked.

"Yes, like Greg," I said. "Which was how he could make a Concorde or a weapon or a helicopter appear by magic. He shrank them down and carried them in a pocket, then grew them whenever he needed one of those toys. That's why he blindfolded Theo—he shrank you all so he could get you on the plane without knowing what he was doing. Then he'd take off, fly out the air vents or whatever, then grow the plane to normal size once he was out. Supersonic transport in his pocket at all times. An arsenal, always at his disposal. And if he really wanted to make someone disappear, looks like Sam figured it out—they would just disappear, too small to affect anything in the world ever again."

"That's so evil," Friday said.

"Is she talking to you right now?" Sam asked, peering like he could see me next to Friday's head. "Now listen up, Sienna—none of this is gonna matter, y'hear? Why don't you go fly on along and learn to enjoy your new life as a tiny person. Or you could stand back and watch me beat your friend to death here. Either is fine." He stretched, cracking his back, then started to shrink.

"What the h—?" Friday started to ask, but I could see what was happening clearer than he could. Sam shrank, not quite to my size, but probably to a quarter of an inch or less. Before he did, though, he leapt off his back leg, launching into a front kick. It was a subtle move when he was full size, probably didn't look like much of anything, like he was changing his stance. But when he started to shrink, his mass and weight shrank.

His momentum didn't stop, though. His momentum carried him forward, but faster because it was applied over less mass and less weight, launching him at Friday like a bullet.

Sam hit Friday in the chest with a kick, all that force spread over a foot only a centimeter at the impact. I could hear the bone crack in Friday's sternum, and he cried, "Ooof!" probably because he hadn't been hit with the searing pain yet. He was also thrown back a few feet, and Sam appeared again, regrown to full size, grinning at Chase.

"You sure you want to involve yourself in this?" Sam asked Chase. "I do so hate to hit a lady, especially one I ain't been paid to hit."

"I hate to hit a lady, too," Chase said, and she swung at him. "But I don't mind beating the shit out of a cock like you."

He shrank and dodged, reappearing when she had missed him cleanly. She didn't overcommit, though, didn't swing for the fences, probably because she knew Sam's ability to dodge was going to be epic. She swung back quickly and actually managed to elbow him in the jaw, knocking him back a step, before she hurled herself backward to avoid a riposte.

"Well, someone came to play," Sam said, rubbing his jaw.

"And you came to play with yourself," Chase said, coming at him again.

She did admirably, but I knew this fight was going to end up pretty lopsided, pretty fast if I didn't do something to change the odds. "Friday!" I shouted and zipped toward him. He was getting back up, clutching his chest, wheezing from the kick he'd taken. I came right up to his ear and shouted.

"Friday! You have to get back in the fight!"

"I ... can't ..." Friday said, moaning. "I ... don't know how to fight ... that ..."

"Dammit, you giant wuss," I said, "that woman is throwing herself on a hand grenade meant for you." Chase was falling back, quickly, against an assault she knew was coming but couldn't see, because Sam had once again disappeared. "She's going to die trying to save you, and you're sitting here rocking in your little cradle. Now listen to me, shitbird—this is war. Stop being an enormous baby, quit filling your diaper and crying, stand up tall, grow your fricking muscles, let your testicles drop, and *sound your battle cry.*"

"My ... battle cry?" His face was all screwed up, and I could tell he was both confused and genuinely trying not to weep.

"Yes," I said, trying to figure out how to rile his dumb ass up for this impossible fight, "your battle cry. Let it ring over the field of conflict. Go to war, Friday. Go fight."

"My battle cry." He sounded stronger, pushing to his feet. Chase was leaping in a back flip as Sam blipped into existence for a second, launching himself after her again. She was doing a masterful job, some serious prequel trilogy Jedi gymnastics skeelz being exhibited there, but Sam was after her like a heatseeking missile, and I knew how it would end if something didn't change fast.

"I call to war!" Friday shouted. "I call to war!"

"That's not really a rallying cry," I said, "but okay, get riled. Go after him. Go—"

"I sound my cry over the field of battle!" Friday shouted, his shirt shredding as he grew his muscles. "Hear me!"

"Okay," I said, "now get after him. Make this fight happen."

"Hear my battle cry!" Friday said, growing until his muscles looked like they were going to pop, and he took a deep breath before letting out a bellow that they could probably hear in Florida. "DICKS OUT FOR HARAMBE!"

"What kind of battle cry is *that?*" I asked. "That's an internet meme!"

But he charged.

I wanted to believe in Friday's rage, his power, that somehow when he charged in—even after that … that … battle cry, I guess—that it was going to change the course of this fight. That he was going to catch Sam at an inopportune moment, pound him in the jaw with enough force that the assassin was going to die right there, a victim of fury … and apparently an internet meme.

Friday came at him like an out-of-control bus. I couldn't see Sam, but I knew he was there by the way that Chase was dodging and ducking and generally trying to predict the next attack from what was basically an invisible enemy. She was good, but no one's that good, especially when your enemy isn't big enough to generate any real sound.

Chase caught a hit hard in the side and went down, flipping over as Sam reappeared, looking triumphant. He showed up right in Friday's path, smirking down at Chase.

And Friday was only feet away, stampeding toward him.

Sam looked over in time to see Friday coming when he was a foot from running Sam over. Sam didn't waste time; he disappeared just as Friday was charging through, and I wondered if Sam was going to take the hit, get launched into the stratosphere.

Nope.

Friday hit something, all right, right in the gut, and it was like seeing that a train derail. He crashed, his forward momentum stopping like he'd run into a wall, and then his ass and feet backflipped over and Friday went flying off like gravity had ceased, into the air like a punted football.

"And the field goal is good," Sam said, reappearing as Friday soared above a hundred feet, hitting the apogee of his arc and flying onward, crashing down to a landing somewhere in the forest beyond the lumberyard. Sam made a clucking sound of amusement. "Well, looks like there goes your champion. Sad to say, since he's the one I'm here to kill, we're going to have to wrap this up—" And he reared back to hit Chase.

"Shit!" I said, gunning my speed to supersonic as I flew at him. I might make it in time, but what was I going to do when I got there? Wolfe strength might allow me to smash through him, but I doubted the efficacy of the effect given how small I was. A bullet would have been the size of a house to me right now. My light nets were useless, my mental powers—well—

"Bjorn!" I shouted.

No effect, Bjorn said. *Nice try, though.*

"Harmon, does that go for you, too?" I asked.

I can read his mind, but affecting it while this small is difficult, to say the least, he replied, and then added a very uncharacteristic, *Sorry.*

"Bastian, if we go dragon we'll be—"

The size of a pillbug, maybe, Bastian said. *Still too small.*

"Shit," I said, almost to Sam, "that leaves—"

Gavrikov.

In a lumberyard? Bastian asked, sounding like he was in disbelief. *Did your brain fall out of your head when you shrank?*

"Why? What's wrong with using my fire powers in a—"

Sam was reaching back, about to leap at Chase, and I knew from what he said that he intended this to be a killing blow. My time was out, and I had one play available to me.

"Gavrikov, NOW!" I shouted, about to crash into Sam. My only hope was that I could burn him enough with a maximum blast of fire to distract him, maybe hurt him when he shrank.

I lit off like a candle, propelling an explosive blast of flame off my body, my skin, letting it sweep outward in an unstoppable wave. It was big, comparatively, it was bright, probably even large enough that an observer could have seen it, looking like a firefly lighting up in the middle of the day.

My flames reached out for Sam, catching him as he was shrinking. I heard his agonized scream as they caught him, big enough to actually do some damage to him. He twisted and writhed as he flew, his momentum carrying him forward—

And he slammed into Chase's arm, which she'd somehow covered by bringing down her lightsaber and turning it into a shield that protected her from forward attack. She knelt behind it, head down, forearm out and blocking her as tiny

Sam, a little nova of fire, slammed into the shield and bounced off, Chase absorbing the blow like a Spartan in the battle line.

"Yes!" I shouted, exultant. "Got you, you little basta—"

No, no, no, Bastian said, causing me to have a moment of doubt. *You shouldn't have done th—*

"Why can't you play with fire in a lumberyard?" I asked, looking down at where Sam had fallen, somewhere far below, out of sight. Something was glowing, sparking, going brighter, along his trail toward the earth, like a meteor streaking up from the ground. Which was weird, because Sam couldn't fly, but—

The flame twisted and grew, moving in a sort of slow motion, like synapses on a brain scan, expanding outward. It took me a second to process that I was watching a chain reaction of some sort, and a second more to realize—

There were wood particles floating in the air around me. Huge, in fact, the size of little floating lanterns.

And way more flammable.

A wave of fire washed over me as the wood particles ignited. It was somehow worse than being caught at the edge of a nuclear blast, mainly because I was small and caught in the middle of this massive combustion event. "Gavrikov!" I shouted, turning on my flame absorption from pure instinct when the fire came rushing for me, howling like a living storm, an inferno consuming every particle of wood that permeated the air around me.

It took a few seconds for it to reach its crescendo, and I took in a lot of fire during those seconds, absorbing the heat and trying to stymie the growing explosion. When I felt like I'd taken in all I could, I opened my eyes, thinking maybe— just maybe—I'd headed this thing off before it got bad.

Nope again.

The air around me was hot, dry, the logs in the pile and on the conveyor where Chase had been working when Friday and I had arrived were on fire, along with some of the machinery. Other piles elsewhere in the yard were similarly aflame. A forklift blew up about a hundred feet from me, its propane tank combusting and the concussive wave of the explosion driving me what felt like a mile backward, toward the edge of the yard, flipping through the air.

When I righted myself again, I had a good view of what I'd done.

The whole place was aflame, the sky already black with choking smoke, and the flames were rising higher and higher, consuming the lumber piled everywhere. It was like I'd been dropped right into a vision of hell, everything burning, the hot, dry air wafting off the rising conflagrations. I blinked my eyes against the raging heat, afraid to look away from the spectacle, orange and red light dancing in all directions as the flames continued to spread.

And that, Bastian said, *is why we don't play with fire in a lumberyard.*

47.

Augustus

With what felt like all the energy in the world shooting at me, I started to panic a little bit. Neon green glowing beams of light came at me from the right, a fiery red beam from this attacking meta's eyes came at me from the left, sandwiching me between a, uh ... well, a red place and a green place. It was a Christmas of laser-esque death, except this was the kind of gift you wanted to pass along to someone you really hated. Like Charles Manson, or Roman Polanski.

But neither of those bastards were there to take the hit for me, and I was about to be neatly bisected by energy beams, so instead I went back to the well and grabbed at the first thing I did have control of.

Which happened to be the concrete beneath our feet.

My control over concrete is imperfect, because only about twenty percent of the elements in a slab fall under the scope of my powers. That made seizing a chunk of it somewhat difficult, like trying to hold onto a human being who's been oiled up and is trying to slip your grasp. Not that I've ever tried, uhh ... You know what? Never mind.

I focused my attention on the ground beneath my enemy's feet. I couldn't even see him behind the glare of his powers cutting toward me, he was just a shadow in the distance. Lifting a hand, I seized the twenty percent of the concrete I could control in a three-foot circle around where he stood and six inches below ...

And lifted it as hard as I could, ripping it out of the ground.

It wasn't a perfect move. It broke apart as soon as I got it clear of the factory floor, but it also ripped the footing right out from beneath my opponent, sending the green beam and the red laser jetting up into the air. He sliced a segment out of the catwalk behind me and I heard it hiss and then drop, clanging as it hit the ground.

I pulled the ground from beneath him like it was a rug beneath his feet, but when I finished, it was flaking like crazy, all the earth elements hanging in my floating grip and all the chaff busting off in a powdery cloud. I came at him with what I had and concentrated it together tightly, throwing it at his face like a punch.

It dusted him hard, knocking him back, but it didn't put him down. I threw it forward again, working on another segment of concrete, trying to sift it a little better so I got more of what I could use and less of the crap that I couldn't. I kept up my attack, and my opponent didn't like that much. He lifted a hand and it started to glow blue, plasma wafting off it in a burn of heat so intense I could feel it ten feet away from him.

He lifted his hand as I came at him again with my gravel punch, and met it in midair. There was a crackling noise like a skillet spitting a little dot of butter straight to a boil—

And suddenly, I couldn't feel that gravel fist anymore, because Mr. Energy had reduced it to its base elements, which were out of my sphere of control.

"Dayum," I muttered, already working to rip up more of the floor. I wanted to rip deeper, get to the earth itself, but the slab was way thicker than it would have been in a normal warehouse this size. They must have built it industrial strength because of the weight of the chemical vats.

"Move!" Reed shouted, blowing our attacker back a step, launching him around a vat. Our opponent shot a parting blast at Reed, who threw up a hand to block his face. The green energy beam caught him right in the wrist, a glancing blow that filled the air with the smell of something being burned. Reed cringed, and when he turned I saw his sleeve had been burned away and there was an inch-long gap where his skin looked like it had just disappeared, revealing muscle tissue beneath.

"Reed, you—" I started to say.

"*Move!*" Reed shouted as another blast of green came zipping at us. He grabbed me by the shirt and yanked me forward. I stumbled behind him as he hauled ass for cover, another red laser shot the diameter of a fence pole chasing after us and ripping apart a console in a shower of sparks.

I followed him, not stopping until he did, damn near running into him as he came to an abrupt halt in the shadow of a shattered catwalk. The factory had definitely taken some damage, and pieces of metal were everywhere, lying in pools of chemicals, a wash of different ones mingling like rivers running together all over the floor. "What are you stopping for?" I yelled, and then I saw.

"What the hell are you two doing?" Scott was standing in our path, next to Jamal, the two of them good and covered in some sort of chemical mixture. Jamal looked like he'd sweated green, big globs of liquid on his glasses.

"Running from trouble while we regroup," Reed said. "I suggest you do the same." And he started to detour around Scott without so much as an explanation or a question about what had happened to the two of them.

I followed him, slapping Jamal on the shoulder. "You're going to want to be running when this dude we were fighting comes around the corner in a second. He's bad news."

"Yeah, well, we got some bad news of our own standing here," Jamal said calmly, not even wiping the moisture off his glasses. It looked thick all up and down his shirt, too, like he'd gotten doused.

"This guy is a two hundred on the energy projection side of metahuman ability," Reed tossed back, continuing to move toward the back of the factory and only slowing a little to address them. "On a scale of one to ten, guys. He's trouble."

"Yeah, I can feel him," Scott said, standing riveted to the spot. "That's the problem with being in a desert environment, not a lot of moisture in the air, and these chemicals being

249

outside my control ... only a couple sources of liquid in this place. It gives me some clarity."

Reed just stopped dead, because neither Jamal nor Scott was heeding our warning. "Clarity? Scott, this guy is going to vaporize your ass if you don't move it!"

Scott held out a hand, waiting for Mr. Energy coming around the corner. Like he could stop it, as if he was Neo and those laser beams were bullets. "Don't worry, Reed ... I got this."

Reed looked like he was fighting the temptation to run, to get the hell out of there and let Scott experience this ever-closing hell for himself. I knew how he felt, because I was feeling it myself, coupled with a desire to grab Jamal by his nasty-ass wet collar and drag him along with me as I beat feet for the damned hills like a sensible person, one who knew that his mama would kill him if he let his brother get wiped out by a dude with laser beam eyes.

But something about preppie boy's demeanor, his calm assurance, and Jamal's steadfast refusal to run in the face of Reed and me telling him to GTFO made me hesitate. It was a pretty stupid idea, one that flew in the face of all my best instincts, but I stood there with them, every muscle in my body clenched, waiting for something to happen.

Mr. Energy came around the corner, his hands all aglow. He was charging up a blast, the kind that I could see already was going to go big, not home, and it was going to take half the damned building with it. The reflected glare of anger and hate glowed in his eyes, shining under the flickering light that was growing from his hands, the luminescent intensity growing stronger as he let the energy build, and build—

His face jerked in pain, and suddenly Mr. Energy's big-ass blast started to fade, the intensity going down like someone had started sliding a dimmer switch on his light show. He spasmed, sticking his chest out, throwing his head back like he wanted to howl at the moon. "The hell ...?" I muttered. "Is he turning into a werewolf?"

"No," Jamal said. "Wrong monster, wrong side."

"What are you talking ab—?" I only got out that much before the answer came, in a rather spectacular fashion.

Mr. Energy's chest burst open in a cloud of dark red fluid, a hundred veins bursting all at once and carrying all of his blood out of his body in a massive expulsion of liquid. The dark red cloud coalesced and writhed like a living thing, pulled toward Scott and his waiting hand. It floated there in front of him, little dots of extraneous material dripping out of the cloud as the elements of the blood he couldn't control expelled themselves from the part that he could.

"Holy hell!" I shouted. "You just became Count Dracula's wet dream!"

"I don't know which was grosser, what he did or what you just said," Reed said.

"He just drained a man's body of all its blood, this ain't a tough choice," I said as Mr. Energy's exsanguinated corpse pitched forward lifelessly. He didn't even move or twitch, nothing.

"I think the real moral of the story here," Jamal said, "is that you shouldn't mess with a super Poseidon in a dry environment unless you want to become a blood donor in a very major way."

"Did you do that before?" Reed asked, pushing past me to stand next to Scott, who was still holding the cloud of blood in front of him. It wasn't as big as I would have thought it would be.

"Yeah," Jamal answered for him, "he got three of those guys over there that were trying to kill us." He gestured behind us, and I turned, noticing for the first time that there were three bodies on the floor, drenched in red like Scott had just let the cloud go over them once he was done emptying them out.

"I don't know what to say besides *damn*," I said, looking around. I eased back in the direction we'd been going before. The factory had gone silent, not a sound but the spray of chemicals out the side of ruptured vats in the air, no hint of further opposition waiting anywhere around us. "And ... I think we won."

"Good," Reed said. "Because ... I don't know how much more of that," he nodded at Scott and the cloud of floating blood, "I want to see. Ever."

"You think that's bad," Jamal said, "wait 'til you see what he does with it once he's—"

As if to perfectly illustrate the point, Scott moved his hand and the cloud of blood splattered against a nearby wall with a sick noise like someone had thrown spaghetti against it, a rich sound of thick liquid that had a little element of a sucking noise to make it all the worse. And as if that weren't bad enough, it looked like he'd smashed someone against it and turned them into a splatter painting.

I felt a little sick in my guts. "Did you have to do that?" I asked, watching Scott seem to come out of a trance.

"Did you want it splashing around your shoes?" he asked, balling his hand into a fist and then relaxing it, over and over.

"No."

"Then yeah, I had to do that," Scott said. "The room's clear now. No other hostiles. Or anyone, actually."

"Good," Reed said, looking around like he didn't quite believe Scott. I couldn't blame him. That was the sort of thing that tended to change your opinion of a man, and not for the better. Reed looked like he was anticipating an ambush, too, but he kept his head about him. "Then I guess we're done here."

"But not with this group," I said. "Not if there are more of these guys out there, like Omar, in the distribution channel."

"No," Reed agreed. "And we're going to get after them—as soon as we clean up this mess with the local PD." He lowered his head, and adopted a hard look, like someone had stepped on his junk. "But if we keep this up—"

"Please, please, don't let 'keep it up' mean we watch Scotty rip the blood out of more peoples' unresisting bodies," Jamal said.

"He was very definitely resisting," Scott said. "Right up 'til the end."

"—If we keep this up," Reed said, talking over both of them, "... there are ten names on our list in the eastern US. If we can get after them today, with a little electronic aid from J.J. and Abby ..." A small smile of satisfaction emerged, like he hadn't just seen a dude's blood ripped entirely from his body, "... then we might just see the end of this organization by tomorrow morning."

48.

Sienna

Everything around me was on fire, and you'd think I'd be used to that, like it was some perfectly normal status quo for me.

But it was not.

"Shit," I said.

Everything's on fire again, Eve crowed. *You really have a way about you, you know? You should visit a fireworks store next, really cement your reputation for sowing havoc with a pretty display of sky snakes in red, blue and green.*

Or you could go the Guy Friday route and red, white and blue it up, Zack said dryly.

Those are my colors, too, technically, Harmon said, *though I prefer them a bit more understated rather than as a full blown display, garishly lighting up the night sky.*

"Hey, guys, let's not lose sight of the fact that everything is burning and our new replacement supervillain is still lurking out here somewhere," I said, trying to get them—and myself—to focus. It was kind of distracting being in the center of a massive inferno. I may have been immune to the burn, but the smoke still bothered my eyes and threatened to overwhelm me.

Do you hear that in the distance? Harmon asked.

"Hear wh—"

Harmon boosted my hearing somehow, maybe tapping me into Chase or Sam's head for a second. But a distant sound I'd perceived only barely over the roaring flames a moment ago became a lot starker and clearer in an instant.

Police sirens. The cops were coming.

"Good thing I'm microscopic right now," I said. It wasn't actually a good thing, obviously, but in the realm of tragedies and problems I was dealing with, it seemed like the answer to a rather sizable one—dodging the cops when they came out in force.

I lagged a little, dropped a hundred feet, and caught myself just in time to avoid a flaming particle of wood that was burning in the air like an ember on the wind.

Watch yourself, Gavrikov said, *you just used a tremendous amount of your energy trying to start and then contain the flames.*

"No wonder I feel exhausted," I said, trying to keep aloft. "At least now I know that trying to keep this place from burning down at my size is pretty much a fool's errand."

Yes, now you can just give up and fly off, Eve suggested.

I looked over the scene and realized that Chase was stuck in the middle of two particularly ugly conflagrations, wood piles that were tipping over, spilling lit tree trunks around her. There was a pall of black smoke over her, and she was coughing furiously, head down, her lightsaber shield working to protect her from the flames nearest her.

"Yeah ... I really can't do that," I said and darted toward Chase. I couldn't just leave her here, trapped, unable to see where she was going. I flew straight for her ear canal, trying my best to absorb some fire as I went. It went about as well as me trying to put out this entire place with nothing but some tears, but I tried it anyway.

I zipped into Chase's ear and shouted, "Chase! It's Sienna!"

She was coughing so furiously, I wondered if she'd heard me. But then she stopped that barking, hard cough for a second and said, "I can't see ... anything ..." And she started hacking again.

"Dammit," I muttered. I couldn't really do much of anything at this size. I was way, way too small to be able to affect her, push her in any direction. Still ... I could at least see ... "We need to go to your right. There's about a fifteen-foot gap of open space before another flaming log pile. I think you can get out that way."

"… Okay," she said between barking coughs, and started staggering in that direction, holding up her saber shield against the heat of the nearest blaze. I could feel it from inside her ear; the shield wasn't helping much that I could tell.

Chase staggered, and I bounced around a little inside her canal, hitting a waxy buildup. "Yuck," I said, trying to keep close to the exit so I could dart out and look, watchful eye ready to call out the next turn. "Okay, another couple feet and then a hard right turn … that's it … stop. Now walk forward …"

She was staggering, head down, which gave me an angle to pop my head out of her ear like it was manhole cover. Or actually, more like the Millennium Falcon coming out of that cave in the asteroid in *Empire*. Either way, I had enough of a view to be able to call out the next direction. "Take a left!"

Chase staggered, dipping a little lower. The smoke was getting thicker, wind shifting directions. She launched into a terrible cough, a series of hacking barks that forced me out of her ear because her head was moving too much. She sagged to her knees, sounding like she was going to lose a lung.

"Shitty shit shit," I said, trying to figure out what I could do to help her. She was stalled, and the fire was closing. I was just too small to push her along, or help her …

Too small in your current form, Bastian said. *Maybe if you were just a touch bigger …*

"Damn," I said. I'd rejected the idea of going Quetzlcoatl earlier because the size differential didn't seem like it'd make much difference, but what other choice did I have? In the bigger form, maybe I could at least give her a push, some guidance that didn't involve me shouting in her ear like a miniature case of tinnitus or a quieter version of the souls in my head. "Yeah. Okay." I flew out of her head and darted around her back. "Here goes nothing …"

I could feel the change coming. My arms started to stretch, becoming the wings of the dragon, and my legs pulled together, melding to form my long, snaking tail. I felt my nose elongate like a snout, brushing against Chase's back, pushing against her—

And suddenly, she felt very, very small against my nose, because she was stuck between my nostrils and just above my jaw.

What the hell? I called out in my mind, trying to figure out if Sam had gotten to her, maybe shrank her down just as I was growing to dragon size. But no, it was more than that; the flames that had surrounded me were getting smaller, the black clouds that once blotted out the sky were shrinking, and I could see the trees past them, just barely, again, as my head, and Chase on my snout, extended beyond the perimeter of the lumberyard fire.

"Whoa!" I roared as my explosive growth flung Chase free of the flames and into the woods, where she landed in a roll and came up coughing, eyes bleary with tears. "I think dragon form just cleared up my shrinkage problem."

And left you with a brand new one, Harmon said, voice tinged with alarm.

"What new—"

Something hit my wing and rocked me sideways, ripping a hole in my flank as it spun me over, lifting my snake belly up into the air. A line of stinging pains ran along my side from my tail to my lungs, punching in hard like needles or—

Bullets.

I caught a glimpse of the trouble as my body rolled with the attack, a bunch of black SUVs and Army Humvees with mounted weaponry chattering at the entrance to the lumberyard, just ahead of a legion of fire trucks. They had a whole damned task force out there, FBI and military, fifty troops and law enforcement guys, all firing on me.

My wing got chewed up in a machine gun blast and something else tore off my tail, causing me so much pain I screamed in a dragon roar as I dropped, falling back into the cloaking fire beneath me. Hard impacts tore across my shoulder as I changed back into human form involuntarily under the withering storm of bullets. I was bleeding from a hundred wounds, and I hit the gravel and lay there, coughing up blood, the smoke around me threatening to devour me in the blackness of the cloud.

"Wolfe ..." I coughed, blood running freely down my chin.

Hurrying.

Hang on, Harmon said. *Help is on the way.*

"There's no ... help for this ..." I said, running a hand over my chest. There were so many pitted marks in my skin, so many wounds ... blood was flowing out like waterfalls, hot, sticky liquid running down me. "... if I heal ... try to run ... they're gonna ... shoot me down ..." The sound of thousands of bullets filling the air above me still rumbled over the licking of the flames on either side.

Hold on, Harmon said. *Just another minute.*

"I don't ... think it matters," I said, eyeing the nearest fire. The wood pile next to me groaned. It was going to topple over any second, a machine gun chipping away at it and sending embers sparking into the air around me.

Job's not done, Bastian said. *Come on. Up and at 'em.*

They just ate up our dragon form with enough gunfire to kill an army, Roberto, I said. The wounds were starting to knit on my chest. *How did they even get here so fast?*

Apparently they picked you up over Canada, Harmon said. *They were already en route before this started.*

"Oh," I said, staring up at the sky. I could see a hint of blue somewhere between the black clouds. It seemed nice. A nice place to be on a day like this. "They're ... not going to stop, are they?"

Harmon was slow to respond, and when he did, he didn't sound very satisfied at the answer. *No. Not this time. Not anymore.*

"Friday was right; they really are going to grind me down," I said, the back of my head all the way down to my heels feeling the bite of the hard gravel where it rested against my naked skin.

Come on, Eve said. *We have things to do. We still have to save that idiot from assassination. And frankly, your shoulders could use more work.*

"I don't know, man. This is getting pretty outrageously

257

tough. I think this is the part where most people would throw in the towel."

You are not most people, Bjorn said.

The wounds were gone, but the blood and the pain had stayed, mingling with the bite of those rocks against my skin. "No, I'm not," I said, morose, looking once again at the logs about to topple over on me. Tons of weight, landing solidly on me. Felt like an appropriate metaphor. "And I never will be one of them again. Not after all this."

Ten seconds, Harmon said.

"Ten seconds to what?" I asked, the lumber at my side straining and cracking. I waited for the answer, but it did not come, so I just lay there, waiting for the lumber to fall over on me. I doubted it would kill me, but sooner or later maybe the bullets would, or the task force would enter the lumberyard and find me, pumping me full of lead.

Here it comes, Harmon said.

"Greaaaaaat," I said, and something touched me right on the midsection, like a poke in the belly. Sharp but short, I looked down, an uneasy feeling at whatever it was. "The hell?"

The pain of the gravel in my back lessened in a second, one of the grains seeming to grow into a boulder and shoving me upright as I shrank, again, down to tiny size. The pain in my abdomen grew more pronounced as I got smaller, the lump manifesting as a human figure, feet on in my stomach.

I lit up and he jumped back, yelping to avoid being burned as I covered myself in a jumpsuit of fire. The sudden addition of flame and the fact that my body had shrunk to his size let me see him, finally, for who he was, even as he stared at me, a perfect standoff.

"Greg Vansen, you dickweed," I said, suddenly resolved to at least kill his ass before I checked out, "this is all your fault."

"I had absolutely nothing to do with this," he said, looking around frantically, "and in fact ..." he looked greatly disquieted as he stared around himself, looking at the flaming ruin of the lumberyards, "... I came here to save you."

I stared at him, he stared at me, and only thing I could think of was: "... Say what?"

49.

Greg

"What are you even doing here?" Sienna asked before she even gave him a chance to clarify his last remarks.

"I told you," Greg said, burning slightly, and not from the flames around him. He hated being asked the same question more than once. "I'm here to save you."

She thrust a finger out at him. "Save me? Your pal Sam is the one who damned near killed me here. And you yourself dropped a nuclear bomb on me less than twenty-four hours ago. I ought to skin you and offer it to a microbe as a coat."

"As much as that might scratch your charitable itch," Greg said, looking at the pile of burning lumber to his left uneasily, "that would leave you trapped here with a rather sizable police force trying to find you so they can kill you."

"And that differs from what I'm dealing with now how?" She looked weary enough that he wondered if she'd even be able to walk or fly, though her ensemble of a flaming toga hinted that she was perhaps not utterly exhausted.

"I can get you out of here." He pointed to a small thing circling slowly around them, the size of a bee.

She peered at it, squinting. "Is ... is that your Concorde?"

"On auto-pilot, yes," Greg said. "We'll need to shrink down, then I'll grow it and get us out of here—"

She looked around for a moment, seeming to weigh her options. "Yeah. All right, fine. I accept your temporary truce. Get me out of here in miniature or whatever, because I need a damned nap post haste."

"Fine," Greg said, reaching out and touching her on the arm. "Come here," he said, and he concentrated.

It wasn't using his powers that taxed him; it was shrinking while guiding them on the appropriate trajectory to end up on top of the Concorde as it slowly orbited, the size of a buzzing insect to them, already shrunken, and thus microscopic to anyone else. He held her securely on the arm, and she let him guide her, flesh extinguished so he could grip her with his gloved hand.

She stared at the leather encased fingers he wrapped around her upper arm. "Good call, bringing the gloves."

"Preparation," Greg said simply as he landed them expertly on the top of the Concorde, then shrank them between the plates on a top hatch, then grew them again once inside.

His feet thumped down on the carpeted interior of the Concorde inside the passenger cabin, and he immediately turned to sprint toward the cockpit. Leaving the Concorde circling in the middle of such dangerous environs went against all his instincts, and he swiftly flipped off the autopilot, taking the controls again, and sending the plane skyward.

"How did you find me?" Sienna asked, plopping down in the co-pilot's seat without even asking, her skin appearing wherever she touched the seat, her flame leotard pulling back to avoid setting the seat on fire.

Greg eyed her, swallowing his irritation at her bare flesh on his seat. Better than burning them up, he supposed. "It was fairly obvious where you would go next. You'd already visited Jon and Theo, after all. Chase was the next logical step."

"Yeah, but how'd you find me in the middle of a flaming lumberyard?" she said.

He shrugged. "That thing you did earlier, when you crashed my Comanche ... it felt like that."

"Hmph," she said as he pushed the throttle to maximum and the Concorde started to climb. "Like a voice in your head, telling you what to do?"

"More subtle than that," Greg said. "Smaller, perhaps …
I don't know how to describe it. There are some leftover
blankets from this plane's days in passenger service in the
back if you want to cover yourself. I don't think I have any
clothes that would fit you on the plane." He did back at
home, or ones that could be modified to fit her, but here –
well, transporting a naked woman that wasn't his wife was
not a contingency he had ever prepared for.

She looked him over. "I dunno, Greg. You look about
my size."

He turned his attention forward, irritation rolling over
him. "You might want to strap in. And mind the seatbelts."

"We can't leave yet," Sienna said, tensing, pushing herself
out of the seat. "We have to save Friday."

He couldn't help it, he took his eyes off the instruments
and stared at her, dumbstruck. "… Why would you want to
save Friday?"

"Because it's the best day of the week, duh," she quipped
right back. "You know I'm talking about the guy you're
trying to k—"

"Of course I picked that up," he said, flushing in
annoyance. "I meant … why are you bothering to save him?"

"Because I have to save him," she said, looking straight
ahead again. "Why are you saving me?"

Greg froze, open-mouthed. "… I don't know," he finally
said. "Your friend, Bruce … his contract was cancelled, at
least for me. And I never had one on you."

"There's a difference between not killing us and going
out of your way to save us," she said, not letting up from
staring at him.

Greg felt his cheeks flaming as he held tight to the
controls. Couldn't she see he was flying a plane? There was
no time for silly questions right now.

Though … that, perhaps, was not a silly question.
"Because," he said at last, wrestling a little with the stick as
he went for altitude and grew the plane a little to make it
easier, goosing it up to the size of a handheld model, "… it
felt right."

"Weird," she said mockingly. "Friday—Bruce—

261

whatever—he ended up in the woods over there." She gestured in front of them. "Keep low to avoid the storm of bullets flying around."

"Roger wilco," Greg said, shrinking the plane slightly. Taking a bullet at their size would mean complete devastation followed by a probable crash at extremely high velocity. He guided the Concorde through a cloud, speeding it up slightly as the embers of fire floated through the air in front of them, and they emerged out the other side shrunken down again. It was a game, shrinking and growing objects, one that Greg had learned to play masterfully throughout his career, always trying to time it to coincide with when people weren't looking. That was how one cultivated a reputation as a magician, after all.

"Over there," Sienna said as they broke out of the black smoke. Trees were down ahead, snapped cleanly at the top, something having plowed through them on its way back to the earth.

The Concorde carried them through the woods, Greg growing it just a little now that they were clear of the lumberyard and the seemingly endless volley of bullets therein. He leaned forward and looked past Sienna; the police perimeter was well back, and he watched a few black-clad figures trying to shuffle by beneath them, completely unaware that their quarry was slipping by overhead, no larger than a bird to them.

"I'm taking us down," Greg said, bringing the plane down in a slow spiral toward the earth. "I'll shrink and go to autopilot. Then I can step out and retrieve him."

"How the hell do you do that?" Sienna asked. "You can't fly …"

"I just step out and grow, so the fall becomes a step," Greg said, matter-of-factly. "Then shrink when I reach him, reduce him along with me, then grow enough to jump to the plane—"

"Sounds complicated," she said, rolling her eyes.

"It's easy once you practice," he said. "Like any complex process, practice makes—"

"Yeah, just go do what you need to do," she said. "I

guess I'll wait here and … stare out the front window as we go in very tiny circles."

"Have fun with that," Greg said and shrank as he leapt for the seam at the front window. He passed through and grew again a second later, once he was clear of the Concorde, taking care not to grow larger than the flight path of the miniaturized plane. That was half the difficulty; staying conscious of small objects that you needed as they moved around a battlefield, and also making sure that any other combatants didn't run into them. It was for this reason he seldom put anything like the Concorde on autopilot when stepping out. Usually he preferred to land first and place the plane back in its protective case in his pocket before engaging in any sort of fighting.

But, this was a different sort of scenario, and he'd certainly practiced to make sure that he was ready for it.

Greg grew to roughly a foot in height and landed on Friday's leg, prompting a mild grunt. He then shrank again, and took Friday with him, shrinking the man down to the point where he fit in the palm of Greg's hand. Greg himself was ant-sized, which made Friday at his current volume somewhat smaller than a grain of sand. "All right," he said, talking to the insensate figure in his palm as he pulled a small cartridge out of his pocket and expanded it. It was a carrier he'd designed to carry human beings in small form in his pocket, complete with a very tiny oxygen recirculation system with a backup, as well as heavily padded sides to protect against the inevitable bumping that came from being so small and carried on a larger person. "In you go," he said as he tipped Friday inside and shrank the whole thing back down again, slipping it into his breast pocket and clipping it there, the whole thing now no longer than a pen.

"Well, Greg," came a drawling, familiar voice from behind him, "I'd ask you what you're doing there, but I think we both know." He spun to find Sam standing there, taller than him as almost ever, regarding him with a dangerous look.

"I'd ask you what you're doing here as well, but we also know, don't we?" Greg stood up straight and subtly applied a few inches of height. It probably wasn't subtle to Sam, but being smaller than Sam always made Greg uncomfortable. "You took up my contract with McGarry."

"Maybe if you hadn't botched it so darned badly …" Sam shook his head. "I have to thank you, though. McGarry pays real well. I've been trying to get into his good graces for years and he's kept me on the outside. Guess you've been his fair-haired boy for so long he's gotten real used to having a smart, fully-capable Atlas at his fingertips for wetwork, because the minute he was done with you he whistled me right up."

"Imagine how disappointed he'll be to learn you're not that capable," Greg sniped.

"I may not be quite as fancy as you," Sam said with a grin to mask that hostility burning in his eyes, "but I know how to get a job done. Like I know, for example, that by smashing your pocket I'm going to win the day."

"But you'll have a hell of a time proving it," Greg said. "And it seems to me you've also had a head start violating the same terms of the contract that got me fired—you shrank Sienna Nealon and left her that way. McGarry led me to understand that killing her was a very definite no-no."

"Awww, I just shrank her for a spell," Sam said. "She found her own way out, so I don't know what you're squawking about. Seemed fine to me."

"She was about to get killed by the government agents swarming over this place," Greg said, "but sure, I suppose. 'Fine' has many subjective meanings."

"I'm about to lose patience with you," Sam said. "You lost the contract. Why are you here grabbing that boy and helping that girl? This ain't your dogfight, Greg, unless you're taking on hard luck cases out of the charity of your heart now … and I think we both know you ain't got a heart."

"Whereas we both know you don't have a brain," Greg stung back, leaping and growing as Sam reached for him. Greg had in his mind the direction the Concorde had been traveling and the rough speed in relation to the size. As he shrank, he found that indeed, he had been right on target, and landed on the body of the plane with a thump before sliding down and shrinking once more, entering through the gap between the airplane body and the passenger door, returning to his normal size a fraction of a second later.

Sienna Nealon looked back down the aisle at him as he landed. "That is a neat, if slightly creepy, trick."

"You should see what I do for an encore," he said, unclipping the storage unit containing Friday and offering it to her as he slid back into his seat and fastened the restraints. "You might want to hold on."

"Why?" She took the cylinder. "Are we about to—hey, is that Sam?"

"Yes." He took the Concorde off autopilot and pushed the throttle down. He was likely to need the additional speed very, very soon.

"I think he's—is that a Stinger missile in his hands?" Nealon's face was pressed up against the glass like she was suctioned to it.

"Almost certainly. Let me know when he fires." Greg took the stick and started to climb, pressing for altitude as he traded speed for it. He couldn't quite go supersonic at this size, but that would shortly become irrelevant.

"I see a launch bloom," Nealon said. "He's gotta be—I think he's a little bigger than us … the stinger is streaking toward our engine—"

"Yes, that's what it does," Greg said.

"Uh, okay," Nealon said. "So … what are you going to do about it?"

"Something impressive," Greg said, already tweaking things more to his liking.

He grew the Concorde, first to the point where it was the size of a model airplane, much, much larger than the insect-size it had been a moment earlier. With the added size transferring to added thrust, it cleared the trees in seconds. That done, he grew it even larger, back to the size of a normal plane and even slightly beyond.

The Concorde blew out of the area as it broke the sound barrier, leaving the clearing—and the airborne Stinger—far, far behind it. The forest receded into a green path that Greg couldn't see within a couple seconds, even standing up and trying to look back. They were thousands of feet in the sky seconds later, and he started to reduce the size of the Concorde to prevent tracking shortly thereafter.

"That ... was ... yeah, whoa," Sienna said, looking back. "How big did you make the Concorde just now? Because it seemed huge."

"I grew the Concorde—and us—to roughly four times normal size," Greg said. "It was a precaution."

She was studying him carefully, putting it together. "Because of the government agents."

"Because of their bullets," Greg corrected. "They could have, after all, put a considerable number of holes in the airframe. Increasing the size of the Concorde also increased the scale of the thrust, which allowed for a fast getaway and less time for them to aim at us, albeit at the cost of a larger target for those seconds we were within their range."

"But their bullets wouldn't do nearly as much damage to us or the plane at four times normal size," she said. "Because that'd make me ... like ... twenty feet tall. A 9mm bullet would be like a pinprick."

"Exactly," Greg said.

"Huh," she settled back in her seat. "So ... what do we do now?" Her unease showed clearly on her face, in the way her lips were a stiff line once she finished speaking.

"We'll need to change planes soon," he said. "An abandoned road will do. I have an airframe I've modified to look like a Predator drone. Hopefully that will allow us to blend into the background noise as they put up every kind of airplane they've got in an effort to hunt you down."

"Yeah," she said quietly. "Seems like I've really called down the thunder this time." Her face flickered into irritation. "Thanks for that, by the way."

He stayed stiff at the controls. "If you're waiting for me to apologize for not actually killing you or doing you much in the way of actual harm, and then saving your life afterwards ... you could be waiting quite a while. If you don't like me, you may also feel free to step out at any time and take your little friend with you." He waved a hand at the cylinder she still clutched in her hand.

Sienna stared down at the cylinder. "He's really in this?" She lifted it up like she was going to give it a shake.

"I wouldn't do that if you like him alive," Greg said. "It's padded, but he's minuscule, and you have metahuman strength. Turning it into a centrifuge will have predictable results on his flesh and bone."

"I guess I've got to handle him with kid gloves, then," she said, holding the cylinder daintily. "So ... what else is new?"

"What's new is I just saved your life," Greg said, shrinking the Concorde as he spied a country lane in the distance. It was paved, and would do nicely for a landing strip. He could feel her glare burning into the side of his head. "And that ... is very, very new ... at least to me."

50.

Sienna

Riding along with Greg Vansen was a trip, and I mean that in the sense of the word that is very literal—we were riding, in a shrunken plane, across the country—and also in the way that everything was extremely, exceptionally weird.

Because I was shifting in size from that of an enormous Sienna giant to the size of a bug, sometimes within seconds, and entirely out of my own control.

"Your little fake drone seems to be making good time," I said as we crossed the loping plains of Illinois. Ahead, I suspected, was metropolitan Chicago, though I couldn't quite see it yet.

"It's actually a real drone," he said. "I just stuck a cockpit in when I removed one of the remote piloting systems. I seldom use it, though, because it's so much slower than the SR-71 or the Concorde. Blends better, though, in a crowded sky."

"Yeah," I said, feeling a tug of sadness. "I get the sense that the sky over America is going to be crowded for a good long while yet." I didn't take the obvious path and hammer him with the fact that it was his own damned fault for implicating me in a miniature nuke attack, because he'd already expressed a total lack of remorse for that. And since he hadn't actually killed any other human beings in said attack, as much as I wanted to rip his throat out for screwing me over, I was having a hard time working up the motivation to do so, especially since he was presently protecting my ass from a government that was trying really hard to draw and quarter me in the modern style.

"Mmm," Greg acknowledged stiffly. He was a really short guy by nature, stocky and stout, kinda like me in that regard, and probably within an inch of my natural height. He'd apparently tailored his planes to adapt to that height, though, because every one of the pilot seats seemed to have been raised a few inches. It was a strange thing to notice, I suppose, but I noticed it.

"Okay," I said, changing tacks, "so I'm calling you Hank Pym or Scott Lang. You choose. Generous, huh?"

He didn't look at me. "Hank Pym," he said softly, almost before I finished the sentence. When I left a pregnant pause for him to elaborate, he took the invitation. "Hank Pym was a brilliant scientist who created countless inventions. Scott Lang was just a thief." He pursed his lips hard. "I hate thievery, especially thievery for monetary gain."

"Didn't you … steal this drone?" I asked, wondering if you could drown in irony. I hoped not. "And your planes? And helicopters. And—"

"Yes," he said, swiftly and impatiently. "But not for gain. They're tools. And I always chose the ones heading for decommission, preferring to restore them myself through my own tinkering. So I suppose I stole from the boneyard of the military and a few companies here and there, but … nothing that anyone was going to consider a great loss to their bottom line."

"Including that nuke?" I fished.

"The nuke was from a program called SADM—Special Atomic Demolition Munitions," he said, taking on the air of a professor giving a lecture, "they were designed as suitcase bombs. I also stole some of the old Davy Crockett field artillery nukes. Yes, they were all headed for decommissioning. They were also generally small, a kiloton at most in their natural size. Of course, I reduced the one I aimed at you, or else it would have blown up considerably bigger." He sounded a little defensive about it.

I decided to detour around the argument I saw because

… what was the point? "So … you can't control insects, can you?"

He hmphed, and I realized it was a very, very muted chuckle. "No. I looked into it after I discovered the full scope of my power as an Atlas, but it was … well, impossible. You see, ants communicate by—"

"So you're an Atlas?" I asked. I laid my head back on the headrest and found it very comfortable. Like he'd regularly had company in his plane trips and refurbished the chairs accordingly. When he nodded, I said, "I've fought an Atlas before. In Minneapolis, once, close to the end of the war. He didn't shrink."

"He could have," Greg sniffed. "Most Atlases are simply idiots, though, like most metas and most humans. They never see the value in the small, only the big. Personally, I reverse the calculus and find it works much better. When I discovered my power included the ability to shrink not just myself but others and objects as well, it was like opening a door to endless possibility."

"Which you decided to parley into a career as an assassin," I said.

"Yes," he said softly.

"Why?"

"Because it pays better than being a cell biologist," Greg said. "Or an entomologist. Being good at what I am good at … pays better than heroing, I would imagine." He gave me a sidelong look. "And certainly better than working for any of the paramilitary organizations that I tried to contract with before settling on this freelancing path I've been on the last few years."

"You might be surprised how well heroing pays these days," I said. I'd approved the payroll for the new agency, after all. It was rich because I'd wanted it to be, and the good news was it was pretty rapidly becoming self-sustaining thanks to all the jobs they were picking up from local and state governments.

"Perhaps," he said. "Ultimately I just decided to become the best in my chosen field. To use conventional weapons— but have everything I need on hand. Immaculate preparation, ready for nearly any contingency."

"You didn't seem too ready in Portland," I said.

He grunted his displeasure. "I was not informed that Bruce—Friday's—accomplice was you."

"Or when you tried to kill him in the river before that."

"His being a metahuman was withheld from me as well. As you know, that is crucial information in dealing with a dangerous subject—"

"Or above the Sierra Nevadas—"

"Fine," he cut me off, "dealing with you has been a humbling exercise in empirically finding the holes in my contingency plans. Are you happy now?"

"Well, the government is after me now in record numbers, so … no, I'm not super duper happy at the moment." That thought settled like a worry on me, one that was bound to persist past the current crisis. "Don't suppose you'd like to stand up and take credit for that?"

"To whom?" Greg asked.

"The media, the government," I said. "Anyone who'd listen?"

He cocked an eyebrow in surprise but kept his focus on the planes unfolding beneath us. "Who do you imagine would want to listen to that tale, exactly?"

Intentionally or not, I think he might have had something there. "Damn you," I said.

He kept staring straight ahead. Maybe it was his way of expressing remorse. "I don't think anyone would take notice even if I were to broadcast a full confession on YouTube, complete with demonstrations of my ability, and my additional nuclear stockpile in the backdrop—you know, for color."

"Why do you think I said, 'damn you'? I know a truth when I hear one." I sighed. "Still, you could at least try."

"I'll take it under advisement," he said, and we both knew the advisement period was over. I didn't have a lot of faith that a full confession would do much good. The hornets' nest was already fully engaged in being pissed off at Sienna Nealon right now; it was highly unlikely that they'd put their stingers away, at least in the short term.

271

"Least you could do after trying to kill me," I said, knowing that it wasn't close to the least he could do.

The least he could have done was leave me to die in Montana under a hail of bullets the like of which probably hadn't been seen since … hell, I don't know. Pick a big battle in a big war with hundreds of participants, because there were a lot of bullets flying at me in Montana. More than the US had seen in one place on our soil since the Civil War, I would have guessed.

"I'm not trying to kill you now," he said stiffly, once again justifying himself. "I'm not even trying to kill your oversized and under-intellectual boyfriend—"

"You keep insulting my honor like that and I'm going to gut you just as a warning to others."

That elicited a brief smile. Because he didn't think I was serious, I guess. "Sorry."

"An actual apology," I said. "Amazing. Did it hurt?" We settled into a few more minutes of silence until I came up with another worrying thought. "Since Sam is your buddy … is he going to know where to find you?"

This caused Greg to shift uncomfortably once more in his seat. "No. I had a series of safe houses across the country that I used when he and I … worked together. I taught him some of my strategies, tried to take him from the path of being a stupid Atlas who only went big to—"

"Becoming small and lethal and an invisible danger to people everywhere," I said. "Thanks for that, by the way."

"You're welcome," Greg said, playing the straight man. "I shut down those safe houses after we parted ways slightly less than amicably. I haven't been back to any of them since, and I never revealed all my locations to him, or in fact …" He looked sullen for a moment. "… ever told him my real last name." He looked right at me. "It's not actually Vansen."

"Smart move," I said. Really damned calculating, more like. But when you're an assassin, I suppose it only made sense to hide your identity even from potential partners. "I mean, deceptive as hell, but … smart." I looked out the thin viewing slit. The city of Chicago was stretching out in the distance ahead, the far western suburbs already underneath us. I noticed we were descending, and also, possibly, shrinking. It was tough to tell this far from the ground. "How'd you two hook up?"

"I took him on after my last partner … moved on to other … work," Greg said, the words coming in fits. "We ran across each other in the course of work early in my career moving between those unaffiliated paramilitary groups, and when … my other partner …retired, I looked him up."

I didn't press him to fill the Swiss-cheese holes in that story. Not like I had a lot of leverage over him right now anyway. The suburbs were getting bigger and bigger, spreading out under us, and I realized that, yep, we were getting smaller. And closer to the ground. The houses were looking pretty swank, too, well-kept and newly refurbished. They looked like they were out of a John Hughes film. "Where are we going?"

"I only have one safe house left," Greg said tightly, "so we'll hole up there while we plot our next move." He brought us lower and lower, and we continued to shrink. I suspected we were no more than a foot long at this point, as we crossed into a neighborhood where the houses looked like they were probably very old and very expensive.

"Looking like a pretty nice safe house," I said. "Most of mine have been dives, because they're cheap and I'm budget conscious. But you go in style. I'd say I like that, but since you make your money killing people …"

Greg tensed as he brought us in even lower. We skimmed over the roof of a two-story brick house, probably only about three feet above it, but it seemed a lot farther given how tiny we were now. "I do what I have to."

"Pfft," I said, poking him again. "You don't have to kill people." He gave me a sideye. "What? Is that because I kill people? I did it in the course of law enforcement." Mostly. Especially these last few years.

"It doesn't really matter now, does it?" Greg asked. "Because apparently … I'm now out of business." He'd brought us down even lower, through the high trees that hemmed in the neighborhood yards. We were aiming at the

273

wall of a white paneled house, heading straight for it.

"Um. Um. Um." I was pointing at the wall we were going at, traveling at the speed of several hundred miles per hour, unable to quite articulate the words.

Greg didn't look over at me. "Hmm?"

"We're—uh—the wall—"

The plane continued to shrink as we headed toward what looked like a small vent mounted to the outside of the structure. It got huge in front of us, massively huge, to the point where instead of being in danger of hitting the wall, suddenly it felt like we were going to be swallowed up whole by the darkness on the other side.

"And ... now," Greg said, as a light flipped on in the vent. We easily slipped between the covers and came in for a soft landing on a runway that felt so enormous it might as well have been an outdoor landing strip in Utah.

The Concorde taxied to a stop and I was left sitting there in the co-pilot's seat, staring at the complete nothing anywhere nearby. "Well ... this is a really nice safe house you've got here. Kinda empty, though."

"You think so?" Greg allowed a rare smile as he held on to the stick.

"Yeah, I think s—oh."

The world had once again changed outside my window, the walls that had seemed hundreds of miles away now only a few football fields in length from me. There were planes lining one side of the room, which now looked like a massive hangar. I looked to my right and found a row of various cars and old military vehicles. I counted at least one M1A2 Abrahms main battle tank, a few prototypes I'd never seen before, a Soviet T-72, and a host of other vehicles from the military, like an MRAP. Another section was lined with helicopters, and along the far wall what looked like a small rack appeared to hold model boats ... which I suspected were real boats.

"For someone who prides himself on not being a thief, you have kind of a lot of stolen merch here, guy," I said, giving Greg a pointed look as he ran through his post-flight checklist and taxied the plane into a spot that seemed perfect for the Concorde.

"Like I said," Greg blushed furiously, flipping his switches, unable to hide his embarrassment now that I'd seen his Fortress of Solitude, "I believe in being prepared."

51.

Augustus

My day had been long, starting with the raid in Nevada in the morning and working our way back across the country. We'd rolled up eight out of the ten names on our list of plumbers, hitting them like they deserved to be hit and finding that—big surprise—every single one of them had been packing meta powers.

"That last guy didn't play fair," Jamal said, holding a damp cloth to his head. He'd taken a blade hit right to the forehead from some guy who seemed to be able to pull them out of his skin like porcupine quills. Spontaneous generation of blades wasn't a power I'd ever seen before, but it beat the hell out of the next thing he'd done, which was to turn his coffee cup and the coffee inside into hardened steel, which he'd bounced off Jamal's forehead at high speed.

"Duck next time," Scott said lightly, rustling the bushes as he stretched. We were hiding on a stretch of road outside Durham, North Carolina. Darkness had fallen already, and there weren't any street lights this far out. We were a thirty-odd-minute drive from the Raleigh-Durham airport, and the city had faded surprisingly fast.

"Ha ha," Jamal said, pulling the cloth away from his head. He'd stopped bleeding a while ago, the big baby. "When do you think this guy is going to show up?"

"Casey said any time in the next hour." Reed was staring into the darkness, down the road. We'd had our receptionist back in Minneapolis spoof her number and book an appointment with the plumber in question, giving them an address down a road with no exit. Now we were just waiting, and hoping that word hadn't gotten out yet to the last few members of this organization still free that they were getting rolled up hard today.

"Where's our last stop again?" I asked. It was a little chilly in the North Carolina woods, and silly me, I'd heard Vegas this morning and nothing else, so I hadn't brought my coat. I rubbed my arms, the thin material of my dress shirt doing nothing to keep me from freezing my ass off.

"Southern Alabama," Reed said, "but if Team Two keeps up their current pace—"

"The B team, you mean?" Scott asked.

"—They might get to mop up that mess before we get there," Reed finished, undeterred.

"How's it feel to bust up a massive criminal conspiracy to mess with US law enforcement by giving sketchy people superpowers?" I asked.

"Ask me when it's done," Reed said, all clipped and pissy. He threw a very disapproving look over his shoulder at me. "You're not supposed to jinx us like that."

"Man, we could fail right now and we've already busted up their production facility and seventeen out of their twenty distributors," I said. "Andrew Phillips is going to get on TV tomorrow and take full credit for this, you know. He's going to brush right past the fact that the FBI had nothing to do with any stage of it and just throw himself right into the honey."

"True story," Scott said, and when he took a glare from Reed, "What? You know it is."

Jamal frowned, and for the first time in a couple hours it wasn't because of his head injury. "This was us and local law and state law enforcement all the way, and he's going to jump in and declare victory to distract from the fact he's probably having zero luck with catching Sienna. Bogus."

"'Bogus'?" I looked at my brother. "You been cribbing language notes from Bill and Ted again?"

"Keanu Reeves is the man," Jamal said without shame.

ROBERT J. CRANE

"You see *John Wick*?"

"Those movies are pure badassery," Scott said.

"Yeah, well, I hope you all display some of that yourselves tonight," Reed said, and then corrected himself: "More of it, I guess, since you've done pretty well today." What had started off as a shot, he amended to make a compliment. Not bad.

"I personally could use a drink right about now," Scott said.

"Turn on the spigot, waterboy," I cracked.

"I was thinking whiskey, actually," Scott said, "which is another substance I have no control over—"

"Car coming," Reed said, shushing us. "No ... van." I could almost see his ears perking up as he listened. "A hundred yards out. Get ready just in case."

"Man, we have not heard a car in the hour we've been out here," I said. "This is probably the guy."

"Guys, actually," Reed said, squinting into the dark. "Van has a driver and passenger."

"Time to cowboy up," Scott said. "Party of two, your reservation is about to be cashed in."

"How do you cash in a reservation?" I asked.

"I don't know," Scott said. "I thought it sounded cool."

"Sounded like it didn't make any sense," Jamal said.

"Uh, incoming, peeps," Reed said. "Serious business here? Reservations and cash ins and all else aside?"

"Cash me ousside, howbow dah?" Scott asked.

"Does that girl get a royalty check every time someone says that?" I asked.

"Probably be the only money she ever earns," Jamal said.

"You better watch out, she's feisty, she'll probably come looking to kick your ass if she hears you talking like that," Scott said. By now the three of us were totally ignoring Reed, his dark face turning redder and redder as the van drew closer.

"We're ready for 'em," I said to Reed, just to keep him from popping a vein out or something. "Just playing with you, Reed."

"Good," Reed said, "we wouldn't want a repeat of what

278

happened in Colorado now, would we?" He pointed that one right at me.

"Nah, we wouldn't want me to save a whole town and fend off a bad guy," I said under my breath. He didn't look back, but I knew he heard me.

"Who wants to stop them?" Reed asked. The van was only twenty or so yards away now.

"I got the front tire," I said and lifted a hand.

"I'll get their alternator," Jamal said, shuffling on his knees over to me.

"Say goodbye to your radiator, boys," Scott said. "Also, those windshield wiper sprayers are about to go crazy."

I waited a second, and when Reed didn't reply, I said, "You should shut off their AC. Really show 'em who's boss here."

Scott and Jamal both cackled, and I reached up and crushed the van's tire with a blast of gravel right out of the road. It popped in a burst of air, and then all three other tires blew out, too.

I caught Reed smirking. "There's air in the tires too, Augustus."

"Their electrical just fried out," Jamal said.

"Doubt they can see much of anything now …" Scott said.

"Ooh, here comes one of them now," Jamal said. "Dude looks pissed."

The dude in question did indeed look pissed. He got out of the van and practically ripped off the door. There was meta strength there, no question. "I think that's confirmation enough," Reed said, rustling the bushes.

Our opponent looked right at us, and I knew Reed had made a serious mistake. "Oh, shit," I said, "I think he—"

"Heard me?" Reed stood up. "I noticed."

"No," I said, using the earth I was standing on to launch me into the air. I did the same for each of them, but a second too late. "He felt it, Reed! He's a—"

The bush rustled again, and I knew what was happening even as I propelled myself skyward.

This guy? This guy was a Persephone. He'd felt our

presence through the plant when Reed touched it.

"Gahhhhh!" Scott said, branches wrapped around his neck like twisting fingers.

"Get ... us ... out ..." Jamal struggled to say as I hovered over the van.

"Yeah, yeah, I'm on it—" I started to say, ready to uproot the plant and be done with it.

But I didn't get a chance.

Because a blast of water like a knife sliced through the chunk of ground I was levitating on and it broke apart. I fell forward, narrowly missing getting chopped in two by the geyser of pain. I hit the roof of the van and bounced, rolling off the opposite side to where my friends and Mr. Persephone were. I vaulted back to my feet with the help of some gravel and dirt, and found myself looking at a very familiar face, positioned in the passenger door.

"Well if it isn't my old buddy Omar," I said, putting up my hands and getting ready for the fight that was about to come my way. Omar wasn't smiling; he looked pissed as hell, like he was ready for round two to go different—and deadlier for me—than round one had. "Looks like you were wrong, Reed!" I doubted he was paying any attention to me now. "Looks like this is going to be Colorado all over again ... 'cept this time I'm kicking your ass."

52.

Sienna

"You got a bathroom around here?" I asked as I stepped off the plane and into Greg's mighty, mighty fortress of hangardom/solitude/museum of plundered military history. He'd modified some clothing he had on board so that it fit me, barely – a shirt and pants that were kinda like capris, but they worked, albeit uncomfortably. I looked back up at him as I took my last step down off the ramp to find him staring at me blankly, and not because of my ill-fitting wardrobe. "Seriously? Fine, I'll just go on the plane."

"You can't," he held up a hand to stop me from going back up. "The lavatory shuts off when the plane does."

I shrugged. "So start it back up again."

"Well, it needs maintenance," he said, "and I don't want to strain the batteries." He looked a little guilty.

I rolled my eyes, looking around the brightly lit hangar. It looked a little like the inside of an electrical box, the sort you'd install plugs in, but completely emptied out and with a giant vent placed over it that was completely shut against the wind. I figured Greg must have really shrunken us in order to get us and the Concorde between those plates, because there was no way his miniature menagerie would have held up very well if even a slight breeze got in here. "Fine. Where do you go?"

"Well, wherever I want," he said, looking a little annoyed by the question. "I can shrink to the point where it's such an inconsequential amount of volume—"

"Yuck. And I was just thinking it was a really nice place you had here, you know, considering it's literally a hole in the wall." I looked around again, hoping that maybe a Porta Potty would pop up, like magic. "What about in the house?"

"No," he said, shaking his head violently, "that won't work at all."

"Well, if it flushes, it'd work just fine for me."

"We can't," he said, still shaking his head like he was trying to expel Sam from hiding in his hair or something. "It's too—dangerous." He must have realized how lame that sounded, because he reddened more than I'd seen him do thus far.

"Dangerous?" I almost laughed. "Dude, you live in Shermer, Illinois. The worst danger you'd face around here is Emilio Estevez taping your butt cheeks together in the locker room, or maybe the Wet Bandits burgling your house." I scowled at him, my need to pee rising. "Did Emilio Estevez tape your butt cheeks together, Greg? Is that why you're so anal retentive?"

"Look, you can just go wherever in here," he said, taking a step toward me. "I'll shrink you so small I won't be able to see you and just—go to town."

"No," I said. "Also, other than going dragon, which I'm pretty sure would return me to normal size and through the wall of your house—"

"It would, yes. Molecular change returns you to your original proportions."

"—how are you going to get me back to—whatever pin-head size I am now after I get done taking a mini-pee on your floor? Still ewww on that, by the by."

He spoke slowly, like he was spelling out for me, a clear idiot, the most obvious thing in the world. "I would wait a reasonable period of time and then check on you—"

"Peeing out in the open, in the middle of the floor here, while shrunken, and then I have to wait for you while dodging the puddle of my own pee, when I'm done?" I said. "A world of no, no and HELL NO. This ain't happening. Show me to the bathroom in the house."

"This isn't—we can't—" Greg started to stutter, which made me think I'd gone and blown a hole in his logic circuits.

"Sure we can," I said, starting to search for the exit. There was a door way, way over on the far wall, and I had to assume that led somewhere. I darted over to it, opened it wide, and zipped out.

"Wait!" Greg called after me. "You can't just—"

I found myself in a human-sized office, and I was very much still not human-sized. I was guessing I was maybe the size of a gnat's leg, which was kinda disquieting. "I can and I'm about to, Greg. Get me to normal size and find me a toilet before I pay you back for all these attempts to kill me by doing some suburban renewal I know your neighbors won't appreciate."

"But I saved your life!" he shouted after me, scrambling toward the door.

"And I appreciate it," I said, "but my gratitude is balanced both by the realization that you've made my life—which you saved, thanks for that, again—so much harder by getting a nuclear incident blamed on me, and oh, also I'm about to pee myself because you're being a dick about not letting me use your bathroom." I looked at him with a blazing irritation. "Solve my immediate problem and I'll forgive you for causing my other, longer-term, intractable one, okay?"

"Fine!" he shouted, stepping right up to the door to the office. There was a thousand-foot fall to the carpet awaiting him if he jumped out, but if I had to guess, he made that jump all the time, growing to full size before he hit the floor. It was probably like taking a normal step for him. "Fine, I'll—hold on—"

He stepped out and touched my shoulder as he went. The world changed around us, everything seeming to shrink in perspective, the office appearing normal-sized within a second or so. My feet brushed the carpeting, and I went ahead and stopped my hover, my weight setting on the balls of my feet.

Greg was standing in front of me, looking severely put

out at having to invite me into his home. He wasn't just looking daggers at me, he was looking Scottish Claymores at me, such was the breadth of his irritation. "This way," he snapped, and walked me to the door of his office, pausing to look out. It was cracked just a smidge.

"What the hell is going on in here?" A female voice said, opening the door before Greg could stick his eyeball up to the crack for a check. A woman shoved it open and Greg dodged so as not to end up with it planted in the middle of his forehead. She stepped in at meta speed, voice hushed as she took him in with a glance and said, "You're not supposed to be here."

"I wouldn't," he said, "but—I—" Greg's hands flailed uselessly as he tried to find the words to explain himself and failed in flustered uselessness. "—she—" He pointed at me.

The woman turned her head casually, like she was just following his pointed finger, and saw me, nodded, then turned back to look at him. A second later, it seemed to register with her that I was there, and maybe also who I was, because her head snapped back around, fast enough that I feared she'd go Exorcist and spin it all the way around in her haste. "What. The. *Hell.* Greg?" She whirled back on him, and then looked back at me like she couldn't believe what she was seeing.

"Hi," I said, "I was just looking to use your bathroom."

53.

Augustus

We kicked it off right. Omar came at me with spears of water ripped right out of the air, and I threw up a dirt defense torn out of the ground as I did one of those gymnastic leaps sideways. Water- knives shot over and around me, one missing my thigh by about an inch. I landed low, my dirt shield obscuring me from Omar's sight. That was going to be the secret of my success, making sure this dude couldn't see me.

"Aug … gust … us!" Reed shouted from over past the van. I had forgotten about them already, all tangled up in my own stuff.

"Sorry!" I shouted, and ripped that plant out of the ground by its roots, carrying a small mountain of soil off with it. I shot it right at the last position I'd had for the Persephone driver. I heard a grunt and I guessed that he'd jumped out of the way followed by a thump that shook the van as I slammed that wad of dirt and plant into the side, knocking the van several inches toward me.

Flashes of lightning sparked and lit the night just out of my view on the other side of the van, but I was already focused back on Omar. I'd done all I could for my boys, now I was going to have to do all I could for me.

I took down my dirt shield for a second and caught Omar looking across the hood of the van, trying to see what was going on there. I got his attention back pretty quick with a buckshot blast of gravel right to the gut straight out of the roadway. He screamed as it hit, and then lashed back at me with a thousand needles of water.

I threw my shield back up and jumped high. It looked like a daggered rainstorm was going on beneath me, like the wind had blown it hard sideways. I knew if I'd been there to take it, it would have ripped right through me and left me looking like a pincushion.

Omar brought down a cascade of water from somewhere above, maybe up the hills, maybe from a creek nearby, I didn't know. All I knew was that suddenly I was dealing with a lot more H2O than I'd planned on and jumped on top of the van as it roared down beneath me like an angry river.

Topside, I had a clear view of the fight on the other side of the van. Persephone Man was really giving it to Reed, Jamal and Scott, which might have explained why none of them had come to join me. Scott had a shield of water up, attacking from one side, Reed was ripping the wind at Persephone from another, and Jamal, separated from the other two, was fending off three plants that seemed to have gained sentience, coming at him and brushing off his lightning attacks like they were nothing.

"Uh oh," I said as Omar jumped up on the hood of the van to face me. He was swirling the water around the van, and I had a feeling in about two seconds I was going to get overwhelmed, surrounded and slaughtered by it. And my boys weren't going to be any help because they were too busy fighting for their own lives.

I felt out into the distance. There was good earth all around us; I could have made a golem, maybe an army of golems, fought it out with this guy from here to Durham and back again. But I'd done that once before and a city in Colorado had almost paid the price. Omar was a bad, bad man, and he wasn't going to run away this time, I could see it in his eyes. He was grinning, knowing he and his partner had us on the ropes.

So I reached out a little farther, found the thing I was looking for, and summoned it toward me with all my strength.

"You can't stop us," Omar said with a grin as the water started to snake up around my ankles. I was going to jump, but it got me too quick, I was distracted for just a hair too long. "You're going to die right now, because you're not strong enough. Which is just as well for you." He chortled under his breath, like he was privy to a real good joke he didn't want to share. "You would never have survived the awa—"

The boulder I'd pulled from about two hundred feet away came sailing in right then, five feet wide by two feet tall. It made a whistling noise as it roared toward us like it was fired out of a piece of field artillery, and Omar didn't even have time to turn before it struck him right in the upper body, turning his entire torso and head into a giant SPLAT! mark on the rock. His legs and hips stood there for a second, surreally standing on their own before gravity took hold and they went tumbling off the van like they'd gone all wobbly.

"I beg to differ on that 'strong enough' thing," I said. "Guess we're just going to have to agree to disagree."

Omar's water released around my ankles, flowing off the van now that he'd let loose of it. "Scott!" I shouted, and looked out for the blond man in the midst of the battle in front of me.

He was already doing his thing. Scott yanked the water under his control and sent it right around Persephone, encasing him in it. The plant man was freaking out, the entire forest up in arms.

"Quick!" Reed shouted, "put him out before the last march of the Ents kills us all!"

Jamal sparked a blast that surged into Scott's water bubble, blue electricity coruscating around it. Within the lit sphere, Persephone Man jerked and spasmed until he went still, and the sounds of the forest died down around us.

"Is he still alive?" Reed asked as the chaos turned to silence, and the moon broke out of the clouds above to cast the entire scene in a pale, silvery light.

"I doubt it, man, I cut ol' Omar in half," I said.

"Not him," Reed said, holding his throat where the plant had throttled him. "I meant Sir Poison Ivy. I can see your boy is roadkill."

"Weak pulse," Scott said, letting the water slip away from the Persephone. "He'll probably heal fast, though."

"Get a dose of suppressant," Reed said, and I saw Jamal trot off to the car to fetch our medical bag. "Let's wrap this up." He sidled over toward me as I hopped down from the van. "So ..." he looked at the severed lower body splayed out on the road. "... that was the guy that gave you hell in Colorado?"

"Yeah," I said, "sorry if you wanted him for questioning. I get the feeling from how he played this, he might have been a higher up."

"Well, he was going to kill all of us," Reed said, still idly stroking his throat. "Speaking for my own ass, which has been saved because of you ... I'm grateful. I think you made the right call." He shook his head at the remainder of the corpse.

"Thanks, Boss," I said, kinda sincerely and kinda sarcastically. "Can I get some PTO for this?"

"Probably real soon," Reed said with the ghost of a smile. "After all, if we just smashed up the entire distribution network for these people piping fresh meta criminals everywhere in the US ... seems like we're bound to experience a precipitous drop in trouble, right?"

"I don't know about that," I said. "Seems to me if someone's gone to all the expense and trouble of doing this once ... we kinda need to strike off the head of the serpent in order to kill it good and dead, you know?"

Reed lapsed into silence. "Mark McGarry. That was his name, right?"

"That's what Cassidy said." I watched as Jamal came trotting back with a syringe, making his way over to the Persephone and giving him a stick with it. "Guess we have to rely on Abby and J.J. to dig him up, though, right?"

"Yeah," Reed said. "I suspect. After all ..." he chuckled, "... it's not likely he's just going to drop into our laps."

54.

Sienna

"I just want to say," I said as I stepped back into the office after relieving myself to find Greg and Morgan, his wife, apparently (I'd caught her name as I headed for the bathroom), "this is maybe the most awkward situation I've ever seen."

Greg just gave me an evil look, and Morgan didn't seem to know how to react.

"Mommy? Is that Daddy?" A little blond boy came wandering in, parking it next to me and looking up. His face was wide and open, and he was staring right at me. "Who are you?"

"This is a friend of Daddy's, apparently," Morgan said, voice tight with strain.

"More of an ally of convenience," Greg said, almost apologetically. I had no idea whether he was apologizing to me or to Morgan. "Morgan ... please, can we talk?"

"Hey, uh ... little blond child," I said to the kid, who was looking up at me like an idiot for not psychically guessing his name, "maybe we should give your mom and dad some room to talk."

His name is Eddie, Harmon said in exasperation. *You could ask, you know.*

I don't kiss babies and shake hands like you, I snarked, *for obvious reasons.* "Uhh, Eddie, I mean."

"How did you know his name?" Morgan looked like she

289

was about ready to rush to his side.

"She has a telepath in her head," Greg answered for me, all slick like he was trying his hardest to smooth things over after what I imagined must have been a hell of a fight. However much trouble Greg had apologizing to me, he looked like he was ready to throw a thousand of them at her feet like rose petals. He turned to his kid. "Please … why don't the two of you go off and play while your mother and I talk, Eddie?"

I thought I was having a bad, Forest Whitaker eye reaction to the implication of me watching a kid, but Morgan went absolutely bonkers. "You're going to send our son off with *her* as the babysitter?" Half an octave higher and all the windows would have broken.

"Good point," Greg said after a moment's consideration. "There are things to take into account, precautions …" He looked at little Eddie and said, very seriously. "Son, Sienna is a succubus. Make sure you don't touch her while she watches you."

I gave him a sour look. "Gee, thanks for the vote of confidence in my competence."

Morgan's eyes just about popped out of her head. "I didn't mean about her being a succubus! I meant she's …" Here her voice fell, like Eddie couldn't hear her if she whispered, "… she's killed people!"

Greg actually let out a soft laugh. "Well, really, Morgan … who among us hasn't?"

"Your son, I damned well hope," I said, "because I don't babysit killers for free. Unless they're stuck in my head."

Low blow, Wolfe said.

"Language!" Greg and Morgan both hissed at me at the same time.

"What, I'm speaking English," I snarked quietly. *Damned great English,* I kept to myself to the assorted laughing of the souls in my head. "Uh, Eddie," I said, when I caught sight of their lack of amusement, "come on, let's go … play, I guess." I patted him on the back to guide him out of the room and he went along with me. I meta whispered to Morgan, "I don't know what you've heard about me, but you have to know I don't hurt kids."

That didn't seem to reassure her, at least not based on the panicked look on her face as I left and followed Eddie out of the office toward a staircase near the bathroom.

"So …" I asked as we started up, his little feet thumping on the wooden stairs, "… what do you want to do?" I had no idea what kids did, other than bottle flips these days. I mean, I couldn't even remember being Eddie's age. Even knowing as little as I did of how adult relationships worked, I was anticipating some fierce meta whispering from Morgan and Greg the second they thought we were out of earshot.

"My mom said you killed people," Eddie said, looking over his shoulder at me as we walked up the stairs.

I searched for the diplomatic reply to that for a fricking kid, and came up with, "Uhm … yeah, she did say that."

"So you really killed somebody?" Eddie asked as we rounded the banister at the top of the stairs and entered a long white hallway with doors on either side. His tone was alarmingly overawed and lacking the basic preservation instinct most people I'd known possessed.

Was it hot in here? It felt hot, and I tugged at the collar of my poorly-fitted shirt as I searched for an answer, finally saying, with all the requisite guilt of lying to a child, "Maybe once or twice."

Eddie took that in as he ducked into a bedroom to our left, a taupe room with white baseboards and beige carpeting that was almost completely clear of any obstruction, save for a Lego set that was being carefully built in corner of the room. All the pieces that weren't on the creation were separated into piles by color, and while I couldn't quite tell what the hell it was supposed to be, because either it was still in its infancy or I was just oblivious, it seemed to be lovingly put together.

Other than that, the room was clean, the white dresser to my left and the double bed with frilly metal to my right, all made up and in perfect order. Either Morgan and Greg ran this kid with a whip, enforcing strict discipline and cleanliness, or he was one buttoned-up little dude.

"So what was that like?" Eddie asked, rounding on me

once we were in the room.

I plopped down in front of the closet and found the carpet pad a lot more comfortable than I would have guessed. "Um, well, they, uh ... they died very quietly and ... ahhh, painlessly ..."

You are such a liar, Eve laughed. *And to a child, no less! Pathetic.*

"No, I mean how did you kill them?" Eddie asked, sitting down next to his Legos and messing with one of the piles that had slightly toppled when he'd sat down. He scooped it all back together, answering for me the question of who exactly was running this kid and his spotless room.

I blinked. "Uhm ... how would you guess I killed them?"

His eyes lit up. "I bet you ripped their guts out with a knife! And that there was blood everywhere—"

"Oh, gah—no," I said, shaking my head furiously. "No, there was no—no blood."

You are getting really good at lying to this child, Wolfe said. *Perhaps you should stop. Acquaint him with the real world, and all its faults and flaws ...*

Sure, let me describe for him how I killed—oh, I dunno, Nadine Griffin, I thought back at Wolfe. *Drowning is such a pleasant way to go.*

"Well, then how did you do it?" Eddie asked. "Did you cut off their heads?" He seemed thrilled at that idea.

I tried to recoil in horror at the tiny psychopath sitting in front of me. Leaving it up to his imagination was way, way worse than most of the kills I'd actually made. "No! Uhm, well, there was this one time in Atlanta when these guys who were soldiers of fortune—uh, mercenaries—were hired to kill me. And they jumped out of a van—"

"What kind of van?" Eddie asked. "Like, white? Black?"

"I don't remember," I said, losing a little patience, "but they came jumping out with guns and started shooting at me, so I uhm ... shot back with fire of my own."

"Like, how?" he asked, staring at me with intense interest.

"Like this." I lit up my hand for a split second, let it burn, then snuffed it.

"Whoaaaa!" Eddie was on his feet in a second. "That is

so cool! That is way cooler than anything, even a bottle flip or an EX Pokemon card!"

"Uhhhh … thanks, I guess," I said, hoping that those were, indeed, cool things. I mean, I'd seen bottle flips and they looked pretty stupid to me, but he must have thought they were cool.

"You want to watch me build my Legos?" Eddie asked, turning back to his little construction project.

"Sure," I said, settling back on my haunches. Man, Greg and Morgan had invested in a nice carpet pad here. It was really comfy, like, better than most of the beds I'd slept in the last few months. At least since my time at the resort in St. Thomas.

In the last two days I'd been shot at, a lot. I'd been nearly nuked. One of my safe houses had been straight-up wrecked. I had the government after me harder than maybe ever before, and it didn't look like they were going to play anymore games with bringing me in.

And now I was taking shelter in the house of the guy who was responsible for a lot of the shit I'd suffered through the last two days, a man who'd seemed like he was going to kill me until, oh, three hours ago or so.

Now I was watching his child build Legos. "What kind of set is that?" I asked.

"Marvel Superheroes," Eddie said, not looking up from his labors. I guess the allure of hearing me talk about murdering people had already worn off. "It's from *Age of Ultron*. It was on discount because it's old."

"Old? It came out like two, three years ago," I said, laying sideways across the floor, using my own arm as a pillow. "Though, I suppose, given that you're five, that was like the Mesozoic to you." I paused. "The Mesozoic was—"

"I know," he said breezily. "It has to do with dinosaurs. I like dinosaurs."

"Cool," I said. "Dinosaurs are … very cool." I yawned.

"Yep," he said, fitting a couple pieces together. "You know what I like best about dinosaurs?"

"No …" I said, slurring my words. Man, this carpet was comfortable.

"It's that they ..."

I didn't catch his answer, at least not that I remember. I passed clean out, right there, drifting off to sleep on the floor.

55.

Greg

"What the hell is this?" Morgan hissed once the sound of Sienna and Eddie walking up the stairs had receded. "Why is she here?"

"Because I saved her life," Greg said, trying to figure exactly how—and how bad—this was going to be for him. Obviously they had not parted on the greatest of terms last time, but Morgan's fury was such that he had never encountered from her before.

"You—what?"

"I told you I clashed with her," Greg said, trying to keep the strain out of his voice, stay matter-of-fact, stay cool, keep this from naturally escalating the way Morgan seemed to want it to. She had reasons to be upset, of course.

"You tried to bomb her to death," Morgan said.

"Yes, and the press and government seem to be blaming her for that."

Morgan's eyes swelled, threatening to pop out of her head. "Because she's a murderer!"

"So am I, so are you," Greg said calmly. "It looks to me like she's seldom killed anyone who didn't deserve it at least an iota."

"I'm trying to extract us—our family—at least me and Eddie—from this lifestyle that you're digging deeper into," Morgan said, gathering a head of steam.

"I'm not," Greg said. "I'm trying to get out, too. Truly."

"Then what the hell is she doing here?" Morgan's voice hit another high note.

"That's part of me digging out," Greg said. "I have, evidently, caused her … problems …"

"To say the least."

"… and her … friend? Compatriot? Colleague—I don't know what they are to each other. But he was the target McGarry assigned me."

"You didn't bring him here, too?" Morgan asked. She did not sound pleased. "Everything you told me about him suggested that Bruce or whatever his name is was dangerous, a carnival sideshow at the best of times."

"He's in her pocket," Greg said, gesturing in the direction that Sienna and Eddie had gone. "So he's hardly a threat at that size. But—listen—"

Morgan's face crumpled, close to tears. "Why? Why can't this just be—why can't it just be over?"

"Because when you threw me out earlier—and said what you said," Greg spoke, the words fumbling from his lips, "it gave me great pause, Morgan. You were right, of course. In that moment, I saw myself the way that you have been seeing me, the way that Eddie has—and I hated what I saw." He deflated a little, slowing down his words. "I saw that I have become something … that I never set out to be. Something that I never wanted to be."

"What did you see?" Morgan asked. "Of yourself?"

"I saw myself as a monster," Greg said. "The person who … who steals the oxygen out of the room when he's in it. I don't want to be that person to this family. When I'm not around, you and Eddie—it's bright, like sunlit day. And then I step into the picture and the clouds roll in and everything turns dark. I see that now." He lowered his head. "I'm becoming like a more angry, perhaps more patient version of Sam—minus the charm."

Morgan greeted this with a nod. "You do lack the charm." When he gave her a wounded look, she shrugged almost apologetically. "Well, you do. But on the plus side, you don't fake it like he does. And I don't think you have more patience—at least, not here. Not with people. With things, with process, maybe, but ... not with Eddie."

"I concede that's true," Greg said. "But ... what I see ... is not what I *want*." He looked around the house. "What we've built here ... this ... foundation of our lives ... I have come to agree with you. The price is too high. Too much for the toll it's taking on our family." He swallowed heavily. "On me. I wasn't always like this."

"No, you weren't," she said.

"I want to change," he said quietly. It was silent save for the thumping of his own heart. "Do you think ... do you think it's possible ... that I could? Or is this ... fully ingrained in who I am now?"

Morgan sagged against the wall, a mixture of relief and weariness writ on her face, bags seeming to form under her eyes. "Greg ... you're one of the most capable men I've ever met, if not maybe the most emotionally unaware. *Can* you change? Yes, I think you could. If you really wanted to."

"I truly do. More than anything," he said. "I don't want to be who I am now." He looked up at her. "I don't want to do this anymore. And if it means we have to leave this place, move somewhere smaller, live on less ... then I am with you, the trade-off is fair. Worth it. I could become an engineer, perhaps. Maybe a cell biologist." He smiled faintly. "There are some things I could contribute to that field, I think, that no one else could. I don't promise it will be an easy road, though—"

"I don't really care," she said, leaning her head back and laughing from exhaustion. "This hasn't been easy. Keeping things together here, knowing what you're out there doing ... none of this has been easy. Trying to inject light into our lives while your work brings neverending darkness ..." She lowered her head. "I don't care what you do or what you make as long as you stop crushing your soul in the process. We can live with less money." She sighed. "We can't live as a family with you like that anymore."

He eased over to her, slowly, to give her a chance to retreat. She stood her ground, looking up at him with that same tired relief in her eyes. He took her hand, gently. "Then you won't have to. That's ... part of the reason I went after

Sienna and ... Bruce or whatever he calls himself these days. Friday, I suppose."

"Why Friday?" Morgan asked.

"I ... have no idea," Greg said, almost laughing at the absurdity of it. "I don't know why he called himself Bruce Springersteen before, or Percy Sledger ... it's all ... he's a ridiculous man."

"Why did McGarry want him dead?" Morgan asked, leaning forward, putting her head on his chest. She breathed into his neck, and he felt ... alive. Relieved. Reprieved, even, like he'd slipped the noose he'd been in, at least for now.

"I don't know," Greg said, "but Sam is after them now. McGarry hired him."

Morgan stiffened against him. "He won't stop until they're dead."

"No," Greg said, putting an arm around her back. Morgan slipped his grasp, looking up at him with undisguised alarm. "No, he won't."

"Can he find them here?" Morgan asked. "Can he find us?"

"I don't think so," Greg said, "but we should probably leave tomorrow just to be safe."

Morgan pulled away from him shyly. "I already packed up most of the house. Shrank it for easy transport."

Greg just stared at her. "You were going to leave me."

She stared back, then broke away from his gaze first. "Yes."

He took a deep breath. "I'm glad you didn't."

She wrapped her arms around him again. Their almost total lack of height differential didn't bother him this time, not when it let her kiss him on the lips so easily, so gently. When they broke, she said, softly, "We left Eddie in the keeping of the FBI's Most Wanted fugitive."

"He's probably fine," Greg said, a little uneasily. "But all the same—"

They both beat a hasty path up the stairs. When they reached Eddie's door they found it open wide. Eddie was lying down in front of his Legos, head down, asleep on the carpet. Sienna was across the room, laid similarly, as though one of them had mimicked the other.

"We can't just leave him like this," Morgan said.

Greg crossed to his son, and carefully, gingerly, picked him up and carried him to the bed. He laid him in it, and then covered him with a quilt. Eddie barely stirred, opening his eyes sleepily for only a moment before closing them again after locking eyes with his father. He did not show fear, and snuggled against Greg's arm as he moved him.

"Maybe there is some hope after all," Greg murmured as he withdrew his arm, careful to transfer Eddie's head to the pillow.

"I'll sleep in here tonight," Morgan said, creeping up to his side and slipping into the bed next to Eddie. "Just in case."

"I'll need to keep watch until morning anyway," Greg said, making his way quietly over to Sienna, shrinking as he did so. With great care, he removed the cylinder containing Friday from her pocket, reducing its size to slip it from her without disturbing her. "Just in case Sam develops a brain and manages to find us." He returned the cylinder to its previous size.

"What about her?" Morgan whispered, nodding at Sienna. "Are you just going to leave her there?"

Greg thought about it for a minute before answering. "Yes. I'll ready the rest of the house, and ... we'll come up with our plan for what's next after everyone is awake tomorrow. I'm sure that won't be easy, given the state she finds herself in, hounded on all sides. But for now ..." He stared at the woman in the middle of the floor, her face relaxed, exhaustion having claimed her, "... for now, yes ... we should just let her rest ..."

56.

Sienna

I awoke to someone poking me, sun making its way through my eyelids from some source outside my consciousness. My shoulder ached from sleeping on a floor for hours, my neck had a little crick in it, and the feeling of a steady tap of someone's finger against my shoulder made me want to roar to my feet like a lion and break their damned hand. "What the hell?" I growled, rolling over to find Guy Friday about to nudge me with a finger again. I caught it just before he poked me in the boob, thus saving his life again.

"Language," Greg hissed from just over Friday's shoulder, scowl on his face and a look of fatigue under his eyes. I doubted he'd slept.

I looked around the room and saw Morgan lying next to Eddie, looking just as scandalized at my use of the word hell. Her son was dead to the world on the pillow next to her, I saw as I floated to my feet, his mouth open and his right arm laid over his mother's face in a very unnatural way. That didn't seem to bother Morgan nearly as much as my little swear; she was probably used to catching an elbow or two from Eddie when sharing a bed with him. "What?" I asked. "He's not going to learn the mildest profanities in his sleep, okay?"

"Shhh," Greg said, and beckoned me forward, out of the room. Friday tiptoed along comically while I floated out, leaving Morgan and Eddie to snooze, I guess. Or Eddie to snooze and Morgan to cuddle. "We need to plan," Greg said once we were all safely on our way downstairs, still taking care to be quiet.

"I suppose," I said, yawning. "Probably can't stay here in Hughesland forever, after all. Though I could use a day off, Ferris Bueller."

"Har har," Friday said as we reached the ground floor and stepped into a living room that was bare to the walls.

"So now we know Greg's secret," I said to Friday. "Turns out all this time he was Mr. Little and you were Mr. Big." I grinned, because I found it funny. Friday just stared at me blankly. "Mr. Big was a character—"

"From *Sex and the City*," Friday said. "Carrie's true love. I got it."

I raised an eyebrow. "You're an interesting fellow sometimes, Friday," I said, looking around the empty living room. I hadn't been in here last night, so this all came as a slight surprise.

I looked around questioningly, and Friday, surprisingly, answered. "Greg's bailing out. Because of Sam."

"I thought you said he couldn't find you here," I said.

Greg was more subdued today than yesterday, and I chalked it up to worry and lack of sleep. "I don't think he can, but my family's safety isn't worth the risk. I'm starting over again anyway. Leaving here will perhaps make it a cleaner break."

"You leaving behind the luxury life of the assassin?" I asked, watching his reaction. The fact that there appeared to be peace between him and Friday should have been mind-boggling, but Greg had probably explained what was up over a beer or something, as guys weirdly did, and I expected Friday was probably all, "It's cool, bro," and they were fine with each other. Weirdos.

"Yes," Greg said.

"Good choice," I said. Not like I was in a position to turn him into the feds for murder and assassin-work anyway, being way higher on their priority list than he would ever be. I was living in a weird space these days, more disconnected from the law and justice done by the government than ever before, and more renegade-y than I would have preferred.

Oh, who am I kidding? I always liked being judge, jury

301

and unaccountable executioner, though I preferred to do as little of the last bit as possible.

"I'm willing to give you a ride anywhere you'd like," Greg said, "but after that … we part ways. I need to go get to the business of establishing my new life and while I'm sympathetic to your predicament—"

"Lemme stop you right there," I said, "because maybe we can help each other out. This Sam guy … is he a pro?"

Greg's eyes blinked a few times in calculation. "Yes, I suppose."

"So he's not going to do an assassination for zero money, right?" I waited for the answer, because my plan hinged on it.

"If someone he hated crossed his path, he'd kill them, but … no," Greg said, "I doubt he'd continue hunting you down if the contract was off the table." His eyes lit up. "Oh. McGarry."

"Is that your boss?" I asked. "Former boss, whatever?"

"Yes," Greg said. "He's—"

Ding dong.

Company's here, Harmon said. *And, possibly, an answer to many of your woes.*

"That's foreboding," I said.

"Just ignore it," Greg said, frozen in place. "It's probably just UPS."

"We should answer it," Friday said, eyes strangely fixed in place. The doorbell rang again, like whoever was waiting on the doorstep was in no particular hurry but wanted to remind us they were, indeed, there.

"No," Greg and I said at the same time, and he went on, "I have a small camera on the porch." He beckoned us toward his office.

When we stepped in, I noticed he'd packed pretty much everything except for the TV and a few odds and ends that I suspected he planned to leave behind. Even looking at it, I couldn't see the place in the corner of his office where the door to his secret hideout was mounted in the wall. Damn, that sucker must have been tiny.

"This is a pinhole camera," Greg said, "shrunken to impossibly small." He clicked the TV on, and it showed us a

302

clear color image of the front porch, though the resolution looked a little funny, probably due to the camera being so small.

On the front doorstep stood a man, dressed in luxurious suit, with silver hair and a perfectly groomed mustache. He had a pleasant look on his face, patient …

And he was instantly familiar to me.

"I don't know who that is," Greg said. "He could be working with Sam."

"I don't think so," I said, peering at him. I was ninety-nine percent sure I knew who that was, but he was so damned out of place compared to where I'd last seen him, thousands of miles from here, that I couldn't quite believe it at first.

Then the man turned, and looked straight at the camera, favoring us with a muted smile, and I knew it was him.

"Announcing Alistair Wexford," Friday intoned, clearly the speaker system of choice for communicating our visitor's message straight to us, the knucklehead, "Foreign Secretary of the United Kingdom."

"What?" Greg asked in disbelief.

"Wexford's a telepath," I said, inclining my head toward the monitor and counting on Friday to see it, which meant Wexford would. Wexford mirrored my motion back to me, letting me know that, yes, he was watching us just as we were watching him. "I met him in London a couple years back when I got tangled up in a murder mystery involving some members of a group called Omega that I used to, uhmmm … run. Sort of."

"What the hell is he doing here?" Greg asked, as overheated as I'd ever heard him. He was clearly not prepared for this contingency, and it was freaking him the eff out—or as near to it as Greg probably got.

"He comes bearing a message," Friday said, with a bit of an English accent, "and an offer for Sienna Nealon." Wexford smiled on the monitor, and somehow I felt just the slightest bit of reassurance. Like maybe there was a way out of all this. "And perhaps … a solution to your current dilemma."

57.

Back in my place in Minneapolis I slept like the rock I'd mashed Omar with, waking to the sounds of the city already in motion. I showered, dressed, and headed out to Eden Prairie in my Mercedes, rolling on into the office just after nine. I figured normal working hours could be a little flexible after yesterday's craziness, and apparently I was right, because once I nodded and passed Casey, our receptionist, I found Scott and Veronika were the only ones in so far. No sign of Reed, which meant while the boss was away, the paperwork could wait in favor of play.

"What's up, preppie boy?" I asked Scott as I poured my first coffee and rolled over to his desk.

"Nothing," he grunted, leaning back in his chair at his cubicle. "Thanks for the assist last night. That Poseidon you clashed with ... he was tougher than me. I couldn't even get a grip on that water he was using."

"Yeah, he was a real badass, all right," I said, blowing the steam off the surface of my coffee. It'd be a while before it was safe to drink. "That Persephone was no joke, either. You ever seen Kat turn an entire forest against someone like— heh." I stopped to guffaw.

Scott smiled. "You just got the joke of her last name, didn't you?"

"Yeah," I said, looking up as Jamal came wandering in, Colin blowing the papers off the desk a step behind him.

"Yo, you two."

"When are we going paperless?" Colin growled, zipping back around and picking up his mess. He disappeared out the door for a second and returned with small rocks that he placed on the top of strategic paper piles to keep them from blowing away. "This is such a waste."

"Of what?" Scott asked. "Your time?"

"Of natural resources," Colin said, "to say nothing of the chemical waste from the process. And the forests don't need any additional help getting plowed down." His eyes flashed. "Especially after what Sienna did yesterday."

I paused with my nose over my coffee. "Yesterday? You mean the day before, right? The LA thing?"

"No," Colin said. "It was all over the news this morning."

"Yo, Casey," I called out there, "did you get the paper this morning?"

"No," she called back around the corner.

"Waste," Colin growled. "Get a digital subscription on your iPad."

"You know it takes electricity from burning fossil fuels to charge those up, right?" Jamal asked with the ghost of a smile.

"What'd Sienna do yesterday?" I asked, waiting for someone to enlighten me.

"She had a standoff with federal law enforcement in Montana after she blew up a lumberyard," Reed said tightly as he strode in with a purpose, and not a happy one, it didn't look like.

"Targaryens ain't got nothin' on her," Jamal said, "they ought to put the words 'Fire and Blood' on her sigil."

"Listen up, people," Reed said, striding up to his office door and turning around. "I know we had a big day yesterday—a tough one, but a good one—but this isn't the time to slack off."

No one spoke up, so I went ahead and threw in my two cents. "Uhh ... all we have left is the paperwork, man. That and tracking down the boss of this whole thing, McGarry, which ... I mean, unless Jamal or J.J. or Abby gets a line on him ... we're kind of done, right?" The three of them had taken a stab at finding McGarry yesterday, and apparently they'd come up real dry. Like Death Valley dry. Cassidy had placed him in motion, flying somewhere, but we hadn't been able to track him at all, which had left Jamal with a real scowl.

"Then we need to get our paperwork done," Reed said, producing a chorus of groans from those of us who'd bothered to show up on time or close to.

"Lame," Veronika pronounced.

"In case you didn't just hear me," Reed said, and he was clearly laboring under a lot of misplaced anger, "my sister just set off the entire national security apparatus again yesterday. We might have had a great day yesterday if not for her stealing all our thunder and turning it into a shitstorm for metahumans even tangentially connected to her. Like us." He glanced around, that raw anger seeping out. "So, in order to atone for her sins, we're going to process through every bit of paperwork those local law enforcement agencies want out of us. Today.

My heart sank, and I could feel the morale in the room going with it. "We are celebrating our victory with a few hundred pages of paperwork each."

"Kid me would not have been excited to know how much paperwork adult, superhero private-eye me has to do," Scott said, drifting back in his chair and looking at the ceiling.

"Somehow they leave all this out of the cop shows," I complained. "Probably because it's about as exciting as watching putty harden."

"Well, get to spackling," Reed said, turning around and heading into his office. "It's not like I'm getting a free pass on this, after all." He scooped up a pile off his desk and waved it around. "See? This is mine." It was about two inches thick. "Now ... get thee to work, people. Let's get past this and get back to making a name for ourselves that's not dependent on whatever dumbass thing my sister does on any given day." He slammed the door lightly behind him.

"Somehow, I get the feeling this isn't just about processing paperwork," I said. And no one answered, but I could tell they were all in agreement, as I headed back to my desk to dig my way out of this mountain of reports.

58.

Sienna

"You're pretty damned far from home," I said to Alistair Wexford as we all stood a little awkwardly around Greg's office. All his furniture was gone, which contributed to the entire scene being more uncomfortable yet.

"Yes, I don't tend to cross the pond all that often," Wexford said, looking around at our other guests with cool regard. He smiled, a little hint of warmth in a most peculiar situation. "But of course ... these are special circumstances."

"How did you show up right at my door?" Greg asked, watching Wexford with blatant suspicion. I couldn't blame him for that; Greg was already about to run like hell before some random stranger showed up on his doorstep looking for the FBI's Most Wanted fugitive.

"When Ms. Nealon and I met on her last journey to London," Wexford said smoothly, still wearing that faint smile, "I made a connection with her mind that I was able to renew once I reached these shores to home in on her, as it were. And that led me to your door, good fellow." He looked around. "I suppose since you've packed, you wouldn't happen to have any tea, would you? And perhaps some chairs to make this conversation just a bit easier?"

"I could ... probably dig something up," he said, watching Wexford intently.

"That's a good chap," Wexford said with a smile. "And Friday? Do give Gregory a hand, will you?"

Friday nodded, looking like he was still a zombie well under Wexford's control, following Greg out wordlessly. He even closed the door behind him, leaving Wexford and I in the office, alone.

"I haven't seen you in years," I said, "and you just show up out of the blue, looking for me."

"Well, I noted your situation had taken a turn for the dire," Wexford said with a trace of unease detectable beneath that British reserve. "I come on behalf of Her Majesty's government with an offer."

"You're making me an offer?" I pointed at myself, like it wasn't obvious with just the two of us in the room. After he'd bloodhounded his way to me across the Atlantic.

"We are aware, in the circles in which I run—" he started.

"Meaning the metahuman elements of the UK government," I said.

"You Americans certainly are blunt, aren't you?" he said with a charming amount of understatement. "Yes, the metahuman elements of the UK government. The new PM is fully briefed and aware of your situation. He feels you've received—how do you say it? A bad rap."

"I can't argue with that," I said. "Even before this whole nuclear bomb thing."

"Yes, a most unfortunate occurrence," Wexford said. "Still, even before that, the truth of the Eden Prairie incident—I believe they call it at the high levels of your government—was well known and completely ignored in favor of such specious theories and frankly, mad explanations that cast you in the worst possible light. I have been lobbying on your behalf for a kind of asylum over these last few months. Unfortunately, the last Prime Minister had simply too much on her plate to consider, ahem … intervening in such a small matter. Her words, not mine, I assure you."

"Yes," I said, "it's certainly not been a small matter to me. Not these last few months."

"I imagine after the death of President Harmon and all his efforts to destroy you, it's been a bit lonely," Wexford said with something approaching a note of regret. "In any case, the new Prime Minister, Everton Daniels—he has finally heeded my constant harping … and he wished me to offer you a safe haven in the United Kingdom."

"Wait … what?" I leaned forward as Greg entered the room again, bringing with him something small in the palm of his hand. He touched it with a finger and a chair appeared, which he promptly set behind Wexford, who sat down in it very gracefully, without so much as a look. Greg put another one behind me, and two more to form a nice little square in the middle of the nearly empty office.

"He's offering you a way out while the heat's on here," Friday said, coming back into the room with two cups of tea, piping hot. He handed the first to me, and I took it, not really knowing what the hell I was doing, then gave the other to Wexford, who accepted it with his customary grace and settled back to give it a good, long sniff. If he disapproved, he didn't evince it in his expression. "You can go to England and hang out over there."

"The US and UK are allies," I said. "And the US Government is hunting me like a dog. How would you explain that away?"

"I think we could overlook our extradition treaty just this once," Wexford said, blowing gently on the steaming cup. "In exchange for perhaps a favor or two of your usual variety. We seem to be having an artificial rise in the number of metahuman crimes in the UK as well, and … tragically, thanks to the EU regulations on the matter … no one to help us police them."

It was a damned good thing that Greg had brought me a chair, because I leaned back in it now pretty heavily. This wasn't the sort of offer I'd expected to come my way, and damned sure not from a guy I hadn't seen in years. "Okay," I said, absorbing the logic of it all. "But … why me? There are other metas who you could hire."

Wexford paused, his teacup still steaming, hiding his smile. "I do hate to see a good person get a bad run of luck. It seems to me … you could use a break. And fortunately, after many months of lobbying, it seems the PM agrees."

I leaned back again, taking it all in. It was like a perfect gift handed to me, and naturally, I was looking for the strings, the bad horse teeth, the army of Trojans that was going to come bursting out—pick your metaphor. After what happened in LA, the Montana incident was just the beginning of the hell that was bound to be headed my way. The US Government had tasted blood, and with the media in a frenzy about me being the worst thing to happen to America since the advent of reality TV, me being attacked relentlessly was going to be the new normal.

I didn't even have to think about it for very long. "Yes," I said. "The answer is yes." My eyes stung a little bit at the realization I was having to basically flee my homeland. "But ..."

"But you want to wrap up this last job before you go, yes?" Wexford cocked his head at me and took a little sip. "Naturally. I'm here to provide a limited amount of aid in that regard as well."

"Wait," Friday said, "so ... what are we doing now?" He looked right at me. "You're leaving?"

"Not until I make sure you're safe from Sam the incredible shrinking a-hole," I said, "and his boss, McGarry."

"Yes," Wexford said, "Mark McGarry. Bit of a blight upon humanity, that fellow. I can provide you with his current whereabouts, courtesy of MI6."

I raised an eyebrow at that, and Greg said, "If you know where he is ... I have a modest proposal for what to do next."

Wexford smiled faintly. "I do hope it doesn't involve eating Irish babies." He paused as Greg frowned and Friday openly gawked at him. "It's from Swift."

"Taylor?" Friday asked, frowning. "Damn. She must take her beauty regimen seriously, eating Irish babies. Probably really good for fair skin."

Wexford cringed. "It's from Jonathan Swift, actually."

Friday stared at him blankly. "Is that Taylor's brother?"

"Sam is mean," Greg said, jumping right in so none of us had to sit there and work to disassemble Friday's idiotic misunderstandings, "but as you pointed out," he nodded at

310

me, "he won't waste his time working for free. Remove McGarry, you remove the money that drives Sam. He won't be happy, but without the contract, he won't waste his time hunting your ..." He looked at me like he was trying for my approval, "... friend? Compatriot?" He looked helplessly at Friday.

"Near stranger?" I offered.

"BFF," Friday said.

"... He'll be safe, whatever he is," Greg finished.

"All right," I said, nodding slowly. "So we go after this McGarry ... and take him off the board. Case closed."

"Yeah!" Friday pumped his fist. "Then I get to go back to ... uhm ... sitting around ... doing nothing, I guess. Lame." He looked at me. "And you get to go to England. Which is totally kittens, except for the teeth over there." He looked at Wexford. "Do you guys not have dentists?"

"Tired joke, that," Wexford said, looking at the ceiling to avoid the question. He looked to me. "Where do you wish to begin?"

It didn't take me more than a second. "Where's McGarry right now?"

"I thought you might take the aggressive tack," Wexford said, and he pulled out his phone, studying the screen for a moment. "He is presently on a transcontinental flight to Newfoundland, where he will refuel, and then hop across the ocean on his way back to the nation of Revelen." He looked up at me and smiled. "It seems your brother and some of your old friends tore apart his entire organization in a series of stunning raids yesterday. It's left Mr. McGarry scrambling for safer ground." He put the phone away. "I should warn you ... should he reach Revelen, he will be nearly impossible to apprehend."

"Revelen ... again," I muttered. "I'm about tired of that country always being a pain in my ass."

"You going to war with a nation state?" Friday asked. "Because that would be cool. Like something out of one of my stories."

I raised an eyebrow at that, because ... it might just be like one of Friday's stories. "Not today. Let's bag McGarry and get this assassination business over with." I looked at Greg. "How do you feel about attempting a midair assault?" And I could tell, by his smile, that he felt as good about it as I did.

59.

Greg

Greg knelt down next to the bed where Morgan lay beside Eddie, and her eyes fluttered slightly open to look at him, the morning sun shining in through the window behind him.

"Morning," Morgan whispered softly, trying not to wake Eddie.

"Good morning," Greg said. He half expected to see Sam appear at any moment, out of some darkened corner. It was an irrational fear, unlikely to happen, of course, but then, probability had been shot to hell over the last couple of days, had it?

"Are you leaving?" Morgan asked. She sounded warmer about it, almost regretful, something he might not have been able to imagine a day earlier. After the fight.

"We're going after McGarry," he said. "If we can remove him, Sam will be working for free."

"He won't like that," Morgan whispered.

"Yes, I expect he'll go find something else to do at that point," Greg said. "Something that pays."

"He might not," Morgan warned. "He's not like you, Greg. He holds a grudge hard. You know that."

"Hm," Greg said, almost smiling. "Would you say he's even pettier than I am?"

"Less fastidious," she said with vague amusement, "more hot-tempered. He won't get hung up on the little details the way you do, but he'll get mad about you doing this to him when he's just worked his way into McGarry's confidence."

"After his failure yesterday, I doubt McGarry is feeling much confidence in him," Greg said. "After this … we won't need to worry about it anymore."

"Be careful," Morgan said, putting her hands on his face and pulling Greg close to kiss him.

"Hide in my workshop with Eddie until I get back," Greg said as he withdrew after the kiss. It felt warm and wonderful, a lively promise he couldn't recall feeling in …

Years.

"I will," she said, shrinking and rolling off the bed so as not to disturb Eddie. She regrew at Greg's side. "Why don't you … carry him, though?"

Greg looked down at Eddie. Morgan was perfectly capable of lifting a five-year-old and carrying him to the tiny, hidden door in his office, shrinking down and getting him through …

But … he couldn't miss this opportunity, could he?

Greg leaned down carefully, shrinking his arms until they were sandwiched between Eddie and the sheets, and then expanded them again, lifting his son off the bed carefully, gently bracing his little blond head against Greg's upper arm. Eddie moved a little, then snuggled in.

He carried his boy down the stairs with care, making sure that he never once rustled him out of sleep …

And relished every minute of it.

60.

Sienna

"I'm gonna be happy once this is over," I said to Wexford, who was strapped in next to me in the Concorde. "I could use another nice little vacation, and merry old England in the middle of summer seems like just the place. Especially if I can stop trying to hide who I am with these ridiculous disguises." I wasn't wearing one right then, but only because I had Greg up in the cockpit, ready to shrink me in case we ran into any trouble.

"Well, you can't exactly parade through the streets of London," Wexford said. "Some discretion will be expected. We can turn a blind eye, but if you become too ... loud, shall we say, our position will become ... difficult, in relation to diplomatic matters with the United States."

"I'll try to keep from causing an international incident," I said dryly. "Still ... the offer is appreciated." Wexford inclined his head toward me. We were in the front of the passenger section of the plane; Greg was in the cockpit, along with Friday. I couldn't see Greg from where I was sitting, but I had a feeling based on the volume of chatter from Friday—it sounded like a monologue—that Greg was probably not having one of the best days of his life. "And it'll be nice to put this annoying case behind me." I narrowed my eyes. "Say ... you don't happen to have a reason in that MI6 report for why this McGarry guy put the hit out on Friday to begin with?"

315

Wexford took a deep breath, which, coming from a guy so British and uptight he might have been carrying an undeployed umbrella up his ass for safekeeping, was a pretty solid cue that he was holding back something. "It's not in the report, no."

I stared him down. "But you know, don't you?"

He squirmed a little in his seat. "I do. Friday, as you call him, knows as well. He is aware of precisely why McGarry wishes him dead."

I felt all the blood drain from my face. "I'ma kill his ass right now." I clenched my fist. "I have been through hell these last two days, and followed every one of his bullshit stories with him—and he's *known why all this time?*"

Wexford put a hand on my wrist, a brushing, gentle one that got me to simmer down for a moment as he put on his best sympathetic look. "He doesn't hide this secret—and it is, as you Americans might call it, a 'doozy'—he doesn't hide it out of malice toward you." He wore a warm, empathetic look that wouldn't have been out of place on Dr. Zollers's face. "He hides it out of shame."

"Friday has no shame," I said, but uncertainly.

"Oh, but he does," Wexford said. "Much shame, in fact. His entire persona, all his bluster, it's all a mad effort to hide his feelings of deepest inadequacy—of intellect, of prowess, of social skills. You could scarcely name a category of belonging where your associate feels he excels, other than perhaps in raw strength. Even there, he would pale in comparison to your abilities."

"But he—" I started to say.

"We're coming up on McGarry's plane now," Greg called from out of the cockpit. He sounded pretty damned cross, like someone (Friday) had twisted up his pubes. Which was a shame, because he'd looked all relaxed and happy right before we'd left. "Two minutes."

"You're not coming aboard with us, are you?" I asked, shedding my seatbelt and stepping past Wexford into the aisle.

"I believe I'm better remaining here," Wexford said with the trace of a smile. "I'm not much for physicality, but I'll be watching and lend a thought if things get out of hand."

"Do you consider it likely they will?" I asked, looking out of the window. There was a Gulfstream IV below us and ahead, a plane I was intimately familiar with from having flown on it more times than I could count.

"He has bodyguards," Wexford said. "Very strong ones. Enhanced with additional powers from a chemical source I believe you're familiar with."

"Revelen." I cursed again. "Any chance you'd care to share what's going on there, behind the old Iron Curtain?"

"We'll discuss it on another occasion," Wexford said, "a more … opportune time than now." He smiled once more, as Greg came stomping out of the cockpit, his eyes threatening to roll back in his head, with Friday a couple steps behind. "After all … you have work to do right now."

61.

Blowing into the passenger cabin of Mark McGarry's plane involved a neat little skydiving maneuver, with Greg riding my back and controlling our size, and Friday clutched in my arms, rolled up like he was about to do a cannonball into a pool. We battled through the howling wind outside to fly right through one of the seams in the airframe, and then, POP! We were in the plane, staring at a seething Mark McGarry, who didn't look at all like I thought he would.

I was expecting an old fat guy with a three button suit, a cigar, maybe bald, you know, a typical diabolical arch villain.

Mark McGarry looked like he was in his late twenties, with black hair and olive skin, a frown of deep impatience on his face. He was wearing one of those Reebok jogging suits that were probably really expensive but still made you look like you just got in from a run or from the gym. It was a look that screamed, "Bro douchebag," to me.

"This is gonna be fun!" Friday shouted, and McGarry's brow creased. He heard it, but it was probably so distant and tinny he wasn't putting two and two together yet.

"Now!" I shouted, and Greg grew us back to normal size at McGarry's feet.

Or at least, I thought he did. Apparently, I didn't think this entirely through, but fortunately, Greg did.

He stopped growing us at about half size, which was good, because Friday was already yanking himself out of my grasp and bellowing as he flew at McGarry's face. My skull thumped against the bulkhead, and I felt Greg sliding off in order to avoid being crushed.

"Lose some altitude!" Greg shouted at me as a half-sized version of Friday went screaming into McGarry's face like a dwarf lusting for blood. McGarry, for his part, was screaming right back, probably from being attacked by what looked like a very bulky child. "You're smashing my head against the top of the cabin."

"Sorry," I said as Friday got hold of McGarry. There was some serious face punching going on there, I could see, as I drifted downward. Greg started to grow the two of us again, and once we were back to normal size I settled us on the thin carpeting that covered the floor of the Gulfstream. "I'm just not used to this shrink and grow thing."

"It takes some adjustment," Greg said apologetically. He was watching Friday, as was I. Dude was really going to work on McGarry, whose pretty face was not looking quite so pretty. Greg shouted, apropos of nothing: "Mark McGarry! Any last words?"

I let that dramatic question hang in the air for a minute as Friday worked McGarry. I watched for a few seconds, then winced. "Friday," I said, prompting mini-Friday to turn around and look at me. He was pretty feral at that point, so I put a lot of command in my voice to get him to lay off. "Don't kill him. Go to the body for a bit."

"Okay!" Friday chittered, and man, he back to punching McGarry in the gut. McGarry, for his part, was still screaming at being attacked by something so small and vicious.

"Looks like a pitbull attacking a yuppie on his way to spin class," I said.

"Help me!" McGarry screamed in between punches. Friday hit him right in the breadbasket with a devastating cross and McGarry said, "OOF!" and then stopped talking for a couple minutes.

"Pilots coming at us," Greg said, looking out of the corner of his eye. "Probably bodyguards, too."

"Wexford warned me he had a couple." Greg was right. The cockpit door was open and the flight crew was stepping out, menace on their faces. One of them had an arm that started to glow, like he was channeling energy through it, ready to rumble on the plane.

"Yeah, no," I said, and shot a light net with a little extra gusto. It peppered him right in the face and knocked him over with the force of the blast, sealing his head to the deck. I did the same to the co-pilot, but he got bonded to the back of his seat.

"I'll finish dispatching them," Greg said, striding off toward the front of the plane, "non-lethally," he added after a pause, as though he needed to reassure me of this for some reason.

"Cool," I said noncommittally, "you do that." I heard a mighty whack of Greg's fist against a downed pilot's jaw and winced. He might be doing the non-lethal thing, but it wasn't going to be a painless one.

"Please make it stop!" McGarry screamed, and I stepped over to pitbull Friday and yanked him off.

"Let me at him!" Friday growled, still swinging his tiny fists. Looking at him more closely, he was less than half size, more like a third or a quarter, because I was holding him several feet off the floor by just dangling him out from my body.

"Okay, McGarry," I said, "you know who I am?"

He took one look at me and nodded, dabbing with a nylon sleeve at his nose, which was dripping blood. "You're Sienna Nealon."

"Not that it matters, I guess, since Friday was already doing a number on you," I said, "but if you know me, you know my lack of reticence to use violence on people who deserve it—"

"I didn't do anythi—" he started to protest.

I swung Friday toward him and the miniature schnauzer in my hand upped the intensity of his swings. Even though he was attacking nothing but air, it was air that was a lot more proximate to McGarry's face than it had been a second before, and McGarry seemed to catch the implication, because he shut up. "Don't give me those lies. I will let this little pitbull loose and watch him eat your eyeballs with a peanut butter sandwich."

Friday stopped for a second, dangling completely still. "I would not eat his eyeballs on a peanut butter sandwich. That's just nasty."

"It's an expression," I said. "You'd probably do worse to him."

"I'm just going to punch him until he can't breathe right anymore," Friday said. "Maybe do the tango on his junk—"

"I will tell you whatever you want to know," McGarry said quickly. "Within reason."

"Who hired you?" I asked.

"Uhm, I don't entirely know," McGarry said, "but they're a consortium based in Revelen. I'm not supposed to know that." He swallowed heavily. "But I do. And now so you do. So … can I go?"

"Who was your contact person?" I asked.

"She went by the name Juno," McGarry said.

That trilled a little note of worry up my spine. I'd known Juno, the real Juno, who typically called herself Hera. But she was good and dead, and I'd watched it happen, which suggested to me it was probably a codename. "What else do you know about her that you shouldn't know?"

"Very little," he said. "We never met, only talked on the phone. She's in Revelen. She has deep pockets. She gave me all the money to set up the US operation, and gave me guidance on what to do with it, how to run it, some specific commands …" He swallowed visibly, Adam's apple bobbing up and down.

"What kind of specific commands?" I asked.

"She told me to have him killed," McGarry pointed at Friday. He swallowed more heavily. "And to make sure you didn't get killed." He looked right at me.

"Interesting," I said. "Keep going. When did you last talk to her?"

"This morning," McGarry said with a heavy gulp, and then he just stopped.

"What did you talk about?" I asked, trying to prompt him along.

McGarry looked around, like he was trying to find an escape, like he might want to jump out of the plane. "She asked me to schedule ... uhm ..."

"What?" I asked. "A prostate exam? Because I'm about to have Friday perform one on you, fully submerged." I held up mini-Friday again.

"I am not going up there," Friday said.

"You might just if he doesn't answer this question," I said, and Friday went super pale. But not as pale as McGarry.

"She wanted me to take out a contract with a local assassin against the people who ... arrested our entire organization yesterday." McGarry gulped hard.

My blood went cold like the plane had dropped away and I'd been left out in the frigid air at 20,000 feet. "And did you?" I asked, ice in my voice.

He nodded. "I contracted it to Sam Bennett."

"That is very bad news," Greg said from behind me. I hadn't even realized he'd rejoined us.

"When is he going to do this?" I asked, feeling the chill seep through me.

"As soon as he's able," McGarry said. "This ... it took priority over assassinating your friend here." He nodded at Friday. "As far as I know ... he's doing it right now."

62.

Augustus

"Hey, Kat, how you doing?" I asked, taking a respite from the stupid paperwork and cracking my knuckles. She was the last of us to arrive, everyone else already with their heads down, the occasional grumble about the annoying differences between paperwork contrived by different locales filling the air along with the infrequent swear word.

"Ugh, I feel terrible," Kat said, flouncing over to her cubicle and flopping into her chair. "Filming all week and those raids yesterday and now this today." She made a show of yawning. "I feel like I should have my personal assistant doing this, but silly me, I gave her the week off, so she's back in LA having fun and I'm soldiering on through forty degrees and a mountain of this." She inclined her head toward the stack of paperwork on her desk.

"Yeah, no one suffers like you, baby," I said, and she gave me a withering yet amused look. "Except for the rest of us."

She grabbed a spare piece of paper, wadded it up into a ball and threw it at me.

I blocked it with my forearm and chuckled. "That stack ain't getting any smaller, and you still have to do it even if you toss all of it at me."

"Don't tempt me," she said and sighed, making a face as she disappeared behind the cubicle wall. I could sympathize. This was going to be an all-day thing.

63.

Greg

"We are on course for Minneapolis," Greg said once they were back aboard the Concorde, McGarry bound in white nets of light, a strange spectacle not akin to anything he could recall seeing at any point in his rather illustrious career.

"How far away are we?" Sienna was plainly tense, cracking her knuckles nervously as she slipped into the co-pilot seat. Lord Wexford and Friday were in the passenger compartment with the unconscious, netted-up McGarry. The pilots had been left on his plane, one conscious and one not, with Sienna promising to unbind the conscious one as soon as they'd made good their escape.

"We're over upstate New York now," Greg said. "I can try and lose us in commercial traffic, but …"

Sienna's mouth was a tight line until she spoke. "They're canvassing the country with overhead satellites for objects moving at supersonic speed, so if we push it …"

"They're likely to notice us and respond, yes," Greg said tightly. The feeling of a clock counting down to danger was imminent, and strangely gripping, given that he didn't even know any of the parties involved in this particular drama save for Sam, who was the antagonist in the equation.

"How fast can we go without getting their attention or getting big enough that they notice?" she asked, still quite pale.

"I don't know," Greg said, "but I expect we're about to

find out." He hesitated. "Shall I push it to the limit?"

"Maybe," she said, stroking the console on the side of her seat. "Is there any way we could get there faster, with less danger?"

Greg pursed his lips. "Perhaps. If we switch to the SR-71, it's possible. The aircraft's profile is less likely to be noted by ground-based radar, but we're still visible to overhead satellites. It can go Mach 3.3, which we won't, because we'll be smaller, but it beats the Concorde's 2—"

"Dammit," she said, thrusting her head against the seat back. "This is …"

"Intolerable," Greg offered.

"My fault," she said.

Greg felt the puzzlement roll through his brain, prompting the question before he could stifle it. "How is it your fault? It seems to me your friends decided to cause this trouble of their own accord, going after McGarry and his operation."

"Because it's my fault," she said, offering no further explanation. "Maybe I should jump out, race for Minneapolis myself."

"If you do that," Greg said, "you risk bringing the danger of the law against your friends, not just the danger of Sam, who is almost certainly making his way there more slowly than we are. Trust me when I tell you that he does not possess the ability to pilot a plane, and certainly does not have a supersonic aircraft. The clock you imagine ticking down to your friends' deaths is most assuredly not moving as swiftly as you think."

"Nice logic," Sienna said, rolling her head against the rest to look at him with a bleakly cynical smile. "How does that usually work when it comes in contact with irrational emotion, in your experience?"

Greg let his mouth fall open to answer, then smiled. "A very excellent point."

She smiled, wanly. "You seem like a relentlessly pragmatic person."

"A useful attribute in someone who is tasked with dealing death," Greg said, checking the instruments. "And thank you, I think."

"So ..." she said, "... why do you always ask, 'Any last words'? before you kill someone? Or try, at least? It seems sentimental. Kind of a time waster, isn't it?"

Greg drew a deep breath. "It is sentimental, I suppose. My mother was the meta, though she kept it quiet. She had my ability, but tended toward what most Atlases did with it—grow only, because big is good and small is ... insignificant." He blushed as he said it. "When she would remonstrate me as a child, she used to swell. I thought I imagined it, until I looked back later, once I knew about her powers." He shook his head. "But that's neither here nor there, I suppose, because the reason I ask that question is ... is my father.

"He was a human. A government scientist." Greg subtly eased up the throttle, pouring a little more speed and making the Concorde just slightly larger. It would shave a few minutes off their arrival. "He was assassinated during one of the brief spells during which the Cold War went slightly hotter, during which our two governments, the US and Soviet, used unaffiliated metahuman agents as cats' paws to keep things quiet and on the level. They found him at his desk, dead, slumped over—he'd never seen what killed him coming." Greg thought of the image soberly; he'd seen it in a government file once he'd gotten old enough to use his powers to ferret out the truth of what had happened.

"So, I ask my ... victims," Greg said with great distaste, "if they have any last words ... because I don't think he got a chance to have any." His mouth felt very dry. "I don't know what he would have said if he'd had the chance, but ... I like to think ..." He swallowed hard. "Well, I don't suppose it matters what I like to think, since ..." He laughed weakly. "I suppose instead of following in my father's footsteps, I've followed in the footsteps of whoever killed him." He touched his forehead and found it wet. "I always thought that was ironic, with a sort of ... amusement." He swallowed, and tasted bile in the back of his throat. "Now I wonder why I thought that it was anything other than wretched."

"I wonder about that, too," Sienna said, lifting her head off the rest and regarding him curiously. "You could have left with your family after we pulled the plug on McGarry. You could have tried to call Sam and dissuade him by telling him the money had dried up, then gone your separate way. Instead ... you're charging into battle with us. Doesn't seem like your style, since you're not being paid, either." She leaned forward, putting her chin on her hand. "Why are you doing this, Greg?"

He stared straight ahead, out the window, into the banks of clouds that lurked just outside. He was trying to keep them hidden from satellite observance as he pushed the throttle up, but the Concorde shuddered from the adverse conditions. He ignored it. "I don't know," he said quietly.

"Well, regardless of the reason," she said, standing up, "I guess ... I can pretty much forgive the crap we went through before if you can help me save my friends." She paused at the cockpit door. "Still, though ... I hope at least you know why you're doing this, because it's bound to be dangerous." And then she left, wandering into the passenger compartment with an aimless shuffle to her step, plainly killing time until they got there.

Of course you know why you're doing this, that smooth voice said in the back of his head. It was so familiar, the name almost on the tip of Greg's tongue. *It's because you saw yourself for who you really are—a villain—and now you want redemption, both in your eyes and that of your family.*

I don't know what you're talking about, Greg said.

You can lie to yourself, if you'd like, the voice said, so slick, so sure, *but don't bother to lie to me. How long have you looked in your son's eyes and seen that fear lurking there, afraid of his own father, of what you've become? That horror in your wife's eyes as she looks at you, through you, and sees your innumerable sins?*

Greg swallowed again, trying to choke back that feeling of bile welling up, revulsion raging in his blood like a poison.

Don't worry, the voice said. *You'll feel better once this is done. Once you've taken that first step. Because ... let me tell you something about redemption, a lesson I've learned from personal experience. Redemption ... is not a destination. It's a journey to right the wrongs you've committed, as best you can.*

Something about the way the voice spoke brought to

mind a peculiar association—an American flag. Greg shuddered, wondering where that had come from.

But see ... the wrongs you've done, they never go away completely. The scales ... they don't balance, exactly. The pain you've caused doesn't just vanish. The human wreckage you leave in your wake doesn't just disappear once you start doing the right things. The people you've harmed ...

The voice trailed off for a moment, and then began again, a little weaker, a little ... choked. ... *Once you see inside the lives of those you've harmed, those you've tried to destroy ... it changes your perspective, doesn't it?*

"Yes," Greg whispered, looking over his shoulder. Sienna was standing there, talking to Friday ... and Greg felt a strange swell of guilt for what he'd done to them. To her, specifically, her exile impending, thanks to him.

Redemption is a journey, the voice said again. *Atonement, amends ... they don't come immediately. You'll be working on this for quite some time, Gregory. Maybe the rest of your life. But the good news is ... maybe soon, even ... you'll be able to look in your wife's eyes and that worry will be absent. Your son will be able to look at you without being deathly afraid. If you actually change.*

"I want to," Greg whispered, a single tear trickling down his cheek. He should have been embarrassed at his weakness. Should have rushed to mop it from his cheek. But he didn't; he left it there like an external reminder of all the reasons he had to be ashamed.

I know, the voice said, smooth, sincere. *I can see it in your mind. In your heart.*

"Who are you?" Greg said, adjusting the speed upward again.

Just the voice of experience, he said, growing quieter and quieter. *And of a fate you had best hope you never meet.*

Somehow, Greg knew that now the speaker had left him alone, in the cockpit, with his thoughts. Greg stared through the windshield at the clouds ahead, and pondered the future, that prick of tingling fear at the words the voice had said, about redemption, about his family, about atonement. And he kept nudging the speed up a little at a time, until he could move it up no more.

64.

Sienna

"We're over Minneapolis," Greg announced as I slid back into the cockpit with him. Friday and Wexford remained behind because there was only so much room up front. "Five minutes 'til we're in a pattern over the office complex you flagged."

"Okay," I said. "What's our plan?"

"I'll bring us down to a hundred feet over the building, shrink the plane and put it in a holding pattern on autopilot," Greg said, fingers dancing over the console in front of him, doing who knew what. "We'll drop as we did before, and warn your friends—"

"They can't see me," I said, though saying it out loud was like a dagger through my heart. "The FBI will have the office under surveillance. If they catch a glimpse of me there …"

"All right," Greg said, frowning as he adjusted his planning. "That complicates things."

"What about Sam?" I asked. "How's he going to play this contract?"

That caused Greg's frown to deepen. "He lacks my … subtlety at times. If this were a single-person assassination, he would likely shrink to enter their body while wearing scuba gear, follow their blood flow to the brain, and grow, simulating a massive aneurysm—"

"He would ride their blood flow?" Every part of that statement gave me the heebie jeebies.

Greg was back in straight professor mode. "It's a very simple way to assassinate, and because it looks like a natural cause of death, typically is one of the cleanest methods we could employ—" He must have caught me looking at him in horror, because he pulled back pretty hard. "And is quite disgusting, obviously."

"But he won't do that here?" I asked.

Greg shook his head. "Too many targets. It won't look like an accident if ten people die of an aneurysm. For this ... he won't bother with subtlety, because you can't make this many deaths look like an accident, at least not easily. Even a gas leak explosion might not kill the targets, given that so many of them are metahumans. He'll need to be thoroughly destructive, especially lethal, and most accidental means simply don't possess the effectiveness of intentional, targeted means—guns, bombs, etc. He'll opt for the latter, counting on his abilities to screen him from any implication in the murders, and allow the undoubtedly countless people with an axe to grind against your friends to shoulder the blame during the investigation."

It took me a few seconds to unpack everything Greg said there. "So you're saying ... he's going to go big on the kill method, and he's basically counting on his powers to shrink and the fact my homies have lots of enemies to keep him from ever getting caught for this?"

"Exactly."

I swore under my breath. "So ... how's he going to do it? The killing?"

Greg shrugged. "I don't know exactly. When someone hires us, it's almost exclusively for covert kills, the sort for which you don't want blame to come back on you, and that—preferably—don't look like a kill at all. I can't recall ever working a mass hit like this with Sam. I don't know what he'll do, except to say that he's not a particularly shy or subtle fellow."

"Great," I said, lapsing into thought. Sam was like an invisible spirit of death, reaching out his hand for my friends, and I had to go try and defend them, all without being seen.

"We're over the drop zone," Greg said a few moments

later, and I looked up to see that we had definitely shrunk again, buildings in the distance looking like mountains, even though I knew from photos they were small office park buildings, no larger than a few hundred feet in length. They looked like worlds unto themselves, which, I supposed, at this size … they sort of were. "Shall we?" Greg asked, stepping out of his seat and letting the plane fly onward. I suspected that at this size, it could fly for about a hundred years without hitting anything.

"If you don't mind," Wexford said, "I'd like to get out now. I need to catch a flight back the UK, after all, and, ah … just in case things go wrong for you …" He looked at Greg. "Well … I'd rather not spend the rest of my days as a microbe. I hope you understand."

"I can drop you around back of the building," Greg said with a nod. "You should be able to find transport from there."

"Excellent," Wexford said. He nudged McGarry's bound form. "What shall we do about this fellow, then?"

"Oh, I've got a plan for him," I said, heaving him to his feet. "At least, after this is over. But I don't need him running off before then, so I think … maybe we just shrink him and leave him so tiny that even Sam won't be able to find him." I shrugged. "That way, if anything happens to us, he can spend the last minutes of his life running from a giant ant while it tries to make him dinner."

"Seems fair," Greg said with a shrug, grabbing the bound McGarry and pulling him close.

"This is going to be totally kittens," Friday said.

"What?" Greg looked at him like he'd been dropped on his head a few too many times.

"He's saying it's going to be awesome," I said, as Greg shrank himself, McGarry, Friday and Wexford small enough that they could fit into my pocket. The scale thing was kind of cool, I reflected, in that once he started shrinking me to fit between the airtight gap in the plane's door, they'd all remain proportional in size to me as I was now, safely tucked away in my pocket until I started to grow again once I was out and flying. I'd have to be careful to remain upright, though, or risk them tumbling out and down to their deaths.

"Can I say awesome again now?" Friday squeaked, now no bigger than my hand as I scooped him up, careful not to touch his skin and placed him in my right breast pocket. I put Wexford in next to him, then grabbed Greg, who was holding tight to McGarry, and put him in on the left pocket. Now they all had a front row seat to our descent.

"Sure," I said wearily, "knock yourself out. Say 'awesome' again. A million times, if you like."

Friday seemed to think about it for a few seconds. "You know what? I think I like saying, 'This is going to be totally kittens!' even better!"

"I miss the days when one prepared for a moment like this by saying, 'Once more unto the breach, dear friends,'" Wexford said.

"It's the twenty-first century, dude," I said as I readied myself before the door, about to hurl myself and these others through a microscopic crack in it before facing death and danger again, one last time, before I left the city—and country—of my birth. Maybe for good. "Also, there's that part later in the passage about closing up the wall with our English dead, and you're the only English here, so …"

"An excellent point," Wexford said. "Let it be 'awesome,' then. Or whatever alternative you favor."

"Yeah," I whispered. "This is going to be totally kittens."

But somehow, maybe because of all the worries and thoughts churning in my mind … I wasn't all that convinced.

65.

We flew out of the Concorde and down to the office building below, stopping behind the brick structure in an isolated spot to let Greg grow Wexford back to his usual size. The Brit strutted off with his inimitable confidence, and once we'd dropped McGarry, still bound up and shrunken to miniature size, in a spot on the sidewalk against the wall just outside the door to the agency's new office, in we went, Greg, Friday and I.

My first thought when we shrank to slip through the door was ... damn, I was paying for a nice place. Not to say our old office was a crap sty, but it wasn't as nice as this. I'd seen the blueprints for the buildout, and I even knew the name of the full-time secretary we passed in the lobby was Casey, but knowing these things isn't the same as seeing them, and it cause a pang of sadness as I flew toward the hall to the bullpen.

If I thought I was struck by sadness in the lobby ... well, it was nothing compared to what I felt once we made it into the bullpen.

"I'm growing us to ant size," Greg said from my back. "We should still escape notice, but it'll make traversing longer distances easier. Sam likely won't go any smaller than this anyway, because he can't fly."

"Good to know," I said, keeping my emotions bottled like a Sprite someone had shook up like a fiend. There was definitely some emotional carbonation threatening to blast out. From where I flew, a few feet above them, I could see all my friends: J.J. and Abby, working side by side in a cubicle in the corner, Augustus with his head down over a stack of forms like he was an accountant, Jamal a couple desks away playing with his phone while ignoring the stack of paperwork sitting in front of him. Kat looked like she was asleep at her desk, Scott was diligently working at his, the frown on his face that look of concentration he got when he didn't know what he was doing but didn't want to ask.

"How's it going, guys?" The voice cracked over me like a thunderbolt out of a cloud, the speaker standing at the entrance to his office. Seeing him there in his suit, with his hair all styled up in his ponytail, arms folded because he was Mr. Serious and *in charge* ...

It was my brother, Reed. I felt a jolt run through me, and I swallowed hard to keep that emotion safely down, where it belonged.

"Oh, we're just dying of joy out here," Augustus said. Always ready with a good shot, that guy.

"Can we hire an administrator to do this for us?" Scott asked. "You know, to save time." He reddened almost imperceptibly, and I knew it was because he didn't want to admit he was in over his head on whatever he was doing.

"You need to take us lower," Greg said. "Sam will be moving across the floor when he comes."

"Right," I said, launching us into a dive. "So ... the plan is to fly around these cubicles in slow circles until we see him, then ... kick his ass?" I was barely holding my shit together, and spelling out our absurd plan helped take my focus off the fact that almost everyone I loved and cared about was within twenty feet of me.

And I couldn't say a word to them.

I should have listened to Zollers, I said in my head, longing for someone, even the wretched souls imprisoned in my skull, to hear me. *I should have dreamwalked to them. Talked to them. But I didn't.*

Why do you suppose that is? Harmon asked. He seemed to be taking the lead now when it came to my psychological well-being.

I don't know, I said, shutting down the thought before it

334

had a chance to choke me up. *I don't want to talk about this right now.*

All right, Harmon said softly. *But ... later.*

"Sure," I whispered, sniffing and shaking it off. He wouldn't let me forget, that much I knew.

"Hey, guys," Friday said, "I think I see Sam."

"I don't think Sam could have made it here yet," Greg said, giving off a sniff of his own.

"Yeah ... I think that's him." Friday pointed at a spot on the carpet.

I strained to look where he was indicating. The carpet was a commercial standard, not a lot of height to it and shaded pretty dark. The fibers looked huge even at the height of a foot, which is where we were flying. "I don't know how you'd see anything at this distance."

"He's right there," Friday said. "Right fricking—" He waved his hand and I brought us down, not really sure why I was trusting Friday to—

Oh, shit. There he was, Sam, walking through the low-pile carpet like he was making his way through marsh grass, trudging along halfway across Augustus's cubicle entrance. "He's here!" I said, bringing us down low.

"How did he get here so quickly?" Greg asked as we came down for a landing, interposing ourselves right in Sam's path.

"You think you know me so well, Greg," Sam called into the twenty feet or so of space between us. Or more like a millimeter, actually. "But I'm not a stupid guy."

"You're trying to kill my friends," I said, "and you're about to do it for zero dollars, because your contract has been voided by the untimely disappearance of Mr. McGarry."

Sam just stared at me. "Y'all took out McGarry?"

"That's right," I said, ignoring Greg's insistent tug at my sleeve. "You're now a charitable organization if you go through with this. Also, I will personally annihilate you."

"Sienna," Greg said softly, "I was all in favor of cutting his financial incentive to kill us and then informing him at a distance, but this is an entirely different thing. You've just copped to hitting him right in the bank account. I don't think he'll take that well."

"Greg's right," Sam said, "and incidentally, the reason I know I'm smart? Greg doesn't choose to work with dummies."

"That's right!" Friday said. "We're all geniuses."

Everyone just sort of stopped, stared at Friday for a second, hulking in his place behind a carpet fiber the size of a small tree, ignored him in order to make ourselves feel better about our own intelligence, and moved on back to the war of words that seemed to be heading toward an actual war. "If you try and go ahead with this," I said, "not only are you going to end up with nothing, but I'm going to make it my mission to turn you into something that will get sucked up by the cleaning lady tonight when she makes her rounds with the vacuum at ten PM. There's going to be no win in this for you, Sam. But you can still break even by walking away. Hell, we could even be generous and give you a ride home."

Sam just stood there, staring at the ground. "I'm afraid you got a part of that wrong," he said, shaking his head. "See ... I went all in on this, thinking I'd have a chance to impress Mr. McGarry, make up for not killing your pal Friday, uh, yesterday." He made a funny face as he realized the verbal contortion he'd just made, but went on. "I sunk a lot of my own money into making this job come off smoothly, perfectly, and now that you've gone and cut the old monetary umbilical cord ... seems to me I'm pretty well screwed." He grimaced. "I wish you hadn't done that, because now ... now I'm in a real fine mess. In fact, you might even say ..." His voice hardened, and he looked super pissed, "... I got nothing left to lose."

"Don't do something even stupider—" I started to say.

But it was too late. Sam reached into his pocket and pulled something out. It was a small case, and it grew in front of us, the item he'd shrunk going to full-size—or at least our size—in less than a second ... and suddenly we all knew where Sam had invested his money on this job.

And it was, to borrow Wexford's cribbing of the

American word … a doozy.

A rank of a hundred soldiers—hired mercenaries— blossomed in front of us like those mythical sea monkeys that you were supposed to just add water to. Except these were real-deal guys, human beings with assault rifles, formed up in a rank like an army ready to march, their guns up, pointed at us.

And there were way, way too many to miss.

66.

Augustus

"Hey, Jamal," I hissed, sticking my head up over the wall of my short cubicle, "do you have an extra set of headphones?"

My brother paused, turning to look at me over the cube between us, filled by the irritable Angel, who had her head down and was blatantly ignoring us after catching my sideways glance. "Nah, I don't have another pair. Why didn't you bring your own?"

"I forgot I was going to be doing paperwork all day, for the rest of my life," I said, sagging back down in my chair. My stack still looked like my wallet these days: thicker than I would have ever believed. "Man," I sighed.

I thought I saw something move out of the corner of my eye and spun around. I stared at the carpet next to the entry to my cubicle. I would have sworn I'd seen something there a second ago, but there was clearly nothing going on.

With a shrug, I turned back to a witness statement from a town in New Hampshire that was particularly dense. "Who writes this shit?" I muttered, stretching my fingers before I picked up my pen and got back to work.

67.

Greg

Greg watched in horror as Sam deployed a hundred seasoned mercenaries and they opened fire, barely getting his hands on Sienna and Friday in time to shrink them low, already tiny bullets flying over their heads like he'd witnessed in that Montana lumberyard.

"Why is my life just a series of people constantly shooting at me?" Sienna asked as the air above them churned into a frenzy of bullets, the shots ringing out like thunder around them.

"I think it's because you always belittle and demean people," Friday said seriously. "You're reaping hard that nasty crop of sarcasm you're perpetually sowing."

"Shut up and stop accurately assessing my personality quirks," Sienna said, grabbing him again as Greg hopped onto her back, zipping them forward around the stalks of carpeting fibers that stood above them like pillars of the world. "Let's go whip Sam's ass and go home."

"What about these poor mercs?" Friday asked. "You're just going to leave them tiny to die in the carpeting?"

Sienna's face twitched. "Yes. Because I'm hell on mercs. It is known."

"Cold," Friday said as they veered past a fiber of carpet bigger than any redwood Greg had ever seen.

"I've done worse for less reason," she said. "Maybe they'll find their way over to J.J.'s desk and live a meek subsistence on crumbs dropped from his snack hoard and the occasional spill of Mountain Dew and Red Bull."

Greg held on tight, taking care not to touch her skin. "Believe it or not, food doesn't taste nearly so good when you're shrunk. And it causes mighty bouts of indigestion."

"A worthy fate for these assholes," she said, sweeping low and between them. "Diarrhea to death."

Ahead, Greg could see Sam, reaching into his pocket and deploying another load of soldiers, these a quarter the size. "We have a problem," he said, pointing.

"Shit," Sienna said. "How many of these guys is he carrying?"

"I don't lack for enthusiasm!" Sam called as they shot toward him. "I loaded up on mercenaries. They're going for dirt cheap right now, almost like someone hasn't been cutting 'em down like wheat lately the way they used to."

Greg looked down at Sienna and caught Friday looking up at her. She reddened a little, and said, "What? I've been on the run. And gentler. Though that era seems to be coming to a rapid close."

"I need to stop Sam," Greg said, "while you two deal with these toy soldiers. Otherwise, who knows how many of them he'll pull out?"

"Need a toss?" Sienna asked as Greg slid forward, shrinking to fit in her hand. "Or are you just tired of riding on my back?"

"More A than B," Greg said, "so if you'd be so kind …"

"Thanks for flying Sienna air," she said, and Greg felt himself shot from her hand on a glowing web of light. Sam was just ahead, reaching into his pocket again, and Greg grew as he approached, the net of light fading as he came to his old foe, extending his leg—

He caught Sam just as his old friend was trying to shrink, Greg's foot in his ribs causing Sam to stagger, dropping whatever he'd had in hand a moment earlier. "Shit," Sam said, returning to roughly the same size as Greg. Sam swiped at his head, mopping up a bead of sweat. "This is how it's going to be, is it?"

340

"Yes," Greg said, throwing himself forward at Sam, striking him in the midsection with a punch as the two of them tumbled down, shrinking as they fell, "this is how it's going to be."

68.

Sienna

"Hey," Friday said just after I threw Greg toward his rendezvous with fate—or at least Sam.

"What?" I asked, stopping in time to avoid plowing into a carpet stalk. There were about a hundred soldiers behind us, a hell of a lot bigger than us, too. I could hear them tromping, trying to catch us in a hurry.

"How are we going to fight these guys when we can't shrink or grow?" he asked.

"Well, I can grow into a dragon—" I started to say, then realized—no, I couldn't. Not without returning to normal dragon size and completely flattening my agency's office building. "Uhm ..." I said.

"Fire?" Friday asked. "Like, blazing hot—"

"I'm not starting a fire in here," I said, "and besides ... they'd probably see at least the flashes in the carpet and notice something going on. I do have these light nets, but ..." I caught a glimpse of one of the soldiers; he was a giant compared to us. I barely reached his knee. "That's probably not going to do a lot against a hundred targets this size." I ran through the sequence; I could retreat, I guess, flying up to the ceiling, but that wouldn't win the fight, and Greg would be stuck down here. If Sam won, I'd be really badly placed to stop him ...

Which left the Warmind ...

Against this many of them? Bjorn asked. *And of this size? I*

342

don't think I can help you here …

"There are a hundred more even bigger than these guys just a little further back," Friday reminded me, oh so helpfully.

"Well, hell," I said, "I'll admit it—I'm fresh out of ideas."

A deep sigh filled my mind, a smug, paternalistic, I-know-you-need-me sigh that I'd kind of anticipated. *Fine,* Gerry Harmon said, *there's no need for drama.*

Oh, are you willing to help? I kept a wary eye on the incoming hordes of mercenaries. I could hear them crashing their way through the forest of carpet.

Yes, Harmon said, like he was some poor, put upon, long-suffering soul. *Let me introduce you to the wonder that is telepathy. Because clearly … you need some assistance.*

"I'm going in!" Friday shouted, tearing out of my grip and hulking out as he hit the ground running. He swelled, muscles bulging, probably getting about as wide across as one of these guys was, but only a third of the height.

"Wait!" I shouted, but he was already running toward the fight that was coming our way.

Some competent assistance, Harmon said.

"Oh, shut up and help me win this fight," I said, sweeping toward Friday and the mercenaries.

As I came blazing around the corner and got ahead of Friday, something curious happened. It was as though my mind … opened up. Like a fog was lifted, and suddenly I could see around the corner, could see past the next fiber of carpet standing like a tree blocking my path. I could feel things, see things, know things that I wouldn't have been able to a moment earlier. The nearest merc in front of me had an itchy trigger finger, had already fired a dozen rounds because his squad leader had told him to. He had his gun down, searching for prey that was low to the ground …

I went high and came down on him. He saw me just in time to want to let out a scream of panic at the tiny human shooting toward him, but I stifled his panic and rocked him with a perfectly placed hit to the jaw that put his lights out. He sagged, and I came up and smacked the squadmate just behind him who'd caught sight of me but hadn't said anything yet because I had shut down his speech.

Two more guys came bounding up behind him, and I could see their intent to fire before they did. Through their eyes, I could tell the aim path of their guns, and I moved accordingly, dodging as they shot. I turned down their perceptions—

I'm *doing that, actually.*

—Whatever, Harmon turned down their perceptions, and they were suddenly blissfully unaware of each other as I dodged between them and they blew each other's brains out. Meanwhile, back in the tight cluster behind them, a subtle adjustment to the hearing centers of the next squad coming up made them all think that the gunshots had come from behind them—

I hit them while their backs were turned, beating their asses in a frenzy, fighting these giants that were four times my size while pasting them with metahuman strength that allowed me to shatter bones and hit like a bullet. They would have screamed and cried, but I made them hold it in, crippling and killing them the way I could now tell they would have happily done to me if they'd but had a chance.

Friday came charging past with a merc clutched in his arms, looking a little like an ant carrying away a morsel three times its size, singing the song "Runaway Train" at the top of his lungs. Which I had to turn down in the perception of two of the nearing squads. "Is he singing …?" I asked as he tore past.

"Be my Eric Clapton in this duet!" Friday shouted, throwing the soldier in his hands up in the air. The guy smacked off a carpet fiber and came flipping back down, landing fatally hard. He did not move.

"… No," I said as I dove toward the next squad. I was going to take these assholes apart. If Friday didn't beat me to it.

69.

Greg

"It was always going to come to this, wasn't it?" Sam asked as Greg wrapped his hands around Sam's neck and started to squeeze.

"Pretty sure," Greg said as Sam whipped a thumb at his eye. Greg broke his hold and tossed Sam back to avoid it, but Sam started to grow.

The world around them was a frightening spectacle at this size. Motes of dust drifted by like asteroids running across the heavens above them. The slightest breeze could move them at this mass, and Greg considered it lucky that the air conditioning and heat didn't seem to be running, and that the door to outside wasn't in this room.

Greg slapped a hand on Sam's, gripping him tight, then stopped him from growing.

Sam just stared at him, straining like he was trying to lift something a few tons too heavy for him. Finally, he stopped. "Well, damn. You never told me it worked like that. What is this? Like a thumb wrestling contest? You win, so I can't shrink or grow while you're running the show on me?"

"Something like that," Greg said, and plowed him in the face with a hard hit, growing as he did so. So long as he held on to Sam, Sam couldn't use his power, which meant that Greg could just grow to the size of an adult compared to Sam and smack him around like a misbehaving child.

Sam shook his head, a little shadow of blood staining his

upper lip. "You look like you've done this before, Greg. You give your kid a good smack every now and again when he lips off at you?"

How does he know about Eddie …?

Greg froze, not catching Sam's grin until it was too late. He brought his hand down on Greg's wrist and a shock of pain ran through it as Sam broke the hold and grew a few inches, smacking Greg across the face as he did so.

He didn't know … he was just talking until he hit a nerve …

"I don't like this side of you, Greg," Sam said, tromping toward him as he swelled in size. "Feels like you're denying who you really are. You're acting all weird, throwing in with your marks, people you're supposed to be killing."

"The contract was cancelled," Greg said, picking himself up and trying to match Sam as he grew, wiping a trickle of blood off his own lip. "And I don't like any side of you."

"That cuts me right to the quick," Sam said, coming at him again with a hard punch that Greg shrank to dodge. "Hits me in the heart, you know."

Greg flicked at his fingernail, and the pistol he habitually hid right underneath it. He made it swell as he knocked it loose from the place where it sat buried in his skin, lifting it up as he drew aim on the center of Sam's chest. "No, but this will."

He fired and Sam grew swiftly, trying to outrun the damage of the pistol shots. Greg grew as well, trying to match it, but he knew already he wasn't having much luck. The bullets were pinpricks and little else, and if Sam kept going …

"Gimme that," Sam said, swiping for the gun. Greg shrank it out of his grasp and reached up, tagging Sam in the mouth with another punch that rocked him back a step. "You know," he said, rubbing his jaw, "you hit pretty hard for a little guy, Greg. I always thought it fit real well that you went the opposite direction of most Atlases with your powers—you know, given how stunted your ass is by nature."

"Now who's cutting who to the quick?" Greg said, elbowing Sam as he made another clumsy attempt at physical combat. This was something of an impasse; Greg had tools he could use, of course, but they'd keep changing sizes. Sam had a slight advantage in that it probably wouldn't bother him to go big, big enough to maybe even destroy the building like Godzilla, but Greg couldn't allow that. It would draw the sort of scrutiny he wouldn't care to deal with.

"Well, you took the legs out from under me by taking out McGarry," Sam said, dodging backward and stopping. They stood facing each other, both of them acknowledging the standoff. "That was a real blow to my future prospects. Hit me right where it hurt, I'll admit." Sam grinned. "Maybe now I'll do the same favor—hit you right where it'll hurt, take away one of your new friends—" He smiled and darted off, growing all the while, zipping around the corner toward where they'd left Sienna and Friday behind—

70.

Augustus

"Anybody else hungry?" I asked, sticking my head up above the people all ensconced in their paperwork, focus down. The bullpen was like a funeral home in the middle of a wake, no one daring to raise their voice—until me. "I'm thinking I'm going to go to Punch and get a pizza. Anyone else want one?"

"I'm good," Veronika said, still working diligently. She'd been damned quiet today, and she didn't even look up now. Something was stealing her feisty.

"Think I'll get takeout from Manny's later," Scott snarked at me.

"I'm good," Jamal said.

I paused when they stopped talking, wondering if I was hearing a faint buzzing noise. I looked around, trying to find the source. I'd thought I'd heard it a few minutes earlier, super faint, from somewhere near the entrance to my cubicle, but ... there was nothing there but empty carpet.

"All right," I said, shaking off that weird feeling, "well, if anyone wants anything—"

"Text me your order," Colin said as he shot to his feet, "I'll save you the carbon." And he blew past the entrance to my cubicle at warp speed, sending a wind through that I had to block with my body to keep it from destroying my stack of papers.

"Damn, man," I said as the place started to settle down

348

once his windy ass passed through, "I just wanted to get out of here for a little while."

"Send him your order and get back to the grindstone," Reed said from behind me, barely stifling a grin. "Come on. We get through all this crap, I'll take you all out for drinks tonight to celebrate."

"Yay," I said, settling back in my chair. Something moved again, out of the corner of my eye, at the entrance to my cube. I spun in my chair and stared. Huh. Just a ratty piece of commercial carpeting. Nothing going on there. Shaking my head, I went right back to work, counting the number of forms I had to file before I could call this day done.

71.

Sienna

INCOMING! Harmon screamed as I was wrecking a squad of guys on the far side of the battlefield. The carpet was really working to my advantage in giving cover, and so was the fact I could fly, because for some reason these idiots seemed to think they were in a real war, in a real forest, and that people couldn't swoop down on them from above. The good news was they weren't learning, because they were dying too fast to.

I looked up when Harmon screamed his warning right in my head, but it didn't do a bit of good. Something blew past like the shadow of a demon rising up from hell. Something smashed the carpet forest next to me, but I was already heading low before it picked up again and was gone, leaving a bunch of guys squished in its wake.

But that wasn't the only effect of the hell beast that had just ended the world slightly to my left. The thunderous impact had rocked the ground beneath, a compression wave of sound flattening the soldiers who weren't affected by it directly, and launching the others into the air from the earthquake effects.

"Friday!" I shouted as I saw him tumble by, a hundred feet off the ground. I reached over and snatched him before he hit his apogee and started sailing back to a crushing death below.

"Whew," Friday said as I realigned my grip so as not to

absorb him, "that was starting to get really ugly. What do you suppose that was?"

"A foot, I think." I thought immediately of Colin Fannon, the speedster. He'd probably blown past in a whirlwind of action, and damned near cleaned us out in the process.

"Anyone left alive down there?" I asked, circling low again.

Not many, Harmon said. *Greg and Sam were behind the cubicle wall over there, but they're headed back here—oh, no—*

"Wha—" I started to ask, but didn't get the chance.

As I came in for a landing, Sam lunged at me from behind a blind carpet fiber corner. I hadn't even known he was there, now that I was out of telepathy mode. He came at me like Superman, fists forward, and I snapped into a defensive stance, throwing Friday to the side in one smooth motion.

"Wheeee!" Friday shouted as he flew laterally.

I put my hands up as Sam came closer and closer. It was a standard move, designed to allow me flexibility to bat away a strike, to catch a punch in my hands, and to lift my arms and wrists to use as shields against battering blows.

Sam ... didn't do any of those things.

He shrank before my eyes, nearly disappearing as he shot toward me. I wasn't quite quick enough to smack him like a fly, and he sailed under my guard—

Sam struck me in the chest, perfectly placed between the ribs, breaking through the skin and entering my body like a bullet.

"No!" Greg shouted, coming around the corner. "No!" He took one look at me, eyes falling right to my wound, and he paled visibly. "He's—he's in your bloodstream." He looked up right at me, like he was pronouncing a death sentence, "He's ... he's inside you now."

72.

Greg

"How rude," Sienna said, a look of irritation flashing briefly across her face.

Greg couldn't find it in himself to laugh, nor to cry, though he did feel closer to the latter. Hadn't he told her? Hadn't he warned her about Sam's means, his common method of killing? He was sure he had, thought it had stuck in her mind. How could it not? Inducing an aneurysm? Hell, Sam could just grow in her heart, destroying it completely. She was so small right now, no one would ever find the body.

"This is a catastrophe," Greg whispered, looking back up at her, unable to quite catch his breath. He was about to witness this woman—this brave woman—die in front of his eyes at the hands of cowardly Sam.

"Tell me about it," Sienna grunted, sighing.

"I'll—I'll go in after him," Greg said, taking a step back, ready to jump into the wound. If he could get in there in time, maybe—

"Hold up there, cowboy," Sienna said with a weary sort of patience.

Greg just stared at her, gawking. Did she really not understand that death was sweeping through her veins right now, heading toward her heart or brain? "But—"

"Catch me," she said, and lifted a finger—

Which she then lit on fire—

And rammed right into the hole between her ribs.

She didn't scream, but only because she passed out within a second of sticking the flaming finger between her ribs. The sick, searing smell of meat cooking made Greg take an involuntary step back, so that when she toppled over, unconscious, he couldn't even catch her—

"Gotcha," Friday said, darting in behind her and breaking her fall. He had her in his arms and laid her down, across the base mat under the large carpet fiber tree that stretched above them.

"What did she do?" Greg marveled, staring at the hole in her side. Blood bubbled out, steaming, and a couple seconds later, a small, almost invisible little lump washed out—

Greg snatched it up, growing it in his fingers until it was doll-sized. He stared at the burned skin, the hanging body limp in his grasp. "Oh."

"That's your boy Sam, right?" Friday asked, still kneeling next to Sienna's head.

"Yes," Greg said, staring at the lolling little corpse as though it would spring to life and start cursing him, a tiny leprechaun with a drawl. "Did she ... boil him to death in her own blood?"

Friday guffawed. "That sounds like something she'd do, yeah."

He stared down at Sienna, who lay flushed and unmoving upon the matting. "Is she going to be all right ...?"

Friday glanced down, and ran his hand over her forehead. "Yeah. Wolfe's probably—"

Sienna sat up suddenly, her mouth gaping open and a smoke ring puffing its way out. "Hot damn," she said, and then launched into a fit of coughing that she only stopped once she caught sight of the corpse of Sam perched between Greg's fingers. "Oh, good. I was worried he'd get stuck in my body and I'd recirculate him until he started to rot. Give me assassin blood cancer or something. That cannot be good for your health."

"Not as bad as an aneurysm," Greg said, lifting Sam up to look him in the eye. They were open, staring, his face nearly seared off. "Or a heart attack."

"Hey, can I see that?" Friday asked, hand extended.

Greg took a look at Sam's corpse, then offered it to Friday. "Yes. Why do you wa—"

Friday snatched it up and then slammed it against the latticework of the mat. The body broke into pieces and Friday laughed. "Kittens! That was so cool."

"Ugh," Sienna said, getting to her feet. She was still looking a little flushed, so Greg came to her side and offered her an elbow. She shook her head, and stood there, getting her balance. "So ... I think that's the end of the mini-mercs."

"Yup," Friday said. "And we wiped out Sam the Spam. No, wait—Sam the Sham? Sam the Sham-Not-Wow?"

"We saved your life, Friday," Sienna said wearily. "And that of everyone else in the room." She looked around, though it was near impossible to see anyone from here, them being so small. "Not that they'll ever know."

"Mmm," Greg said, nodding. "This feels ... curiously satisfying."

"Welcome to Team Good Guy," Friday said, clapping him on the back hard enough to nearly send him flying into the carpet fiber they were beneath.

"Yeah," Sienna said, "you'll like it here. We've got cupcakes. And unicorns, maybe. I don't know, something cool." She seemed to be reserved, holding something back. "So ... we've got one last thing to do before the job's done ..."

73.

Augustus

I worked until I couldn't handle working no more, couldn't dot one more I, cross one more T, and I stood up and said, "That's it! I'm taking a break!"

"Take a break then," Veronika said, not lifting her head. "You're a big boy. No need to be a drama king about it."

"Yeah," I said, no one else speaking up, "I'm gonna go … get a breath of fresh air or something … maybe have a talk with an actual person and not a paperwork drone … like y'all," I gave 'em a shot.

"Let us know if the real world is still out there," Scott said, leaning his head back against his seat. "All I have seen in my life and all I have known is the bite of a pen at my fingers and the rough touch of paper forms at my hand."

"And you thought I was dramatic?" I tossed at Veronika as I weaved my way out of the cubicle farm and toward the lobby. "Also, where's Colin with my pizza? Because the Flash does this in like two seconds."

"Colin has to pay," Veronika said. "With a credit card, because paper money is just so—"

"Yeah, whatever," I said, throwing a hand back at those poor people still laboring under their forms. Craziness. It was a beautiful May day outside, and we were all stuck inside doing this crap. I looked out the front window as I popped into the lobby. Casey looked up at me from her phone as I came in, and I said, "See? You got the right idea. At least you're playing Solitaire or something. Those guys in there," I waved back at the bullpen, "they are crazy. They're all doing—"

The glass window to my left shattered as a human being came sailing in, unconscious, and hit the ground, rolling slightly until he hit the wall with a thump. Once I overcame my initial shock, I shouted over Casey's screams, "Yo, guys! We got something here!"

I dropped down and grabbed the man who'd flown through our window. He was all cut up—no surprise after what he'd just gone through—but as I rolled him over, I stared at his face. Felt like I recognized him instantly, and the name hit me in a jolt as Scott came busting around the corner first, and I looked up at him as he came to a stop, Jamal right behind him, followed by the others.

"Yo, you guys," I said, pointing at the bleeding man on the floor, "I think this is Mark McGarry." I looked out the window, searching for a sign of where he'd come from, but there was nothing there. "Special delivery, I guess ..."

74.

Sienna

"Boom," I said, already on my way back up to the Concorde circling above, "that's how it's done."

Greg was riding my back as usual, but we'd left Friday on top of the plane. "What do you want to do now?"

"I don't know—" I started to say, but was interrupted when something—someone—went whooshing past, straight up into the sky on a platform of rock.

Augustus.

He was riding it up toward the nearest low-hanging cloud, like an elevator into the sky. "Yo!" He shouted at the cloud, like an old man who had a bone to pick with it. "Sienna!"

We both watched him zip up there, and Greg said, "You know, I think that fellow believes you're up there instead of down here."

I sighed. "Yeah."

"Sienna!" He was really hauling ass for the cloud. Like he could have caught me riding a self-made meteor if I'd really been trying to fly away from him.

"What do you want to do?" Greg asked.

I knew exactly what I wanted to do, but did I dare? "I guess … I should go talk to him, huh?" I waited for Greg to be the voice of reason, talk me down from it. "I mean … he's just going to keep yelling at clouds if I don't, right?"

75.

Augustus

"Sienna!" I said as I flew into the cloud, white haze surrounding me, cold air nipping at my nose. "I know you're up here."

"You caught me," a voice said behind me, and I whipped around to see her standing there, her hair darker and slightly shorter than when last I'd seen her. She looked … tired, though I suppose that shouldn't have been a surprise. "How's it going, Augustus?"

I just stared at her as she hovered a little closer to me. "That's all you've got to say to me? After all this time?"

"I know it feels like an eternity since you've had the pleasure of my company," she said with a wan smile, "but it's only really been about six months. I'm sure you're trucking along okay without me."

I opened my mouth to rebut that. "Of course I am. But … you just threw a dude through our window, and you don't even stop and say 'hi'?"

"That's for your own good," she said. I didn't think I'd ever seen Sienna this … drained, emotionally. She looked a little dead inside, and maybe more than a little outside. Fit as hell, though. "I'm a fugitive, Augustus, and your paycheck comes from state and local governments that want your help maintaining law and order. I don't think being seen with me would help your cause much."

I just stared her down. "Come on, girl. We were friends.

You got me into this. I wouldn't deny you in front of the world right now. I know you didn't do what they say you did. You're innocent."

"Innocent might be trying to carry the point a little far," she said. "But … thank you. For believing in me."

"Jamal said you were working with him a couple months ago," I said.

"… And?"

"I dunno," I said, shrugging my shoulders. "I don't know what you're doing."

She laughed, but it lacked any joy or authenticity. "I'm running, Augustus. Far from here. Halfway around the world, in fact, as soon as we're done talking."

"I heard you were saving Friday's life," I said. "That true?"

"It has been saved," she said. "The job's done. I kept him from dying at the hands of an assassin so that he could meet his inevitable end when he sticks his junk in a bowling ball exchange again."

I felt a world of questions bubble up there, and I didn't want to ask any of them, or know the answer to them. "Part of me wants to say you've changed … but another part thinks maybe you haven't. Not that much. You were always guarded. Now you just seem … I dunno. Like you're a castle. Ain't nobody getting behind those walls."

She just hovered there, staring at me, and finally, she parted her lips a little. "I'm so sorry, Augustus. My life … it's in ruins. Destroyed, still burning … and anyone who gets close … they're going to get burned, too. You're doing a good thing here," she said, looking off to the side, as though there were someone else waiting for her in the clouds. "You're making a difference. What you did to McGarry's organization … it'll save more lives than you can count."

"Yeah," I said, feeling a little tightness in my chest. "What's it going to take to save your life, Sienna Nealon?"

I thought I saw a little glimmer of a tear in her eye, and it took her a while to answer. "I don't think I believe in miracles anymore, Augustus."

"That's depressing," I said. "You know … your brother

is down there. I could whistle him right up, give you two a chance to hash things out face to face—"

"No," she said. "I need to get out of here." Now she was like stone, settled, a gargoyle in the middle of the clouds. "And you should get back to your paperwork."

I frowned. How'd she know about that? "So ... you're going somewhere, then?"

"Nowhere you should know about," she said, a drift of puffy cloud coming between us, causing her to fade. "Go live your life, Augustus. And don't worry about me. I'll be fine."

The drift ran over her and when it passed, she was gone.

I let my rock carry me back down to the ground, stepping off as I let it rejoin the landscaping at the office park.

Reed watched me landing, standing outside, staring up into the sky. He gave me a canny look, kind of piercing. "You see anyone up there?"

I opened my mouth and started to say, "Yeah, your sister," but I killed the words before they even reached my tongue. "Naw," I said instead. "Looks like whoever did this is long gone."

He stared at me for a minute, and I wondered if he was going to accept the lie. Finally, he just nodded, and said, "Just as well." And when I cocked my head at him quizzically, he said, "If we knew for sure who did it ... it'd just be more paperwork ..."

I didn't quite laugh at that, just tried to plaster a fake smile on my face as sirens sounded in the near distance, the cops on their way to pick up Mark McGarry from our custody, and tried to ignore the sick feeling inside as we prepared to put this case to bed for good.

76.

Safe back inside the Concorde, I let myself breathe for a moment after my conversation with Augustus. Greg was bustling around in the cockpit, preparing to take it off autopilot, though he was waiting for a destination from me ...

And from Friday, who was leaned back in the front row again, hands behind his head, looking for all the world like he'd just won a big battle singlehandedly.

"If you get any more relaxed, I would swear you'd need a cigarette for the first time in your life," I said, taking a seat across the aisle from him. When he didn't get the joke, I moved on. "So ... where are you headed next?"

"I might bum around town here for a little while," Friday said, shrugging his small shoulders. He blinked, then smiled at me. "Heyyyy ... can I put my mask back on again now?"

"Not just yet," I said, and he stopped, hand thrust into his pocket already.

"Oh," he said, pulling his hand back out, mask gripped tight in his fingers, like a black do-rag in his skinny digits. "So ... I guess you're ready for your payment now ..." When I stared at him steadily, he elaborated. "You know ... the name of the person who told me where to find you?"

I stared at him, watching his reaction. "It was Harmon, wasn't it?"

Friday's face fell. "You knew?"

361

"I suspected," I said, doing a little lean back of my own.

Guilty as charged, Harmon said.

I'll take, 'Things I don't want to say to an arraigning judge for $1,000, Alex.'

Hahah, Harmon said. *It's good to maintain your sense of humor about these things.*

"If you're going to stay in Minneapolis," I said to Friday, "I've got a safe house nearby. I'll give you the address and where the key is, and you can stay there for a while. Grab a spare phone out of the stash, too, if you want."

Friday looked at me with these big, kind of watery eyes. "I … I don't know how to thank you for everything you've done for me."

"I do," I said softly, and leaned closer to him. "Wexford told me that you know why McGarry was trying to have you killed."

Friday seemed to shrink before my eyes, even though I had thought he was already as small as he got. "I … okay. You deserve it, I guess." He looked down at the mask on his lap. "But … can I put this back on first?" He looked at me pleadingly.

"Sure," I said, and waited as he put the mask on.

77.

Friday

Sienna note: I think this might have actually happened.

Bredoccia, Revelen
Eastern Europe
December 17, 1989

The Iron Curtain was falling, knocked off its rod by the Soviet Union crashing down on its mouldering foundations. We didn't really know what we were doing at the time, only that we were participating in history as it was being written. Most of the time during that period, we were waiting in the wings, waiting to see what would develop, almost as if the people planning our ops didn't have any better idea than anyone else what was going as things started to fall apart.

But the day they sent us into Revelen ...

Well ...

The revolution was already churning its way through the streets when we parachuted in one moonless night. We could see the torches burning down in Bredoccia, the capital, but we were tasked with infiltrating a castle that sat up on a hill in the nearby mountains. Apparently during the days before World War II, before the Communists had taken Revelen, the whole country had been run from that hilltop chateau.

And as we parachuted in behind the walls that night ... I could easily have believed it.

The place was in disrepair, towers falling down, their blocks crumbling and moss-covered. I could see them as Jon guided me, cradled in my parachute, right into the drop zone atop one of the walls. As soon as I landed, he zipped off and got Theo, doing the same for him. Chase was next, and finally Greg showed up on his own. We stood there, in the dark, the power to the entire country cut for all I knew, staring into the sheer blackness of the night, and Greg beckoned us forward, our metahuman eyes guiding us as we stole into a door in the castle wall.

"Voices down," Greg said, whispering meta-low. "Keep our formation tight. Our objective is a meta being held in the basement dungeons by the local authorities. Extract and I'll exfiltrate us. This whole thing should only take ten minutes. If we get separated, we meet here. Anyone not here in ten minutes gets left behind." His eyes seemed to flash in the dark, and we all took him seriously.

We descended into the castle, tiptoeing and trying to keep up. It was so dark, and my eyes weren't adjusting as well as the others. They felt like they were watering, like I was in an eternal squint. I bumped into a wall and Jon swore under his breath at me.

"Sorry," I whispered. "I'm sorry. I can't see. I think I need glasses."

"Didn't you bring NVGs?" Theo hissed at me.

"What?" I asked.

"Just follow me, fool," Theo said, and he was moving again.

I tried to follow him, really I did. But I went around a corner, where I thought he'd turned just a minute earlier, and ...

Theo was gone.

The hallway in front of me was dark, no sound echoing down to suggest they'd passed through. I fumbled my way down, hands scraping across the stone walls until my probing fingers found a wooden door and it swung against my slight pressure.

Light cracked out, spilling over the hallway, and I blinked in surprise at the intensity of it. I opened it further, the hinges squeaking as I stepped inside, my AK-47 drawn and ready to fire—

"What is your name?" a calm voice asked as I stepped into the room. The light came from a single lamp by the window, and a man sat in a chair behind a tall desk, long, thin fingers cupping a very old book in front of him. His hair was near black, slicked along the sides and top of his head. His hair met in a dramatic widow's peak on top of his forehead, and his eyes rolled over me—

Oh, God. His *eyes*.

They were glacial blue, and they found me like they had lasered through the darkness and seen me coming before I'd even settled on the outside wall. His lips were stiff, stern, no hint of a smile on them. His suit was old too, but immaculate, the shirt beneath perfectly white.

"I asked you your name," he said, closing the book quietly and placing it upon the desk in front of him. He gestured to the AK in my hands. "Put that away. You don't need that."

"Okay," I said, and tossed the AK-47 off to the side like it was six-week-old chimichanga. I looked after it as soon as it was gone, sudden panic setting in.

Why had I just thrown away my gun? My only gun?

"What is your name?" he asked again, infinitely patient.

"Y-yancy," I said, barely getting the words out between chattering teeth.

"A polite answer to a polite question at last," he said, long fingers stroking his chin. "You are an American, yes?"

"Y-yes."

"Yancy the American," he said, rising to his feet. He was so much shorter than me. "And, Yancy the American ... are you a metahuman?"

"Yes."

"Mmm," the man said, slipping around the corners of his desk as though almost ephemeral, passing through them. "What is your power, Yancy?"

"I'm a ... Hercules." I felt so small, so ashamed in that moment. I couldn't decide why I was answering any of his questions, why I had thrown my gun away. I felt so insignificant, like I would somehow slip between the floorboards and fall into the castle's darkest dungeons, never to be seen again.

Never to see the light again.

"What is your father's name, Yancy the American Hercules?" the man asked again, smoothly, silky voice filled with that infinite patience.

"I …" I shook my head. "… Wh-what's *your* name?"

He raised an eyebrow at me, then smiled, and it made me shiver like he'd opened the windows and somehow all of Antarctica had poured in. "Curious. I have … so very many names, Yancy. Many you would not have heard of. Perhaps a few you would have. My most famous was Vlad. The least? It hardly matters. A name is simply a way to allow your reputation to precede you." He drifted around the front of his desk. "But we hardly have need for that now, do we, Yancy? Because … it hardly matters that you know my reputation, does it? I mean … do you need to know anything more of me?"

I found myself shaking my head. "No, I … I think I … know all I need to about you."

The man smiled, wolfish, delighted … and it almost made me fall to my knees, ready to beg for my life. "Now, Yancy … what is your father's name?"

I swallowed hard. "Simon." My knees were quaking, threatening to make good on my desire to beg. "Simon Nealon."

SLAP!

OW! What the hell was that for? I'm telling you the damned story you asked for!

Bullshit!

It is not! I'm telling you the truth! *whisper* This time.

You never told me your last name was Nealon!

Because it's not! Ow, my cheek. That really hurt! It was my dad's name, and I never even met the guy!

That's my last name, idiot!

Yeah, so? Lots of Nealons in the world.

Yeah, but Simon Nealon was my grandfather, you twit! And he was a Hercules!

Oh. Wait. So … does that mean …?

It means, if you're telling the truth …

You're my damned uncle.

Wow. Weird. I didn't think I had any family left.

… Yeah. Weird.

So should we like, hug, or something?

… Why don't you finish the story?

The man stood there, staring at me. His smiled had vanished. "I knew Simon Nealon. It was a shame about what happened to him in London." He lapsed into silence for several minutes, a silence I felt absolutely no need to break. When he spoke again, it was as though he'd made a serious decision. "I will let you live, Yancy the American, because of my past associations with your father. Next time, though," and he wagged one of those long fingers, giving me a glimpse of a fingernail that looked like iron grafted to his cadaverously thin digit, "you will not be so lucky."

"Th … thank you," I said, bowing as I felt myself unfreeze from the spot. I started walking backward, urging myself to go faster, to break into a run, to hurl myself out his door into the dark hallway, anything to get away from him, to get away from those eyes, that face …

"Go in peace, Yancy," he said as I escaped through the threshold. "And do not come back to Revelen again."

"I … I won't," I said, shaking my head fervently. "And—I—I won't tell anyone about you. Ever."

"That would be exceedingly wise," the man said, and with a wave of his hand the door closed in front of me, clicking shut as though it had never opened in the first place, not a hint of light spilling out from the cracks.

When I caught my breath, I turned and ran blindly up and down staircases and passages until I burst out onto the roof. I ran in a circle until I was sure I'd found the place where we came in. I sat down right there, hugging my knees to my chest, trying to keep from sobbing … and the team found me there a few minutes later, when they came back up.

I didn't speak for two weeks.

78.

Sienna

I was stroking my forehead as Guy Friday finished his story, my head spinning because at least two of the little factoids that he'd dropped on me during that story were burning up my brain from the inside.

One … he was my damned half-uncle.

Two … I was pretty sure the guy he was describing was the metahuman equivalent of the boogeyman, taking credit for the name of 'Vlad,' probably meaning Vlad the Impaler, a.k.a. Dracula. Which was an awfully dramatic thing to put on your resume, but …

After all the shit I'd caught from the nation of Revelen these last few years … a big, spooky boogeyman who thought of himself as Dracula …

Well, it started to make an awful lot of sense.

"None of the others saw this guy?" I kept my voice quiet. Greg was still messing around up in the cockpit. Maybe he was giving us our privacy, I dunno.

Friday shook his head. "No. None of them had a clue why I was catatonic for two weeks after the mission. They all thought I was just cracking up or something. But I physically couldn't speak. It was like my mouth wouldn't open. I woke up screaming at night, had tremors, night sweats …" He looked down at his feet. "I couldn't tell anyone what I saw, and none of them suffered what I did … no, they didn't see him. I know that. If they had … I wouldn't have had to say a thing." He looked at me, a cold dread in his eyes that I hadn't seen even when he'd shown up wet and bedraggled on my doorstep in Portland, terrified of Greg killing him.

"Well?" Greg asked from the cockpit door, standing like a pillar right in the middle of it. "Have we made any decisions about where to go yet?"

"Friday's staying here in Minneapolis," I said quietly, half-buried in my reactions, a tumult of emotions and thoughts.

Greg took that in stride. "Very well. I can bring us down to just above the ground and step out with you, if you'd like."

"That'd be good," Friday said, standing up. I got the feeling as he did so that he was trying to shed the dark sensation of fear, and everything that revisiting the memory of the man he'd met in Revelen had dredged up in him.

"Are you ready to go?" Greg asked.

"Hell, yeah," Friday said, voice cracking a little as he pulled himself together. "I got some chicks in town I want to catch up with, if you know what I mean." He nodded ferociously. "And I think you do."

Whatever negative effect telling me his story had had on him, it looked like it had passed. I got to my weary feet and said, "Good luck. And, uh ... so long ... Uncle Friday."

Friday was hard to read with that mask on, but he kinda drooped for a second and then got really still. "So, uh ... I'm not really familiar with the protocol on having a, uh, niece ..." He put his hand behind his head and scratched the back of his mask. "Do we ... like, shake hands, or ...?"

"Come here, you big goon," I said, and dragged him down in a hug. I did see a hint of surprise in his eyes as I pulled him to me for it.

And it felt surprisingly good, since it was the first one I'd had in months.

79.

"So you're on the straight and narrow now?" I asked Greg as we jetted along toward Chicago. He'd offered to take me to the Atlantic Coast, but I'd passed on that. He wanted to get back to his family, and I was so tired I was going to bed down in a safe house I had just outside Chicago. Tomorrow I'd make a speed run up to Canada and then head east, crossing the Atlantic faster than the US Government could send jets and drones and missiles to intercept me.

I hoped.

"Prudence would seem to demand it," Greg said, adjusting the Concorde's course. "Having seen what holding to the assassin's way has done to my family ..." He shook his head. "It'd take a more stubborn man than I to not see that now ... now is the time to let go."

"Good call," I said. "You know, a lot of people, they tend to hold to that stubborn pride way past the point when they ought to tap out." Internally, I squirmed slightly as I said it, mainly because the words seemed to apply almost as much to me as they did to Greg.

"People confuse me," Greg said, a surprising amount of feeling in his voice. "Assassinations were simple, for the most part. Dead human beings? Easy to understand. Their agency is gone, they don't move ... or confuse you ... or have unexpected outbursts of emotion ..."

"We talking about your family when it comes to those unexpected outbursts of emotion? Or you?"

He seemed to catch his breath. "I always prided myself

on preparation and perhaps, my coolness to any concern. Because of the preparation, you see. When ready for nearly anything, almost nothing discomfits you."

"Tell me something," I said, leaning closer, "did you prepare for parenthood?"

Greg just froze. "No. I mean ... I read some books, but ... once I got past the first year ... I sort of assumed I knew what I was doing. The same goes for marriage."

"Well, I've never been married—or a parent, though I have just found out I'm a niece again, for whatever that's worth—but I don't think you can learn most of that stuff from a book, Greg." I leaned back in my seat. "At the risk of mouthing off when I don't exactly know what I'm talking about ... just go live your life, man."

He stared at me. "You think it's really that simple?"

"I get that you want to be prepared for everything," I said, "but somehow I get the feeling ... that's not been working out so well in family life. Am I right?"

"Yes," he said stiffly.

"I don't know," I said, "maybe change tack. See what Morgan thinks? She seems like a reasonable lady, other than that really harsh prohibition on swearing you guys have going on. I think you'll learn more from listening to her and what she wants, what she thinks is best for Eddie than you would reading a hundred books."

He blinked a few times at his control. "You know what? I think you just might be right."

"Yeah," I said, settling back in my seat as the lights of Chicago's skyline appeared on the horizon. "I just wish it did me more good in my own life."

80.

I settled down to sleep that night in my safe house, the bed hard and lumpy beneath me. I didn't love it, and sleep didn't come easy, restlessness threatening to make me toss and turn all night …

But eventually I did fall asleep, and I managed to keep my mind on one person as I did so.

"Well, well," Reed said as he appeared in the black-edged world of the dreamwalk. "And here I thought I was about to have some nice, peaceful, dreamless sleep."

"Yeah," I said, unable to stop myself as soon as I saw what he was wearing, "clearly you did not dress for company."

He looked down, and his face found every single shade of blush it could apply and then some. He was wearing a heavy cotton bathrobe and fuzzy slippers, and I couldn't control my laughter.

"Laugh it up," he said as I chortled at his attire, "any night but this one, I might have been prepared for you. But tonight … yeah, I wore the fuzzy slippers. You know why? Because they're comfortable, and I was out two seconds after I got into bed."

"I'm sorry," I said, still trying to keep from laughing my ass off at him. "I, uh … it's always kind of a dicey thing barging in on people in their dreams, y'know."

"Yeah," he said tautly, wrapping his muscular arms over his chest. "So … what brings you into my mind this evening?"

"Well," I said, "... I had a talk with Augustus earlier."

Reed stiffened, no mean feat considering he was already pretty well at full ATTEN-HUT! "Is that so?"

"Yeah ... and Augustus is not the most subtle guy in the world, but the gist I got is ... he thought we—that you and I—should talk. And I figured he would have told you about seeing me, so ..."

"So here you are."

"So here I am. To talk. Because ... he seemed to think we need to."

Reed just stared at me before lowering his eyes, not to look at his fuzzy slippered feet, but at the general darkness that was the floor. "Augustus thinks I'm mad at you."

"Oh," I said. "Are you ... mad at me?"

Reed drew in a deep breath and let it all out before speaking. "No. I'm not mad at you, Sienna, but ... it's been six months." The last part came out in hard accusation. "Six months since Harmon screwed you over. And you've talked to Jamal, Scott, Kat, hell, even Friday ... but not me?" He kept those arms snugly folded in front of him. "So ... no. I'm not mad at you. But I do wonder ... they can find you, but I can't? They get to talk you, but ... not me?"

"It's never been an intentional thing," I said. "I didn't help any of them find me, by the way. I was hiding from everyone."

"I guess I suck at detecting, then," he said, "because I've been looking ... and the only place I've seen you is in the agency paperwork."

It was my turn to stiffen. "I don't know what you mean."

"Oh, come on," he said. "Jonsdottir? It took me two days of rolling that one around before I said it out loud. John's daughter. Lamest pun ever."

Now I was blushing. "Okay. That was perhaps an indulgence I shouldn't have taken—"

"I'm more interested in where you got the money," he said. "Because setting up this place—twice—couldn't have been cheap."

"I kinda ... drained Omega's accounts a couple years ago," I said. "Figured it was mine since technically I was their last Primus."

"And what did Janus think of that?" he asked.

"Dunno. Didn't ask. Haven't seen him since, though, what with him being in London, so ..." I didn't feel a need to mention that I might see him soon, though. Very soon.

"You're a real pile of ..." he started.

"Shit?"

"... Secrets, Sienna. Secrets. You're my sister, not my enemy."

"Sorry."

"No," he said, putting a hand up to his brow. "Look ... I know ... last time we saw each other ... South Dakota ... that can't have been easy on you, either. With me hunting you because of Harmon ..." His voice trailed off. "Look, Isabella keeps telling me that it's not my fault ... what happened to me when Harmon was in control. That it's not my fault I betrayed you."

I felt really small, like Friday in front of Vlad small. If Greg had shrunk him first. "I know."

He looked up, and there was this deep well of anguish in his eyes. "But I still did it. There's a little part of me, too, that wondered ... if maybe you did believe it was ... it was my fault."

"No one knows better than me at this point how badly Gerry Harmon can mess up your mind, your life," I said, shaking my head. "It wasn't your fault. I never blamed you, once I knew what was going on. Because we're, y'know ..."

He took a step toward me, almost experimentally. "Family?"

"Yeah, that," I said, not looking up.

"So ... why haven't we talked until now?" Reed asked, maintaining that foot or so of distance still between us.

"Because I usually don't know what I would say to you," I said, letting it all kind of spurt out. "There are times when I'm ... just bored. Netflixing, reading, idle. And I watch stuff that I know you like and I think, 'Oh, man, I have to talk to Reed about this' ... except I can't, really ... because I'm a fugitive and you being seen with me would rip your life apart. End the agency. End the good it can do with you at the helm, so …"

"But you're talking to me now," he said. "And no one's watching. We could have talked about … I dunno, what have you been watching?"

"Uhm, well," I said, trying to remember, "I caught up on the *Gilmore Girls* revival."

He stared at me with smoky eyes, but I caught a glimmer of pride. "Excellent choice." He relaxed a little. "But … why haven't you dreamwalked to me until now?"

"I have this kinda problem," I said, "and I've talked to Zollers about it—"

I saw the flash of disappointment from my brother. "Zollers, too, huh?"

"You're not making this any easier."

"Sorry," he said, with real contrition. "Go on."

"I don't find it easy to ask others for help," I said. "Like, if anyone asks me, friend or almost a weird rando from the 'net—"

"Like Friday."

"Like Friday, yes … I'm there. I'll help them, especially if it involves metahuman shenanigans. But when I get in deep … I turtle up. And especially now, where there are real, honest-to-God consequences if any of you get seen helping me … yeah. I'm in my shell, and reaching out? Feels impossible sometimes. The longer I waited … the harder it got to … pick up the dreamwalk phone and mosey on over." I bowed my head. "I'm sorry, Reed. I just … I'm a loner. For all my years fighting with the team, I'm still the girl who retreats into the box when trouble comes, because the instinct is to think there's no one here with me when it rolls around."

He reached out for me and dragged me close in my second hug of the day. And even though it wasn't real … it still felt good. "We're family," he said. "We're supposed to watch out for each other. Trouble comes your way, I want to be there for you."

"How does an aiding and abetting felony strike you?"

"Like a long jail sentence in the Cube," he said, still holding me tight. "But if you really needed me … damn, I would hope you'd call. Because I'd be there. For you. Really, I would, Cube be damned." And he held me tight, his warmth against me, sweet comfort that allowed some of the troubles I was looking into, some of the worries of what was coming tomorrow … the big thing that was coming tomorrow … slip away, if only for a moment.

And the moment ended before the hug, because I remembered something. "So …" I said, "… in the vein of that that whole, 'we're family and watch out for each other' thing … but without having to worry about jail time … there is one thing you can do for me … well … for family …"

81.

Greg

Finishing packing the house hadn't taken too terribly long. Morgan had done most of the work before he'd arrived home with Sienna and the others the day before, and the small incidentals he picked up during the night were already almost loaded by the time he had arrived. Moving when you were an Atlas was the simplest of things, after all; no truck needed, just a small box you could put everything in.

"Are you sure you want me to bring all this?" Greg asked, his entire workshop shrunken into the palm of his hand. Removing it from the wall had been easy, but he'd had to take great care to bind everything down first, which had been last night's efforts. "I could just leave it behind."

Morgan looked at him from the co-pilot seat of the Concorde as they cruised on autopilot above the yard. It looked like twenty thousand feet of height from here, but they were really only about ten feet up. "Just in case," she said. "Who knows where the road will take us?"

"All right," Greg said, and then looked at their sole passenger, who was sitting in the seat with Morgan. "Where would you like to go, Eddie? To start our … new life together?"

"I want to go to the moon," Eddie said.

The literal part of Greg's brain burned, but he kept a tight lid on it. Morgan smiled, reassuringly, and Greg said, "I don't think I can get us there with this plane, son. Where else would you like to go?"

Eddie lowered his head, giving that some deep thought. "Legoland?" he asked experimentally.

Greg blinked. It wasn't an unreasonable request. "I think we can oblige that. It's in Florida, isn't it?"

"Yes, it is," Morgan said, stroking Eddie's arms and making him shiver and giggle. "Near Tampa, I think?"

"Tampa!" Eddie said. "I want to go to Tampa."

"Then Tampa it will be," Greg said, taking the plane out of autopilot and angling it up. He smiled, just slightly, as he looked over at Morgan and Eddie. "And maybe, someday ... well, I'll work on that moon thing."

82.

Augustus

"So ..." Reed said as we all stood around in the bullpen the next morning, not really addressing the elephant in the room, "... I noticed that, uh ... no one really got all their paperwork done yesterday."

"Yeah, having the head honcho of the criminal organization we were busting get tossed through our plate glass window yesterday kind of broke up the buzzing paperwork party," Veronika said. "I guess it's hard to get your focus back after it starts raining bad men."

"Tell me about it," Angel said. "Casey called in sick today. Says she's thinking about not coming back. Didn't know it'd be like this."

"Did no one tell her the last office got blown up?" I asked. "I mean, this ain't that big a town. Feels like something she should have known coming in. What's that thing the Romans say about the buyer being aware?"

"Caveat emptor," Jamal said, and I just shot him that look for being a showoff know-it-all. "What? Can we talk about the other thing now? The elephant in the room?"

"Uh, yeah," Reed cleared his throat.

"I'm not an elephant," Guy Friday said, all hulked up almost to the ceiling, "and that's not a trunk!" He burst out laughing, slapping his knee because he was doubled over. "Oh, I slay me." He straightened up, all serious again. "But really, guys, hey, it's great to be here. Thanks for having me."

"So, most of us know Friday already," Reed said, looking like he had swallowed a really big, bitter pill, maybe one that was designed to be taken rectally, I dunno. "And for those who don't, uh ... what's your real name, Guy? I've only ever heard you called Friday, and I'm pretty sure Sienna stole that from somewhere."

"Marshall," Friday said. "Matherson. And remember the 'son' part because it's super important."

Scott frowned. "Isn't that Eminem's real name? But, you know, without the 'son'?"

"Nooooo," Friday said, "it's totally my own. But I'm a huge fan of 'Love the Way You Lie.' That song is so *kittens*!" He shouted the last word, like it was supposed to mean something.

"This feels like as good a place as any to leave off," Reed said, a faint aura of exasperation hanging over him. "Everybody welcome, uh, Marshall, or whatever his name actually is ... and try and get that paperwork done so I don't end up having to walk around like the guy from *Office Space*, whining about your TPS reports." With that, he disappeared into his office and shut the blinds, probably to continue his emotional breakdown, since he'd already gone and hired Friday.

"It's nice to meet you," Angel said, extending a hand to Friday.

"Not as nice as it is to meet you, sexy legs!" Friday said as I started to walk away. I'd known Angel for a few months, and I didn't need to see what was coming next.

Crack!

"Good thing metas don't scar easy," Jamal said, cringing away from what I was sure had been a truly righteous strike by Angel against Friday's masked face.

"Hey, I got a question for you," I said, undeterred by the sickened look on Jamal's face. I didn't want to look back, because for all I knew, Angel was about to take all the paperwork in the office and insert it into Friday the way Reed should have taken his enormous pill this morning. "How do we prove Sienna Nealon innocent?"

My brother looked around like he was expecting

someone else to come flying through a window. He motioned me over to his cubicle and fiddled with his phone for a second, then sat down heavily, beckoning me to lean down. "Look ... ArcheGrey swore there was some kind of evidence out there but ... there's a whole can of worms from that, and not earthworms, either. Like acid-spewing worms from *Star Trek*."

"Like a horta?"

"Yeah, something like that," Jamal said. "The evidence is being actively covered up. And after LA, you're going to have a hell of a time finding anyone with any kind of signal boost who'd be willing to get the word out there, even if you did find it."

"Isn't that what the internet is for?" I asked.

Jamal just laughed. "You are so charmingly naïve, bro. The internet's just a repository. It could already be posted on YouTube for all we know. Unless anyone can find it, it would just remain an incredible snuff film with zero views, and Sienna would continue to languish in the wilderness."

"So ... there's got to be something we can do," I said. "You know, we're detectives, technically—"

"Did we get a PI license with this gig?"

"—so it's kind of our jobs. Right?" I waited for him to say otherwise, though I didn't think he would.

"Yeah, you're right," Jamal conceded. "And ... I've done a little digging, but ... I ain't found an end to the wall, if you know what I mean. It keeps going down, no way out."

I stared at him blankly. "I don't know what that means."

"I means I haven't found anything yet," Jamal said. "But I have looked some. And ... we could ask for help, if we had the funds. Cassidy Ellis is out there. Or Arche, if I could ever find her. Doubt she'd help for free, either, though."

"Naw," I said, "for now, this is just us. We do this. A conspiracy of two."

Jamal screwed up his face at me. "... 'Conspiracy'?"

"You know what I mean. We do this alone. Secret-society style. Because if you're right, and someone's trying to hide this stuff ..."

Jamal nodded. "If they're willing to bury her ..."

I nodded. "That's right. Then they'll more than happy to bury us. We keep this tight for now. Secret. And we find out what's going on, who's behind this." I looked around, half expecting Scotty to stick his head over the cubicle wall any second. "And maybe ... just maybe ... we'll figure out a way to clear Sienna's name."

83.

Sienna

I made the Atlantic Coast without incident. No missiles shot me down. No planes blew me out of the sky. No one flew alongside me and yelled at me over a speaker, warning me to turn back and return to American airspace, or else.

If the US Government knew I was leaving, it seemed they were pretty content to see my ass go.

The air turned colder, belting me in the face like a punch as I went "feet wet" over Newfoundland, and started crossing the ocean. I cast a look back at the Canadian coast, which was receding quickly, then lapsed into thought.

Harmon, you ass.

You needed something to do, Harmon said, and I could hear a weary sort of self-justification in his voice. *We hadn't talked yet about Friday's little revelation of who had brought him to my door.*

You needed direction, Sienna, Wolfe said.

Purpose, Gavrikov added.

"I didn't need to have everything go to hell in the United States," I said out loud, disappointment outweighing my anger. "You blocked me at every turn so I could do it myself, but your trail of breadcrumbs ended up being liberally doused in nitroglycerine that blew up in my face."

An unfortunate side effect, Harmon said, *and one I am truly remorseful for. I was ... worried about you.*

"And you didn't see the nuke coming?" I asked, my teeth already chattering. It was only getting colder the farther I got

383

from land.

No. I would have warned you if I had. I didn't have a truly solid grasp on Greg's mind until after that.

"So were you the one responsible for his sudden change of heart?" I asked.

Not entirely, no, Harmon said, a little cagily. *He was destroying his own life, and he knew it. He lacked the capacity to change as fully as he might have wanted to. He's an inflexible fellow. I ... helped him to bend a little more than he might otherwise.*

"Well, at least you knew enough to stop digging once we were well and truly buried in the hole," I said. "What about Wexford? Did you send for him?"

No, Harmon said. *I've never met him before that I recall. Telepaths don't really have much sway on each others' minds, unless they grossly outclass each other in terms of power.*

"Like Zollers does with you?" I took the opportunity to grind a little salt in that wound while I could.

He's not that much stronger than me, Harmon said, *but he caught me at a time when I was trying to control a great many minds. He was trying to control none. I was overmatched.*

"And Friday?" I asked. "Did you know he was my uncle?"

He didn't know he was your uncle, Harmon said. *And no, I didn't dumpster dive into that brain, I stuck to the surface and teased out only the most applicable secrets while letting you do your—your thang,* he sounded really weird saying that—*for the rest of them. And just so you don't doubt ... I concur with your assessment of his last confession. What he told you about that castle in Revelen ... as near as I can tell, it's real. And the level of fear that man made him feel ...*

Yeah, I said. *I picked up on that. He'd never felt anything like it in his life.*

To say the least. Friday, while a great many things ... dullard, pitiful fashionista, compulsive liar ... he is not an obvious coward.

"Adds another cherry on top when it comes to my reasons to go to Revelen for a little visit, though, doesn't it?" I asked.

I would not suggest that, Gavrikov said.

You don't know what's waiting there, Wolfe said.

"Do any of you?" I asked.

Silence.

"Fine," I said. "They lost all their US goodies anyway. I can wait until another day to deal with them, I suppose." My cheeks felt like they were frozen blocks of ice. "I've got a flight across the Atlantic anyway. Might as well set down somewhere friendly and just chill for a bit. Relax, maybe. See what Wexford has in mind for me. Kick it old school for a while, take out some dumb, street-level meta criminals."

Sounds like fun, Wolfe said.

"Yeah," I said, "it ought to be a ball."

I looked back as the continent of North America started to fade from my sight, disappearing over the horizon as I flew into the grey skies ahead. I looked back for as long as I could, even though I knew I was looking at Canada, not the USA, because … for my purposes, it was near enough.

Feeling homesick? Harmon asked, gently.

"No," I said, lying blatantly and daring him to call me on it. I blinked icy tears out of my eyes as I took my last look at the place of my birth.

Not last look, Wolfe said. *Just leaving for now.*

"I know," I said, but when I blinked again, more tears rushed down my cheeks, and I looked again, though now all I could see was ocean as far as the horizon stretched.

Something about it felt final to me, in spite of what they'd said.

Like I'd never see home again.

Sienna Nealon Will Return in

HUNTERS

Out of the Box
Book 15

Coming July 25, 2017!

Author's Note

Thanks for reading! If you want to know immediately when future books become available, take sixty seconds and sign up for my NEW RELEASE EMAIL ALERTS by visiting my website. I don't sell your information and I only send out emails when I have a new book out. The reason you should sign up for this is because I don't always set release dates, and even if you're following me on Facebook (robertJcrane (Author)) or Twitter (@robertJcrane), it's easy to miss my book announcements because...well, because social media is an imprecise thing.

Come join the discussion on my website:
http://www.robertjcrane.com!

Cheers,
Robert J. Crane

ACKNOWLEDGMENTS

Editorial/Literary Janitorial duties performed by Sarah Barbour and Jeffrey Bryan. Final proofing was once more handled by the illustrious Jo Evans. Any errors you see in the text, however, are the result of me rejecting changes.

The cover was once more designed with exceeding skill by Karri Klawiter of Artbykarri.com.

The formatting was provided by nickbowmanediting.com.

Once more, thanks to my parents, my in-laws, my kids and my wife, for helping me keep things together.

Other Works by Robert J. Crane

World of Sanctuary
Epic Fantasy

The Girl in the Box
and
Out of the Box
Contemporary Urban Fantasy

Southern Watch

Contemporary Urban Fantasy

The Shattered Dome Series
(with Nicholas J. Ambrose)
Sci-Fi

Voiceless: The Shattered Dome, Book 1
Unspeakable: The Shattered Dome, Book 2* *(Coming 2017 – Tentatively)*

The Mira Brand Adventures
Contemporary Urban Fantasy

Mira Brand and the World Beneath: Mira Brand Adventures, Book 1* *(Coming 2017!)*
Mira Brand and the Tide of Ages: Mira Brand Adventures, Book 2* *(Coming 2017 - Tentatively)*

*Forthcoming, Subject to Change

CPSIA information can be obtained
at www.ICGtesting.com
Printed in the USA
LVOW13s1248230917
549813LV00009B/425/P